ALSO BY KAT & STONE BASTION

No Weddings Series

No Weddings · One Funeral

Two Bar Mitzvahs · Three Christmases

For Valentine's

Unbreakable Series

Heartbreaker · Rule Breaker · Lawbreaker

Forthcoming: *Ball Breaker · Icebreaker*

Highland Legends Series

Forged in Dreams and Magick

Bound by Wish and Mistletoe

Born of Mist and Legend

Found in Flame and Moonlight

THE TRAVELER: Initiate Years

Veil of Realms · Secrets of Alexandria · Panther Rising

Stones of Power · Highland Magick

Half-Baked Holidays

Half-baked Holidays:

A Romantic Comedy Holiday Collection

PRAISE FOR KAT & STONE BASTION

No Weddings and
THE NO WEDDINGS SERIES

"One of the best romantic comedies of the year!"

— *AGENTS OF ROMANCE*

"The No Weddings series is one of the best I have read that follows one couple. Cade and Hannah are both lovable characters, the storyline is real and entertaining, and the banter is fun and witty."

— *LIVES & BREATHES BOOK BLOG*

"I loved it, and I mean REALLY loved it!"

— *ORCHARD BOOK CLUB*

"This is an exceptional series... You find yourself fully engrossed in their world and can't put the book down."

— *BOOKS -N- KISSES*

"The No Weddings series has a group of such amazing characters; you can't help but relate to them and feel the emotion in every situation they encounter. It has been a long time since a story has made me feel that way let alone an entire series!"

— *UNDER THE COVERS BOOK BLOG*

"The story of Cade & Hannah's relationship is realistic, heart-warming, and filled with real-world connections that shook me in a way that few titles I've read this year have managed...I have loved every minute of the No Weddings series."

— *THAT'S WHAT I'M TALKING ABOUT*

Heartbreaker

"This book has definitely earned its five stars and I am just floored right now. The passion is explosive, the story itself is beautiful, and the emotions are so real my heart is ready to burst. Beautiful book. Absolutely breathtaking."

— *ONE PAGE AT A TIME*

"Heartrending, passionate, and captivating! *Heartbreaker* is a riveting page-turner that will leave you breathless with raw emotions, and the need to hold tight to the ones you love!"

— *BENEATH THE COVERS BLOG*

To the wanderers...
May you always find home.

AWARDS & PRAISE FOR KAT BASTION

Forged in Dreams and Magick

First Place – Unpublished Beacon Award
Best Paranormal Romance

First Place – Hold Me, Thrill Me Award
Best Paranormal Romance

**Chosen by FreshFiction.com as their
Fresh Pick for October 22, 2013**

"A beautifully woven tale about love, choices, courage and destiny, *Forged in Dreams and Magick* is one of the best time-traveling novels. Fans of Gabaldon's *Outlander* will love it."

— *BOOKISH TEMPTATIONS*

"I was gripping my iPad like a crazy woman and fanning myself from the smoldering romance. Lawdy!"

— *THE FLIRTY READER*

"Bastion's debut is pure perfection, a combination of romance, magic, emotion, adventure and surprising twists and turns. This is a truly unique romance that should not be missed!"

— *THEBOOKQUEEN*

"HOLY HELL!!! I am so... um... wow! FABULOUS-NESS. *Forged in Dreams and Magick* definitely makes my BEST OF list for 2013..."

— *THAT'S WHAT I'M TALKING ABOUT*

"A story guaranteed to enthrall with lushly detailed travels into times long gone by. Woven with love, passion, magic and legend, the story had me hooked from the very first chapter."

— *READ-LOVE-BLOG*

"Kat Bastion's wonderful debut brings a new voice to the fore. Her voice is strong and unhesitating, very human and real, sometimes young and delicious in her treatment of intimacy and relationship development."

— *FANGS WANDS & FAIRYDUST*

"OMG, Bastion hits all cylinders in this supernatural tale. The layers in the book were fascinating, and I devoured the fun, adventuresome read."

— *LITERATI LITERATURE LOVERS*

Bound by Wish and Mistletoe

"I LOVED it! *Bound by Wish and Mistletoe* is, to my mind, a perfect entry in the historical / paranormal fiction genre and has quite a bit to offer."

— *FAB FANTASY FICTION*

"Kat Bastion has done it again! ... Excellent holiday novella, perfect for a cup of cocoa and snuggling under a blanket in front of the fireplace this holiday season."

— *THAT'S WHAT I'M TALKING ABOUT*

"Move over, Julia Quinn and Sabrina Jeffries! Kat Bastion is an absolutely gifted author and deserves to be recognized for her talent."

— *LOVESHISTORICAL BOOK REVIEWS*

THREE CHRISTMASES

THREE CHRISTMASES

KAT & STONE BASTION

1. WEARY TRAVELER

Cade...

Passengers rushed by in the Philly airport, but they faded into my peripheral. The sounds in the terminal? Background noise. The T-shirt stuck to my chest on the hot mid-September afternoon. Didn't care.

My only focus—Hannah.

And once I strode through the security barriers, there she stood.

Gorgeous.

Dark brown hair was pulled up into a ponytail. Bright hazel-green eyes searched for me. A pale blue sundress stopped midthigh, revealing an endless stretch of toned legs. Territory I intended to explore. Get lost in. Repeatedly.

Her gaze locked onto mine, and her lips curved into a huge smile. Just for me.

Two quick strides later, I dropped my bag and tugged her into my arms. "Fuck, Maestro. I've missed you." Five days on a business trip. Too damn long. But my new consulting business had just begun to take off and Blake Fisher had become a dream client.

Her arms slid around my back, and she clung tightly. Soft lips pressed into my neck, and as she dragged them up, she inhaled slowly.

"Did you just smell me?"

"Mmm-hmm. You smell amazing, spicy, male."

"Glad you like my sweat." Didn't blame her, though. I wanted to breathe her in. I buried my nose just above her ear, taking an addictive hit on a deep breath. "Don't ever change your shampoo." Coconut-mango, she'd once said. I wanted to roll around in it—in her.

A crowd of noisy kids split around us. None of the chaos fazed her as she pulled away, expression fierce. "Never. And I missed you too." Her gaze dropped to my mouth. A beat later, she lunged upward. Her lips crashed onto mine, soft, sweet.

I kissed her. Easy, at first. Then harder. When I gripped her tighter, she leaned further against me. Her hands shot into my hair, pulling at the roots as my tongue tangled with hers. With a low moan, she tugged my lower lip between her teeth, then sucked on it.

Want shot straight to blinding need, zero to sixty. But I held back, dimly aware the authorities frowned upon standing sex in the middle of an airport terminal.

A couple of minutes later, breathless from nearly mauling each other, I lowered my forehead to hers. "Seriously, I need a shower. I have stale airplane all over me."

Her tone lowered, sexy. "You need me all over you."

Better images snapped into my mind than us fully clothed and groping. Her naked. Straddling me. "*Yeah*, I do. Love that dirty mind of yours." I eased back and blew out a hard breath. "Let's get outta here before we get arrested."

Her lips curved into a sly smile as she slipped her hand into mine. "For naughty thoughts? Guilty."

I picked up my bag and let her lead us toward the parking garage. "No. I'm seconds away from filthy-as-fuck actions. You. Me. The nearest wall. A sturdy counter."

She glanced over her shoulder, and I sucked in a breath. Her expression was a mixture of all my favorite things about her: amused, innocent...naughty.

I dropped her a heated look. "Parking garage is becoming a real possibility."

She stopped at the doors that led outside and pressed her lips together, fighting a smile. "Behave. We'll have plenty of one-on-one time later. I promise to make the wait worth your while."

I gave her a hard kiss, then growled against her lips. "It always is."

When we got to her car, she dropped the keys into my hand. I grinned. The '67 Mustang Fastback had been an inheritance from her grandfather, and she treasured the gift. So did I. The car had been well taken care of. Loved.

None of her family remained. Her mom died when she was in high school. Her grandparents passed away within the last couple of years. Her dad had been MIA from before she was born.

I was her family now—we were, my family and good friends. And new friends she'd made.

After we made out like hormone-charged high schoolers in the car for a few more minutes, we drove out of the parking garage, through airport gridlock, then onto the expressway. And I finally began to relax.

Thank God for the modified sound system in her car. The speakers blared the rock playlists on my phone. Journey's "Don't Stop Believin'" switched over into the grittier Nickelback's "Gotta Get Me Some."

Fuck yeah, I do.

Hannah reached for the knob and turned the volume down. "How was Miami?"

I merged into the outgoing lanes of traffic, then glanced at her. "Muggy. Hot. Good trip, though. Blake has great potential with the portfolio he owns down there."

"Bars and nightclubs, right?"

I nodded. "And a couple of five-star restaurants right on South Beach."

I got off the expressway and moved into the center lane, planning to go straight to her house. She pointed further ahead toward the road that led to my neighborhood. "We're going to your house."

"We are?" Not what I had in mind. My plan? Naked. Shower. Her bed. Maybe a kitchen island. The floor. No dog. No roommate. No interruptions...for hours.

She nodded. "I have a surprise for you."

Well, okay. She was forgiven. I could deal with a short detour.

In front of my house, an unfamiliar dark car was parked at the curb, idling. Someone stood at my door about to knock, but he turned when we pulled into the driveway. He held insulated silver carriers in his arms.

"Pizza?" I glanced at Hannah, then cut the engine and opened my door.

She got out as I grabbed my bag from the backseat. "Yep. I'm not cooking tonight."

Hannah owned and ran a bakery, Sweet Dreams. She was also a Culinary Institute of America trained chef. And, due to a tradition we'd started when I'd patiently pursued her, she typically cooked dinner for me and my two closest friends several nights a week.

When we reached the door, Hannah unzipped her purse while the guy rattled off the total.

Confused, certain that pizza prices hadn't quadrupled in the time I'd been gone, I shook my head. But Hannah didn't bat an eyelash as she handed him seventy-five bucks, including tip. Then she grabbed my bag from me with both of her hands, and the guy shoved four pizza boxes into mine.

"We having a party?" I scanned along the curb and down the side of the street from where we'd come, not seeing any other cars.

She opened my unlocked front door. "Not exactly…"

The entryway inside was dark. Hannah tossed her keys into the entry table bowl. I dropped my bag onto the floor just beyond it. Low voices murmured in the background, then two barks sounded out. Seconds later, Ava, Hannah's and my German Shepherd pup, rounded the corner from the kitchen and greeted us. She trotted alongside Hannah as we walked toward the kitchen, but once Hannah finished rubbing her ear, Ava doubled back to me.

"Hey, girl. Happy to see you too." I balanced the pizza boxes in one hand and leaned down to rub her scruff. I didn't have to bend far; she was almost seven months old, nearly full grown. Her tail beat rapidly against my thigh.

I stood, then whistled low, assessing the kitchen. "Nice. Cabinets are finished and the counters are back on. Looks like they're all done up here." A couple of months ago, a pipe had burst behind the dishwasher, flooding the kitchen, living room, and basement. Our remodeling crew had been working nonstop to complete the repairs and restoration.

"That's not all." She opened the door to the basement.

Ava bounded ahead of us, and we followed her down the stairs.

The lights were already on. In my absence, the furnishings had been brought in. Some were brand new, replacing things damaged beyond repair, others refinished and reupholstered. I set the pizzas on the bar's granite countertop and crossed over to the refurbished pool table. "Love the color." I ran my hand over the black felt my roommate, Mase, and I decided to lay down over the slate instead of the typical green. The carved wood frame had been sanded and stained a dark mahogany.

"Cade!" My sister Kiki sprung up from the group seated in front of a new flat-screen TV that had Sunday night football blaring. She collided into my side with a hug.

"Hey, sis." I kissed the top of her head, then arched a brow at Hannah. "You don't call this a party?" I glanced around the room. "And where are all your cars?"

Ben, my best friend and business partner in Loading Zone, the bar we co-owned, turned from where he sat in a leather club chair. "Not when there's football. Then it's just game night. And we parked a few doors down. Hannah's idea."

Busted, Hannah shrugged with a smirk before Kiki tugged her toward the TV area. My other two sisters, Kendall, the baby girl but two years ahead of me, and Kristen, the oldest, sat on our old sectional, which had been refurbished back into a healthy black leather.

Mase got up from a side chair and headed toward the food. "A party has balloons. Music. Cake."

I shoved him, causing him to stumble sideways a step. "Thanks for the update, smartass." He knew we were party experts with the successful event-planning company my sisters and I ran: Invitation Only.

He gave me a mocking smile. "Anytime. You need business advice, I'm your guy."

I flipped him off. Hey, I missed the crazy fucker. Had to show him some reunion love.

Not really hungry, but needing to make sure Hannah had what she needed, I found the box with her favorite pepperoni and cheese and slid four slices onto a plate. I grabbed a couple of beers from the fridge, then made my way over to where she sat in an oversized leather chair.

She got up, took a beer and the plate, then pushed me into the chair before sitting onto my lap. I wrapped my arms around her, mumbling into the curve of her neck. "Not sure how long I'm gonna last before that one-on-one time you promised."

She gave me a soft kiss. "Game's at the beginning of the fourth quarter. Won't be too long. But I wanted to be sure you saw the basement. Mase had Joe move everything back in earlier today." Our contractor, Joe, had performed a miracle restoring all the damage in two months. It helped that he had the blueprints from our first remodel of the kitchen a couple of years ago, right after I'd bought the place.

"Thanks, Maestro. Feels good to have our basement back." I squeezed her hip, taking a look around the room that had been the most damaged in the flood. Water had rained down from the ceiling. Nearly everything down to the wall studs had to be replaced.

She nodded toward the corner of the room, then bent down, whispering into my ear. "We may need to do a private inspection of the closet later." I'd initially had the closet installed as a heartfelt gesture and slight joke. She and I had our first heated encounter in a church supply closet.

I gave her a hip a gentle squeeze. "I'm beginning to like *later* better and better."

"You home for a while?" Kristen asked.

Glancing up at her, I gave her a short nod. "Yeah. I'm home until the first." I let out a relaxed sigh, happy to have family and friends around me, in spite of the long travel day and my need to get Hannah alone. It felt great to be home.

I'd been gone on various business trips on and off the last couple of months. Miami had come on the heels of New York, Chicago, and Portland. To complete my consulting commitment on all of Blake's bar and restaurant holdings, I had several dozen cities yet to go. But he hadn't given me a time deadline, so I worked them around my other clients into a schedule that would span into December.

Kristen grabbed the remote and turned the volume up a notch. "Good. Saturday we can meet to go over events I've lined up through the end of the year."

"I'll put it on the calendar." That was the other reason to pace myself. Invitation Only still needed my attention in an advisory capacity and in running some of the events. Kristen had agreed to handle most of them while I got my consulting business off the ground.

Hannah offered me her slice of pizza. I bit off a third of it while she held it for me.

"Good," Hannah murmured in my ear while I chewed. "I've got lots of scheduling of my own to do with you."

Hannah was the most important reason I worked hard to keep things balanced. In the last two months while our relationship strengthened, we'd spent as much time together as we could. But after trying to handle too much a few months ago, and almost losing Hannah in the process, I made sure my schedule revolved around her every chance I had control over it.

The game continued on. The Seahawks were playing at home. My sisters, Ben, and Mase made random commentary.

"Look at how those pants grip that ass," Kiki breathed, fanning herself.

Kendall shoveled popcorn into her mouth, then mumbled around it. "Number twenty-four? Running back. Right?"

"Nope. Eighty-four," Kiki corrected.

"Tight end." Kristen's one and only loaded comment.

"I'll say." Kiki sighed.

I groaned. "If sex talk about players doesn't stop, I will ban all females from game night."

Kiki stuck her tongue out at me. Kristen fought a smile.

I rolled my eyes. They knew I could never ban them from anything. I loved them too much. Pranks though? *Fair game.*

The Seahawks won in overtime, we'd polished off the rest of the pizza, and everyone finally made their way out. We said our good-byes, then I closed the door while Mase took Ava out back.

Impatient, I pulled Hannah into my room, shut the door, and turned around. She gave me a playful smile as she backed into the center of the room to stand beside my bed.

I stepped forward and tugged one of her dress straps off her shoulder. A thin, black bra strap remained in place. "Off."

She bit her lip. "My dress?"

Tease. I gave her a hard look. "Everything."

"No shower? What about stale airplane?"

I growled. "We're about to get very dirty. You on me now. Shower after."

I pulled my phone out of my pocket to put it on my desk.

It vibrated in my hand, the screen lighting up with the ID of an incoming caller.

Blake. With the excitement of seeing Hannah and my family and friends, and the distraction of the game, I'd forgotten about the report I'd promised him tonight.

Hannah tossed her bra at me. The scrap of lace landed on my shoulder. I glanced up.

With a wicked smile, she swiveled her hips. All she had on were her high heel sandals. Her breasts swayed, her nipples hardening.

I swallowed hard. "I have to answer this. I'll be quick."

She nodded, sat on the bed, then crawled backward into the center and sprawled out. "Fine. But with me, you better take your sweet time, Mr. Michaelson. The rest could take all night."

I let out a slow breath, staring hard at her, *dying* to touch.

Frustrated, but dedicated to my commitments, I clicked the phone on. "Blake."

"Cade. How did the trip go? I didn't see an email."

"Went well. I've got some suggestions I think you'll be pleased with. Will tomorrow work?"

"That would be fine. Do you have room in your schedule next week for an extra trip?"

"Phoenix? I hadn't planned on that until the first."

"No, San Francisco. At Fisher Holdings, company headquarters. Should be a quick turnaround. One night. Two if you want to relax and recharge before your return flight."

Hannah's brows imperceptibly furrowed. I kept her in the forefront of my mind as I thought about next week's calendar items: strategizing with Ben before Loading Zone's quarterly meeting, a new client appointment regarding the possibility of a start-up, Kristen's meeting request on Saturday. "How's Thursday? I'll catch an early-morning flight. Stay one night. Fly back Friday."

"That would be great," Blake replied. He'd been easy-going with his requests of my time: always respectful of my other responsibilities, never coming across as demanding or entitled. "I'll have my secretary make the flight and transportation arrangements in the morning. We'll email you the details."

Hannah arched on the bed, her hand cupping a breast. Her fingers pinched a nipple and her lips parted on a gasp. Her gaze was locked onto mine.

"Sounds good. We'll talk more tomorrow." I hung up and tossed the phone onto my desk.

Her other hand trailed lower, fingers sliding through trimmed dark hair. She let out a low moan, her eyelids fluttering shut.

"Bad girl." I unfastened my belt.

Eyes opening only halfway, she bit her lip, then exhaled. "Just the way you like me."

"True." She was bad in all the best ways, good everywhere it counted.

Her gaze drifted to my phone. "Plans to leave already? You just got back."

I stripped my shirt and jeans off. "No. No talk of plans now. Only thing on my mind—me on you."

Her attention shifted to the erection jutting toward her. As I approached closer and crawled over her, she licked her lips. "Not me all over you?"

I nipped her earlobe and slid my cock through her wetness, pressing down on her. "That too."

A soft moan escaped her lips as I flexed my hips. She slid her hands down my back, then gripped my ass.

"Done." I grabbed her hips and rolled us.

She inhaled sharply, then collapsed her upper body onto my chest as she straddled me.

Without releasing my grip, I arched up against her. "Hot as it is to watch you touch yourself, I want to be a part of your orgasm."

Her breath caught as her body shuddered. Pressing her palms against my chest, she pushed herself up. Bracing her weight, she curving her pelvis as she slid over my cock. "You want me to *take* my pleasure...on you."

The tip of my cock caught at her entrance. I held my breath as she paused there, taking me into her heat only a fraction.

My voice grew hoarse. "Fuck yeah, I do."

A split second later, she slammed down.

A groan ripped from my throat as pleasure shot through me.

I pinched my eyes shut, or I blacked out. Either way, Hannah was wrapped around me. So I was safe. Taken care of.

Home.

2. DIRTY WHEN WET

Hannah...

C ade had a tortured expression on his face.

I smiled and lifted my hips, nearly pulling off of him. "You like me on top."

His eyes drifted open. "I love you any way you want to be. As long as you're with me."

He looked beautiful, willingly pinned under my slight weight. Almost-black hair had ruffled in our play. Eyelids were half closed over darkened blue eyes. His strong jaw, shadowed with stubble, clenched.

"I'm with you. Don't ever doubt it." Sometimes I wanted to pinch myself to believe it, but never once in the last couple of months had I wanted to be anywhere but in his protective arms.

On a shaky breath, I pressed my hips down once more, but slower, while I skimmed my palms up his muscular chest, lowering my upper body over him. My lips brushed against his the moment I hit bottom again—or more accurately, when he did.

Exhaling, I groaned at how completely he filled me. The experience was at once shocking and comfortable. Vulnerable and safe.

His hands slid slowly up my outer thighs, then he gripped my hips, holding me down.

When I tightened my inner muscles, his cock, hot and hard deep inside me, twitched.

"Tease," he growled.

I smiled against his lips, kissing him softly. Only once he gave himself completely into our kiss did his hold on my hips relax. I began to move, slowly pulling my body up, right to the tip, then easing back down, taking him deep inside me again.

We made slow love, one of the many ways we came together sexually. Heated meaningful looks were exchanged as our bodies reunited. Our emotional bond almost charged me more than anything physical between us.

He gave me the reins, letting me ride him at my pace. When I stayed down on him, rocking to a rhythm that wound me tighter, he shifted his hands to my ass, clutching me hard. My breathing grew ragged. Panting turned into low moans with every exhale.

Right when I hovered on the edge of release, Cade began thrusting hard, scattering the focus I had on an orgasm just out of reach. His gaze locked onto mine the second he stopped. His grip on my hips held me fast, rendering me immobile. I gasped for air as a tight ache coiled through me. When I thought I couldn't bear the tension any longer, his cock twitched inside once more. He thrust deeper. And I screamed, shattering.

On a final hard thrust, Cade came on a loud growl, his pulses mixing with the last of mine.

After a shuddering breath, I collapsed onto him.

Awareness filtered back into my brain in fragmented pieces. "Holy shit," I whispered. "Did I just scream at the top of my lungs?" The details were fuzzy.

He wrapped his arms around me. "Yep. No biggie. Mase knows we have sex."

Flushing hot in mortification, I slapped his chest. "But he didn't need to *hear* it."

He cleared his throat. "Would you like me to gag you next time?"

Giggling, I settled back against the heat of his body while he tightened his arm around my shoulder. "No. Maybe I need to be more aware. Bury my face into a pillow or something."

Tipping my chin up with a finger, he captured my lips, kissing me long and slow. "I love you unaware right before you come, when you come. Sexy as fuck."

"Mmm..." Our aftermath ebbed into a wonderful place. I felt peaceful and protected. Loved. His breathing slowed, deepening. After being separated for almost a week, I didn't want the moment to end. Didn't want to get up and pee. Or shower. Even though I needed to do both.

Long minutes later, I eased away from him. He didn't move a muscle. His jaw had slackened. With a smile I couldn't help, I pulled his black T-shirt on. Satisfied with the hem hitting me just below midthigh, I tiptoed out into the hall.

Light streamed out from the kitchen, and after I went to the bathroom, I took a detour before heading back to Cade's room. Mase sat at the kitchen table, eating something in a bowl. Ava was sprawled out on the floor beside him. When I stepped into view, she lifted her head and thumped her tail in a furious beat on the floor. But with her excellent training, she didn't move from her spot.

I smiled and crossed the room, then bent down to rub her head. "Hey, girl." After a moment, I stepped back and took a deep breath, looking Mase in the eye. "I...didn't keep you up, did I?"

From under shaggy, dark blond bangs, he pegged me with a hard stare. "What would keep me up?"

I pressed my lips into a firm line, trying not to laugh. "If you don't know, we don't need to discuss it."

The corners of his lips twitched. "Nope. We're good."

Mase was such a great guy. He treated me like a beloved sister. "Thanks again for helping to get the basement squared away now instead of next weekend."

"No problem. Was a great idea, actually." He spooned what looked like cereal into his mouth.

"Just wanted Cade to have some great news at home after being away for five days. Was his longest trip so far." I stared at his bowl, certain I'd seen a bright-colored flash. "What are you eating?"

"Granola and orange juice. Want some?"

My stomach roiled. "Sounds delicious."

"Liar. You look like you want to puke."

I grinned, shaking my head. "Enjoy your gastronomical brilliance. I'm going back to bed."

"'Night, Hannah."

I padded down the hall, opened and shut Cade's door, and stripped off his T-shirt before settling back into his side. He moved, turning toward me before caging me in his arms.

On a contented sigh, I closed my eyes, grateful—that he'd enjoyed his surprise enough to wait until all our company had left, that he'd been blown away enough by our private homecoming to pass out cold.

I pressed a kiss to his forehead and drifted to sleep in his arms.

SHOWERS DIDN'T HAPPEN until the following morning, if you count 3:00 a.m. as morning, as opposed to middle of the night, like normal people. But I had to be at Sweet Dreams in an hour.

To my amusement, Cade refused to let go of me this time when I tried to sneak away from his firm hold. He mumbled all the way down the hall about the insanity of having to get up.

He ducked his head under the hot shower spray and still hadn't opened his eyes. He also hadn't stopped touching me. Hands, lips, and teeth had traveled across every available spot, stroking, kissing, sucking, nipping.

When I slathered soap across his chest, his eyes opened. Mischief glittered there. "My turn."

I squirted a dollop onto his hand, and he made a great show of sudsing up between his palms. Then he held my gaze as he separated them and covered my breasts with the foam. He cupped them, lifting gently, then massaged slowly, pinching my nipples each time he made a full circle.

I groaned, then closed my eyes as I dropped my forehead onto his chest. "Cade, I have to go into work. We don't have time."

One of his hands slipped down my skin until his fingers slid between my legs. I shuddered and leaned further into him, losing my balance—and my will to resist him.

"We always have time. How long do you shower?"

Had he asked me a question? I couldn't think with the way he stroked me. Hot ache and blinding need had become all I could focus on.

He stopped moving. "Maestro, think. How long are your showers?"

"Fifteen. Twenty." I bit out the words, all I could manage.

"Plenty of time. I'll have you clean and satisfied in twenty."

After that, I lost track of time. The fingers of his one hand pinched and teased my nipple. The other, stroked me on a vertical ascent to ecstasy. When my breath caught, my orgasm edging into reach, he suddenly turned me around, bent me over, and thrust into me.

I gasped for air.

His fingers returned to my clit, rubbing in fast determined circles, while he pulled back and thrust deep in a pounding rhythm. Ache fired into searing pain seconds before waves of pleasure rippled through me. My scream tore out before I could stop it, echoing on the tiles surrounding us.

Cade tightened his grip on my hips, increased his pace, and came hard on a growl right after me. His upper body slowly molded to my back, his hot skin warming me far better than the shower spray. After several labored breaths, he folded his arms under me, pulled me up, and gently turned me.

Before I could process thought, he embraced me and captured my lips in a hard, insistent kiss. But then his lips softened, exploring, teasing. While I still struggled to catch my breath, he kept me in his arms, reached around for the soap, and squirted some out.

Without ever breaking complete skin-to-skin contact, he soaped my entire body, every crevice, nook, and cranny. He even lifted each foot and slid a soapy finger between each toe.

After an intense sexual experience I hadn't expected, he ministered to me in the most intimate way. It touched my heart, the amount of tenderness he showed in caring for me.

He stood, then gently urged me into the spray before rinsing every last soap bubble from my body. Relaxed to a level I couldn't remember in recent history, I turned back toward him, tilting my face up. My gaze met his.

So much emotion shone back at me. "I love you, Hannah."

He'd said the words before. They weren't necessary now. But after missing him badly for days, the passion behind them burned through me.

"I love you," I whispered. And I did. With all my heart.

Days gone at a time didn't matter. Absence only intensified what I felt for him.

But the longing for him until he returned? That was the hardest part.

"I'M WALKING YOU OUT," Cade muttered.

"No, you're not. Don't be silly." I ran my hands up his still-damp chest. Thin black pants clung to his hips—all he'd put on. I pressed a kiss over where his heart beat, then pulled back and tugged on one of my clean T-shirts over my bra. From the drawer he'd given to me for sleepovers, I grabbed a pair of tan cotton shorts and quickly pulled them on, then zipped and buttoned them. I snagged a pair of white socks and closed the drawer. "You're half asleep and sunrise won't happen for a few hours. Go back to bed."

When I turned, he swayed on his feet, and I pushed him backward. He gripped my hips, yanking me with him. "Tuck me in, then. Read me a bedtime story."

I landed on him, straddling his hips. I smiled but shook my head. "No stories. I have a suspicion they'll take a sudden turn toward pornographic. Then I'll never get to work."

With care, I shifted my weight to one knee and spun off of him. I perched on the edge of the bed and pulled my socks on.

After stretching out lengthwise on the bed, he handed me one running shoe, waited until I'd laced it up, then gave me the other.

"So, Blake called you away again?" His telephone conversation from last night pinged back into my brain.

"Yeah." He yawned. "San Francisco."

The sheet had tangled beneath his legs. I tugged it free, then pulled it up over his legs and chest. "Only one night?"

He held my gaze with half-lidded eyes. "Only one. Gotta get back to my girl."

I smiled. "I like that."

"Hey, you tucked me in."

"How about that?" I brushed a rogue lock of hair off his forehead. "If you're good today, I'll even read you a story tonight."

His eyes widened, darkening. "Promise?"

I gave him a soft kiss. "Only if you're good."

As his eyes drifted shut, he murmured. "I'll be good at everything possible..."

The last words were barely breathed out. I pressed a kiss to his temple, then grabbed my purse, turned off his light, and slipped out the door, closing it behind me.

By 8:00 a.m., a legion of cupcakes had been created. My two dedicated employees, Chloe and Daniel, were masterful in keeping up with our growing orders. And scurrying between countertops in the middle of a sea of colorful iced cupcakes we'd just finished, they made me proud.

Chloe began loading the first transfer board with maple

glazed chocolate pecan cupcakes. "You know, we're going to need to hire someone else. Soon."

Daniel stepped away from the baking area and pulled his hairnet off, setting his inky black Mohawk free. "Two. Two more employees." He skimmed a hand from front to back, to get his hair to stand more upright.

"Great. Can you find two *exactly* like you? Then will you interview, hire, and train them?"

"Now, there's a thought. Anyone who survives the interview without staring at Chloe's assets or my metal makes it to the final round."

I huffed out a laugh. "We could sell tickets."

Daniel referred to Chloe's well-endowed rack and his piercings. Both of my employees were attractive college-aged kids who expressed their uniqueness on the outside. Chloe accented her fire-red hair with makeup and outfits which swung either Goth or rockabilly, depending on her mood. Daniel, with his ears, nose, and eyebrow piercings, and tattoos that peeked out from under his shirt, dressed in what could only be described as clean-cut rocker grunge.

And they were both quick as whips and gentle as pussycats.

Daniel took the first transfer board from Chloe while she loaded a second with black forests. I picked up a board that I'd already loaded with classic red velvets and followed Daniel up front. Chloe trailed right behind me.

I considered their plea for help. "You're right. We're almost splitting at the seams. Any new orders, and we'll be working nights and weekends."

Chloe shook her head as she came around the other side of the display case and squatted down to fill in the bottom row. "No can do. I've got school. So does Daniel."

He dropped a heavy look at me. "And a life beyond cupcakes."

Point taken. "Yes. I'll put an ad out this afternoon."

Chloe stood, set the transfer board on the top of the case, then dusted off her hands. "Would it be okay if we sat in on the interviews? I know you were joking about us hiring, but I'd love to make sure all our personalities click."

Daniel gave a short nod, agreeing.

"Absolutely. Check your schedules and let me know when you can do it either first thing on a Saturday or a Tuesday or Thursday late in the afternoon." Those were the times our shop slowed with walk-in traffic.

The door opened, jarring the small bell above it. In walked two beautiful women about my age. Both wore chic suits, the willowy pale blonde in charcoal with a frayed black-and-pink tweed trim, the curvy brunette had on a burgundy jacket over a pencil houndstooth skirt. The blonde had long, straight hair, sleeked back into a wide barrette. The brunette had a shorter pixie cut, the longer locks on top purposefully tousled wild.

The brunette's eyes widened the moment she saw me behind the counter. "Hannah!"

"Elyse!" I rounded the corner for the near-tackle hug I knew was coming so she didn't take down Daniel and Chloe with me. I opened my arms wide, and we collided into a sideways embrace. Elyse was a title company sales rep and one of our regular customers. She'd also become an incredible walking billboard, networking our name out to everyone who fogged a mirror.

"Hey, Elyse." Daniel and Chloe said in near unison.

"Hi, guys! This is my new trainee, Kylie. I've taken her under my wing to learn the ropes. This is Hannah" —she gave me a squeeze— "Daniel and Chloe."

Daniel gave a short nod. "I've got your order boxed and ready in the back." He disappeared to get the three boxes Elyse picked up every third Monday of the month for the real estate luncheon her company sponsored.

Elyse turned away from me, set her purse on the counter, and pulled out her credit card while Chloe rang her up. "Kylie's territory will be northeastern Philly. Mine's southeastern. But we each have an office near Glenhaven, so she'll be able to order here for our events too."

Glenhaven was our quaint suburb community, attached to the greater Philadelphia metropolitan area. We were close enough for retail conveniences, yet sprawled far enough out on the fringe to keep us away from most of the city hustle.

I leaned toward Kylie, glancing up. Her skyscraper stilettos sent her slender body into catwalk-model territory. "You have experience in marketing?"

With a short nod, she smiled. "They say I'm a natural. Command the room, tell them what they want to hear, they're yours."

Behind us, the bell above the door tinkled again. "Sound business advice." The low timbre of a familiar voice caressed my ears.

Cade.

The two girls spun around, gasping when they caught sight of him.

My indrawn breath was slower, calming the riot of reactions my body had around him. When I turned, his focused gaze rested squarely on me. He held a tray of four coffees.

Pulse hammering, my smile widened. Images of our early-morning shower flooded into my mind. A flash of heat speared much further south as I took a steadying breath. "Hey there, stranger."

Had my voice sounded breathy? Elyse and Kylie exchanged glances while Chloe printed out a credit card receipt.

Daniel chuckled. "Hey, Cade."

Finally, Cade tore his loaded gaze away from me. He gave Daniel a chin up. "Hey, Daniel."

Cade swept his gaze across the room at all the faces staring at him. "Am I interrupting?"

Taking the tray of coffees from him, I pulled one loose and handed it to him as I shook my head. "No. Elyse is a friend of mine, the title company rep I've been telling you about."

She extended her hand, gold bangles clanking at her wrist as she shook Cade's. "Nice to finally meet you, Cade. This is Kylie, a new hire I'm training."

Chloe rounded the corner, leaning a hip against the edge of the counter. "Know of anyone else looking for a job? We're hiring as of today. Wanted: responsible, brilliant, fun, and *must* love cupcakes."

Cade's gaze swung back to me. "Really?"

I stepped closer to him, grinning as his expression turned from surprise into pride. He'd been a dedicated consultant in the launch and growth of Sweet Dreams, offering invaluable advice. "Just decided this morning. It's time. And I don't want to face a mutiny." When I turned, Chloe and Daniel were nodding, vigorously.

"Nice meeting you all." Elyse gave Kylie one of the boxes and slid her arms under the other two. "We've got to head out or we'll be late for the meeting. Still doing lunch Wednesday?"

"Yes." I raced toward the door, but Cade beat me to it, opening it for the girls. "Lila's at 11:00 a.m.?"

Elyse nodded. "Sounds perfect. See you then."

I folded my arms across my chest, leaning into Cade's side as we stood in the open doorway. "Great to meet you, Kylie. You should come too."

Kylie glanced at Elyse, who gave her a firm nod before stowing her two boxes into the backseat of her Mercedes. Kylie then handed her the one she held. "Sure. I'd like that."

"Great. Good luck with the new job."

She beamed a smile at me. "Thanks."

Cade let the door close. His body heat singed through my thin T-shirt. As my internal temperature rose, I glanced at the counter. Chloe and Daniel had disappeared, probably in a race to catch up on our jam-packed day.

I nudged my hip into his solid side. "I have to go. I'm desperately needed back there."

A dark lock of hair fell onto his forehead when he gave a slow nod. Piercing blue eyes held mine. He pulled me into his arms, his warm strength surrounding me. "Just wanted to say 'hi.' Can't stop thinking about our shower."

I swallowed hard as I remembered it in vivid detail. "Me either."

He bent down, his voice a low growl. "Make sure you get extra dirty today."

Fighting a smile, I leaned into him. "Oh? Why's that?"

"Today feels like a two-shower day."

3. TAKING CARE OF BUSINESS

Cade...

My mood soared. The wakeup soap-down started the day on a fucking spectacular note. But seeing her eyes light up when I walked into a room? Always hit me hard and deep. Kept me going for hours—days when my work demanded it.

Hannah made me look forward to coming home.

All the trips, carving out a career I'd been born to do, were the culmination of my life's goals and education. Sure, work pulled me away, but it also gave me something to share with her.

The recent months had been an adjustment. Our new relationship had been tested—trauma from her ex, meddling from mine—but we'd survived. Then we'd focused on quality time. Stability. Us against the world. Or at least, us fighting for our space within it.

On my way to my new consulting office, I swung by Loading Zone. The bar didn't open on Mondays, but it served as Ben's office seven days a week; he took administrative operations to a whole new level—art-form territory. If it was daylight, he'd be there.

I parked the Jeep that Mase and I shared beside Ben's Escalade, then pushed through the back door. Heavy metal clanged behind me when it slammed shut, bouncing echoes off the concrete floors and rusted-metal walls. At artistic Kiki's insistence, we'd refurbished the abandoned warehouse into an "industrial-grunge" bar. Whatever she called it, customers loved the vibe. Magazines raved. And money flowed—all that mattered.

Odd. Silence filled the place. I stuck my head in Ben's office. Empty.

"Ben?"

A grunt sounded out from up front.

His shadowed form slumped over the counter from behind the bar. Backlighting under the liquor shelves gave off the only light in the dark room. A bottle of scotch and a shot glass stood beside his hand, but he just stared at the inch of counter space between them.

"You okay, man?" I crossed the room. I'd never seen him so...off.

He shoved his hand into his thick mass of black hair, messing it up further. When he glanced up at me, dark eyes pegged me. "Been better. Stacy dumped me."

"Ah. Sorry, man." That explained it. Ben's first long-term girlfriend. She'd been quiet. But then, so was he. From what I'd seen of them together, they'd gotten along fine. "What happened?"

Finally he grabbed the scotch and poured the shot. "Want one?"

Bracing my arms on the edge of the bar top, I shook my head. "No, thanks."

Without expression, he eyed the amber liquid, then

slammed it back. "Seems I'm more committed to my work than to her."

I barked out a laugh. Couldn't help it. "This is news to her?"

He ran his tongue along his teeth. "Apparently. I've been driven all along. What she liked about me—right up until the point it took me away from her."

Unsure what to say, I waited. Listening worked when words failed. But when he poured a second shot and set the nearly full bottle back down, I grabbed it. "Changed my mind. I will have one with you." The man needed backup, and I could handle one drink and still drive.

He gave me a sharp nod and grabbed a shot glass. Then he slid it over.

Bartender muscle memory had me pour the shot without looking, my gaze fixed on my friend. Hard to tell if he was hurt or confused. Probably some of both.

Slowly, he straightened up from the slouch he'd been in. Gaze fierce, he narrowed his eyes at the scotch. Like the damn thing held his absolution. Then he grabbed it, raised it up, and stared at me. "To being true to who we are."

"Fuck, I'll drink to that." I raised my glass, then tossed it back with him.

Women couldn't change men, no matter how badly they wanted to. Or how hard they tried. Creatures of habit, we were set in our ways, down to our bones. Could we be softened around the edges? Sure. Even a dog could be housebroken.

But Ben and I had been bitten by the business bug. Shit was addictive. Taking something from an idea to creation to success—we both excelled at it.

Only problem? Ben hadn't found the woman meant for him. Or he would've tried harder.

Me? I'd become invested in Hannah. Balance for me was nonnegotiable.

He sighed. "I'm good. Freedom has its perks." Ben's expression changed, relaxed. His double dose of scotch had already begun to take the edge off.

I swiped the bottle from the bar top. "Yeah. Like flavor of the week." How Ben had operated since college. Girls flocked to him with his dark, edgy look. Broody was a one-word descriptor. Mysterious, a second. Behind the quiet exterior, his mind was razor sharp.

When I moved behind the bar and returned the bottle to its shelf, he didn't argue. Except on rare occasions, we had an unspoken agreement not to drink our own stock. Or abuse the responsibility of being bar owners. A bigger motivator for Ben? History. Alcoholism ran in his family, had torn his parents apart. He respected the killer for what it was. And I supported him when needed. But every other time he'd drank hard liquor had been when we were partying—not when shit hit the fan.

The universe had an odd way of balancing. While I rode my relationship high, Ben got nailed into a serious low.

Intent on distracting Ben and accomplishing what I'd dropped by for, I grabbed both glasses and washed them in the sink on the end. "You cool with moving the quarterly meeting to next Monday?" I pulled out a clean, folded towel and upended the shot glasses on it.

He leaned back against the bar, crossing his arms. "Week from today?"

"Yeah. I'll be out of town the following. Unless you want to wing one without me."

"No way. Loading Zone is ours. We do it together." His entire demeanor changed. Filled with purpose, he headed back toward his office as I followed. "I'll email the crew."

By crew, he meant everyone from the bartenders to the doormen, DJ to the janitor. Each one attended quarterly meetings, actually rescheduled their lives around them. Because they didn't just work here—they profit shared. Not because they owned a piece of the company; it was simply our business model. We brought in team members and gave them a vested reason to help us succeed.

I leaned against the doorframe, watching Ben as he flipped open his laptop on the desk. "Okay. Cool. I gotta head to the office. Need to send a report to a client and schedule the next week. You good?"

"Yeah." The hard stare he shot me was filled with emotion, heavy. The kind with words that didn't need to be spoken.

I clapped him on the shoulder. The guy was made of steel. "Call me if you need anything."

"Thanks, man."

The gray morning had been raindrop free, but a mineral tang hung heavy in the air. Windows down, the drive to the executive suites building took ten minutes—long enough for the cool air to clear my brain. I needed the neutral reset after the high of Hannah and low from Ben. Only way to think straight for work.

I walked across the marble floor and nodded to the building receptionist, who sat behind her tall mahogany desk in the lobby. The newer building was only partially leased, and I saw no one else on the way up to the third floor. After a low ding, the elevator doors opened. Two steps into the hall, I stopped with a grin.

Beyond the glass front wall of the office, the newly hired secretary slid a giant orange orchid from the center of the coffee table toward one corner. She pulled back, assessing. Then she gave it a quarter turn before she fanned out three magazines, probably the entrepreneurial ones I'd instructed her to order.

Swallowing down my smile, I opened the door. "Looks great, Cassandra."

The earthy theme had been Kiki's idea. With all the cold steel and concrete at the bar, I hadn't argued. The leather chairs were a light brown. Prints on the side walls were ancient-looking botanical sketches. A looped beige rug sat under the seating in the reception area. Dark walnut flooring spanned everywhere else.

"Thank you, Mr. Michaelson."

"Cade. Call me Cade."

Cassandra straightened taller beside me. Then my consulting partner, Simon, walked into view from the supply room with several manila file folders in his grip. He gave us a chin up, turned his head, and tapped the Blue-tooth earpiece—universal signal for "I'm on the phone." Without breaking stride, he disappeared down the hall and his door clicked shut.

"Such a shame when he doesn't talk," Cassandra said. *Breathlessly.*

I dropped a deadpan look at her.

Oblivious, she sent a dreamy-eyed stare toward his office. "He's British? He looks like an Arabian prince."

Great. My one place to escape all the female sex talkers, and I'd inadvertently hired one to fill the void. My sisters would die laughing if they had any clue.

When Cassandra made no further comment, nor any sign of moving from her awestruck pose, I shifted around her, into her line of sight. My expression hardened.

Her brown eyes widened.

Good. I had her attention. "This is a place of business. I expect you to respect Simon for what he is—a top-notch financial analyst and business consultant."

She swallowed hard. Her expression grew stern, and she nodded. "Yes, sir. I understand. It won't happen again."

I sighed, then smiled. "Cade. Yes, Cade."

The hint of her smile crept out, which turned her pretty face into a powerful asset. The sharp brain behind her attractive package would work to her advantage if she used them both correctly.

"Yes, Cade."

"What you to do on your own time, is your affair." I glanced down the hall, uncertain about Simon's views on work and play. "I advise against it though. Mixing business with pleasure rarely ends well."

Thank fuck Hannah and I were the exception.

"Yes, s-I mean, Cade." She gave a final thoughtful glance down the hall. Then, as if the entire exchange hadn't occurred, she moved behind her desk, her demeanor all business. "I have those demographics and business reports you asked me to compile on the Phoenix Metropolitan Area."

"Categorized by city?"

"Yes." She handed me the folders. "With more detail on those with the greatest projected growth."

"Excellent." I took the folders from her. "Hold all my calls until after lunch. I'm heading out of town Thursday and Friday, so we'll need to reschedule my meetings to early next week."

The phone began ringing as she sat at her desk. "I'll take care of it, sir."

"Cade," I muttered as I turned and headed toward my office. Sir reminded me of stiff suits. Unless the word came from Hannah's lips, the only time it sounded appealing—for stiff in a whole other way.

With so much work ahead of me, I closed my door and got to it, starting with the eighty-seven emails in my inbox. Some were about Invitation Only items. Most were either new leads or the dozen existing clients I'd been working on projects with. On and off all morning, I thought about Hannah but kept working through the impulse to call or text her. Didn't want to lose my momentum. Or bother her.

An email came in from Blake's secretary. Flight information. Ground transportation. Glaringly missing, however, were hotel accommodations and an itinerary. I fired off an inquiry in reply.

When I worked right through lunch, efficient Cassandra brought me back a burger and fries from her lunch hour. But since I couldn't eat a messy burger and work worth a damn, I took a break. Wordlessly, she grabbed a beer from my wet bar and set it on a cork coaster on the corner of my desk.

My phone already had an alert message on it from Hannah.

I clicked into the text. Three tiny characters were there.

. . .

I huffed out a laugh. Hannah knew her innuendo-filled reminder would make me smile. Mission accomplished. And those three naughty little dots meant more than textual foreplay. Remembering the fun we had during my slow pursuit of her, I replied.

Miss me, huh?

No reply came through. I bit off a quarter section of burger and stared through the glass-walled conference room, out into the lobby. Nothing came into focus until I blinked my dry eyes several times. It was the longest distance I'd looked at after staring at my computer screen all morning. If I wasn't careful on the eyestrain, I'd end up needing glasses. I grabbed my beer, took a couple of good swallows, then leaned back in my chair, letting my eyes fall shut to rest them.

My phone buzzed on the wood desktop. I put down the bottle and swiped up my phone.

Hannah's reply was worth the wait.

> Missed you bad.

> I'm thinking you like me bad.

> . . .

I blew out a hard breath and replied.

> Fuck yeah, I do.

Her blue typing bubble appeared.

> Busy?

I nodded.

> Very.

She replied.

> Me too. Need to skip dinner. Gotta work late tonight.

Not unusual. For either of us.

> Do what you need to. We'll fend for
> ourselves.

Her rapid reply told me she'd already been typing.

> Would you maybe wanna come over late
> tonight?

I smiled.

> No.

Her reply fired through.

> No?

I typed.

> Not maybe. Definitely.

A pause, then her typing bubble appeared again.

> Great! I'll text you when I leave the shop.

Plans tonight with Hannah gave me something to look forward to, settled me. I typed a good-bye so we could both get back to work and get our after-work plan on track.

> Miss you . . . more.

Her reply volleyed right back.

> Impossible.

When 7:00 p.m. rolled around, my brain stopped functioning. On the ride home I thought about what my life had become. Work and Hannah. The one, consulting, which honed my natural skills at seeing the big picture, shifting perspective, and advising on it, fulfilled a lifelong dream. The other—made the dream worth living.

At home, Ben dropped by to eat with Mase and me. Just the three guys seemed good for Ben after his somber mood at the bar. We ate Chinese food and debated which teams would go all the way in this year's World Series.

Hours later, Hannah's text pinged through.

Ready?

. . .

I clicked off the Ozzy marathon I'd been blaring in my room, grabbed my keys and jacket, and rode my motorcycle over to her place.

She'd left her front door unlocked. I slipped inside and locked it. The silence surprised me. Not a light on in the place. I quietly placed my keys on her narrow entry table and took my boots off.

I found her in her bedroom. She lay curled onto her side on top of the comforter, the mountain of decorative pillows still intact. With care not to disturb her, I moved each pillow, one by one, onto the couch in the small sitting area. A cold draft blew in from an open window above her window seat until I pulled it mostly shut.

In full stealth mode, I climbed onto the bed and wrapped my body around hers. Instinctively, she snuggled deeper into my hold and let out a quiet sigh. Her fingers slowly opened over my forearm, held tight for a second, then relaxed.

A burning ache filled my chest and I kissed the soft top of her ear. Seconds later, I began to doze off as peaceful thoughts filled my mind.

The reason we spent our days apart? So we could come together.

BEST LAID plans with Hannah would never be enough. Actions mattered.

Tuesday night came after another challenging workday. With our busy work schedules, we hadn't seen much of each other since that amazing shower Monday morning. And Hannah had texted she had to work late again, expecting to be busy at her shop past midnight.

But another Hannah-less night stretching ahead?

Fuck that.

Scraping my chair back, I stood and grabbed my plate. "That's it. I'm outta here."

Mase picked up the other half of his legendary sourdough grilled cheese. He stared at the bread and cheddar with narrowed eyes. Like if he wished hard enough, it would turn into something more extraordinary, like beef tips. "Where you going?"

"Where do you think? If Hannah can't break away, I'm instigating a forced work break."

Mase exhaled hard and stood, tossing his grilled cheese back onto his plate. "Well, hell. I'm not hanging around here. It's like the morgue. I'm thinking Laura could use a study break."

"Yeah, good luck with that." Mase's girlfriend was busy studying for the bar exam. And Mase had been a good boy, honoring the forced seclusion she'd finally demanded—because Mase kept distracting her.

He swiped the Jeep keys from the entry table bowl. "I don't need luck. I've got more effective weapons in my arsenal." He gave a quick waggle with his brows.

I shook my head, snatching my bike key from the bowl. The man was in for an adventure tonight. From what I'd heard, hell hath no fury like a studying Laura interrupted.

The ride to Hannah's shop normally took twelve minutes on a light traffic day. I made it in nine, give or take a few seconds. After dinnertime on a slower Tuesday night, the business corridor on the way to Sweet Dreams seemed deserted as yellow street lights began to flicker on.

I parked my bike and spotted Daniel behind the front counter, emptying the contents of the display case onto a flat board. His black Mohawk bounced when he gave me a chin-up as I opened the door.

I glanced at the *Sorry, We're CLOSED* sign. "Want me to lock this?"

"Yeah." Daniel straightened from behind the counter and gave a hard look. "She know you're coming?"

I shook my head. "No. Thought I'd surprise her. Should I worry?"

"We've removed all sharp implements from her reach and stayed out of her way most of the night. Never seen her like this."

Maybe I should've text-teased her first. "Thanks for the heads-up."

"Anytime. Good luck." Daniel returned to loading the unbought cupcakes for the night.

I headed back to the kitchen, remembering I'd given Mase the same well wishes.

The first person I saw in the kitchen wasn't Hannah, it was Chloe, her prodigy baker, with her red hair pulled into a ponytail. She focused on pulling a large bowl from under one of their mixers. Then she raced across the room with it toward a stainless steel counter that held several unfrosted cake rectangles. She nearly clipped my shoulder as she passed. "Hey, Cade." The bowl spun as she slid it onto the counter, next to empty cake pans. "Daniel, it's done!" Without skipping a beat, she began frosting cupcakes with whirlwind speed.

I nodded to Chloe. Then I zeroed in on the person I'd come to see tonight.

Oblivious to my arrival, Hannah hunched over her desk. A deep scowl marred her face as she typed furiously into her phone.

Not wanting to shock her, I took measured steps as I approached and spoke softly. "Hello, Maestro."

A couple of seconds later, she glanced up, blinking. Her eyes widened as sudden panic flashed across her face. "Cade. What are you doing here?"

I reached down, gently taking the phone out of her hands and placing it on her desk before I pulled her from the chair. "Relax, babe. I'm not here to disrupt things."

Her brow creased, and she tried to tug her hands from my grasp. "But you *are* disrupting things. We've got a dead-line to meet for tomorrow, and we're so far behind."

Unhappy at seeing her distressed, but torn between letting her go and seeing what I could do to help, I dropped one of her hands and clasped the other more firmly. Then I turned and led her away from her desk. "Mandatory fifteen-minute break."

A heavy sigh sounded out behind me.

I fought a grin.

When we pushed through her back door, we entered a

small cobblestone courtyard. Light angled out through the shutter slats inside her shop, shining on a brightly tiled bistro table and two weathered white metal chairs. An old concrete birdbath stood in one corner, and in the other, a green ceramic birdhouse dangled from a shepherd's hook.

Hannah tugged her hand from my grasp. By the time I turned around, she'd crossed her arms over her chest.

Far removed from the jovial girl I'd come to know, the woman standing before me now seemed hardened. For a fleeting moment, she resembled the Ice Queen persona I'd encountered so long ago.

Barriers up.

Me on the outside.

I frowned, inexplicably riled. "Hannah, what's with the attitude? We haven't seen each other all day. You act like I'm crashing your party."

A muscle in her jaw ticked. I reevaluated my choice of words. And maybe my spontaneous decision to come here. Had it been selfish? Yeah, maybe a little. Okay, a lot. But I reasoned it was selfish not just for me alone, but for both of us together.

She let out a slow breath through pursed lips, like she held back from blowing a gasket. "You haven't seen me angry, have you? Well, this is it. You knew I was scrambling to make deadlines. I told you I wouldn't make it home until after midnight. That I needed to focus. And yet here you are" —she waved a hand between us— "distracting me."

I fought a smile. "You know, you're *sexy as fuck* when you're pissed." Couldn't help it. She was. Nostrils flaring. Chest heaving. Wisps of hair falling into her face that I knew she wanted to blow out of her eyes.

Instead, she glared at me.

I tried not to smirk. I really did. But I was instantly transported back to all those times I'd made one of my sisters furious with one prank or another and how they would stand there, staring me down, not quite knowing how to deal with me.

Hannah thought I'd showed up to disrupt her. Probably thought I wanted to have sex with her. I'll admit, when I stepped into the courtyard, I instantly scanned possible locations for an explosive fifteen-minute break guaranteed to pound out all her tension. She needed to blow off some steam—I wanted to help.

But my intentions shifted with her mood. She needed me, all right.

I took a step closer, but she didn't budge, her arms still crossed and her body held rigid. With a gentle smile, I wrapped my hands around her elbows. "Use me."

She blinked. "What?"

"You need help. So use me. I have two hands, and I'm trainable. Tell me what has to be done, and let me help the three of you catch up to where you're supposed to be."

Her expression softened, not much, but it was far from glacial. "Really?"

Before I had a chance to assure her of my now honorable intentions, she grabbed my hand and yanked me toward the back door.

I grinned. "So I guess the fifteen-minute break is over?"

She whirled around, colliding back into me. She tilted her head and narrowed her eyes. "Tell me you didn't want to bend me over out here during said 'fifteen minute break.'"

I shrugged, feeling only mildly contrite. "Thought crossed my mind."

She took a deep breath and stared hard at me—like she didn't know what to do with me. And I didn't care, as long as we spent tonight together, *whatever* that entailed.

Her eyes suddenly sparked with humor. "Keep thinking that, *babe*. You have frosting duty tonight. Let's see how good you are with a spatula on actual cake. We'll see if you've earned 'break time' by the time we get out of here."

Even though her words teased of a possible reward, her expression still held a hard edge. She meant business. Play would come later.

Her determination with her business was exhilarating to see firsthand.

And sexy as fuck.

Minutes later, I stood in front of an entire countertop of unfrosted cupcakes. Chloe pointed. "First do the cream cheese on these red velvets. Then the fudge on those chocolate. Daniel will have more frosting ready by the time you're done. Now watch carefully; I'll go *slow* for you."

I shot her a deadpan look. The "slow kid" comment? Not appreciated.

She grabbed a cupcake and a spatula, then iced the top with four efficient strokes. She left upswirls each time she broke contact. "There. Now your turn." She handed me a cupcake.

Across the room, Daniel manned the mixers, adding ingredients while the metal beaters spun in the industrial-sized bowls. On the table beside him, Hannah poured creamy batter into molds.

When I dipped the spatula into the frosting, I caught sight again of my green apron with yellow ruffled trim that Hannah had put on me before I'd had a chance to argue. Daniel wore a plain black apron.

I glanced at Hannah. "You sure my yellow ruffles are enough? Nothing with pink lace?"

Chloe snorted beside me.

I glared at her.

She pressed her lips into a flat line that kept twitching up into a smile.

Hannah set her empty bowl aside before glancing up at me. She arched her brows. "What? Ruffles too emasculating for you?"

I stood taller, rolled my shoulders, and cleared my throat. My voice deepened, "No, I'm good. I've got big enough balls to wear ruffles."

And the crowd burst out laughing.

Hannah stared at me with an unreadable expression that morphed into something resembling part incredulousness and part gratitude. She continued her pointed look and mouthed *thank you*.

I gave her a big smile.

Chloe pointed at the cupcake in my hand. "You frosting that thing, or what?"

I nodded. "Yeah, sorry. I'm on task." And with a few smears of frosting, twisting my wrist with every sweep like she had, said cupcake transformed into an acceptable product.

She nodded, satisfied. "Do both those sections. When you're done, let me know."

Chloe abandoned me and went back to the monumental creation she'd been working on. Even unfrosted, the form took shape as she moved pieces into place. Giant balloons stretched up on one end, and a replica playground with swings, slides, and a merry-go-round stood on the other.

"What's the big cake project?" I asked the room at large.

"A surprise party at The Children's Hospital of Philadelphia," Hannah replied.

Not much more was said after that. We all worked in relative silence for the next few hours, everyone focusing on their tasks with calm efficiency. They had a heavy quiet vibe going. I kept my mouth shut, fitting into their system.

Yet, even with the protracted silence, while the four of us worked, the tension that had thickened the air when I'd arrived eased somewhat.

At half past eleven, everything that had been baked and cooled had been iced. Other cakes were left sitting on the counter or had been stored in the cooler for the following day.

Chloe scrubbed her hands down her face. "You guys good for us to take off?"

Daniel grabbed his keys and phone off of a narrow table in the far back corner. "We'll be in at eight, if that's cool."

Hannah shook her head. "No, you guys went above and beyond. And Cade helped us get some of tomorrow's work done tonight. I'll come in early tomorrow. How's ten sound for you two?"

Daniel gave her a hard look. "No way. You aren't dealing with the morning rush by yourself. Nine."

Hannah smiled. "Fine. Nine would be great."

"Okay. That's better. G'night, Hannah. 'Night, Cade. Thanks for the drop-in help."

I slid my arms around Hannah, who hugged her arms across her middle. "Anytime. Good night, you two."

"Good night!" Chloe shouted from the front after already disappearing.

Hannah sighed in my arms, leaning back against me.

I smiled, kissing the top of her head. "Still mad at me?"

Snorting, she turned around. Amusement fired in her eyes. "I should be. You initially came here with intentions other than helping us. Naughty ones."

"Can you blame me? I missed you." I dropped my forehead to hers. "And I'm kind of addicted to you."

A small smile curved her lips, a touch of remorse flashing across her expression. "Next time, maybe text first."

"Nah. You would've waved me off. Then you'd still be here, and I'd be sulking at home."

She wrapped her arms around my waist. "This was better?"

"Way better. At least we got to be together. Anytime you need my help, let me know. I'm glad you're hiring. You need more people. And rock music. Your kitchen needs rock music."

She laughed.

The easy sound calm me. Aching to touch her, I bent down and gave her a soft kiss.

She smiled against my mouth, then pressed kisses along my jawline, murmuring, "Wasn't there a possible reward for good-frosting behavior?"

I growled low, buried my face into her great-smelling hair, and walked her backward toward that private patio. "Thought you'd never ask."

4. COURSE CORRECTION

Hannah...

S tartling upright in bed, I took a shuddering breath. Heart racing, body shaking, my skin was covered in a thin sheen of sweat. My mind tried to lock onto the fragments of a dissipating bad dream, but the images faded too quickly.

With trembling hands, I skimmed my fingers across the surface of the bed. My fingers hit the warmth of Cade's body. I exhaled slowly, comforted already just by his presence. His help at Sweet Dreams earlier, and our coming together again after both of our busy schedules, made me feel deeply connected to him again, grounded.

But my heart still pounded from the nightmare. Sleep anytime soon would be impossible.

I slipped out of my bed, naked but not caring, padded across the rug, then stepped onto the cold wood floor that led to the hall. I switched on the kitchen lights, fired up a teakettle on the stove, then sat at my dining table. I flipped open my laptop and clicked it on.

Surfing the Net kept me occupied until the kettle began to rumble. Trained in tea preparation from Gran, I poured hot water into the teacup to rinse it, dumped it, then filled it again. From antique tins she'd collected, I chose the lavender chamomile, plucked out a tea bag, and dunked it into the hot water. When the tea darkened, I pulled the bag, dropped it into the sink, and returned to the table with the teacup balanced on its saucer.

Bored with mind-numbing retail shopping and news trolling, I clicked into my email. Several supply order confirmations were there, unopened. I scrolled down with one hand, holding the teacup in the other as I blew on the hot liquid's surface. Kristen had sent an email, an official notice of Saturday's Invitation Only planning session: a barbeque. Two unknown emails were stacked on top of one another, minutes apart in send times. The subject of one said "Contacting You." The second said simply "Your Dad."

Surprised, my hand flinched. Scalding tea singed my lips. "Shit." Licking my upper lip, I nearly dropped the cup back onto its saucer. It clattered loudly. I sighed at my overreaction.

Unthinking, I clicked on the "Contacting You" one.

I found you from a newspaper article. Called your work the other day at lunchtime. You weren't there, but the girl who answered gave me your email address. Hope it was okay to contact you by email. Didn't want to shock you in person. Wanted to be sure.

I frowned. Shock me? Sure about what? Chloe hadn't mentioned anything to me. Confused, I scanned down the list again. I'd accidentally read the second email. I clicked into the first one.

Cade appeared suddenly, squinting. "Bright."

I glanced up.

Six-foot-two inches of chiseled sexiness leaned against the doorframe, hair stuck out in adorable dark spikes on one side. He speared a hand into the other side. With a lazy stride, he crossed the distance between us and brushed a kiss to my cheek. Then he sat, dropped his elbow to the table, and propped his head onto his hand.

Distracted, my gaze returned to the startling emails. I stared in shock at the laptop screen.

His hand slid over mine, warm and protective. "Everything okay?"

I scanned down the content of the email. It was signed by a Paul Gilcrest. My gaze shot back up to the subject line. I swallowed hard, unable to tear my eyes away. "Don't know. Strange emails," I muttered, the only words I could manage as I tried to process what had been sent. I began reading what had originally been the first message.

Cade leaned in, reading over my shoulder.

Dear Hannah,

You don't know me and may not want to know me. But I've known about you since before you were born. Your mom sent me a note with no forwarding address that said she was pregnant, she didn't want me in your life, and that if I tried to contact her or claim you, she'd fight me in court to get sole custody. And seek the maximum amount of child support.

We were already apart at that point. I was young and irresponsible. I didn't have it in me to chase after something I couldn't handle, let alone afford.

Things have changed now. I'm older and wiser. Or so I'd like to think. I have a wonderful family, wife, and two kids. But there's always been something missing in my life to make it complete. You.

If you want to get together, with no pressure or expectations, please let me know. I would love to finally meet you.

With love,

Paul

I blinked. My mouth fell open as I scanned through the message once more. At the end of the email was a standard signature block that included his full name, address, email, and phone number.

"Maestro." His voice was low as his hand squeezed mine.

"I—" My throat locked up. I held tight to his hand. His warm strength tethered me like a lifeline while my thoughts jumbled into a whirlwind.

"Wow." His singular word said all either of us were able to process.

"I have a dad." In utter disbelief, my tone fell flat as my gaze met his.

He shook his head. "No, you don't, Maestro. You have a biological father. A sperm donor, you'd once called him. You've always had that. Only before, he was an unknown. A *dad* raises you, takes you to ball games and ice cream. Your mom and Granpop and Gran were that for you."

I stared back at the computer screen, struggling to have thoughts flow through my brain again. "You're right."

"You ever consider the possibility he might contact you?"

Swallowing hard, I nodded, remembering silly dreams in high school. "Hundreds of times. It was this recurring fantasy I had as a kid, especially after Mom died—she never talked about him."

"And how did the fantasy go?"

A bitter laugh escaped my lips. "Far differently. Not once

did I have him contacting me. I'd always imagined me being a private investigator, sleuthing around to find clues my mom might have left, like a note hidden in an old book or a ticket stub stuffed deep into a forgotten pocket. I even watched *Lara Croft: Tombraider* a million times, thinking maybe my long-lost relative left me a ticking clock hidden in the wall for me to find when the planets aligned."

One corner of his mouth twitched up. "Did you go knocking on the walls of your house?"

The absurd image made me smile. "No. But I did scour through all the books in our house, more than once. Examined the back of every framed picture, twice. Before any garment of my mom's was stored into my closet or given away, I searched every pocket."

"Nothing?"

I looked up into his bright blue eyes. The compassion there warmed my heart. "Not even a scrap. It's as if he never existed. After a while, I stopped thinking he was a person wandering around in the world somewhere. All the scenarios I'd dreamt up where I'd hunted him down, thoroughly researched his life, then approached him when I was ready, faded away. Other than mentioning him to you, I haven't thought about him in years."

He rubbed his thumb along the back of my hand. "Do you feel like you're in a good place in your life to want contact with him now?"

I pulled my other hand from the table, and placed it over his, holding it captive between both of mine. "I'm in the best place I've ever been in my life. I've never been happier."

"But..." He tilted his head. "There's hesitation in your tone."

Smiling, I leaned forward, kissing him softly. "Not about us." Suddenly, the cause of my uncertainty slammed into me. "Why is it every time you and I finally get our footing, some ghost from the past creeps out of the woodwork and haunts us?"

"Dumbfuck and Selfish Bitch," he agreed, evoking our exes' nicknames.

Furious, I shot up from the chair, scraping the wooden legs back, almost toppling the thing. I pointed at my laptop. "What right does this Paul have to wait until *his* life is perfect to show up and screw with mine?"

He leaned back in his chair, watching me with an impassive expression.

Irritated at his calmness, I scowled. "Get pissed off about this, Cade. Join me. It feels great." Pacing back and forth, aware of my nakedness but not giving a damn since he didn't seem distracted by it, I tried to wrap my mind around the surprise that my "biological" father delivered. But I failed to grasp the enormity of it all.

"I'll be whatever you want me to be, Hannah." His voice softened with each successive word. "I don't care about anything as much as I care about you. The ghosts in our pasts can go fuck themselves. Because they won't ever be an issue for us again. Dumbfuck turned out to be a speed bump. Selfish Bitch's meddling was more like a multi-car pileup, but we survived it all."

In the midst of my pacing, I paused at the corner of the kitchen island and glanced at him. "So you think I should make contact with him?"

He slowly shook his head. "I don't think anything. This is a monumental choice to make—too big to decide on an emotional whim. Mull it over. Hell, he had all of your life to think about how and when to approach you. You never imagined this scenario. Take all the time you need to figure out *if* you want him in your life. If the answer is yes, then decide how you'd want that to be."

Calmed enough by his rational words to take a deep breath, I sat down again, leaning into his warm body as he wrapped an arm around me. "I want us first. Nothing that messes with us."

Pulling me close, he kissed the top of my head. "Nothing he or anyone can do will mess with us again. We'll make sure of it. Don't reply to him right away. He said he'd understand if you didn't want to see him. He'd be an idiot not to realize this would be a shock for you. Take a few weeks. Months even. There are no rules here."

Relief coursed through me, tension easing through my shoulders. Quick to explode into full-blown anxiety from past troubles, I'd never had Cade sitting right next to me, literally holding my hand, to help talk me through the frenzied emotional storm.

"I do like being unruly." I huffed out a soft laugh. When he eased back, my gaze met his.

Mischief glittered across those dark blue eyes, and he gave me a lazy smirk. "I do love that about you." He lifted his free hand and trailed his fingers down the side of my neck. "Hungry?"

His gaze drifted down to my bare breasts, lingering as my nipples hardened under his heavy attention, then shot back up, locking onto mine. By the time he took a slow breath, he looked ravenous.

I swallowed hard and nodded, unable to find my voice, my throat locking up.

"Good," he growled. "I'm famished. And wondering what you taste like covered in chocolate sauce."

Emboldened by my own hunger, needing to take charge for a change, I pressed a hand to his chest, shaking my head.

"No. Not this time, Mr. Michaelson. Your turn to be on the menu."

His eyes widened, nostrils flaring, but he didn't argue.

Smart man.

I went to the pantry to retrieve the jar of chocolate sauce. By the time I turned around, he'd jumped on top of the kitchen island and had reclined back.

For a split second, my breath caught. Like a Greek god carved by Michelangelo himself, Cade reclined on the slab of marble, sleek lines of muscle stretching from his legs to lean hips. Strong shoulders and corded forearms shifted as he turned to face me, revealing rippling abs that led to a dusting of hair. In the center of all that muscular beauty, arched the very thing I couldn't wait to drizzle chocolate sauce on, wrap my lips around.

He watched me, the corners of his lips twitching.

Right when my pulse fired faster, as I bit my lower lip and took another step closer, my beautiful man took a deep breath, and the heat of his stare intensified. Until he dropped his head back and shot his arm straight up in the air, striking a pose with all the ego of a man who *knew* he was all that—with the confidence in his masculinity to pull it off.

"Well, hell. Was I supposed to grab a sketch pad?" I bit the lip I'd pulled into my teeth to keep from laughing.

He snapped his head up, pinning me with a hard stare. "Make one move anywhere but straight toward me, use any medium but that sauce on my body, and I *will* tackle you onto the kitchen floor. Then I'll be painting you and cleaning up the mess with my tongue."

I grinned and took another step toward him. "Promise?"

He held my gaze. "Bad girl."

"Always, for you."

As I slowly unscrewed the cap, a sudden streak of disobedience speared through me, and I bolted the opposite direction. And damn, either I'd telegraphed my move, or Cade was preternaturally fast. Because I didn't make it far enough to take a third step. With gentleness I struggled to fathom, he tackled me in midair, spinning us so his shoulder hit the cabinet, and his back, the tiled floor.

The jar jostled out of my grasp and fell between our bodies. He knocked it aside, twisting until my backside hit the cold tiles, my wrists pinned with one of his hands above my head.

His eyes glittered. "All bets are off, Maestro. You had your chance."

I struggled under his hold while he grabbed the tipped-over chocolate sauce making a mess on the floor. With a quick twist of his wrist, he upended the jar and dumped the rest of the contents onto my chest.

Squealing as the slick sauce dripped down my sides and onto the floor, I squirmed, but he held me fast, his strong grip unyielding. And then he just looked at me. His gaze swept down my body and back up again, the seriousness in his expression hardening into something deep and soul-searing.

In that moment, nothing else mattered. Not his business or mine. Not any ghosts from our pasts, nor surprise family trying to insert themselves into our present.

He swallowed hard. "Gotta say, Maestro, this is far from how I imagined my condiment fantasy going down. But you look fucking fantastic on your floor covered in chocolate."

5. ANOTHER OCEAN

Cade...

The plane ride was unremarkable, as most were. Leaving Hannah that morning had been uneventful —I'd been comatose at the crack of dawn when she'd left. Under my phone on her nightstand was a folded note from her, the only evidence I had that she'd kissed me good-bye.

With my early-morning flight, the minutes I'd had to spare before my plane took off were spent with a quick shower at her place, the shoving of clothes into an overnight bag at my place, and a race to the airport on my motorcycle. Sheer luck made me hit the security lines at a random slow point and board the plane before the final call.

Before the last passengers boarded, I sent her a quick text.

Miss you already. Back before you know it.

I watched the empty text box. Would she notice her

phone? Not likely. I blew out a hard breath and dropped the phone down, resting it on my thigh.

A flight attendant's voice sounded over the speakers as the last passengers stowed their luggage in the packed overhead compartments. Instructions were issued, including to turn off all electronic devices.

As I lifted the phone again to power it down, an alert flashed across the screen.

Missed you first. Hurry home. Be safe.

"Sir, you'll need to turn off your phone." The stern glare from the male flight attendant warned me he'd tackle it out of my hands if necessary. Business class passengers must've been breaking the rules lately, leaving the rest of us to deal with the power-entitled enforcers.

I held it up as I shut it down, never breaking eye contact. The guy gave me a curt nod and continued down the aisle to find his next rule breaker.

The flight took just over six hours, then another fifteen minutes while we taxied and waited to disembark at the gate. A smile crept onto my face as I heard electronic devices chime back on. It took almost twenty minutes to navigate through the crowded airport. *Thank fuck* I didn't have to pick up luggage.

Ground transportation had been arranged by Blake's secretary and a large-framed man looking to be in his midthirties greeted me just outside the security gates with a "Michaelson" placard held in front of his chest.

"I'm Michaelson."

"Very good, sir. May I take your bag?" He reached forward, offering.

"No, I'm good." Trust came slow to me. My belongings stayed where I could control them.

Respect and understanding flashed in the man's eyes. "Mr. Fisher assigned me to you for your stay. Let me know if you need anything. Here's my number if I'm not with you."

Confused, I took the card he held out and read it aloud, "Jackson Tomlin."

"The one and only. But you can call me Jack."

"You're not transportation from the airport?"

He gave me a cunning smile that didn't quite reach his eyes. "Oh, I am. I'm also part of his private security detail. He assigned me to you."

Private security. Interesting. "In that case, I'm Cade."

The ride from the airport to the financial district in the heart of San Francisco took thirty minutes. From between buildings, I glimpsed the Golden Gate Bridge, majestic even with a gray cloud cover behind her.

Instead of pulling up to any one of the stately buildings that looked to be architectural marvels, Jackson parked in front of a modern glass building. Curbside, I craned my neck up. The thing had to be forty or fifty floors, easy. "Is this the tallest building in the city?"

The valet took the keys from Jackson and nodded toward him. "Thank you, Mr. Tomlin. Mr. Fisher arrived twenty minutes ago."

Jackson stepped beside me and glanced up. "Not the tallest. But the newest and most square footage of retail and commercial space. Follow me. I'll take you up to his office."

He guided me through a gleaming lobby. People hustled to and from a bank of a dozen elevators. We passed by them all, going to the one at the end where no one stood. Inside, the control panel boasted fifty-five floors. Jackson pressed the number fifty-five.

I examined the back of the suit jacket he wore. No evidence of a holster could be seen through the material, but gut instinct screamed the guy was armed. "You're familiar with the retail and commercial space?" Realtors and business investors used that kind of vocabulary.

As the elevator rocketed upward with stomach-dropping speed, he stepped back, facing me. "Each member of Mr. Fisher's security detail knows every square inch of his building's office space. Best way to protect him is to know him."

"Interesting." And mildly unsettling. Power and money came with risks—common sense. Until now, however, I'd never had a taste of it firsthand in the corporate world. Even my exposure to my father's business dealings had been nothing to this extent.

The doors opened to an expansive lobby area. Fine art hung on the walls, stood on pedestals.

A middle-aged redheaded secretary nodded to us, then lifted her phone. "He's expecting you. I'll let him know you're heading back."

From the few open doors we passed, I could see that large offices lined the perimeter. Several associates with earpieces passed us in the wide hallway, carrying on animated conversations without paying us any attention.

A closed door came into view as we rounded the corner. Jackson reached for the knob as we approached. "I'll be in the lobby when you're ready."

The instant the door opened, Blake stood and came out from behind his desk. He had a full head of silvering hair, but the man was fit as an Olympian under his five-thousand dollar tailored business suit. "Cade. Great you could make it out here on such short notice."

I smiled, taking his offered hand. "Happy to help, Blake."

"Offer you a drink? Scotch, right?" He walked over to a walnut bar in the front corner.

As barware clinked, my attention wandered toward the floor-to-ceiling windows that spanned two entire sides of the office. "Yeah. That'd be great."

Water from the bay stretched across the horizon line. The Golden Gate crossed along one side.

"Your email didn't outline my assignment." To be prepared for anything, I wore a suit. Brought jeans and two shirts, typically all I needed when assessing a restaurant or bar.

He handed me my scotch, neat, the only way I drank it. "That's because there isn't one."

I turned to meet his gaze.

Icy gray eyes stared back at me, assessing, calculating.

About to take the bait, I opened my mouth, but a knock sounded at his door.

A thin-built man walked in a second later. Wire glasses were balanced low on his nose. Intelligent eyes stared across the large office at Blake, shifted toward me, then back to Blake. "You asked to see me?"

"Yes." Blake clapped me on the shoulder. "Henry, this is Cade Michaelson. The protégé I've been telling you about. Cade, this is my right-hand man, Henry."

Protégé? Had Blake taught me a thing or two when we'd met on some of my assignments? Sure. But it's not like he'd taken me under his wing.

Henry crossed the room, confident, unhurried.

I met him halfway and shook his hand. "Good the meet you, Henry."

Blake didn't move from the windows. "Once we're through with our meeting, brief Cade on the rest of the company, as we'd discussed. He's familiar with the bars and restaurants in the US metropolitan centers. Apprise him of the entire worldwide portfolio."

Henry gave me an efficient smile. "Count on it. I've put together a file with the details."

I turned back to Blake. My mind spun. The click of the door sounded behind me. "No assignment?"

His gaze held mine, unwavering. "Not an assignment. An opportunity. Perhaps, the biggest one of all."

Suspicious, my eyes narrowed. I put down my untouched scotch on a side table. "Clarify, and please make it quick. Vague doesn't work for me. I came here in good faith."

He tipped his head toward me, opening his arms. "I've not breached our agreement."

"Our written agreement entailed my consulting for you. Nothing more." Wharton trained didn't mean I wanted to go corporate. I didn't work well under authority.

"Do you like this office?"

I shrugged, dropping my hands into my pockets. "What's not to like?"

"It's yours, if you want it."

His statement froze my brain. "Your office." My words fell flat.

He turned and faced the bay. "I'm vacating it in a few weeks. Been thinking about retiring for some time now. In August, when Dwight mentioned he knew an up-and-comer on the East Coast, opportunity appeared to be knocking on both our doors."

The man had lost his mind. I picked up the scotch and tossed it back. Since Blake's delusion had his office becoming mine, I crossed over to the bar and helped myself as if it was. I poured a double while I wrestled with the implications of his offer.

"You want me to have your office." I stared at the amber liquid in the heavy crystal glass.

"Yes."

I turned toward him. "Because you want me to fill your shoes? Run the company?"

"That's exactly what I want you to do."

"I think the thin air up here on your fifty-fifth floor has affected your judgment." Fucker was insane. I tossed back the second round. "You're making no sense. I'm fresh out of grad school. I have no experience running a worldwide corporation. You must have hundreds of people better qualified working for you already."

"I do. But none of them are you."

My jaw clenched. I'd only met the man a month and a half ago. "Why me?"

"You're trained just like the hundreds of more qualified people under my employ. But they lack something crucial that I had when I started this company. Other than me, you possess it to a degree beyond anyone I've encountered."

"Which is?"

"Genius-level instinct and innovative execution. You see things on the micro and macro scale in a simultaneous instant. You're cautious, taking necessary but efficient steps to prove what your gut tells you. Then you act decisively, never second-guessing."

I crossed my arms and dropped him a hard stare. "None of your employees can do that for you?"

The slow shake of his head never pulled his gaze from mine. "Not one. I don't want to turn the reins of the company over to someone who can't improve it from where it stands. None of the people in my employ have all the talents required to do so. You do. What you have can't be trained into someone."

I let out a slow breath, mulling over his words. "You're asking a lot. Running a worldwide corporation has never been on my radar."

"For the right price, any course can be altered."

I huffed out a laugh and shoved off from the bar. "Blake, you've been around too many corporate sharks."

Blake countered, "Eight figures a year has a tempting appeal." His expression never changed.

Okay. That got my attention. I ran my tongue over my teeth, then grinned. "Is that pre-tax?"

Blake mirrored me with his own smile. "To start. You'll take over my salary, but year-end bonuses are structured on performance. You apply your skills to the company on a larger scale, continue to make every aspect of it more efficient the way you've been doing one business at a time, sky's the limit."

Too good to be true normally was. Yet his offer was an unheard-of dream job for any graduate. And I did have a knack for business consulting. Polishing a business to outperform itself, or its competition, had become an addictive rush.

"The office is on the wrong coast."

His calculating eyes narrowed. "Your girlfriend, Hannah."

I gave him a slight nod. No way in hell I would leave her behind.

"Women follow the men they love. It's a true test of a relationship. Trust me, I've been there. And didn't you tell me she runs a bakery? Plenty of those in every city."

I growled low at Blake's chauvinistic comments. He might've figured me out on a business level, but he had no clue about my values. Hannah was no ordinary woman. She had built an amazing bakery of her own. Made cakes that were museum worthy. I wasn't about to tell him that, though. None of his fucking business.

When I didn't reply, his expression became unreadable, hardening. "The terms of the offer are drawn. Hard copies are in the files we left at the company brownstone, including the general duties and responsibilities of the position. As I mentioned, it's essentially what you've been doing, only on a larger scale." He stepped forward, extending his hand. "I have to head to an investors' meeting. Take the weekend to give the idea consideration."

Unable to make sense of the mess of thoughts in my head, I shook his hand. My aggressiveness came from being caught off guard. No reason to fault the guy for revealing his secret in his own way. "I will. But I intend to grill the fuck out of Henry for all the dirt you've got buried. Is he up to the task?"

Blake laughed hard and clapped me on the shoulder as he turned to leave. "Do your worst. Henry survived me."

Alone in the large office, my gaze swung out to the bay. Thoughts raced in my mind, then froze when the possibilities tangled. How would Hannah react? What would she think?

What did I think?

That one was complicated. Easy, in that I'd never wanted to be completely immersed in corporate life. I liked operating at an arm's length, consulting. Complicated as shit, in that I'd come to get a rush every time I analyzed a business, figured out its weaknesses, solved the puzzle of how to make it stronger. To do that every day on a larger scale? And get paid north of a cool ten mil? My brain froze over again.

The greatest problem? I'd never seen myself as an employee in my plan. Wait...CEO ran the show. Except

Blake was off to an investors' meeting. People he answered to. Yep. Complicated. I needed to clear my head.

Hannah.

On autopilot, I pulled out my phone and dialed her.

She picked up on the second ring.

"Hey."

I exhaled the breath I'd been holding. "Hey, you. Watcha doin'?"

A soft laugh filtered through the phone. Her voice lowered, "I'm being entertained by the interview session."

"Ah. That's today?" I walked over to Blake's desk and leaned against the edge. Background chatter sounded out over the phone.

"Apparently. Chloe and Daniel commandeered the whole process, and to see what they could do, I gave them carte blanche. They've done an impressive job. Fifteen initial candidates were whittled down to three in a couple of hours. How are things going there?"

"Interesting."

"*Good* interesting?"

"*Bizarre* interesting. And good. Maybe. I'll tell you all about it when I get back. When I figure out all the details myself."

"Where are you?"

"In Blake's office on the fifty-fifth floor."

"Can you see the Golden Gate?"

I pushed off the desk and walked to within inches of the spotless windows. "Yeah, it's incredible. The city is below and all the streets seem to lead to the bay. View is amazing."

She hummed. "Sounds amazing."

"Would be better with you in it."

She huffed out a short laugh. "How could I be in that view?"

"Up against the glass. Hair a mess. Me holding you. Looks fucking spectacular in my mind."

Sudden silence came over the line. I heard a door close. "Better find a way to get me there and steal Blake's office for a while. I'll bring the bottle of window cleaner."

I exhaled a slow breath. "Damn, woman. I love guttering thoughts with you."

She was teasing. But little did she know how close her voiced fantasy came toward potential reality.

Blake's offer fell more into the realm of possibility.

6. NEEDED DISTRACTIONS

Hannah...

I stood by the bird bath in the dappled shade of the charming courtyard behind Sweet Dreams, pulling my lower lip into my mouth—the lip Cade had sucked and tugged lightly with his teeth when he kissed me good-bye early this morning. I ended the call with Cade as the butterflies in my stomach began to settle and a warmth spread through my chest. I couldn't stop grinning.

After slipping the phone into the back pocket of my shorts, I stepped through the back door and returned into the kitchen. I didn't feel one stitch of uneasiness in leaving the interview process to Chloe and Daniel. From the moment they walked in with me as we opened up for the day's baking, they were all business.

"It says here you're taking night classes. Which nights?" Chloe asked. They were on the last interviewee of the three finalists. The other two were waiting out front.

The timid brunette gave a single nod. "My night classes are Tuesdays and Thursdays from 8:00 p.m. till 9:30 p.m. I have two morning classes on Mondays, Wednesdays, and Fridays."

"What's your schedule for those classes?" Daniel asked, jotting down notes on a clipboard that he had perched onto his folded leg.

I returned to the end chair I'd been sitting in and watched Chloe and Daniel with a bit of awe. My fun-loving employees had transformed into an interviewing team to be reckoned with. Both sat in their chairs, dead-serious expressions on their faces, inches between them with their united front.

The brunette, Gina I thought her name was, flicked her gaze to Daniel. "First thing in the morning: one class at 8:00 a.m., the other 9:15 a.m." Gina stared at Daniel, her expression hardening. "Ask me what you really want to know."

Whoa. So not timid, after all. Little Miss Meek had some feistiness underneath.

The corners of Chloe's lips twitched, and when she lost the battle with her smile, she raised one of her crossed arms and covered her mouth with her hand. Daniel's jaw clenched and his eyes narrowed. But he did that every day when Chloe got him riled. I imagined him calculating his odds of survival with Gina and Chloe.

He leaned forward, resting his forearms on his jeans-clad thighs. "Will your schoolwork, or any extracurricular activities, interfere with the schedule we've explained?"

Gina gave a slight headshake but held Daniel's gaze. "I want this job. You need someone to open three days a week, close on two, and the occasional Friday or Saturday night event job? That's perfect for me. Mornings can be Tuesdays, Thursdays, and Saturdays, if that works for you. Any other day, I can work a closing shift."

Daniel gave a curt nod at Gina, then glanced at Chloe as he arched a brow. "Anything else?"

Chloe took Daniel's clipboard and scanned it for a moment. "How much notice do you need for event nights?"

Gina narrowed her eyes in thought. "I don't have a boyfriend, but I do like to go out with friends on the weekends. If you could give me five to seven days' notice, that'd be cool."

"No problem. And you don't have issues working late on some nights when you don't have school?"

Gina's brows raised. "You mean, am I interested in overtime pay? No issues. I'm there."

Daniel barked out a laugh. "Yeah, she's gonna fit in here just fine." He swung a glance my way. "What say you, Boss?"

I grinned at Chloe and Daniel, happy they'd thoroughly vetted and interviewed the candidates but deferred to me—the paycheck provider—for a final decision. "I say thanks for conducting such a great interview."

I stood and offered a hand out to Gina. "The job is yours if you want it."

She smiled wide, jumped up, and shook my hand. "Thank you so much, Hannah." She glanced at her two interviewers. "I'll be on time, work hard, and learn fast. You won't regret it."

Gina extended her hand out to Daniel, and he shook it while giving her a warm smile. "We're looking forward to it."

Chloe shook Gina's hand next. "Welcome aboard." Then she glanced at me. "Midday tomorrow an okay start?"

The front door bell jingled, and I stood while swiping my purse off the desk. "Fine by me. That's my lunch date. You guys good to complete the paperwork and hire the last one?"

Daniel's eyes widened. "Either one? Our pick?"

I gave him a hard look. "You two insisted on running the interviews. Take them all the way. I give you authority to hire either. Both are well qualified, and if you like them, I do. Besides, you two are the ones training them and working closely with them. Choose which one you prefer."

"Hannah! You back there?" Elyse's disembodied voice sounded out from the front.

"Be right there!" I shouted before glancing back at the threesome. "So you guys good?"

Daniel waved me off. "Yeah, go. We got this."

I had no doubt they did. In the eight months since I'd brought Chloe and Daniel on, they'd practically become partners in Sweet Dreams, if dedication and commitment counted for ownership shares. And having two more loyal employees to handle the growing demand meant I got to spend more time with Cade. Something we'd been short on lately.

A sharp pang of longing hit me as I walked up front. I missed him. We'd made time when we could, but early mornings weren't his thing and late nights weren't mine. The in-between times got sucked up by our businesses. Hopefully things would settle soon and we could carve out some couple time.

"Hannah Martin," Elyse chided the second I rounded the corner. "How could you have kept us in the dark about your boyfriend?"

I blinked, glancing at Elyse, then at Kylie. "What?"

"The boyfriend. Cade." Elyse arched her brows and dropped a knowing look at Kylie.

Kylie leaned forward, lowering her voice. "The Italian sex god."

I burst out laughing, then quickly ushered them out the front door, past the last two interview candidates who sat on the couch. "Go. I'll be right there." Elyse and Kylie turned around on the sidewalk, waiting.

I glanced back over my shoulder at the potential future employees, relieved the near sexual-harassment bomb had been diffused. "Chloe and Daniel will be right with you. You two good? Need water or coffee?" Although a twinge of guilt hit me about abandoning my post while my employees hired our new help, pride washed it away in knowing they could handle the task and wanted to.

Both of the young women shook their heads. One held up a water bottle we'd earlier provided. Daniel would be outnumbered no matter which candidate they hired, but then, he'd handled everything with an ounce of humility and a gallon of professionalism, with just the right amount of humor and teasing thrown in. Much the same way Cade handled being outnumbered with his sisters and me.

The thought brought a smile to my face.

The moment I stepped out the door, Kylie stared at me. "You were just thinking about him weren't you?"

I rolled my eyes and walked past them toward Lila's. "Who? How do you know?"

With quick clicks of their skyscraper stilettos, they appeared on either side of me. Elyse nudged into my shoulder. "Italian sex god. Keep up, Hannah. We only have an hour and a half for lunch. If we explain everything, we'll never get the dirt."

Kylie grinned. "Your dreamy-eyed look is a dead giveaway."

Against my will, images of my scorching Sunday night with Cade popped into my head. Monday morning's heated shower. Tuesday's after-bakery sexcapades...

My cheeks flushed hot. *Yep. Definite sex god.* "He's not Italian. I don't think."

"Notice how she didn't deny the sex-god part?" Kylie teased.

After a few more minutes of grilling about Cade, I turned and stepped onto the meandering cobblestone path through Lila's garden. Her fall flowers were in full bloom now, deep violet asters stealing the show in the borders. Her maple tree had just begun to turn a fiery red.

Lila rushed out the front door of her café and onto her porch. Her ruddy cheeks framed a broad smile. "Girls! 'Bout time you showed up. My gossip nerve's a twitchin'."

I grinned and hugged the curvy woman whose snowy hair had been pulled into a loose bun, who easily could've been my grandmother but had become and dear friend and confident. "Your gossip nerve sparks constantly. Lila, this is our new friend Kylie. Elyse is showing her the sales-rep ropes."

"Well, come on." She guided us inside the café's cozy farmhouse interior. "You all look too thin. Order something hearty. We have an Italian panini on special."

Elyse gave me a pointed look. "Italian seems to be on the menu today."

"I'm fairly certain Cade's not Italian." His dark hair and olive skin must've thrown them.

"What's his last name?" Kylie asked.

"Michaelson."

Elyse whipped out her phone and started clicking.

I hung my purse on the corner of the chair back. "I have to pee."

"English," Elyse supplied.

Kylie scrunched her face. "English sex god doesn't have the same ring to it. What else could he be?" She snapped her fingers. "Greek! He's definitely a Greek sex god."

I groaned in defeat. "Fine. Make him whatever nationality you want. But he's *my* sex god." They burst out laughing as I abandoned the table to go to the washroom.

And I couldn't stop smiling. *My sex god.* His faithful worshiper missed him. I pulled my phone out of my back pocket, flicked on the light in the bathroom, and closed the door.

I sat on the antique wooden chair in the corner, surrounded by more of the same décor of her café: white-washed wainscoting up to a chair rail, pale gray walls that held black-and-white photographs, a burgundy sunflower in a vase on a corner table.

My phone screen showed a missed text from Cade:

Miss you, Maestro.

I typed a quick message, hit SEND, and placed the phone on the chair before peeing.

Miss you more, my Italian-English-Greek sex god.

After washing my hands, I picked up the phone and grinned at his reply.

What? Wait. I don't want to know, do I?

I pressed my lips together.

Nope. Lunch with the girls at Lila's. You've gone international.

A quick reply fired back.

Or you have.

I bit my lower lip.

I'm craving international now . . .

The reply bubble came up as he typed.

exhales slowly

I took a deep breath and blew it out, imagining the heated expression on his face.

Gotta go. But I intend to worship you. On my knees. Soon.

A single word came through.

DEAD

When I opened the door, Willard, Lila's brother, called out from the back. "Oh, almost forgot. Jessie called again."

As Lila walked by, she let out an unusual, heavy sigh.

"You okay, Lila?"

Her face brightened back to her typical sunny expression. "I'm fine."

Uncertain, I narrowed my eyes. She and I had become good enough friends for me to pry a little; we usually filled our time together sharing personal stories and solving business challenges. "Are you sure?"

She gave me a serious look. "I may have to close down the restaurant for a whole week in October."

My eyes widenened. "Why? Is something wrong?"

"Oh, no. My girl's about to have two more babies, and her husband got called away on one of his covert-operation assignments. He'll be gone at least a month. Doctors are plannin' to induce on the 21st.

"But why close down the restaurant? What about Willard?"

She glanced back at the kitchen with a wistful smile. "Willard's good in the kitchen. He keeps calm with me around barkin' orders at him. But he ain't no manager. Not sure what he'll do with an idle week."

"Don't you have three waitresses? Can't one of them cover for you in a managerial role?"

"Nah. They ain't got the experience, nor the inclination."

I did a quick calculation of dates and my schedule. "I'll do it."

"Do what?"

"Be you for the week." I gave a confident nod.

"That's absurd." Her hand flew over her heart, like she had to hold it back.

"No." I put my hand on her arm. "It's what friends do for friends. You need me? I'm yours."

Tears glittered in her eyes. The next moment, Lila threw her arms around me in a crushing hug. "Thank you, Hannah. You're a godsend."

As soon as she eased her hold, I took a deep breath and pulled back. "It's the least I can do."

The caring woman had become more than a friend, she'd become the closest thing to a mother figure I'd had after Gran died. I would be there when she needed me.

"Hey." I curled onto my side later that night, buried under my covers, the bluish glow from my phone the only light.

"Hey yourself, sexy." Cade's deep voice soothed me.

I rolled over onto the pillow he used, burying my face into the indentation to inhale his scent. "Not sexy as fuck?"

A low chuckle rumbled. "Oh yeah. That too."

Silence followed. I could hear his breath. If I listened closely enough, maybe his heartbeat. Or was that mine? It beat for him, and maybe that made them one and the same. I let out a long sigh. "I miss you."

"Miss you too, Maestro. Like you wouldn't believe." His slow words were heavy.

I smiled. "Make me believe it tomorrow."

"Me between your legs? Done. Might take a while."

"Oh, why's that?"

"If I begin at the soft skin inside your ankles, one kiss for every little thing I missed about you while I was gone..."

My mind raced seconds behind my heated pulse, body already aching for his expert touch. "Mmm...sounds divine."

A sigh sounded out. "Gonna have to take a rain check on it being tomorrow though. Didn't want to stay another day, but I need to. If the flight's on time, I'll be able to meet you at Kristen's barbeque."

"Everything all right?" The serious tone in his voice piqued my interest.

"Yeah. I'll fill you in when I get back. Not sure about all the details yet, but if everything checks out, my job description might change."

"Job description? You're a consultant."

"Blake wants me to be more, offering me an obscene amount of money to tempt me."

I smiled. Cade was brilliant. Everything he touched turned into shining platinum. And his dream had always been to create businesses, optimize those already running. "Does he really need to tempt you with riches?"

A long pause weighted the conversation. "Yeah. He does."

My mind whirled. Cade wanted something, and he didn't. For the first time since I'd known him, when business was everything he lived and breathed, he sounded seriously conflicted.

But I believed in him. And I knew what having a dream in every fiber of your being did to someone. I'd realized mine with Sweet Dreams. Cade had already launched a business with his wildly successful bar, but I got the sense he was meant for greater things. His genius seemed attuned to it.

"Cade?"

"Yeah?"

"Follow your heart. Do what you're passionate about."

"Will you be by my side when I do?"

My chest burned at the uncertainty in his voice. "Always."

7. PARTY PILEUP

Cade...

"No fucking way. We are *not* doing three Christmas parties at once." My scowl deepened.

Hannah threaded her hand into mine. I calmed. A degree. She squeezed gently, but said nothing. Kristen unzipped her jacket and glanced at Kendall and Kiki, as if looking for backup. She found none. My comrades just chilled on Kristen's deep seating patio furniture with mildly amused expressions. Jason gave her his husbandly support, his way—he flipped burgers one at a time on their massive barbecue grill, took a swig of his beer, but ignored my outburst.

I snorted and leaned further into Hannah. We hadn't had a moment to ourselves in the last twenty minutes since I'd returned from San Francisco. I needed that alone time with her. Knowing it was only about ninety minutes away, and on the far side of some awesome burgers and company, was all that was keeping me sane through this ridiculous conversation. But I'd promised my sisters support with Invitation Only, and they were important to me too, no matter how crazy their agenda.

Ava bounded back onto the patio, tail wagging, blue rubber ball in her mouth.

Mase took the ball from her and rubbed her head. "Good girl." Then he beamed it halfway across the enormous yard, sending it bouncing alongside Jason and Kristen's barn. The dog raced after it.

Laura, Mase's girlfriend, commented as she leaned against his side, "I don't know who's getting more exercise, you or Ava.

"What are we discussing again?" Ben came in by my left shoulder, cold beer bottles between the fingers of each hand.

I took one. "The insanity of running dual parties."

Kendall gave me a smug look. "She said three, Cade. Triple parties. Follow along."

I glared at her, gave her a smartass smile, and flipped her off, my middle finger hidden by the neck of my beer bottle as I held it toward her.

She blew me a kiss.

Needing to find some thread of rationality, I glanced back at Kristen, our ringleader. "Seriously, Kristen. Didn't we learn our lesson after the last multiple-party fiasco?" I certainly had. "No way in hell am I risking Hannah and me again over the chaos of multiple events—Hannah comes first for me."

I gave Hannah a hard look of love and devotion. She smiled, leaning her head onto my shoulder.

Kristen plopped down onto the chair beside us and grabbed her yellow-lined notepad and pen, tapping the tip of it on her chin. "No need to. We've been managing fine all summer with you jumping in when you're in town." She shrugged. "Plus, we'll make the clients each choose separate days."

I inhaled the faint scent of my defeat in the air, grumbling. "Separate days would be better." I tried not to smile. Kristen stared hard at me until the corners of her lips twitched.

We loved the banter. It was a part of our sibling MO. I was proud as fuck of Kristen and what she'd accomplished with Invitation Only. We all did our promised part, but she ran the show. The company was her baby from the get go, inspired by the renovated barn in her backyard. And kicked off by a successful inaugural party last New Year's Eve.

"Who wants toasted buns?" Jason turned our way as he pulled his baseball cap off, exposing a mess of blond spikes before he flipped it backward.

Unanimous shouts followed before I leaned into Hannah. I growled low into her ear, "I'm so toasting your buns later."

Her eyes widened a fraction. Then she glared at me, whispering, "Behave."

I smirked. Her irritation was an act; I caught the lustful spark in her eyes.

She shook her head and leaned forward, grabbing the Hawaiian iced tea I'd made for her earlier. She hummed with pleasure as she took a few long pulls off her straw.

"Go easy on that, Maestro. It's deadly if not respected."

She grinned before sucking down one more swallow of the strong tropical drink. Then she put the glass back down. "I'll make it last. But you should be careful giving me drinks that taste so damn good."

Kiki nodded and held up her identical hourglass-shaped drink, as if toasting. "Right?" She'd already downed half of hers.

Kristen snapped her fingers. "Hellooo, planning an event here."

"*Events*," I corrected, reluctantly getting on board with the idea.

She ignored me. "How do your dates look in the first half of December?"

"Five minute warning!" Jason transferred the toasted buns from the grill to a platter while Ben stood beside him, slapping cheddar slices onto half the burgers. Mase had moved onto the grass, wrestling a stick from Ava's mouth.

I pulled my phone from the table and scrolled through the calendar, which was an interesting exercise when I had no clue how my December looked. Less chilly in San Francisco, I suspected. But I went with what I had now. "I'm good the 6th, 13th, and 20th. All Saturdays." Weekends seemed the safest bet.

Kiki shook her head. "Can't do the 6th. I'm having my first botanical show at the gallery."

Kendall clicked through her phone. "What about Friday the 12th, Saturday the 13th, and Saturday the 20th?"

One by one, everyone checked their calendars and nodded in agreement. I marked the days. All that could be done with such a long timeline. But there was only one way the triple-party thing could happen. "No way am I point man on all three. One. I'll take one event."

I slung an arm around Hannah's shoulders. "Besides, I need time with you. No overcommitting." The two bar mitzvahs had been a gut-check lesson in taking on more than I could handle. And the potential job a coastline away—still up in the air without discussing with Hannah—made me want to take things slow and steady.

She turned toward me, her expression calm as she whispered, "Thank you."

I exhaled. The whole relationship–balance thing seemed to be clicking into place.

Kristen gave a sharp nod. "Wouldn't have it any other way. Cade, you take one, I'll take one, and..."

Kristen and I glanced at the other three.

Kiki snorted and stood from the couch, waving her arms as she shook her head. "Don't look at me. I'm the artistic one."

Hannah got up and wrapped her arms around Kiki's shoulders. "Count me out. I'm the cake maker."

Kendall remained seated and tilted her head, considering. "Sure, I could handle one party. Who are the clients?"

"Clark and Trina Anderson, Phoebe Rutherford, and Amelia and Ferdinand Constantine."

Kendall leaned forward. "I call dibbs on the Andersons. And tell her you've slotted her party in for the 13th; I'm not going first or last."

Nearly choking on my beer, I pulled the bottle from my lips. "It's not a race, Kendall."

"But it will be a competition. You know those country club women. They will each want their party to be the best of the season."

"Heads up, people. Lunch is on," Jason called. He and Ben stood at the head of the outdoor dining table. The end held the platter of burgers. Colored ceramic bowls spanned down the center of the table, the nearest one filled with Kristen's favorite Caesar salad.

Mase returned from the kitchen, drying his hands in a paper towel. He put his arm around Laura. "Hey, if they aren't hungry, more eats for us."

"Be right there!" Kristen typed furiously into her electronic tablet. Then she put it aside and scanned her yellow-lined notepad before she flipped to the next page and jotted a short note. "Hannah, you okay with three unique holiday-themed cakes in that tight of a time frame?"

She nodded. "No problem with this advanced notice. I'll schedule Daniel and Chloe to help at each event."

I stood from the couch, staring hard at her. "You sure, Maestro? That's a heavy load during the holiday rush."

Hannah smiled wide and nodded. "Yep. We hired two new employees."

I crossed the patio, gathering her into my arms. "That's great news. But if you ever need last-minute help, you know I can ice a mean cupcake."

She kissed my cheek. "You'll have your hands plenty full with party planning, Point Man."

I dropped my lips to her ear. "I'll make sure my hands are plenty full of you too."

Kiki passed by us, voicing quietly, "I'll help too."

"Yeah?" Hannah broke away from my hold and nudged into Kiki's shoulder, grinning.

Kiki nudged her back. "Yeah. I'm not going to be the odd musketeer out. Besides, I need something to take my mind off of Darren."

Darren? Only Darren I knew was the DJ at Loading Zone and some of Invitation Only's events. I arched a brow, but Kiki had turned, heading toward the dining table. Confused, I glanced at Hannah. "Do I even want to know?"

"No." Kiki and Hannah said in unison as we made our way to our seats.

Shaking my head, I silently agreed. As far as Loading Zone rumor had it, Darren played a wide field with no intention of changing. And Kiki? No part of me wanted to know details of her playtime.

But although Kiki was strong on the outside, she also had a fragileness beneath the surface. Now wasn't the time or place to broach the subject, but I made a mental note to talk with her privately to remind her I had a broad shoulder she could lean on, if she wanted or needed.

The balance I sought in life included all my family. And even though my sisters had crossed the line in the past with harassment and pranks, they were still blood. We looked after each other.

Kristen took her notepad to the table. "Which client do you want, Cade?"

When Jason glared at her, Kristen mouthed, "*Sorry.*"

Jason gave her a soft kiss. "It's okay, babe. But you're done." He swiped her notepad and pen from her hands.

"Hey, give those back!" She tried to snatch her stuff back, but Jason stood and raised his arms, holding the items out of her reach. When she began to stand on her chair, Jason hurled them toward the patio area we'd just occupied. The paper notepad landed with a smack on the couch; the pen hit the wood decking with a click, then rolled under a chair.

Typical Jason–Kristen squabble: friendly fire with love under the surface of it.

I grabbed a cheeseburger, then loaded a huge glop of potato salad onto my plate, thinking about how Jason worked out of town most of the time. And their marriage was solid. More affectionate than most couples who spent all their time together. *Could that setup work for Hannah and me?*

Reining my thoughts back to Kristen's question, I shrugged. "Don't care which client is mine, but the 20th would be easier for me. I've got two consulting meetings and a client's grand opening happening the first week of December." What I knew so far, anyway. "So the more planning time for me, the better."

Kristen sighed and sat back down while Jason rubbed

his hand on her back with a triumphant grin. She gave me a slow nod. "Okay. I'll check with the clients to confirm dates, then send you all an email once I have the calendar set."

My attention settled back on Hannah. Kiki whispered something to her that made her blush. Hannah's gaze lifted to meet mine, a sexy smile curving her lips.

I flicked a glance at Kiki. "No sex talk at the table."

Kiki raised her hands, feigning innocence. "I said nothing."

I coughed out, "Bullshit."

Kiki and Hannah laughed.

Uh-huh. I knew their minds. Comments about football players in tight pants. Kiki fooled no one.

My mind working at lightning speed, I glanced across the table. "Kristen, on second thought, see if the Constantines are available for the 20th." Time was a scarce enough commodity. An extra week of planning? Priceless. So would be having the last say with the last party of the year, especially with the Constantines.

Then my gaze returned to the one who mattered most to me ahead of the holiday-event chaos. Her bright hazel-green eyes reflected pure happiness back to me.

I hoped she felt the same after I broke the news about the job offer of a lifetime.

8. MILES APART...
MINUTES TOGETHER

Hannah...

"Cade!" I tugged hard on our clasped hands, but he wouldn't slow down. Or release his death grip. "Where are you dragging me?"

"We need alone time. It can't wait any longer."

I glanced over my shoulder at the ongoing barbeque on Kristen's patio. Everyone stared at us with curious expressions. Of course, it was after the peals of laughter had died off.

"I barely finished eating."

We slowed as we approached the dock by the pond. "You put your fork down."

I gaped at him. "It was a good two inches above my plate when you yanked me up. It *clattered* down."

Finally we stopped, and he pulled me into his arms. The expression on his face was boyish, mischief glittering in his eyes. "At least you dropped it. I'm safer out here without a sharp weapon in your hands." His voice lowered as his gaze drifted down to my lips.

My eyes narrowed. "Will I need a weapon?"

His answer was a sudden kiss, hot and demanding. Then he slowed his pace, becoming tender, teasing. My body heated from the inside out, and I melted into him. It wouldn't have mattered if I'd held a weapon or not. His touch stripped me defenseless.

Long strokes of his tongue, slow sucks and sips of my lips, sent sizzling energy everywhere. But a deep ache settled low in my belly, then lower.

"Wow," I breathed when he pulled away. "You really did miss me."

"You have no idea." He stared at me with intensity.

I let out a slow breath, trying to calm my rioting body. The solid heat of him wrapped around me felt like the most amazing thing in the world. The audience on the patio? Forgotten.

When I turned my face and pressed my cheek to his rapidly beating heart, I absorbed our surroundings. "I remember this dock."

He pressed a gentle kiss to my forehead and took my hand, led me to the end, and tugged me down to sit in the same spot where we'd cuddled on Valentine's Day. "Me too. A girl once unzipped her coat and offered me warmth on a bitter night."

How true. We'd both flayed our scars wide open that night—confessed the sins of our exes.

But another memory overshadowed that darkness. "The beginning of us happened that night." I leaned my head onto his shoulder. "Here on this dock, back on that cleansing night, our hearts first connected."

Only now, the sun shone brightly instead of the nearly full moon. And rather than feeling separate and alone, we'd become one another's.

He threaded his hand into mine and looked across the pond toward a grove of trees, where aspen and maple leaves had begun splashing their hues of gold and crimson. When he turned back to me, his brows raised. Doubt filled his expression.

I nudged my shoulder into his and tightened my hold of his hand. "Talk to me, Cade. You can share anything with me. In fact, this seems to be the place for it. Maybe it's magic."

A warm smile softened his face. "You're the magic, Maestro."

"There you go. See?" I kissed his cheek. "You can tell me anything. I promise only good things can happen." We'd come so far with Cade trusting in me, telling me everything, even the little items he hadn't deemed important. And with every new thought we'd shared, no matter how insignificant, we'd grown closer.

After a deep breath and slow exhale, he scooted a bit, turning to fully face me. "Okay. Here goes. Blake offered me his job."

I blinked. Thoughts jammed as I tried to comprehend what he'd just said. I'd clearly heard him wrong. "What do you mean 'his job?' Doesn't he *own* the company?"

"Not the ownership part of it. The running part of it. He wants to retire."

Still not quite comprehending, I gave a slight headshake. "But he's just met you."

"That's what I said. But apparently, he's been looking for someone like me for years. And when Dwight told him about me, Blake began my background investigation. Then he hired me for consulting on his businesses to get a feel for my work style and ethic. The entire time I've been research-ing, analyzing, and reporting on his companies, he's been researching and analyzing me. The last couple of months have been one giant job interview. Only I hadn't known I'd been applying."

"Wow." My mind was blown. This was so far outside anything Cade had ever expressed interest in before. "His company is huge, right?"

"Worldwide."

"Would you be traveling more?"

"I haven't accepted the job yet."

"But you want to."

"I am seriously thinking about it."

"Why something so big? You've been incredibly passionate about your own consulting firm."

His gaze drifted over my shoulder, unfocused. "I've been wrestling with it for the last few days, sorting out my thoughts—what I want. Fuck, Hannah. This is a once in a lifetime opportunity. His firm is what mine would be in a few decades. Only instead of doing all the hard work of making global contacts and building the business, it already exists. And he's handing it to me on a silver platter."

"But there's a catch," I guessed. I heard the hesitancy in his measured tone. My gaze followed his, out to the horizon. Did the future lie out there?

The warmth of his other hand covered mine. I turned and our gazes locked together, his eyes searching mine. The next words came out just above a whisper, "I'd have to move to San Francisco."

My heart sank—then stuttered. I closed my eyes, trying to hold my emotions back, needing to be strong for him. "If it's something you want to do, then you need to do it. We only get one life. We need to seize opportunities and realize our dreams when we have the chance." I'd done so with my bakery. It had become a dream come true for me. There was no way I would let my fears stand in the way of something he wanted. "Not able to do it from here, huh?"

He gave a gentle headshake. "Wish I could. Blake's corporate headquarters are there. His executives and staff will need face time with their new head of operations. Morale alone would need it during the transition."

Tears welled in my eyes, in spite of my attempts to hold them back. My voice came out the barest whisper. "What about us?"

His expression flickered, like he struggled with what to say. "Any chance you'd want to go with me?"

My mind spun. I couldn't find my next breath of air. So many things tied me to Glenhaven: new friends, my grandparents' home, Sweet Dreams—my dream-turned-reality. And my father. I hadn't yet met him, but I wanted the opportunity to do so. Everything was here. Not thousands of miles away.

But if I stayed...*Cade* would be thousands of miles away.

My mouth dropped slightly open, but uncertainty clouded my brain.

Cade lifted his hand and pressed a finger to my lips. His gaze burned into mine. "Don't answer. You stay here for now. This is your home. It's where my home will always be with you here. I'll fly back every weekend."

I nodded, clinging to his rational words, because my emotions burned hot in my throat. "And I'll stay busy during the week at the bakery." It would keep my mind off of his being gone.

A gentle smirk curved one side of his mouth up. "We'll heat up those text boxes with teasing every chance we get."

I leaned further into him. "You better tuck me in every night with your sexy phone voice."

"Better clear the weekends. Five days straight of sexting

and phone teasing, we'll need a full forty-eight hours to work it all out."

A delicious ache speared between my thighs but was overpowered by the warm pressure spreading through my chest. My heart beat strongly for him and would no matter where he was. "I love you, Cade. I'll be here missing you every moment you're gone and losing myself in you every second you're back."

He exhaled a heavy sigh, shoulders relaxing as he gently dropped his forehead to mine. "We'll be stronger than ever."

I hope so. The distance scared me, but I believed in Cade. Believed in us.

He dropped his head lower, and my eyes drifted shut the moment his soft lips touched mine, thoughts scattering. His tender lips coaxed, teased. I melted inside, feeling safe, loved...craved. The clash of emotions tangled together with our teasing tongues, lust thrumming through me with the fiery heat of his kiss. Leaning closer, I wrapped my arms around his neck, losing myself in everything Cade.

Just then, rapid clicking sounded out and soft fur brushed the backside of my arm. Startled, we both snapped our heads toward the movement right as a black-and-brown blur flew through the air and crashed onto the calm surface of the water. A huge splash misted droplets of pond ick all over us.

I released Cade's hand and gripped the rough edge of the dock, planting myself firmly. "I am *not* going in after her." The last time Ava took a flying leap, it was into his parents' pool. And Cade threw me into the pool after her in good-natured fun because I hadn't leashed her.

Mase and Laura ran onto the dock.

"Not my fault," Mase huffed out. He dropped his hands to his hips, then bent over slightly, trying to catch his breath.

Cade snorted and stood, tugging me up with him. "Not *our* fault. *You* brought her."

Ava swam toward shore, and the four of us filed off the dock, heading toward her. She took two steps, then shook her soaked fur out, splattering us all over again in the process.

Mase leaned in closer. "Her stunt was dog-speak for 'get a room.' I've been training her to do that all week."

Cade wrapped his arm around my shoulders. "Yeah? Have fun cleaning your trainee. Hose is on the side of the barn."

Then Cade led me up the grassy hillside, out of earshot. His lips dropped down to my neck. He branded a trail of scorching kisses toward my collarbone, and I shivered.

"You cold?"

"No." I glanced up at him. "You gave me goose bumps."

His deep chuckle was followed by his lips pressed to my ear, hot breath causing a fresh riot of bumps to break out. "That's Cade-speak for let's 'get a room.'"

I pressed into his side. "We need to squeeze some of *this* into those forty-eight hours."

"Goose bump teasing? Count on it."

On a soft laugh, I shook my head. "Well, yeah. That. But lighthearted family time."

His expression turned serious. "Absolutely. I'm gonna need plenty of that too."

Under his collected exterior, behind the man who chased his dreams and held our love tight, was a brother who needed his family and friends. They were close, and no matter how strong he was in braving a whole new corporate world, he would need heavy doses of his foundation to recharge.

And I would need heavy doses of Cade.

After we said our good-byes, then headed out arm in arm to spend the night at my place, I brought myself fully into the present. If the therapy that had brought me this far —had enabled me to be with Cade in the first place—had taught me anything, it was to be in the moment.

I'd finished worrying about the past. I hoped to banish anxiety about the future.

Every single minute of the here and now was what mattered.

9. HOTTER THAN HELL

Cade...

"I'll take it."

Three simple words. Could've been talking about a loaf of bread or a car.

When I'd said them to Blake, it changed the course of my life. It had meant "I'll take the offer, run your company, make that $14,400,000.00 per year you offered"—which broke down to a staggering $1.2 million every full month I worked.

No matter how insane the number sounded, Blake reasoned that my skills on a global level would make Fisher Holdings ten times that amount. And since I had to sacrifice proximity to Hannah—morning coffees, random lunch hours, nights where if we weren't lost in amazing sex, we were at least in each other's arms—I didn't argue.

The following Wednesday was my previously scheduled four-day trip to Phoenix. Hannah broke her morning baking ritual to see me off at the airport.

We stood outside the security gate, the last bit of airport

real estate where we could still remain together. She pressed further into my arms. "Wish you didn't have to go so soon. You've only been back three days."

"Three and a half." Damn straight I'd been keeping track. Every single minute with her had become more precious. I kissed the top of her head. Inhaled her tropical scent.

She shifted back, then glanced up at me. "You'll call me tonight?"

I bent down and gave her a lazy kiss. "Tonight. This afternoon. The very second my plane lands."

She laughed softly before her lips returned to mine. Gentle kisses followed. Then she pulled away, her gaze hardening. "I will have my phone on ring and in my pocket. Always. Focus on your work, but when you check in, there will be texts waiting for you."

"Oh?" I locked my arms around her, not ready to let her go. "Naughty ones?"

A sexy smile curved her lips. "Oh, yeah. The three-dot variety."

My chest burned. Hannah did that to me. "I love you."

We didn't need to say the words. Both of us felt them down to our bones, but her face lit up every time I said them.

Her eyes narrowed for a split second. "I love you, Kincade Joseph Michaelson. You come back to me safely."

I fought a smile. "Full names now?"

Her hold on me tightened. "Serious business requires it. I need you. Make sure you keep that in mind."

"You listen to me, Hannah Noelle Martin. I will be safe. You make sure you do the same. Any bar hopping with the girls, make sure you have each other's backs. And remember what I told you about drink safety."

She gave me a sharp nod. "Never out of my sight or possession. Only drink anything delivered by a waitress."

"That's my smart girl." I kissed the tip of her nose, delaying the inevitable as the time to catch my flight began running out. Then I rested my chin on her head. "Good-byes suck."

Hannah pressed her face against my chest, squeezed me tighter, and sighed—but said nothing. Different than all the other times I'd left, this one felt heavier. More permanent.

I wasn't just leaving for Phoenix. Boxes I'd packed over the last couple of days would be overnighted to the company row house I'd be living in when I arrived in San Francisco on Sunday. The transition of my stepping into Blake's world would begin first thing Monday.

And I wouldn't fly back to see Hannah again until Friday night.

The crowd of people flowing by us to pass through the security checkpoint began to thicken. A sense of urgency pressed in. The possibility of missing my flight was only part of it.

Gently, I pulled away. But before we broke contact, I kissed her long and slow.

Hannah released her hold and slid her hands between us, up my chest. "You need to go." Unshed tears glittered in her eyes.

I gave her a smile. "Back before you know it. Nine days. We will talk and text every day."

She took a deep breath, then nodded. "And night."

"Count on it. I'm tucking you in."

A huge smile broke out on her face. "You better. I'm addicted to your dirty punctuation."

I dropped a heated look at her as my cock twitched at

the thought. "We need to add a stiff exclamation point to our list."

At the lighthearted shift, she beamed brighter, all traces of the tears gone. "I'll have to find something to surround it with. Tight little parentheses, I'm thinking."

I stared down at her. So many emotions flooded in, words escaped me. After a deep breath, I glanced at the menacing security gate. "Gotta go, Maestro."

Leaning up on her toes, she gave me a last tender kiss. "I'll go first...so you're not turning around in line, trying to get a last glimpse at me."

"Fuck. If you don't, I'll be walking backward the entire time, staring at your gorgeous face."

Pointing at the growing line, she backed up a couple of steps toward the parking garage. "Go. I forbid you to think about dirty punctuation until tonight. You stay focused on your safety and your job." She stopped, took a deep breath, then let it out slowly.

I gave her a nod but made no move toward the line.

Her expression turned serious as she wrapped her arms around herself. "I'll be waiting for you."

The intensity of her words hit me hard as I stared at her. She would be there for me no matter what dream I chased. And she encouraged me to go after them all.

Before I reacted, she spun and vanished into an oncoming throng of people heading my way.

I finally turned to face my new future.

PHOENIX GREETED me with a punch of record heat in the face. Locals claimed it was a "dry heat."

Dry my ass. I sweated like a pig all afternoon.

Living in a place that threatened to hit one hundred degrees six months out of the year seemed insane. But getting in and out of a hot rental car as I surveyed a dozen Fisher-owned nightclubs and restaurants during daytime hours had taught me something valuable: baked Arizonans needed a cool place to unwind after the stifling temperatures. And the more parched they were? The greater amounts of alcohol they drank. Easy money for innovative businesses as long as they were wisely located, well marketed, and efficiently run.

I'd eaten dinner at one of the restaurants before heading to the hotel. And by the time I'd collapsed onto the bed, skin still wet from a quick shower, it was 7:25 p.m. Which meant 10:35 p.m. Hannah time.

We'd exchanged flirty texts all day.

Her first was simple:

· · ·

To which I'd replied:

!

Then I received her wraparound punctuation. Not normal parentheses. Not hard-edged brackets. Fuck no. My girl sent through something curvier.

{ }

While I dialed her number, I stared at my guttered reply.

You know, if you turn those sexy little brackets on their sides, they look like breasts with hard nipples.

To which she'd replied:

LOL. Only you. And only for you.

On the second ring, she picked up. "Hey." Her tone was low, sexy.

I threw most of the blanket aside and pulled the cool sheet over my body. "Did I wake you?"

"No. Ummm...don't think so. Might have drifted off."

"But not *really* sleeping. I get to tuck you in."

"Mmm..." Her hum trailed off into a purr.

Damn, I loved that sound. I sighed, calmness flowing through me. "What are you wearing?"

A soft laugh came over the line. "Nothing."

"My favorite outfit of yours."

She hummed softly again. "What about you?"

"Buck naked. Just for you."

"Wish I could cover your body with mine."

Blood began to flood southward. "Me too."

"Describe the hotel room. So I can picture me there with you."

"It's a casita, actually. At the Royal Palms. Nice resort. Boutique size. Has all these small courtyards and alcoves with Mexican and Mediterranean tile on the walls. Antiques everywhere. Across the room is a curved fireplace with a painted plaster surface. There're two large chairs with a small table between them. I'm on a king-sized bed with wooden bedposts that are carved into seven-foot-tall spirals."

A faint grunt came over the line.

"You okay?"

"Yes. I rolled onto my stomach." She paused. "Those bedposts sound interesting."

"Oh?" My mind raced, trying to catch up to hers. "Why's that? Are you holding onto one? Bent over, maybe?"

Another hum-turned purr. "Or *tied* to it."

Fuck. I swallowed hard. "Hannah, there is no place I'd rather be now than with you. But there is plenty to be said for your missing me."

Her voice lowered, "Tomorrow, I'm going to buy some silk cord."

I shook my head, speechless. Because what little oxygen I had left in my brain was used to imagine Hannah's lush curves, arms held high, wrists bound to the bedpost at the foot of my bed.

I sucked in a deep breath. The room spiked several degrees hotter.

My voice came out a low growl. "*I'm* going to buy us a bed with bedposts."

10. CONNECTIONS

Hannah...

"How do you keep it all straight?"

As Willard chopped vegetables behind me and Lila hovered over my shoulder, I blinked, shifting my gaze between the employee schedule, the duties checklist, and a weekly calendar. Beside those, handwritten instructions were scrawled on several pages of lined notepaper.

During our regular lunch over the past weekend, I'd promised Lila a few mornings of my time to learn the ropes before taking over Lila's managerial role during her trip in a couple weeks. My operation was simpler than hers: deliveries by one supplier once a week, only two employees (four counting my new hires), no checklists.

"Nothin' to it. They all know what to do. The duties checklist keeps the place lookin' spit shined. I'll post the work schedule before I leave. List of everyone's phone numbers are at the bottom."

"You won't need 'em. No one better call in sick," Willard grumbled.

Lila tapped a pen on a third page, which had a weekly calendar of activities. "Food deliveries come Mondays, Wednesdays, and Fridays. Linens on Thursdays. Everything is paid for; all you need to do is sign for it."

Willard coughed out a laugh. When I glanced at him, he pointed a metal, batter-covered spoon at me. "You count every damn thing. Down to the last lemon and every chicken breast."

Lila dropped her hands and gave him a death glare. "You want to manage while I'm gone?"

He huffed and returned to whatever he was mixing up, muttering, "Can't cook and manage at the same time."

"What I thought. You best be nice to Hannah. She's what'll be keepin' this place runnin'."

When Lila rifled through more paperwork on their small desk along the back wall, Willard winked at me. I bit my lip, trying not to laugh. The old man enjoyed riling his sister.

"He's right, though. Once I signed for a meat delivery, eyeballin' the order when we were busy. We were shorted two cases of chicken breasts and a dozen steaks. The delivery guy said we signed for it. His word against ours."

I gasped. "You're kidding. So you got shorted?"

"Yep." She gave a half shrug. "They have quality meats at great prices, and it was the only problem we've had. My own damn fault for not takin' the extra time."

On a headshake, I put a hand on her shoulder. "I will count every item on the manifest to make sure it's all there."

After we went over her daily responsibilities, she poured us each a coffee and we sat at my favorite bistro set by the window. Her café opened in about twenty minutes, which meant fifteen until her early regulars began showing up.

White hair swept up into a bun, steely gray eyes

appearing more perceptive in the morning light, she cast me a knowing grandmotherly look. "Why so glum?"

"That obvious?" I sighed. "Missing Cade, I guess. Both of us worked when he was here, but his being across the country is vastly different. I know it makes no sense, but I can actually *feel* the thousands of miles between us."

"Don't sound strange to me. You're connected to one another. Same with me and my kin."

"You and your daughter?" I took a sip from my hot coffee, letting the rich flavor roll over my tongue as I considered our sudden similarities. We both had close loved ones miles away.

"Yep." She gave a slow nod, her gaze drifting out the window.

We sat in silence a few minutes, staring out at the colorful riot of fall flowers in bloom on the borders of her walkway. The sound of a blender kicked up in the kitchen.

I took a deep breath, dragging myself out of my bluesy mood. "I'll get used to it, I suppose." Even in the last couple of months, things had gotten easier with every successive and longer trip Cade had traveled on.

A revelation filtered into my mind. We weren't the only people I knew who had to deal with long-distance family. "Cade's sister is married to a man who travels for business a lot, and they seem incredibly happy."

Her cheeks plumped with her wide smile. "Each of us finds our own way to deal with bein' separated from a loved one." She patted my hand. "You'll find yours."

All at once, everything hit me—both the rightness and the challenge. One of my many new friends sat in her café, consoling me about distance and family. Out there somewhere was a father I hadn't ever had the chance to know, asking to be invited in. But more powerful than all of that, an incredible man who'd become my best friend, confidant, and lover—more than family—supported me through it all.

Cade and I were over three thousand miles away on a map, yet when I closed my eyes and imagined him, he was only a heartbeat away.

WHEN I WALKED into Sweet Dreams a few hours later, things appeared to be flowing seamlessly. At nearly 10:30 a.m. on a Wednesday morning, you'd have no idea that I'd been gone. The display case was filled with dozens of assorted types of cupcakes, autumn colors splashing across the gleaming wire shelves like a colorful painting.

At our single cash register, our other new hire, Estelle, handled a long line of chatting customers with a happy calmness that rivaled the Dalai Lama's. Yet in the midst of crazy pressure that would've had my adrenaline pumping, she handed the current customer a box of cupcakes and their receipt while thanking them, glanced up and nodded my way with a smile, then shifted her attention to the next in line, a woman holding a toddler in her arms.

Estelle ruffled the little girl's bright blonde curls. "Hello, Georgie."

With a wide grin, I continued on toward the back. Chloe and Daniel were each in different stages of cupcake making, Daniel pouring dry ingredients into one of our two industrial mixers, Chloe frosting a batch of pumpkin spice cupcakes with our popular maple glaze.

Daniel turned the other mixer off, pulled the stainless steel bowl out from under it, and glanced at me as he set it on the marble counter. "Hey, Hannah. How was Lila's?"

Chloe dipped her rubber spatula into her frosting bowl and lifted another cupcake. "Willard ornery again?"

As I dropped my purse onto the desk, a timer chimed on one of the ovens. "I got it." I crossed the kitchen to turn off the timer, grabbed a white kitchen towel, and pulled two fragrant batches of chocolate bacon out, sliding the pans onto our cooling racks. "No more than usual. He's like the boy on the playground who pulls your pigtails because he likes you."

Daniel snorted. "Boys don't pull girls' pigtails because they like them. Who the hell told you that?"

Chloe put down her perfectly iced cupcake, then dropped her hands onto her hips. "Everyone. It's a well-known fact."

He shot a deadpan look at her. "Men 101: when we show a woman attention because we like them, they will know it. When we pull on pigtails stuck to a girl's head? We do because they're there and we can."

I rolled my eyes, but secretly loved their snarky banter. I fought a smile, mumbling, "Let the games begin." When the air current remained charged, I changed the subject. "Estelle is working out nicely."

Daniel poured his batch into silver foil cupcake molds. "Yeah, she is. Sent both of us back here when we tried to help at busy times."

Chloe brought her now-empty frosting bowl to the sink. "And she's a natural back here with the baking. Quick learner, that one."

After tying on my favorite green apron with yellow ruffles, I washed my hands. "What about Gina? How's she doing?"

"Fantastic."

"Great." Daniel's forceful response came a split second after Chloe's.

My chest burned with pride for them. "Sounds like you guys did an incredible job hiring, then."

Chloe stole a glance at Daniel. They locked gazes, and I caught a heated spark. Something stronger than pride sizzled between them. More than coworker respect.

Chloe inhaled deeply.

Daniel's nostrils flared.

They seemed to have frozen for a split second, as if they'd been struck by surprise that they had incredible chemistry. Their intense stare held for a beat longer before they both busied themselves with greater focus.

It took every ounce of self-restraint I had not to burst out laughing. They worked together fluidly. Exchanged heated barbs for entertainment. And whether or not the two of them admitted it, they wanted each other.

A couple hours later, as I sat at my desk replying to vendor emails, my phone lit up with a text from Cade.

Miss me?

I grinned as I typed.

What do you think?

His typing bubble appeared.

I think you need a hit of addictive Cade.

Tugging my lower lip in between my teeth, I typed and hit SEND as I inhaled slowly.

> Massive.

His reply came back.

> Your need . . . or my cock?

I burst out laughing. He probably had that adorable smartass smirk on his face. Cheeks flushing hot, I remembered the teasing banter we had at the faux funeral where things first got really heated between us. I glanced over my shoulder. Daniel and Chloe were staring my way.

On a dismissive headshake, I turned back around and replied.

> Both.

A few seconds later, he replied.

> I vow to satisfy one with the other.

Not a cell in my body doubted his claim. A warm heat spread through me, settling low in my belly, easing into a deep ache even lower. I took a shuddering breath, trying to clear my head. Textual foreplay was something we thrived on —but not in my kitchen with an audience twenty feet away.

> After I pick you up at the airport Friday night?

A quick response popped up.

> You sure about that? No game-time detour with friends?

A powerful resolve rose inside me. Last time was a business trip. This time, Cade had moved. He now lived the entire width of a continent away. The stakes between us—the importance of our bonding with every moment we had—had never been higher.

> I'm certain. No one else. You. Me.

A final reply appeared.

> Done.

FRIDAY NIGHT CAME both in a flash and after an eternity of waiting. I hovered beside the security gates. Any closer and security would scrutinize me more than they already were—like I was someone who wanted to bolt the wrong way through the exit doors to tackle her man in a flying-leap hug and cling to him, refusing to let go.

As it was, I stood off to the side of the flow of traffic, wringing my hands while I bounced in place. Nervous energy never quite found an outlet with me, resulting in my frequent vibration. The more excitement, the greater the bouncing.

Another planeload of passengers flowed through the glass automatic doors, none of them Cade. About to explode with anticipation, I glanced up at the blue electronic arrival boards. His flight number indicated the plane had landed at 7:32 p.m., which was ten minutes ago.

When a sea of people parted around me, I swung my attention back through the doors.

There he stood in the middle of a moving crowd,

imposing with his broad stature, dark hair, and intense blue eyes. His gaze locked onto me, expression fierce, like he'd done battle on the ground, across every state that separated us, just to get to me.

His long strides brought him through the security gate within seconds.

I covered the minuscule distance remaining between us and jumped into his arms with collision force. Without so much as a grunt, he absorbed the impact and spun us around as he gripped me tight. He held me in his arms and moved to the side, whisking us out of the way.

"Damn, I missed the fuck out of you," he growled into my hair as his overnight bag hit the floor with a thud.

I laughed, kissing up the side of his neck, then inhaled deeply, breathing in his spicy scent. I mumbled in between my onslaught of kisses. "Any other swear words you'd like to fit into that sentence?"

He planted me on the ground and kissed me hard. Then he softened the touch of his lips, teasing and coaxing. I moaned, falling lax against him. All too soon, he pulled away.

"No."

What was the question? I furrowed my brow, trying to remember anything before that devastating kiss.

The tenor of his soft chuckle came seconds before he kissed my nose, then picked up his bag. "No. Talk is over-rated. Physical." To punctuate his words, he spun me around and urged me forward toward the parking garage. "Home. Bed. Me lost in your body. From the moment we hit the sheets till well after sunrise."

My body ached at the decadent thought. I glanced over my shoulder and caught his gaze. It blasted back at me, intense, *primal*. Even so, I couldn't stop myself from teasing him. "Not lost in my body the *very* second we walk in the door?"

His nostrils flared and he lunged forward, shoving the door to the parking garage open ahead of us. "Careful, Maestro. I'm a starving man. There are a dozen places to take you between here and your bed."

I threaded my hand into his in the darkened garage, leaning against his solid frame. Heady excitement pounded through my veins. Everything about Cade seemed to have magnified. An indescribable raw edge of danger simmered just beneath his surface, as if his every action and word was barely controlled, nearly uncontainable.

And I'd never been more turned on.

On a slow inhale, I tempted the beast. "Like..."

A blur of motion took my breath away. Pushed, crowded, spun around, I found myself pressed against a dusty concrete wall in a hidden, shadowed alcove, bent forward at the hips. The sudden action was rough and thrilling. Yet every move he'd made protected me, held me. Even as he'd guided and controlled me.

I closed my eyes as his bag thudded hard on the ground. My breath caught at the sound of buttons ripping open on the fly of his jeans. The warm sides of his leather jacket fell forward around me. Strong hands slid up my hips, pulling the thin fabric of my dress with it. "This what you want, Maestro? To take you right here?" His thumbs tugged at the sides of my lace thong—but he hesitated. Waited for permission.

What he tempted me with was dirty, quick and carnal.

Filled with demand.

And something as vital to me as my next breath of oxygen.

I swallowed hard, nodding, unable to find my voice.

Because while the shocking turn of events had gone abruptly physical, there was more. A tidal wave of emotion swelled beneath the stormy surface.

It sizzled in the air, electric.

"Say it," he growled low.

With a gentle scrape over my hips, the lace of my thong edged downward. Seconds later, his cock, hard and hot, slid ever so slowly between my legs. But he stopped just short of where I needed him to touch. Then he eased away. *Damn.*

My body trembled with need. I pressed back, desperate for more. But he gripped my hips hard, holding me immobile.

With measured pressure, he slid forward again. Paused once more.

The torment was intoxicating. And maddening. Ache spiraled inside of me, winding so tight, I risked imploding from the staggering pressure.

"Yes...please," I breathed, begging.

Three quick pumps followed, hard and fast across my clit. My body lit up, the tight coil inside me releasing in a blinding explosion. I bit my lip as waves of pleasure ripped through me. An instant later, he plunged deep. Filling me completely.

A second set of spasms fired off as he moved with force, sliding back, then driving forward. Amid the fresh torrent of ecstasy, I gasped for air, whimpering with every punishing thrust he delivered. And still I wanted more. Craved everything from him. Needed to feel him unravel.

On an animalistic grunt, he tensed around me. Hot pulses fired inside me, mixing with my own that kept coming.

Ragged breaths came from us both as he wrapped around me, his back flush against mine. Dreamy bliss followed, hazing everything around us into some kind of wonderland. In the middle of an airport parking garage, we'd claimed an erotic world of our own.

Vague impressions of his hands sliding up my thighs and my thong being fitted back into place, fringed into my awareness. Slowly I found myself turned, enveloped in his warm embrace. A strong finger touched under my chin, lifted my face.

Warm eyes searched mine as he brushed the hair off one side of my face and tucked it behind my ear. "You okay?"

I took a deep breath, then blew it out as my thoughts clarified. It was all about this. Not the parting of ways, but the uniting—with the force of two unleashed storms crashing together.

A lazy smile curved his lips in concert with mine. Words weren't necessary. He knew. After all we'd been through, he spoke my language.

Another deep breath calmed me by small degrees. Euphoria buzzed through my body, transcending the physical. My heart warmed right along with every pleasured nerve ending. Slowly, my smile widened, happiness threatening to burst me apart.

"Wow." Warm in the protective cage of his arms, legs like Jello but standing because of his strength, trembling still from two magnificent orgasms—the singular brilliant word was all I could manage.

He bent down, and his soft lips kissed my forehead. "C'mon, Maestro. We have eleven other mind-blowing fucks to fit in before we hit those sheets."

My shoulders shook with laughter as he wrapped an arm around me. Then we headed off toward my car as if he'd never left. Yet he had. And we'd been affected. In bad ways and good.

I had no idea how I would survive our next separation. How *we* would. But for now, we would celebrate our deep reconnection.

11. SHIFTING PERSPECTIVE

Cade...

Sex after a long-distance dry spell? *Fucking* amazing. Literally.

At some point in the middle of the night, we caught our breath between rounds of sex. Hannah snuggled deeper into my arms with all her soft curves and sexy-as-fuck purring noises.

"Cade?"

I pressed a kiss to her temple. "Yeah..."

"Could we do a picnic tomorrow?"

Her quiet request shot warmth into my chest. She could've asked for everything I owned, three NFL teams, plus the entire western hemisphere, and I would've brought it all to her on a silver platter. A lazy picnic? "Absolutely."

Toward lunchtime, we finally made it out of bed and showered. We swung by my place to drop off my bag, pick up Ava, and head out.

It was almost mid-October. The colder nights started the fall color change on the trees, but a warm day helped me convince Hannah to wear one of those sundresses of hers. Since she usually worked Saturdays, she'd gotten her loyal employees to cover for her, but warned me she'd have to do some calendaring and emailing on the grass.

Sounded like a perfect day to me.

I turned the Jeep into one of the parking lots at Fairmount Park while Ava barked out the passenger window from Hannah's lap. Fresh air rolled in from the open windows, and I sucked in a deep lungful, excited to be here too.

I shifted the car into park. "You got Ava?"

"Yep." Hannah clipped a red leash to Ava's collar.

I unloaded our supplies, tucking two rolled blankets under an arm and grabbing our cooler with both hands. Hannah slung a beach bag over her shoulder, then cut across the grass toward the sidewalk with Ava.

As they walked ahead, I took quiet notice of Hannah.

Her thin-strapped sundress was green with a pale flower pattern. She wore flat sandals on her feet and had an easy sway to her stride. The smile on her face disarmed me. The woman was naturally beautiful and perfectly clueless about it. Loved that about her.

"Where do you want to sit?" she asked, turning toward me. The breeze blew her hair across her face. When she glanced up the hill, the strands flew behind her shoulder again.

I pointed the corner of our cooler toward a swath of grass where a grove of pine trees offered shade. "What about over there?"

Ava trotted alongside us, proudly heeling beside Hannah. When a young boy walked down the sidewalk with an older Great Dane on a leash, Ava glanced at the other dog with her ears perked forward, but made no move to change course.

Hannah bent down to rub Ava's ear. "Look at how great she's doing."

"Right? I still haven't decided who's prouder of her training, Mase or Ava."

"Good girl, that's a good girl." Hannah rubbed her head once more before standing. Then they broke away from the sidewalk and climbed the slope toward the trees. Ava's black tail wagged a rapid beat against Hannah's thigh.

I sighed, absorbing in everything about the day. *This is what it's all about.*

I planted the cooler on the grass, laid a rolled blanket on the lid, then shook the other onto the flattest section of ground. Repeating with the second blanket, I created a buffer between us and the cold ground, already amazed at the great time I was having. And we hadn't even sat down. *Never thought I'd be one to appreciate parks and trees and flowers and puppies, but love does strange things to a guy.*

"Do you want to eat lunch first?" Hannah looped Ava's leash through the cooler handle.

Ava tested her tether to the limit, finding a sunny edge of grass near the blanket and cushed down. She resembled a canine sphinx lording over the happenings at the park.

"Sure. Might as well relax and eat before digging into work." I sat on the corner of the blanket, narrowed my eyes at the cooler, then at Hannah. "What was so top secret about lunch that I wasn't allowed to see you loading the cooler?"

She glanced over her shoulder, grinning. "While you slept like the dead this morning, I prepared Gran's secret picnic menu for us."

Confused, I blinked. "You made an entire menu this morning? I woke up in bed with you."

After lifting the cooler lid, she shrugged. "Wasn't a big deal. I bought the ingredients yesterday, thinking you'd agree. My body's internal alarm clock woke me at 3:30 a.m., and after few hours of cooking and prep, I crashed back into bed with you." She pulled out clear bags with tinfoil-wrapped packages inside and handed me one. "Seasoned fried chicken, chilled to the perfect picnic temperature."

She grabbed two short Mason jars and lifted one up. "Apple cider coleslaw." She raised the other. "Deviled potato salad."

My mouth watered. "Have I ever thanked you for being a cook?"

"Nope." She popped her *p* with attitude.

"And will any amount of words really suffice?"

She fought a smile, the corners of her lips twitching. "Nope."

"Well, Maestro, I will have to show you, then." I lunged toward her until my lips met the sensitive spot on her neck where it curved up from her shoulder.

She squealed, causing Ava to alert toward us with a soft chuff.

Hannah pushed me away. "Oh, no. Not here, Mr. Michaelson. What will the kids think?"

Grumbling under my breath, I retreated back to my side of the blanket and opened my bag of chicken. "They would think nothing of seeing the birds and bees in the middle of the park."

Handing me a beer, she shook her head. Her dark hair framed those bright hazel-green eyes. "No birds or bees in the park. Lunch in the park. Work in the park."

Smirking, I dragged my gaze down her sexy body. "And plenty of thanking later."

Watching Hannah, I bit into a cold chicken thigh and

groaned at the rich, juicy flavor. After chewing and swallowing, I lifted my brows. "This is delicious. Gran is a genius. And you are *Maestro* in all areas, baking and cooking."

She blushed and shook her head. "It's an easy recipe. Only takes the right amount of care and patience to seal in the juices while frying the seasoned coating into a crisp golden brown."

Her modesty only made her shine brighter. Made her more beautiful.

And I was the lucky bastard who got to be with her.

"Perfection." I grinned. "And the chicken's damn good too."

I devoured half of it before barely taking another breath. Instead of scarfing down the rest in the next inhale, I put it down and grabbed the jar of potato salad. The chunky yellow mixture had dots of dark red spice and pieces of pickle and white onion.

Hannah shifted positions, rolling onto her stomach with her own bag of chicken. She gave Ava treats while I forked a bite of the potato salad into my mouth.

Flavor exploded on my tongue, and I groaned again, eyelids drifting closed. While still chewing, I put down the potato salad and grabbed the coleslaw. Didn't bother to examine it closely, just shoveled a forkful into my mouth. And died all over again.

"Damn, Hannah. You've been holding out on me." I pointed to the electronic tablet beside her. "Cue that thing up to your calendar. We are scheduling in a weekly picnic."

She leaned over and stole a forkful of coleslaw from the jar in my hand. "You're so easy."

Torn over what to put in my mouth next, I looked from chicken to potato salad to coleslaw. "If easy means I will do anything you want for this kind of food, you're damn right I am."

The next few minutes were spent with me polishing off the balance of the food while Hannah played with Ava. Eventually the pup tipped over and stretched out, yawning.

Hannah remained sprawled on her stomach, the slight breeze catching the hem of her dress and pulling it a little higher on her thigh. I glanced behind us, but trees protected our flank. And still, I tugged her dress back down, not wanting anyone to see more than necessary.

Those gorgeous thighs were for my view alone.

Content, I crawled up beside her, joining the lazy twosome. Hannah had her chin resting on her folded arms as she watched people and dogs go by on the sidewalk below.

"Whatcha lookin' at?" I nudged her with my shoulder, aligning my body so my side pressed as close to hers as possible.

She smiled and slid her hand into mine, glancing at me before looking forward again. With a slight nod to the left, she spoke in low tones. "Those two are on a first date."

Following her line of sight, I spotted the couple. "How do you know?"

"I don't, but seems like that's their story. As they walked, she looked everywhere but at him, until she finally did with a slight smile. He reached out to grab her hand, but she didn't realize, so his hand froze halfway there."

"But they're holding hands now," I countered.

"He never pulled it back. He took a deep breath and thrust it forward, lacing it into hers."

I smiled. The dude was nervous. "She's holding tight to that hand he gave her."

"She is."

Another man and woman came over the rise. "What about that couple?"

Instead of answering, she shook her head. "You try."

In their late thirties, maybe early forties, they walked at a slow pace, not touching. But their expressions and stances gave them away. "They're married. Happy being together without the need for holding hands. They come to the park every afternoon to spend time with each other."

Glancing at me, Hannah smiled. "I like that story. How do you know they're married?"

Good question. An even better question would be why my mind went there.

A man wholly against weddings, enough to make a rule banning them from my world, had to examine why two people who appeared content with each other equaled marriage.

I shrugged, unable to answer definitively. "Don't know. They seem deep rooted, stable." I squinted at the couple, scanning their demeanor from head to toe, trying to see them differently than my first instinct. I couldn't.

Two screaming boys, no older than four, maybe five, ran onto the sidewalk from the far right. A young woman pushed a stroller with a pink blanket tucked inside, racing after the little hellions.

I nodded at the chaotic scene. "That's a nanny and her three charges."

Hannah laughed. "How can you tell?"

I snorted, watching how several park goers were about to collide with the wild newcomers. "I've seen plenty of nannies in the high-society circles my parents live in. They bring the children to the park during the day. Gives the kids something to do, keeps the nanny from going insane, and wears out the youngsters for an afternoon nap, all to be refreshed in time for when the parents come home from a busy day at work."

"Huh." Hannah's tone made her seem unconvinced.

The boys weren't looking at the sidewalk, only at each other as they ran ahead, veering around pedestrian obstacles at the last second. They both crashed into our married couple, bouncing off their legs and falling back onto the sidewalk.

Our married couple's expressions turned horrified, and they crouched down to aid the little guys. Bruisers that they were, neither boy cried. They brushed off the help from the adults, sprang back up, and ran off again. The woman with the stroller put a hand on her hip and shouted. The boys stopped cold in their tracks and turned around, faces crestfallen. Like two rule breakers called to the principal's office, they received a reprimand without any sign of affection from the woman. When they continued, the boys walked along with the woman and her stroller, one boy on the left, the other on the right. Martial law had been instilled.

"Ahhh." Hannah laughed. "She's *so* the nanny."

The married couple had clasped hands, leaning into each other. They watched the boys as they disappeared down the sidewalk, uncertainty written all over their faces. I almost laughed. "Now they're trying to decide if they want kids or not."

"And what about you? Do you want craziness like that?" she asked.

I imagined those two running around in a big house, maybe with a couple more brothers. And the one adorable little girl we would have that looked just like her mother. An unstoppable grin stretched onto my face. "Absolutely."

"Well, I didn't grow up in your high-society circles, and I am *not* going to have a nanny."

Chuckling, I gave a single nod. "Got it. No nanny."

I hadn't pictured my future family having a nanny either. My parents did it without help with the four of us, three sisters who would challenge the rowdiest of boys and me— boy enough for them all.

The sidewalk cleared, and we remained quiet for a while. I sighed, calmed by the rare time we'd stolen for ourselves. Closing my eyes, I gently rubbed my thumb over the back of her hand.

Hannah nudged my shoulder. "That's a single father and his daughter."

Blinking my eyes open, I focused on the sole occupants of the sidewalk. The younger man bent down and lifted the little girl up, seating her on a black painted bench.

"What makes you think he's a single father?"

Scrutinizing, her eyes narrowed. "The seriousness in his expression when he looks at her, like the weight of the world is on his shoulders, even while his entire world is there before him."

"Wow." I watched, seeing it from Hannah's perspective.

She swallowed hard. "I know that look. My mother had it with me. Unfortunately, caring for me got to be too much for her, and she held back her affection."

I squeezed her hand at her solemn tone. She didn't talk about her mother much, and never with as much fondness as she did her grandparents. Not wanting to interrupt, I remained silent, letting her share as much as she was ready to.

"I wonder if things would've been different if my father had insisted on being in the picture back then."

She hadn't mentioned anything further about her father after the email—until now. But I knew Hannah had to walk her own path, and it wasn't my place to interfere with that. What she needed was my support each step of the way.

Rather than push, I responded to her statement. "Do you wish things would've been different?"

As the man took a seat on the bench beside the little girl, Hannah shrugged. "My mom worked two jobs. Most nights when she came home, I was asleep. When I woke, she was already gone. Only on rare occasions did I spend time with her, but as I got older, she withdrew more and more."

I sighed. No one got to choose their family situations, but having no father and an absentee mother was a depressing way to grow up. "I'm glad you had your Gran and Granpop."

She nodded. "Best surrogate parents a girl could hope for." The tone of her voice wobbled.

When I glanced over, moisture glittered in her eyes. "You miss them, don't you?"

She sighed, shrugging. "Yeah. Sometimes."

Silence followed. And although Hannah needed to take her time to decide about her father, I also sensed she needed to talk more. So I treaded very carefully into the subject.

"Your father is gently asking to be in the picture now. According to him, which is the only side of the story you have, he didn't have a choice in the matter before, because your mom took the option away from him."

"Yeah." Her gaze drifted back to the sidewalk.

"How do you feel about that?"

She glanced back at me, huffing out a laugh. "Scared to death."

I gave her a reassuring smile and kissed her temple. "We're all scared of the unknown, Hannah. I bet he's scared to death too. It took a lot of guts to put himself out there, hoping you'd be receptive."

Tilting her head, she gazed out toward the horizon. "I hadn't thought about it from his perspective."

"Well, now you call the shots. Instead of your mother making the choice for him, taking away any say he had in seeing you, you're in charge of both of your fates."

Knocking into my shoulder, she snorted. "Gee, thanks. No pressure there."

I smiled, capturing her lips in a tender kiss. "Never any pressure, Maestro. You decide what you want to do. Your father has come to your doorstep, asking to be let inside. If you want to welcome him in, all you have to do is open the door. And even if you do, you get to decide when that happens, how you want it to play out, and for how long you want him to stay."

The corners of her mouth turned up with the hint of a smile as she glanced back at the father and daughter. Both of them laughed hysterically, and the world seemed to shift around Hannah and me, as if we were privy to a scene of what could be.

With a determined expression, Hannah nodded. "I'm going to open the door."

12. NOT JUST A SPERM DONOR

Hannah...

Cade made an excellent point. My father had thrown the ball into my court. I was in charge. But even with the knowledge of the power I held, it didn't make the thought of including him in my life any easier.

Watching the father and young girl on the park bench, seeing their closeness and easy laughter, gave a visual example of what life could be like, made the idea of having a father real. "Guess he's not just a sperm donor anymore."

Cade laughed, wrapping an arm around me. "Not if you don't want him to be."

I kissed Cade on the cheek and rolled over, crawling across the blanket to reach my beach bag.

He sat upright too. "Hand me my stuff?"

My electronic tablet already sat beside me, but I fished around in the bag and pulled out the rest of our things, handing him his phone and tablet. I'd also brought a folder, which I grabbed and opened. Inside was the printed email from my father and a notepad with a pen clipped to the top, in case I wanted to hand write out a pro–con list.

That he left his physical address and phone number at the bottom of the email gave me many options to choose from in contacting him back. But the thought of calling him made my heart race, and I nixed that idea before anxiety shot me into panic mode. Text was an option, but as far as I knew, he only had my email address. And I wasn't certain I wanted to give him any more information about me at this point.

Cade's voice interrupted my thoughts. "Ben. Got the message. Yeah, Lisa said he was causing trouble. Fuck that shit. Giving away drinks is stealing from the house, which means the idiot's stealing from himself. Fire his ass."

When Cade ended the call, he glanced at me.

My hard glare dared him to make another call.

"What?" Looking innocent, he turned his hands up, phone held in one of them.

Lunging toward him, I swiped it from his hand. "No calls."

"Hey. We never said 'no calls.' We said a picnic was cool as long as we can get work done."

"No calls," I repeated, arching a brow.

He raised an arched brow of his own. Dark and imposing, he might've intimidated someone else with his commanding presence, but not me. All it did was turn me on.

"Says who?" His eyes narrowed.

"Me. I'm establishing picnic rules. Only texts, emails, notes and calendaring are allowed. You have a text box in your phone, and I *know* you're well acquainted with the concept. Use it."

His nostrils flared as his eyes darkened. "Damn. I love when you get bossy."

My lips curled into a smirk. "Good. Stay on your corner of the blanket, and quietly fantasize about me getting all authoritative. If you're good, I'll act them out later."

His chest expanded on a slow inhale, his chin lowering even though his hard gaze never broke from mine. That barely controlled primal side of him shot arousal through me so fast I had to take my own deep breath.

His lips twitched. He knew. I knew. And we both knew the other knew. The impasse between us was like a drug—the heady give and take of sexual tension, where neither side wanted to submit, yet struggled to tamp down the urge to tackle the other.

But we were in a public place—definitely more public than the dark corner of a parking garage. And although we could've run off into the woods or made a fort with the blankets, neither of us wanted to frighten the children. Or get arrested.

"Later," Cade growled out, both dark promise and warning.

Satisfied for the time being, I gave him a curt nod, then rolled back over, concentrating again on my dilemma. Now that I'd decided to contact my father, I had to settle on a method I felt most comfortable with.

Needing to remain as secure as possible, because really, short of a DNA test, I knew nothing about this guy who claimed to be my father, I rejected the idea of exposing my phone number or physical address, deciding to email him like he'd done with me. But for some reason, during our gorgeous day at the park, I wanted to write out my thoughts.

Unclipping the pen from my notepad, I thought about

what I wanted to say. Short and to the point seemed the best approach.

> Dear Paul,
>
> Your email took me by surprise. It's taken me some time to decide if I want to make contact with you. Not as any judgment on you, but only because I'm a careful person.
>
> As long as our contact remains positive, I'm open to meeting you. There is a coffeehouse called Old City Coffee on Church Street.

I tapped my pen on my chin. If I sent the email tomorrow, and gave him time to respond, we could probably meet in a couple of weeks. I grabbed my tablet and pulled up my calendar, checking the date.

> If Saturday, October 18th works for you, let's meet there at 11:00 a.m.
>
> Hannah

I stared at my name, then glanced at his email. He signed his "With love, Paul," which was a stretch. He couldn't possibly love me, he didn't know me. But maybe he felt love toward me, or the idea of me, anyway. I felt an absence of emotion toward him—unless uncertainty counted.

Not wanting to second guess my first instinct, I tucked the handwritten draft back into my folder.

Cade typed furiously on his tablet, but glanced up. "That about your dad?"

"Yep." I nodded, turning to face him as I crossed my legs underneath me. I pulled my tablet into my lap, firing it up. "Decided to reply to him by email."

"Smart." He didn't elaborate, as if we spoke on the same wavelength without words.

"I told him I'd meet him at Old City Coffee on Saturday the 18th."

He stopped typing and looked at me, scanning my face. "Want me to go with you?"

I blinked. I hadn't considered Cade coming, and I wasn't sure why. I didn't know if it was because Cade hadn't existed in my life in all the times I'd pictured meeting my father, or if on a subconscious level, I needed to do this on my own.

"I'm not sure. Can I think about it?"

He gave me a warm smile. "Of course. Do what you feel comfortable with. Just know if you want me to go with you, I'm there."

I took a deep breath and exhaled. "Thank you. Your support means the world."

Not wanting to think about long-lost family anymore when the most important person in my life was a few feet away, I put everything aside and closed the distance between us. My gaze held his bright blue eyes. Happiness shone there, and the sight of it spread a buzzing warmth through my chest. "Could we rest a bit? Just lie here together?"

"My favorite thing to do with you." Cade put his tablet down, reclined back, and stuffed my canvas bag under his head while I nestled my head into the crook of his hip.

Content beyond belief, I sighed. The humor of his omission tugged my lips into a smile. "*This* is your favorite thing to do with me?"

His warm hand slid into mine, and he lifted it toward his face. His soft lips kissed my knuckles. "Yeah," he murmured against my skin. "Do I love having sex with you? Fuck yeah, I do. Making you laugh or throw cupcakes at my head? Yes. And yes. But the quiet after, when all we need is to lie together, touch. Absolute favorite time."

Tightening my hold on him, I glanced up. His expression was at once calm and fierce. A sense of rightness filled me, replacing all the longing for him, missing him for the last nine days. My breath caught. Something desperate in me rose up, hard and fast.

"We need this, Cade. Weekends. From Friday night until Sunday when you have to leave. They're mine."

A wide grin broke out on his face. "I'd love nothing more. What about your work?"

Weekends were busy, but I hadn't hired two more employees for nothing. "Chloe and Daniel want to take charge more? Let them figure out the schedule. From now on, I work when you work."

His expression darkened, naughty mischief sparked to life in his eyes. He released my hand and left it resting on his chest as he inhaled deeply. "Then all weekend I get to play with you."

Slowly, his hand drifted down my side over the thin fabric of my dress, along the side swell of my breast, curving into my waistline, tracing the flare of my hip. A sizzling connection charged the air between us—promises of an afternoon filled with playtime.

But beneath the sparking fire burned something deeper, a stronger bond that no amount of busyness at work or distance across a continent could extinguish.

I closed my eyes, committing the euphoria that surrounded us into vivid memory, hoping the image would carry me through the long cold nights we were apart in between all the togethers.

13. ORIENTATION

Cade...

The grind sank in.

All of last week had been spent in San Francisco, bonding with the troops and getting to know the lay of the land of Fisher Holdings. Sunday night, I'd flown to Hong Kong to begin the arduous process of assessing the rest of Blake's companies.

From there Kuala Lumpur. Thursday? Singapore.

Could the assessments have been done remotely? Sure. To a point.

But Blake hadn't hired me to be a computer monkey. And I worked best hands-on.

Besides, face-to-face always cemented business dealings. Foreign management looked me in the eye. Shook my hand. Saw me in action. I didn't come in like some executive cowboy, guns blazing. I watched, asked questions, made key suggestions, with us working together as a team. Respect was earned on nothing less.

Friday morning came with my thoughts on Hannah.

How beautiful she'd find the ocean view from my bed at the Mandarin Oriental. While she was in my arms. As I buried myself deep inside of her. The morning's wood hardened further, and I groaned.

Leaning over, I swiped my phone off the bedside table, mouth stretching into a monster yawn. Although I'd already recovered from jet lag earlier, a flight alert had chimed around midnight, interrupting my sleep to inform me that the first leg of my flight to Philadelphia had been cancelled. An immediate phone call had Maureen, my assistant back at Fisher Holdings in San Francisco, scrambling to get me replacement flights. With the short ride to the airport from the hotel, I had a few more hours to kill.

A loud growl rumbled from my stomach. With sleep-clouded brain cells, I surveyed the oriental breakfast tray made of a grilled fish, white rice, scrambled eggs, miso soup, and folded pieces of thin green paper that according to the waiter was *nori*, edible seaweed. Chopsticks and a fork were lined up beside a dark bottle of tamari sauce.

Yeah. I grabbed two crispy pieces of bacon from my side order plate and stuffed them into my mouth. My stomach needed the familiar before venturing into foreign cuisine.

As I crunched, I dialed Hannah. The good news about being halfway around the world was our time zones were exactly half the day apart. My phone said it was 6:32 a.m. Singapore time. Hers would say 6:32 p.m., only she was finishing her Thursday as I started my Friday.

She answered on the first ring, voice low, "Hey there, sexy."

I grinned. "Your future is calling."

"Oh? My future? What does it look like?"

"*He* is six-two, blue eyes, two hundred pounds of

starving male, who can't wait to make you smile, hear you moan, make you scream."

Silence. "Wow."

I let out a slow breath. "Yeah. Miss you bad."

"Me too." Her tone quieted. "Wait, aren't you supposed to be on a flight right now?"

"Delayed." I scrubbed a hand down my face and sighed. "Means I won't make our dinner plans Friday night. Might not make it for your meeting with your dad." Guilt tripped through me, even though I didn't command the airlines.

"It's okay, babe. I decided to meet him on my own." She sighed heavily. "So no dinner Friday night, huh? No sexy lingerie while I feed you braised beef tips in burgundy sauce?"

I groaned at the entire hotter-than-fuck image.

Her laughter followed. "The dinner can wait. Tell me about your trip. How was the week?"

Whatever paltry appetite I had for cold eggs and fish obliterated, I turned my back on the breakfast, rolling onto my side, and looked out over the gray-blue ocean. "Good. The restaurants and bars are thriving. Real estate investments were forecasted well. The financial components are sound, but with further diversification, they could grow exponentially."

A ridiculous snore rattled in my ear.

"Am I boring you?"

"No. I'm teasing. Sounds wonderful—way beyond my mental capacity, but you sound like you're having a good time."

I grinned. "I am. You know how I love Monopoly." My sisters and I played often, especially when business dealings or serious family matters needed to be worked out.

"You kick ass at Monopoly."

I did. They didn't make me the dog for nothing. "Well, imagine the game on steroids. Corporate strategy on a global scale? Talk about a rush. But even though the bottom line is important, I always keep the customers in mind. The higher some of these corporate executives go in floors on their way to the top, the more distant they get from the ground floor—the ones that support their bottom line."

"That's amazing, Cade. You have a big heart. It will take you far."

A heavy sigh escaped before I could stop it. "Far away from you, at the moment. And it belongs to you."

Her voice softened. "Not far away. I'm with you now."

I closed my eyes, gripped the phone tighter, and imagined her lying here beside me. "Can't wait to see you, Maestro."

A soft hum turned into a low purr. I swear I heard her smile over the phone, slow and sexy.

"Me too. I've got a five course dinner I need to feed you. By hand. While sitting in your lap."

"Sounds perfect, Maestro." Home never sounded so good.

14. COLD COFFEE, HOT TREAT

Hannah...

C ade's return flights got snarled up even further, and his plane hadn't touched down by the time I had to leave for the coffeehouse. From the beginning, he'd been supportive about my decision to meet my father on my own, but he'd insisted on my taking precautions just in case. I sat at a table by the window, but off in the corner, so that no one sat behind me and I could see everyone approaching.

Tapping my thumb on the table, I hit the button on my phone to check the time. Five minutes till. A steaming cup of coffee and a small plate of apple cake sat on the table in front of me. Beyond the tiny patio of the coffeehouse, pedestrians strode by on the sidewalk and down the cobblestone street, oblivious to the monumental event about to take place in my life.

My hand hovered over my phone.

I had no idea what he looked like. Over the years, every time I'd considered searching for clues about a man who'd chosen not to fight for me, I'd decided I didn't want to know.

Now that I knew his identity, the temptation to search him out had been great.

And yet, I still balked.

I didn't want to assume anything about him from a two dimensional image. Any profile or article I might find would be someone else's view about a man I hadn't yet met. And although each of those little threads of information would give me pieces to the puzzle of a man I'd yearned to know all my life, I didn't want any outside force tainting my opinion of him.

And what I thought about him was all that mattered.

"How's your breakfast?"

I jumped and looked up to see the barista. Lost in my thoughts, I'd let a complete stranger sneak up on me. I glanced at the undisturbed cup of coffee, the untouched apple cake. "It's fine. Someone's meeting me, and I thought I'd wait."

He nodded. "Would you like to order something for your companion?"

My gaze shifted to the empty chair. Not only did I not have any idea what the man who'd donated DNA to my existence looked like, I'd had no clue whether he even drank coffee when I'd arranged our get-together.

I shook my head. "I'll let him order when he gets here."

"No problem. Just wave me over when you're ready."

Nervousness fluttered in my stomach, and I tapped the button on my phone again. Three minutes till. Would he be early, like me? Or was he punctual to a fault, like Cade?

The phone lit up with a message from Cade.

Good luck. I'm there with you. Even if only by text.

I grinned, pulling my phone up from the table and typing a quick message.

> Have I told you lately that I love you?

The endearing phrase was one he usually said to me. His blue reply bubble appeared while he typed.

> Nope.

I huffed out a laugh at our conversation reversal, imagining him popping his *p* like I usually did. Warmth bloomed in my chest. No amount of teasing, or switching roles with our phrases, diminished the depth of feeling behind the words. And wherever he actually was, stuck in some airport or on a plane at the moment, he was here with me. Which meant everything.

> Well, I do.

His typing bubble appeared again.

> Me too, Maestro.

I sighed out a long breath, calming a degree from the simple act of Cade reaching out to me.

Still nervous, even with Cade's text support, I picked small pieces off the top of my apple cake, needing something to settle the churning pit in my stomach. Passersby began to blend into one another, students and families, couples and groups of friends, all becoming a kaleidoscope blur as I kept watch for a brave father looking to meet his long-lost daughter.

By the time I'd worked my way through the entire top of the cake in little nibbles, I grabbed the coffee mug that had cooled to lukewarm. I took a few swallows, scanning the inside of the coffeehouse to make sure no one had slipped past while I'd been watching outside.

Refusing to look at the time, I reasoned out dozens of scenarios why he might be late: an unexpected call delayed him; he'd forgotten to gas up his car; reckless drivers had caused a car accident right in front of him, and he had to stay at the scene to give a witness statement.

I took a deep breath and rejected the next one that flashed into my mind. Fate wouldn't be so cruel as to have him *be* in an accident on the way to the event of my lifetime.

Time dragged on. Other scenarios played out in my mind, not the least of which was the simplest explanation. He didn't want to see me, after all.

As my greatest fear manifested itself front and center, my heart grew heavier with every beat. And still, I wouldn't look at the time.

To distract myself, I ate the balance of my cake with a fork. Then I sipped the rest of my coffee as I stared out the window, no longer noticing the people walking by.

I'd been stood up. And as I thought those words, the reasons why no longer mattered.

For the second time in my life, I'd waited for a very important man to show up. And for the second time, a jerk who should've counted himself lucky that I'd been patiently waiting, not only didn't bother showing, but didn't have the decency or the courage to pick up the phone and call.

I hadn't given Paul my number, but he could've called the coffeehouse and hadn't. I'd heard them answer the phone the entire time I sat here, so the phone lines were intact. I shook my head, thinking this is what I deserved for getting my hopes up. In one failed morning, the universe sent me a clear message that my life was complete with the family I already had; there wasn't any room for one more— definitely not someone who would disappoint me on the most important meeting of our life.

And still I sat there, immovable, unable to pull full breaths past the tightening band around my chest. Except this time, no friends and family lined the satin-bowed pews to witness my shame and humiliation. Only total strangers in a coffeehouse, clueless to the extent of heartbreak happening a few feet away from them.

An empty plate with crumbs. A half empty mug, the coffee cold. Those were the images imprinting on my mind as the undeniable realization sank deep.

Against the dark wood grain of the tabletop, my phone illuminated. Finally, unable to delay reality one second more, I glanced at the time on my phone: 11:37 a.m. Like a surgeon who'd given the patient everything she had, I mentally called out the time of death of my lifelong fantasy.

An alert was on my phone from Cade. His message was brief.

How's it going?

Gathering my small purse from the chair and tucking it onto my shoulder, I picked up my phone and punched in the verdict, making it real.

It's not. It never did.

I tossed my garbage, put my dishes in a marked bin, and thanked the barista. By the time I reached the front door to leave, Cade stood in the doorway, compassion etched into every feature on his beautiful face. My heart slammed into my chest, my world lifting back up toward righting itself again.

"Hannah, I'm so sorry." In the tight entrance of the coffeehouse, Cade enfolded me into his strong embrace. "I hope you don't mind that I secretly hung out to make sure you were okay. The second I stepped off the curb at the airport, I grabbed a cab and headed right over."

I shook my head against his chest and took a deep breath, refusing to cry. Cade was solid, real, here in my arms after another five-day stretch of missing him like crazy.

He rubbed my back. "C'mon. Let's get some ice cream."

I burst out laughing, in spite of my misery. "What? Are you trying to kill me now?"

He gave me a nod. "Right. Lactose intolerant. But not liquor intolerant, right?"

Huffing out a hard breath, I shook my head. "Definitely not liquor intolerant."

"Well, then let's go get a feel-good treat for grown-ups, shall we?" He gave me a tight squeeze with his arm around my shoulder and led me down the sidewalk.

Nestling my face into the space where his chest met his shoulder, I sighed and gave a tentative smile, the first twinge of happiness sparking into me in over an hour.

"*You* are my feel-good treat." I tucked a hand into his back jeans pocket. Trying to lighten my mood, needing to grasp onto the joy right here in my arms, I glanced up, taking in his ruggedly handsome features. "My sexy hot treat."

He glanced down at me, giving me a curious look. Then he winked and laughed.

"Easy there, Maestro. No jumping the 'hot treat' in broad daylight."

15. THE MOST IMPORTANT CATCH OF ALL

Cade...

It killed me to see Hannah so disappointed. Two people in her life, men she'd counted on for support and love, had callously stood her up.

The one had been unacceptable.

The second gnawed at my gut, absolutely unthinkable.

An epiphany hit me halfway through our second drink, and I glanced down at Hannah who already had a mellower attitude and a nice pink flush to her skin. "You know, how do we even know that was your father contacting you?"

She shrugged, not looking up from the vodka tonic she stirred. "We don't."

That bothered me. If they ever tried meeting again, I'd sure as fuck make certain he was her father. Hell, I was lucky I'd made it home to be here for her this time—researching the guy out was the least I could do. I sipped my scotch, thinking. "He emailed you to begin with, right? Did you email him while you were at the coffeehouse? Or call him to find out why the no show?"

Her expression darkened. "No. This was his idea. If he wasn't going to show up, he should've called."

Hard to argue her logic. The drinks seemed to be taking the edge off, but her eyes still held a good dose of wariness. She'd been hurt.

But Hannah was made of sturdier stuff than most. She would get through this and emerge stronger for it.

Clanking her empty glass down onto the bar, she raised her hand up and pointed down into it. "Bartender. Fill'er up."

Concerned, I leaned toward her. "What's your limit on drinks?"

She scrunched her face. "Limit?"

"What's the most you've ever had?"

Tilting her head, she raised her brows. "Hard drinks?"

I glanced down as the bartender slid another drink in front of Hannah and pulled her empty away. "Yeah."

She stared into the glass, as if searching for her answer through the clear liquid. "Two."

Great. I'd seen her buzzed on Champagne and drunk on beer, but apparently today she planned on a bender with hard liquor. During lunchtime.

And I couldn't blame her. All I could do was be there for her.

"What's your goal here?"

She turned, regarding me. "What should it be?"

Well, good. At least she deferred to my sober judgment to take care of her when she couldn't. "I think if two's been the most you've had, three's a good hard limit."

Her reply? She lifted her glass to her lips and downed swallow after swallow without taking a breath. When she slammed her empty glass onto the bar, she raised her hand and pointed down again. "Bartender!"

Not wanting to incite a riot, I watched, helpless to ease her pain in any other way. As the fourth drink slid before her and the third empty was pulled away, the bartender made eye contact with me and held my gaze. I gave him a quick nod, and he mirrored the motion.

"Maestro, you're going to make yourself sick."

"Good." She snorted.

I edged up against her from shoulder to elbow, giving her something solid to lean on. "Tomorrow, you're gonna be hurting, bad."

She sighed. "Makes sense. I'm crushed on the inside. Might as well hurt on the outside."

Nursing my second drink with a small sip, I let the smoky scotch roll over my tongue before swallowing. "This morning isn't fatal."

She shrugged. "It feels less severe the closer I get to numb."

When she only took a single swallow of her drink, I sighed in relief. "Have you eaten anything today?"

A curt nod. "Yep. Apple cake. While I got stood up."

"How about after that drink we get you something more substantial? With a good amount of fat to soak up that alcohol?"

"Oh! Could we go to Denny's?" Her face lit up.

Blinking, I laughed. "Sure. We can go anywhere you want."

On a sigh, she traced the rim of her short glass with her index finger. "At culinnnary school, kids talked about hittin' Denny's after gettin' wasted and orderin' Grand Slams at 1:30 a.m."

It took monumental effort not to crack a smile when she started slurring her words. Instead, I crossed my arms and leaned in toward her. "Is that what you're doing? Getting wasted?"

Her brows shot up. "Can I?"

My heart lurched. In the middle of her devastation, she looked adorably innocent, her face bright with hope. I gave her a hard nod. "You can do whatever you want, Maestro."

Dark greenish eyes gazed up at me, glassy with moisture. "Can we order Grand Slams?"

I laughed, wrapping an arm around her. "Absolutely. We can get as many Grand Slams as you want."

She toyed with her glass, taking another sip.

"Why didn't you ever go to Denny's with them?"

She shrugged. "Never went out drinkin' with 'em. Always been a bit of a loner. How 'bout you? Ever been to Denny's after gettin' wasted?"

I nodded. "Few times. But we always ordered mozzarella sticks and onions rings."

"Maybe I should order those too."

As it turned out, four drinks wasn't Hannah's limit. The petite girl, who'd only ever had a couple of mai tais or strawberry daiquiris, apparently had a healthy liver and an iron stomach. I patiently waited until she finished her fifth drink.

She frowned, staring at the polished wood surface of the bar. "Shouldn't my empties be lined up so I can build an upside-down shot glass pyramid?"

"You would, if you were doing shots."

"Oh." She giggled. "My head feels woozy." She looked left, then leaned forward, sweeping her head to the right. "Vvvooom..."

The bartender pressed his lips into a tight line to keep from laughing.

"Okay, Maestro. How 'bout those Grand Slams, now?"

She shifted, sliding off the barstool, and I thrust a hand

under her elbow to steady her. A wide grin spread onto her face, but then her brows drew together. "What's in a Grand Slam, anyway?"

I laughed. "I have no idea. The home run of breakfasts, I guess. A big stack of pancakes, eggs and bacon, I hope. You've certainly earned it with the way you've been going to bat with those drinks."

"Mmm. And waffles? Can we get waffles?" Big expressive eyes pleaded with me.

Drunk as she was, she had no idea. I would give her anything she wanted. "We can order the whole damn menu."

When she took her first step in those high strappy wedges, her knees buckled. Without skipping a beat, I grabbed her by the waist, supporting her.

"Easy there, slugger. One foot at a time."

She glanced back at me over her shoulder, her upper body listing to one side. "What happens if I trip?"

My heart lurched again, and I sighed, kissing the top of her head.

"I will always catch you when you fall."

16. FOOD THERAPY

Cade...

We arrived at Denny's at the tail end of the lunch rush on a Saturday. Kids squealed, waitresses hustled, and a chaotic buzz vibrated through the air. Gritting my teeth at the stress with the frenzied commotion, I glanced down at Hannah.

She beamed up at me like we'd arrived at The Happiest Place on Earth.

A frazzled hostess approached the podium. "How many?

"Two." I squeezed Hannah's shoulder.

She leaned into me, arms wrapping around my waist in a brief hug.

Guiding Hannah in front of me, but never letting her go, I directed her as we followed the hostess toward a table for two in the center of the busy dining room. "Any chance we could snag that corner booth?" I asked.

Holding tight to Hannah's shoulder with one hand, I dug into my pocket with the other.

"That table's for..." The hostess glanced back, her gaze

locking onto the twenty in my hand. "Well, of course. We're lightening up after lunch. That booth will be just fine."

I grinned as she snatched the twenty and slapped our menus on the table.

Hannah flipped through hers, eyes widening with every page that she scanned from top to bottom. "There's no way we could even eat one bite of every menu item. I'd explode."

Unable to help myself, I dropped my chin into her neck, growling. "Better to wait until I can make you explode."

Her cheeks pinked on her already flushed skin. "Right here? In this booth?"

I glanced into the dining room, pretending to survey the possibilities. "Maybe. Think I could keep everyone distracted back in the kitchen by filling an entire menu order?"

She tapped her lip with a finger in thought. "Wonder if" —she hiccuped— "they have a closet."

I blinked. "Okay, that's too far, even for me. No way in hell am I getting you naked in a Denny's closet."

"What about the ba—"

"Nooo," I interrupted. Then I dropped her a deadpan look. My fault for guttering the conversation.

Her lower lip popped out into a masterful pout. All it made me want to do was suck that sexy lip into my mouth. I cleared my throat and tried to concentrate on the menu. "You'd be too loud, anyway."

"What?" Her delicate brow furrowed.

"Your explosion. You tend to scream when you're *not* drunk. We don't want to get kicked out of Denny's in broad daylight for lewd conduct."

Leaning in, she whispered conspiratorially. "Good idea." She hiccuped once more, then gave an exaggerated forward nod. "Better to wait till dark."

Shaking my head, I laughed as I zeroed in on our targeted menu item. "Here we go. Grand Slam. Two of everything: eggs, bacon, sausage, and pancakes."

Our waitress showed up before I finished describing it. "A classic." She smiled warmly.

"Two grand slams." I closed my menu, handing it to her.

"And waffles. Don't forget the waffles." Hannah pointed at the picture on the menu. "But no whipped cream."

Our waitress nodded, taking notes.

"And mozzarella sticks! And onion rings!" Hannah bounced on the booth in excitement.

I snorted. "The classic Denny's buffet."

The waitress winked at me. "Of course. What can I get you two to drink?"

"Orange juice!" Hannah shouted, louder than necessary.

I leveled a look at the waitress. "And coffee. Plenty of coffee."

The waitress winked. "You got it." She took Hannah's menu and disappeared back toward the kitchen.

"I have to pee." Hannah sat back in the booth, her pout back.

I began to slide out but paused when she didn't move. "Well, come on, Maestro. Let's go."

"You're escortin' me, right?" Her lips twitched.

"Right." I gave her a hard stare. "But don't expect to get any action in there."

Smirking about only God knew what, she gave me a glance and poked my chest without much force while I helped her to her feet. "This is the chance youuu've been waitin' for. You get to lift my skirt in the bathroom."

I laughed. "First of all, you're wearing jeans. Second, my wanting to 'lift your skirt' in the bathroom had nothing to do with peeing. Last, but most important, no sex for you until tomorrow."

We made our way through the dining room, heading back toward the entrance side of the restaurant. I silently cursed that I hadn't asked for a table near the bathrooms.

"Awww, come on. I'll be good. Couldn't we have a little sex?"

I chuckled. "There are degrees of sex, now? I must've missed that memo."

She gave me a pleading look when we reached the door to the women's bathroom.

"No. No sex." I snorted, unable to believe the words coming out of my mouth or the location in which they were being said. "Go. Pee. I'll be here waiting. Lean on the walls if you need to."

Almost five minutes later, Hannah emerged, wiping her hands dry in a paper towel as she followed another customer out of the bathroom. She mouthed to me and held her hands up. "Look. No walls."

Not willing to risk her twisting an ankle, I grabbed her hand, shaking my head. "Daredevil."

Shortly after returning to the booth, several platters were delivered to our table. I pulled a Grand Slam in front of me and slid Hannah's in front of her. Thankfully, she dug in, devouring her food in giant forkfuls filled with pancakes and eggs.

Around a mouthful of food, she groaned. "Oh my God. I love Grand Slams."

Her hair was tousled, her eyes unfocused, but she looked adorable with her cheeks puffed full of food.

I grinned. "Not bad for therapy food."

She swallowed down her mouthful. "Therapy food?"

I gave her a nod. "Yeah. A stomach full of good food soothes away what ails us. Like the alcohol."

"No." She pointed her now-empty fork at me. "Alcohol doesn't ail me, asshole men do."

I laughed. "Or that."

She peered at me for a few beats. "You're not an asshole man."

"No, I'm not."

"Don't ever be."

I leveled a heavy look at her, willing the gravity of my words to penetrate the drunken haze of her mind. "I won't."

Satisfied, she gave a hard nod. "Good. So what other food therapy is there?" She took her knife and fork and cut a wedge shape from her waffle, loaded strawberries onto it, then drenched it in maple syrup.

"Thanksgiving. That entire holiday is food therapy." I crunched into a crisp piece of bacon.

"How so?"

"Well, at my house, extended relatives descend and harass the shit out of Dad, which pisses him off. Mom ends up on edge, snapping at my sisters. I stay out of the way, avoiding the craziness, except to help out when needed. But the only thing that calms everyone down from spitting and snarling at one another is the great food at the table."

She arched her brows. "Plus, kinda hard to bicker when your mouth's full of food."

I tilted my head. "Very true."

"Thanksgiving's comin' up."

"It is. I'm hoping you'll go with me. But I'm warning you right now, although I try to avoid the stress, I tend to be surly on that day too."

"I can handle your surl-surli-surliness."

I smirked, torn between laughing at her adorable

stammer and growling at her sexual innuendo. "I know you can."

"Plus, plenty of closets to distract you with," she said with a stone-cold straight face.

Barking out a laugh, I shook my head, unable to believe how fortunate I was. Those idiot asshole men had no clue what they'd discarded.

"That there are. Bathrooms too. I have a feeling this will be the best Thanksgiving ever."

17. AFTERSHOCK

Hannah...

The inside of my skull throbbed. I groaned, cracking an eyelid open to the morning sunlight streaming in while I pushed Cade's leg off of me. He murmured something before snuggling into the bunched comforter. I pushed myself up, needing to pee like crazy.

The room spun as I shifted upright, my stomach reeling. My hand flew up to my mouth, and I took a deep breath through flaring nostrils. After a few seconds, I grew confident that whatever was in my stomach would stay there. I slowly eased out of bed, keeping my head stable as I shuffled across the rug, stepped onto the cold tile in the bathroom, then pulled my pajama pants down.

Huh. Big T-shirt, soft pajama pants, neither of which I remembered putting on.

"Hannah? You okay?" His voice sounded muffled, like he'd rolled face first into a pillow.

Good question. I closed my eyes, assessing the damage. My body felt like shit. My mind, however, had gone numb where thoughts of my father were concerned. Maybe I'd gotten better at compartmentalizing my feelings when it came to monumentally-disappointing men.

Or maybe those had been some damn good vodka tonics.

When I tried to speak, my dry throat locked up. I cleared it before croaking out, "Yeah. Been better, but I'll survive."

I flushed the toilet and stepped up to the sink, turning the faucet on. He stumbled into the bathroom behind me, naked.

Distracted by the reflection in the mirror—the definition to his muscles, his sculpted ass—I let the water run before I realized I still needed to wash my hands.

Soaping them over and rinsing, I dried them in a towel before searching in the cabinet for something for my headache. I grabbed a bottle of pain relievers, shook out two pills, and filled a glass of water before gulping them down.

He flushed, then washed his hands, completely at ease with his nakedness. Then he wrapped his arms around me and kissed my temple. "How about a big breakfast to keep those pills from rotting a hole in your stomach? That is, if you can handle eggs and bacon again so soon after yesterday's Grand Slams."

I gingerly shook my head. "Toast. Maybe half a banana. Something less greasy and more electrolytes."

Cade pulled on jeans, then ushered me out into the hall. "I'll make it all and eat whatever you can't."

My laptop sat on my table, the screen was open but in its dark sleep mode. Curiosity tugging me forward, I slid into my chair and tapped the space bar with the side of my thumb, bringing the screen to life. I squinted, adjusting to the bright light. Without thought, driven by a flicker of hope that burned through my disappointment, I clicked into my email on the chance Paul had communicated again.

There it sat, cushioned by two work emails below it and one above it. Only his all-capped subject line seemed darker, weighing heavy with greater importance. The time stamp showed it had come through while I'd been getting wasted. The subject line said: VERY SORRY.

"He emailed me." My voice sounded reedy.

Cade swore under his breath. "Really?"

He was full-on pissed, yet my reaction seemed smothered, the blank numbness I'd achieved through copious amounts of alcohol remaining. And like an earthquake aftershock, the initial upheaval event had been incredibly distressing, but the follow-up tremors felt like nothing more than an afterthought—and wholly unsurprising.

The rational part of me expected Paul to give some kind of explanation, even a lame one. The girl who'd been stood up didn't care about excuses, though. Heart already crushed, yesterday I'd abandoned the idea that a relationship with my father would be anything worthwhile. Yet still, today, I'd opened the email with that traitorous flicker of hope.

Irritation sliced through my hangover haze, and I scowled at the email, crossing my arms in defiance. "I'm not opening it."

"Okay." Cade opened the refrigerator and pulled out sourdough bread, bacon, and eggs.

Unaccustomed to sitting at the table instead of cooking, but in no condition to operate the stove with the room doing the whole Tilt-A-Whirl bit, I glared at the email like an adversary.

What did Paul expect of me? To give him another shot?

People didn't change. And my father had made the worst possible mistake on his first impression.

Yet in spite of my best efforts to stay angry, curiosity niggled at me. "I'm going to open it."

"Okay." He whisked the eggs in a bowl.

Tapping a fingernail on the edge of the laptop, as if the innocent-looking email had teeth, I hovered the cursor over its subject line. Although the pan on the stove made spattering noises, I didn't look away from the computer screen.

Sighing at my ridiculous hesitance, I clicked on the damned thing, opening it.

I read it through. Then leaned back hard in my chair, seething.

"What does it say?"

I glanced up to see Cade leaning back against the counter, watching me with concern.

"His family had a sudden issue with his meeting me, and he didn't want to upset them."

His eyes narrowed. "Did he apologize?"

"Yeah. Said he was sorry. Asked if I would give him another chance." I shoved the laptop screen shut. "I don't want to go through that again. Once was enough. And I'm pissed that he had all that time to prepare them, years and years to plan this out. But *I'm* the one who gets the shaft when it comes down to who he's willing to upset?"

Between the oven and two stovetop pans, Cade timed breakfast perfectly and loaded one plate with bacon, scrambled eggs and French toast. The one he slid in front of me held sliced bites of banana and dry toast. "So don't. He had his chance. He knew the odds were slim that you'd agree with his first email to you. You owe him nothing." He rubbed my shoulder, then sat beside me.

Tilting my head, I reached over and picked up the

perfect piece of crispy bacon. "Okay, Mr. I-Don't-Cook-Much. Where'd you learn the bacon-in-the-oven trick?"

He shrugged. "Jeep dealership waiting room. Time to kill while cooking shows played on the Food Network. Eighteen minutes. Three-hundred-fifty degrees. Crispy bacon." As he lifted a piece of bacon off his plate, he gave me a self-satisfied grin, then snapped half of it off into his mouth.

I shook my head, smiling at how adorable he was. Then I glanced at my plate, pushing my banana bites around with my fork. "Tell me again what happened last night. Too many details are fuzzy." I finally speared a couple of pieces and forked them into my mouth.

He smirked. "Which ones? Trying to convince me to bend you over in the Denny's bathroom or flashing the waitress?"

I coughed, nearly choking on a piece of banana. "What? I flashed a Denny's waitress?"

Laughing hard, he shook his head. "You didn't succeed. I practically tackled you into the booth, holding your shirt down. But not without your valiant effort to show poor Sandy the goods in the middle of the afternoon."

"Ugh." I groaned. "Remind me to never go into Denny's again."

"What about the lunchtime drinkfest?"

I snorted and gently shook my head. "No. I'm good there too. Did you say something about Thanksgiving?"

He drizzled maple syrup onto his French toast. "I did."

"At your parents' house."

He gave me a sidelong glance. "Yep. If you'd like to go."

I stared at the powder-keg laptop lying dangerously on the table. Then I thought about family—blood relations no one chose, but put up with anyway—and an idea materialized.

"Do you mind if I invite someone?"

He followed my gaze toward the laptop. "Paul?"

I nodded. "I will never meet him somewhere neutral again, trusting blindly that he'll show. I'd rather be in the middle of the people in this world who love me the most, your family—my turf. Do you think that's selfish of me?"

Cade laughed. "No way. I love it. Make him run the gauntlet of my family." He nudged me. "*Your* family. If he even has the balls to show up, we'll put him through the ringer to vet him for you. No one unworthy gets to be in your life."

I smiled, grateful for his protective side. "Thanks. It's the only way I can imagine being comfortable trying with him again."

He took a few swallows of orange juice. "And if you want my opinion, don't count on him showing. And maybe don't tell him to come over until well after the meal will be over. If he shows, he shows. If not, the letdown won't be anything we didn't already expect."

I nodded. "Sounds like a good plan."

"Mind if I have a look?" He nodded toward the closed laptop.

Halfway into shoveling some of his eggs into my mouth, I turned the laptop toward him. He put his fork down and took his time reading the few short paragraphs.

When he finished, he gave me a hard look. "You okay with me checking this guy out?"

"Like hiring a private investigator?"

He tipped his head to one side then the other. "In a way. My dad has a friend who works for a law firm, and he checks people out all the time."

"In legal ways?"

"Does it matter? I'll ask him to check out Paul. He'll get

back to me with what he finds. Then you can decide whether Paul Gilcrest is someone you even want to know further."

"Paul Gilcrest? You remembered his last name?"

Cade gave me a serious look. "After his no-show yesterday, I made it my business to know the name he'd given you. I found the folder you'd brought to the park, which held the first emails you'd printed, and reread them." A sudden uneasiness flashed across his expression. "I didn't mean to step over a boundary—it was only to protect you."

My heart ached at how hard he tried to respect my space, while at the same time, needed to make sure I didn't get hurt. I smiled and slid my hand over his. "No, Cade, it's okay. Thank you for looking out for me."

The private investigator idea sounded subversive. And yet, I needed to know. I couldn't risk inadvertently giving Cade's parents' address over to a complete stranger we knew nothing about, someone who could be a risk to his family or to me.

"Do it. He found out where I worked, inviting himself into my life without warning. I'm fine with turning the tables, finding out all we can about the man claiming to be my father."

"Would you like a DNA sample?"

I burst out laughing, imagining the PI collecting hair or asking for a vial of blood. But then my expression sobered. What did I really know about the guy? Or my mom, for that matter? My mom had chosen not to tell me anything about him. According to Paul, she'd made the decision to exclude him from my life. But I'd always gotten the impression that my father never wanted to be in the picture, and she'd never corrected me on that assumption. I didn't know what to trust anymore. Cade's blatant suggestion was one way to get closer to finding answers.

"Yes." My tone was forceful as a steely determination hardened through me.

Cade choked on the bacon he'd been chewing, coughing and sputtering until he caught a full breath. Evidently, he'd been joking.

I wasn't. Not even a little bit.

EARLY MONDAY HAD ARRIVED FASTER than I'd wanted.

Cade and I had spent our last few hours together in bed Sunday before he'd headed back to San Francisco Sunday night. I would've driven him to the airport, but I'd been hungover, exhausted, and not in any position to argue when he'd tucked me in. My last memory was of his warm lips brushing across mine, kissing me tenderly.

Now I sat in Lila's parking lot while morning's grayish twilight slowly glowed the world into life. I touched my fingers to my mouth, remembering his kiss—heart still reeling from it. The ache in my chest burned into a pang. He hadn't even been gone twelve hours, the heat of his kiss still sizzling on my lips, and already I missed the hell out of him. Exhaling on a slow breath, I cut Josephine's engine and got out.

A car door slammed shut on the other side of Willard's beat-up truck. Through the foggy mist that still hung heavy in the air after a steady overnight rain, a young woman emerged. Sleek black hair hung straight. She wore a basic long-sleeve white T-shirt and pleated khaki pants.

Piercing blue eyes narrowed at me. "Lila's lucky I love

her and Willard," she snarled as she passed by before walking up the cobblestone path that led to the porch.

I bit my lower lip, fighting a smile. From what I'd gathered, Lila's entire staff adored the two of them, and Carole was no exception. The fact that she'd grudgingly set aside her normal waitressing role to be trained as a sous chef under Willard was a testament to that.

Although it was before 6:00 a.m., well after I normally headed into Sweet Dreams, things were already hopping in Lila's kitchen. Sauces were being prepared in an industrial blender. Salad makings lay on a table, waiting to be chopped. A large stock pot sat on one burner of the gas stove, and by the smell of the kitchen, the soup of the day was in the realm of chicken.

A third employee, a high school kid named Reggie, scraped chopped onion from a cutting board into the pot. He glanced up at me, wide-eyed with a big smile. "Hey, Hannah."

Willard focused on pouring a cup of cubed tomatoes into his blender. "'Bout time you showed up. Was about to shut the place down." Only when he turned the thing on, the loud noise whirring above any possible speech, did he glance up at me with spark in his eyes.

The gauntlet had been thrown.

I grinned. *Challenge accepted.*

In the coming hours, and all through the day, I discovered exactly what that entailed.

Customers didn't trickle in to the twenty table café in evenly spaced intervals. They mobbed the front door in packs, waiting for an opportune time to catch us with one of the two servers on a break or an errand.

Doing my best to help fill in the gaps, I timed menus, drinks, orders, meal service, midmeal stop-bys, and check delivery. When things happened smoothly, it was a juggling act of catch-up and smiling customer service. Most of the time, it was flying by the seat of my flaming pants.

Thank God I wore comfortable tennis shoes.

And so, in the whirlwind of my first day as substitute manager, I missed Cade's three texts and forgot to eat lunch. At 3:47 p.m., after the last customer had cleared the premises, I slumped into my favorite table by the window, unable to make it all the way out the door.

I silently thanked Lila for not serving a dinner menu.

The clang of a bowl snapped my attention in front of me. Steaming hot soup wafted up. A plate with a huge turkey sandwich followed. "Eat." Willard glared down at me with wrath in his eyes.

I'd have laughed but could only manage enough energy to lift the soup spoon. "Thank you."

His response was a hard nod before turning away, leaving me to my hearty meal. The moment the first spoonful of salty soup hit my mouth, I groaned at the rich flavor. From the corner of my eye, I caught Willard pause at the hallway that led back to the kitchen.

"You done good, kid," he said, his voice gruff. He disappeared a heartbeat later.

I smiled. Which was amazing, considering how badly my muscles ached from the top of my head to my toes.

My phone vibrated on the table. Lila's name appeared on the screen. I finished chewing a bite of sandwich, then answered it. "You didn't tell me you ran a labor camp."

"Awww...can't be as bad as all that."

Not wanting to worry her when I'd offered to help, I kept silent about my aches and pains. "It's fine. Willard is a well-oiled machine, and your employees are amazing. I just never realized the exhausting whirlwind it is to waitress and manage the restaurant for hours on end. I have new respect for you, Lila."

She chuckled. "Hard work strengthens character." A crackle sounded over the phone as she paused. "Wanted to thank you again for takin' care of Willard. Means a lot to me."

I smiled at her heartwarming concern for her brother. Not the café or her employees, although I was certain they were important to her as well. "Of course, Lila. I'm happy to help."

Tuesday brought more of the same character-strengthening work. Followed by Wednesday, which blurred into Thursday.

By the time I made it home each evening, soaked in a hot bath of Epsom salts, pulled on a soft T-shirt and pajama bottoms, then snuggled into bed, it was nearly 7:00 p.m. and time to call Cade. Was that early for my bedtime? Hell no. I woke up at 3:00 a.m. most days and desperately needed as close to eight hours of sleep as possible.

San Francisco was three hours behind us, so it was only 4:00 p.m. there, but it didn't matter what time I called. Cade always answered.

He picked up on the second ring, his voice muffled. "I don't care what it costs. You're missing the point." A loud voice blared in the background, distorted like it came from a speakerphone. "Crunch the numbers again and find the money for target marketing. You're third in that territory for no explainable reason. That money well spent will gain you market share."

His whisper came across. "Hold on, babe." Silence followed. A door shut.

I snuggled deeper into the pillows, inhaling deeply from the one that smelled most like him. I smiled on a slow sigh.

"I'm back. Sorry about that."

"No apologies. You know I understand." And I did. Mostly. We'd fallen into a routine. Our life had transformed into stolen moments connected by electronic devices. Yet in spite of how badly I wished it were different, it was all we had right now.

"Miss you, Maestro." His voice had lowered, gone rough and sexy.

I didn't answer. Thick emotion threatened to spill tears from my eyes.

"You okay? You've stopped sending me little texts. You haven't told me you've missed me in a while. You do, don't you?"

The concern in his voice broke the weakening dam I'd built and hot tears streamed down my cheeks. I nodded, but he didn't hear me. Not trusting my voice yet, I whispered, "I love you, Cade."

A deep chuckle. "But you don't miss me? Got a hot guy on the side you haven't told me about?"

Damn him. I smiled. And the tears stopped flowing. I shook my head. "Idiot."

"Got you to smile, I bet."

"Yeah."

"So. What's with the silent treatment on the missing issue? Do you or don't you?"

"You know I do."

"Then what's wrong? It's not like you to be so quiet."

Pinching my eyes shut, I exhaled slowly, trying be quiet so he wouldn't hear. So he would believe I was strong. Maybe I could believe it too. "I'm tired. Exhausted tired. My bones are sagging. My hair hurts." Diversion tactics with off-topic truths seemed like a good idea.

"Hair can't hurt, Maestro. It's dead."

"Well, my zombie hair hurts, then."

He snorted over the line. "Woman, you're making no sense."

"I'm going crazy with you gone."

"I love your brand of insanity." A pause came over the line before he let out a hard sigh he didn't bother to hide. "I know, babe. This is hard."

I nodded. "Harder than I thought."

"For me too."

Longing for him, I clutched the phone tighter. "I've stopped telling you that I miss you, because I don't want to dwell on that part. It hurts too much to think about what I don't have: you in Sweet Dreams almost every morning, surprise lunch dates, dinners with you...curling up in bed with you."

"Amazing, mind-blowing, body-rocking sex with me."

"Pig."

"Actually, I've been told I'm hung like a horse," he drawled, his voice thick with sexual heat.

I grinned, then shook my head, huffing out a soft laugh. Those exact words were his reminder of a crazy conversation at a faux funeral so many months ago, when I hadn't been in my right mind and he'd found a way to distract me. The sentiment warmed my heart. "Damn, I miss you, Cade. Something fierce."

"Yeah, me too."

Somewhere deep inside, bravery welled up. My best friend was on the other line. And if I couldn't share everything with him, who could I?

"This is rough, Cade. A *lot* harder than I imagined."

A long, heavy sigh echoed into my ear. "You have no idea how great it is to hear you say that."

I snorted out a soft laugh, then sniffed. "Only you would enjoy my misery."

"No." His voice softened. "Misery enjoys company."

"Yeah?"

"Yeah."

Silence followed. Like we didn't know what to say. Or were afraid to say it. This beautiful frightening tension filled the space, intimate and foreign. Right, and yet at the same time, so wrong.

Images flooded into my mind, all of them silly little moments. So many miniscule things that meant everything. This time when I exhaled, I let the sigh come out full force. No more hiding, no more being strong for him. "I miss you bringing me coffee in the morning."

His deep voice, softened as he whispered, "I miss the smile brightening your face when I do."

"All the little surprises throughout the week."

"Your frustrated little growl when I've coerced time out of you."

I grasped the corner of the pillow, tugging on it. "I secretly loved your manipulations, when you did it just to be able to get time alone with me."

A pause followed.

I waited, hearing my heartbeat in my ears, feeling it thump hard in my chest. My pulse raced at Cade being with me in this moment, closer to me than ever, yet a million miles away.

"I miss being with you, Maestro. Holding you, wrapping myself around you. Being inside you. And after, just breathing with you."

My lungs froze. I counted to three, then let out a slow exhale, one he couldn't hear.

And I don't know what made me do it. Maybe it was all

the little things he'd done for me. Probably it was the big thing he was doing for himself, and for us in the long run. But the small lie came out easier this time, knowing the powerful words were for him.

"You are here with me, Cade. When I'm on your side of the bed, inhaling your smell, hearing your deep voice as it wraps around me, soothes me—you are."

I closed my eyes, wishing it was true. The coldness of the sheet paled in comparison to his hard, hot body. His sighs and growls over the phone were a technological distortion of the richness of his sounds inches away from my ear, his breath heating my skin.

"Yeah, well, prepare yourself for Friday night. Nothing we could do while we're apart will substitute being together, in the flesh, touching, tasting, feeling..." His voice trailed lower.

A groan came from my throat as I buried my face in the pillow, mumbling, "Agreed."

18. SWEET DREAMS...
OR NOT

Cade...

My chest actually hurt. Pain burned behind my sternum. Partly at the tremendous loss to me. Mostly at how the bad news would be received.

The phone rang. Once. Twice. My after-midnight time meant her standing in her kitchen in her tiny robe at 3:12 a.m., getting ready for work.

"Hey, you." Her soft voice eased the pressure. But I cringed, knowing I didn't deserve the reprieve. A kick in the nuts was more in line.

"Hey." Words crashed into each other in my head. I'd run through what I was going to say a dozen times, not wanting to let her down, but knowing I would.

A teakettle whistled in the background, then quieted. I imagined her fishing a tea bag out of one of the tins on her counter.

When the silence grew longer than it should, I jumped off the cliff, coming out with it in one direct truth. "I'm not gonna make it home tonight. A 'sure-thing' acquisition fell apart, and we'll be working on it all through the weekend to try and piece it back together."

Deafening quiet over the phone worried me.

But then she spoke, her voice strong, steady. "It's okay. I've got two more days at Lila's before she's back. Besides, Chloe and Daniel have probably forgotten what I look like, so I'll go into Sweet Dreams on Sunday." Her voice trailed, the strength draining from it. "It'll help to—"

At her voice cracking, I scowled. Fucking job across the country. I began to second guess the decisions I'd made that sounded logical, until they weren't. Not when it hurt people. Not when it made me disappoint the last person on Earth I wanted to.

"Distract you." I finished it so she didn't have to. "I know, Maestro. I'm beyond sorry."

"The Halloween party is tonight." The disappointment in her voice killed me. Clinking sounds followed, like she stirred something into her tea. "You know, I bought a special costume. Not for the party." With every word, her tone changed, a sensual edge taking over. "For you."

There it was—my torture. Not even the real kind I deserved. Not the guilt from her hurt, although I felt it. Not her being honest about how upset she was with my missing one of our promised weekends, but I knew underneath all the bravado, she was.

My penance came in the most appropriate form. A sharp reminder of the things I missed by not being there: every ounce of her sweet and sexy, her slow simmer along with the fire heating it.

Yet in spite of the fact that I deserved so much worse, I took my lashes like any bad boy should. "Yeah?"

"Mmm-hmm…" Her voice dipped lower, husky.

"Care to share? I'm dying here. Give me a fantasy to tide me over."

I wondered if she'd smiled. I closed my eyes, gripping the phone tighter, picturing the little smile she got when she was being naughty for me—a mix between shy and wicked, where one corner kicked up a little.

"I'm dressing as Little Bo Peep. White dress with a corseted top, you know the kind."

Yeah, I did. She'd worn one of those corset tops to our first business meeting. Cunning. And deadly.

My voice came out hoarse, "What else?"

"Thin, lacy straps will be falling off my shoulder. A baby-blue frock covers the dress, which stops just below ruffled white panties."

Holy shit. My mind spun and I groaned, recalculating in a split second the importance of business acquisitions in comparison to the temptation of Hannah in full costume with her sexy-as-fuck tease on.

"Black patent skyscraper-high stilettos…"

"*Dead.* I've died and gone to Heaven. Or Hell."

Her soft laugh made me smile. "No dying yet, Mr. Businessman. I've got plans for you when you finally make it home." She paused. "Oh, and there's a staff."

"Fuck yeah, there is. Nine hard inches." How ironic. Sweet sexy Bo Peep tempting the big, bad business wolf. Didn't know what the hell she saw in me, but what a grateful bastard I was that she did.

"Bad boy." Her chastising tone turned me the fuck on that much more. "It's a shepherd's staff with a little blue bow tied around the curved handle."

My thoughts scanned to all the things I could do to her —would do to her—in that outfit. My throat had gone bone dry. I swallowed hard. "You have no idea."

A heavy sigh followed. "I have to go, babe. I'm so sorry. I promised Chloe and Daniel I'd show up for a few hours to help them with the Halloween cake before Lila's."

"No, don't be sorry. Go. Be amazing you. And I'm the one sorry about this whole weekend." I stared up at the ceiling, pissed the fuck off about life and the "soundness" of my decisions.

"No, really. It's okay, Cade. I understand. I'm the one who encouraged you to follow your dream. Just don't make it a habit of skipping weekends, okay? Please promise me. Your girl needs her time with you."

"Done. I promise. No matter what crazy shit happens over here again, I won't miss another scheduled weekend with you."

"Good. And Cade?"

"Yeah, babe."

"I love you."

The three words were packed with an emotional undercurrent that I felt through the phone. My chest ached even more than before. I took a deep breath and willed all of my heart into my reply, hoping she felt it as viscerally as I did. "I love you."

HOURS LATER, after another all-nighter stuck analyzing the financials of a company demanding beyond top dollar and concluding, yet again, that our final offer would be far less no matter how valuable a resource it would be for Fisher Holdings, I shoved the thick file to the opposite side of my massive desk and leaned back in my chair. A great game of poker would have to be played to make them believe we were all in with the only chips on the table, or it was game over.

I scrubbed a hand over my face and sighed. Sleep. I needed it badly, but my brain was too wired. The sun hadn't yet risen behind the bay, but the sky had begun to show gray signs of life.

Energy gone and needing a jolt, I reached for my phone. Without thinking, I clicked into the text box. But at 4:49 a.m. my time, Hannah would've already arrived at Lila's, helping prepare for another hectic day.

Her last text was from yesterday afternoon on her ten-minute break, before she'd teased me last night about fairytale Halloween costumes as punishment to my never-ending working crimes.

I chuckled, again, as I reread her texted frustrations:

> How is it even possible to break five glasses in four days?

> Curious as to the answer?

> Pickle juice. #5 would be pickle juice on my hands.

Yesterday, I hadn't replied. I'd only called her the moment the nonstop meetings had let up. Today, I lobbed a ball back into her court.

> Sour condiments suck.

> Give me sweet any day.

> And I'll suck harder . . .

I tossed the phone onto my messenger bag, knowing no reply would come through for hours, and flipped open my laptop.

In the next thirty minutes, I opened the two emails that signed the rights away to my former businesses: one from Ben, relinquishing all control in Loading Zone to become a silent partner like my father, the other from Simon, selling my share of our three-month-old business outright. After scanning to confirm each contract was on previously discussed terms, I signed them both and sent them through cyberspace, sealing my career fate.

The finality of the action sank into me as I stared out the windows toward the Golden Gate. The sun now lit the top half of the massive suspension bridge. Yet I didn't feel its warmth or brightness in the anticlimactic moment. In my fatigued, Hannah-deprived state, my thoughts were where the sun had already risen for me this morning—with Hannah.

I shook my head, dragging myself from my thoughts. Being overtired wreaked havoc on my mind. Trying to wind down, in the hopes I might be able to steal a few hours of dead-to-the-world sleep on the leather couch across the room from me, I pulled open the to-do list for the Christmas party I'd committed to.

Over the last few weeks, plans had been formulated, tasks assigned out, orders made. Kristen and Kendall had been hard at work on their parties, sending me updates. I'd done the same, at least to the extent of what I could share of the Constantine's plans. My hosts wanted an unforgettable party. With my event being third, and the last party of the season, but most importantly, with the weekend kicking off my first holidays with Hannah, so did I.

I SHOOK MY HEAD, unable to believe my eyes. "I must be dreaming..."

Hannah dropped her hands onto her hips, looking fucking spectacular. One corner of her luscious lips kicked up into a half smile. "You are."

Unreal as it was, every detail seemed magnified. I wore only a short-sleeved T-shirt, and the cold night air bit into my skin. But it did nothing to calm my heating blood with Hannah inches away. We stood on a red brick walkway leading up to a stately mansion.

My mouth fell open as my gaze traveled down Hannah's shapely legs. Dream or not, every cell in my body wanted to lunge forward. Capture the vision before me.

Instead, I fought the urge. Reason took hold. For now.

"Those are..." I swallowed hard. Words escaped me.

"Mary Janes. Platform, stiletto, Mary Janes." With the twist of her leg, she turned the shoe on its toe, giving me a profile of the black patent leather object of sin.

I growled low, stalking her. "They belong in the air above my shoulders."

"You're obscene." She narrowed her eyes, but the corners of her lips twitched. Her dark eyebrows drew together. "And you're not in costume."

My gaze wandered down her scantily clad body again. "You're sexy as fuck."

She was. White ruffled straps dangled loose off her shoulders. Lace trimmed a tight corset that propped her breasts up in decadent display. A tiny baby-blue dress cinched in at her waist, then flared out.

"Don't need a costume. I'm already your big, bad wolf." My heart kicked up a notch as I leaned to the side, eyeing the fluffy underthings beneath that short skirt. "Are those petticoats?"

Angling her shepherd's staff between us, she shook her head. "No. Pantaloons, I think. And you've got the wrong fairy tale. That's Red Riding Hood. I'm Bo Peep. And no one is going to think you're the Big Bad Wolf."

A smirk twisted my lips. "Covert. Only way I operate. All the better to eat you with."

I took another step closer. She took one back. She glanced over her shoulder, then took one more step on the brick path, heading toward the front door of the house. White smoke billowed from a coffin to our left, spilling over a manicured lawn.

A set of pumpkins by the door had been tricked out to resemble Despicable Me minions. Cute.

And so *very* fucked up in my dream.

Not even wanting to analyze that messed up shit, I took charge again, my gaze swinging back toward the only thing I was interested in. The intriguing spot high on Hannah's thigh, where smooth olive skin disappeared under those ruffled white skirt–shorts.

By the time she turned back toward me, I'd taken another stride closer. "Yeah, I need to learn more about pantaloons. How does one pee in those?"

A breeze carried her tropical scent toward me, and my nostrils flared on a deep inhale. When her arms broke out in goose bumps, I let out a slow breath, trying to control the urge to haul her close and heat up her sexy-as-fuck body. *Patience.* I dropped my head, never breaking our gaze as I edged closer.

She rolled her eyes. "One pulls them down, smartass."

"I thought you'd never ask."

Her eyes widened the split second I lunged.

She spun and squealed, darting left and around a group of people who'd just come out of the house. As luck would have it, Hannah had shielded herself behind a wall of sisterhood.

Really? Therapy would be needed. Lots of therapy.

The one dressed as a devil was Kristen. Kendall had channeled her inner angel, a novel sight to see. And Kiki, wild child that she was, had come as a purple-haired punk rocker.

I stood my ground, lowering my head a notch while staring hard at the threesome. "Stand aside. Give up Bo Peep, or the angel gets it."

Kendall arched a brow, muttering, "Give up the hostage. I do not want to *get* whatever *it* he's referring to." She gestured wildly with her hand in front of the crotch of my jeans.

Everyone burst out laughing as the girls wisely stepped away from my woman. Feeling every bit the Neanderthal who turned Hannah on so much, I chased her into the house, leaving my sisters to follow in our wake.

I stalked her until she stopped and turned at the edge of the room. My gaze drifted down again to her barely legal cleavage, then up to stare pointedly at her. "Better stay glued to my side, Shepherd Girl. I won't be responsible for my actions if anyone looks at you the wrong way."

Grinning wide, she beamed over my possessiveness. "I promise. By your side, all night."

Then she bit her lip, looking coy. I narrowed my eyes at her. "Not joking, Hannah. I'm on the edge of shoving you into a dark closet and staking my claim."

And really, that's where this realistic dream was headed, anyway.

She scoffed. "What makes you think that would stop some guy from making a pass?"

I leaned closer, not bothering to lower my voice with the

loud music thumping around us. "When you smell like me, our sex, and have a hickey on your neck, not even a drunk man with a pea-sized brain would mistake the fact that he'd risk a mauling."

Wide-eyed with shock, she gaped at me. "You wouldn't."

I arched my brows. "Sure as fuck would. Maybe I'll add teeth marks. I am the Big Bad Wolf, after all." I bent down and snapped my teeth close to her ear.

She shivered.

I barked out a laugh. "That turned you on, didn't it, Shepherd Girl?"

A pretty blush colored her cheeks. "Yeah. Kinda."

"Which part?"

She sidled up next to me, whispering just below my ear. "All of it."

"Seriously, this is just a dream?" When I lifted my hand to touch her, the realism ended. The air close to her skin was cold as ice.

She backed away, shaking her head. "You don't get to have me. You didn't choose me."

"No, Hannah." I followed her as she began to vanish. "You're wrong. I did choose you. My decision, this job, will mean a better future for us, secure."

Her image shimmered into the background before everything faded to black.

Loud knocking startled me. I bolted upright, my cheek burning from being ripped off the surface of the desk, and I blinked toward the sound.

My office door opened, and Henry's head appeared as he leaned in. "Sorry to interrupt, sir. You wanted me to alert you when we're T-minus thirty on the next discussion round."

I nodded, swallowing past a cotton mouth. My brain was

still hazed from knockout sleep. "I'm up. Gather the troops in twenty, and tell Maureen to keep the coffee hot and flowing."

Shaken by the dream, by my mind taunting me about what I couldn't have, trying to plant fears about Hannah slipping through my grasp, I growled. "Fuck fantasy dreams." When it ended with my girl disappearing, it was nothing but a nightmare.

I banished the entire episode from my mind, needing to focus on the impending negotiations. But not before I took a split-second note of the dream's fear. That shit came from deep in the subconscious. Only thing real about the nightmare.

"No." I stood and scowled at all the cold glass and steel around me, glared at the entire city glittering in the sunlight. "No fucking way am I going to lose Hannah over this."

I'd had a problem balancing my life before. But things were different now.

Hannah came first. And she supported me. She'd encouraged me to chase my dream.

But sometimes, dreams became nightmares.

19. TRENCH COATS AND GUMSHOES

Hannah...

In the days following Cade's disappointing news that he wouldn't make it home over the weekend, his texts and phone calls had grown different, tense almost. But the tension held an undercurrent of urgency, like every statement held importance, every phrase, heavy with emotion.

Intuition told me the distance between us worried him. Which, oddly, relieved me, because it scared me too. The few months we'd been dating, and the friendship even longer before that, now seemed like the blink of an eye in the face of what stretched ahead.

Every lonely night dragged on like a tortured eternity. Insane longing for him for days on end had turned into a crazed obsession of needing to be with him, touch him, until before I knew it, there I stood, with ticket in hand, boarding a plane. And Cade had no clue.

No time like the present to change circumstance.

After a delayed connection through Minneapolis, resulting in almost ten hours of travel from airport to airport, an executive car service I'd reserved swept me through the dark streets of San Francisco. I'd never been to the West Coast, but I didn't take in any of the surroundings. All my thoughts focused forward—on Cade.

When I stepped into the elevator from the black granite floor of the impressive lobby, my pulse fluttered up in tempo, excitement thrumming through my veins. I pressed the top button, lighting up number fifty-five and took a fortifying breath. The security guard had let me pass with my smile and explanation. Plus my name had already been on their approved list.

My throat went dry, and I swallowed hard as the elevator car flew upward. Out of nervousness, I tightened my belt. Seconds later, the doors opened, and I stepped out, still struggling to come to terms with my wild spontaneity.

I'd never done anything like this in my life.

I blame Cade.

Stilettos I'd worn before, to complete an outfit. The dark bronze trench coat was a splurge from a couple of years ago, a Burberry I'd caught on clearance, even though wearing it today was out of place with the clear weather.

But nothing else underneath was a first.

After my plane had touched down, and I'd changed in the airport bathroom, traveling light had taken on a whole new meaning.

Bolstering my courage, I passed the empty reception desk with smooth strides that I willed to be stealthy, left the stone tile flooring, and quickly made my way onto the plush carpeting of a long hallway. The corner office that I approached, by orientation and our phone conversations, had to be Cade's.

I took a deep breath and grasped the levered handle, pressing down as I exhaled slowly.

The second the door opened wide, all my anxiety about the crazy decision washed away.

Cade stood abruptly from his desk, wide-eyed. "Hannah."

His breathy awestruck surprise made me smile. Subtle lighting in his office was dimmed, more brightness coming from the laptop on his desk than anywhere else. His rumpled hair stuck out every which way, like he'd run his hands through it repeatedly.

The image of him, real and in the same room as me, stole my breath away. Unable to speak, I bit my lip.

Now what?

Cade solved the dilemma by crossing the space between us in seconds and crushing me into his arms. "Fuck, babe. No better thing has ever walked through that door."

Every muscle in my body relaxed in his hold. On my next inhale, I drank in his intoxicating scent, the sweetest hit of a drug I'd badly needed.

When he pulled away, he searched my face, concern etching his features. "Is everything okay? Why didn't you tell me you were coming?"

I gave a one-shouldered shrug. "I wanted to surprise you."

He stepped back and took me in with a nonstop grin. "Mission accomplished. When you'd texted to confirm I'd be working late, I had no idea there'd be a reward attached to my response."

"You deserve a well-earned break," my voice lowered, sounding sultry to my own ears. My impulsiveness had been an exhilarating major step for the careful, sheltered girl I'd been.

In slow motion, he tilted his head, his smile faltering as his attention roved down my body. The moment he reached the stilettos, his gaze shot back up, heating. His fists clenched, then released, like he wanted to do something with his hands, but fought the urge.

After a deep inhale and slow exhale, he backed up, taking measured steps until his backside touched his desk. He leaned against the edge of it and crossed his arms, his rolled white shirtsleeves revealing the corded muscle on his forearms. "Well, hello, Maestro." The deep tenor of his voice caressed my ears. "You're looking *very* seductive today."

His illicit tone caused my blood to heat and flow down like slow honey, warming hidden parts of my body, making them ache for him as if he commanded them. His gaze intensified with a raw hunger as he slowly loosened his ice-blue tie.

My lips twisted into a smirk as I shifted my weight onto one hip. "When you drop by Sweet Dreams, I'm in a T-shirt and shorts, covered in frosting. Thought I'd change it up a little."

He arched a brow as his attention raked down my body once more. "I love you covered in frosting."

I tugged at the belt tie of my coat and bit my lip, getting my flirt on further, dropping my voice, "Well, maybe you'd love me more...in something less."

But the damned belt wouldn't come undone, and I glanced down at the tight knot. Huffing out a breath, I wrestled with the tangle until it finally gave way. When I glanced up, his lips twitched at the corners.

I sighed. "Do not laugh. This isn't supposed to be funny."

He shook his head. "Oh, I'm not laughing. But you *are* adorable."

I scowled, holding the edges of the coat tightly closed as the belt fell open, its ends dangling by the loops at my hips. "I'm not going for adorable." I took a step closer.

He yanked his tie over his head. "How 'bout sexy as fuck, because you've got that going on."

"You say the most wonderful things." I slid my hands into my pockets. "You're forgiven." Then I whipped open my coat, flashing my naked body.

His jaw dropped open, his eyes glittering with lust. He shoved off the desk and stalked forward. Before I took a tentative step backward, he lassoed his tie around my neck. After a deep breath, his voice came out gruff, "Let me earn that forgiveness."

Gazes locked, we drew closer to one another as he dropped the tie, its silken ends feathering down across the bare skin between my breasts. My pulse exploded into a rapid beat, the temperature of the room rising with it.

His hands slid under my coat, over my hips, and clutched my ass. Then he knelt down. Hot lips brushed across my breasts. When his tongue laved over a nipple, I groaned as a shiver traced through my body.

At my low noise, he paused, murmuring against my skin as his lips trailed lower. "Might want to keep it down, Maestro. Not everyone has left and sound carries well through these offices."

I tugged my lower lip into my mouth, nodding. Seconds later, his hot breath fanned across the sensitive skin at the juncture between my thighs, and I bit down on my lip, nearly drawing blood.

He licked me there. Once. Twice. Pleasure speared through me in electric arcs, catching my breath with every touch.

Then all at once, he launched upright, nearly knocking me off-balance. But he was immediately all over me, backing me up as his hands caressed over my breasts and his mouth blazed a scorching trail down my neck.

It was all I could do to breathe and remain upright, but when I stumbled in my heels, he wrapped his hands around my waist, holding me strong and steady, guiding me back, back, until my shoulders hit the cold, unforgiving glass. When he eased away a fraction, his blue eyes had darkened, wild like midnight. His chest rose and fell quickly. His hands skimmed down to my hips, then gripped me tightly.

Yet he didn't make another move. He simply stared at me, as if he couldn't believe his eyes.

And I was right there with him—teetering on the edge of disbelief and fevered excitement.

Taking a steadying breath, I raised my hands and unfastened his belt, never breaking the determined stare we held. So much was there between us, unsaid, as I pulled his zipper down. His cock sprang free and landed in my hand, hot and heavy.

On a growl, he leaned forward and crushed his lips onto mine as I stroked him from base to tip, sliding my hand across soft velvet over hard steel. He shuddered when I paused at the tip and rubbed a gentle thumb along the sensitive underside.

An instant later, his hands dropped under my thighs, and I was hoisted up, my coat falling halfway off my shoulders as I went. His tip slid over my slick entrance seconds before he gripped me hard and impaled me. I cried out, filled, stretched, pulled apart and made whole again in one heartbeat.

Then he began to pump up into me, slow, steady. When he paused after easing back, I opened my eyes, gazing down at him.

He was beautiful, expression tense, awe-filled eyes radiated love and need. Inch by slow inch, he let me fall back onto him. As he raked across sparking nerves, pleasure pulsed through me, and I let out a soft gasp.

The corners of his mouth lifted into the beginnings of a smile. "This view has never been better."

I glanced left, taking in the darkness behind me, city lights glittering down below until the inky black of the bay snuffed them out. The cold window faded away, and suddenly it was as if I was flying, fifty-five floors up.

My gaze swung back to him, eyes widening. "The opposite of claustrophobia."

With a wicked look in his eyes, he pulled back, nearly separating us, then thrust forward with enough force to vibrate the glass. "Want me to stop?" Fully seated, he twitched inside me.

Unable to help it, I groaned. My eyes narrowed as I speared my fingers into his hair, tugging at the roots. "Do *not* stop."

I never took my gaze from him as he sent me soaring higher with every hard drive of his hips. My orgasm curled in around me, hovering at the fringes, teasing me with aching pressure. Every hard precise stroke he made seemed to follow the road map of my sounds, sending me straight toward more incredible pleasure.

And right when I thought I couldn't take it anymore, when every short breath from my lips held a low moan as I stared into his eyes, a coil wound inside me so tight, ache turned into a pinpoint of pain a split second before it shattered into a million sparks of pleasure.

I threw my face into the crook of his shoulder and muffled my scream. A beat later, he pressed his mouth to my neck, and I felt the edge of his teeth. Then he roared against my skin and thrust hard one final time, shuddering as he surrendered to his own intense release.

In the thumping heartbeats that followed, time slowed as we clung to each other. The familiar musky scent of our sex drifted up, wrapping around us in a sensual homecoming as we caught our breaths. His hold on my ass cheeks tightened, and he leaned into me further.

I was trapped between him and the rest of the world by a cold, thin pane of glass. The pressure almost made it hard to breathe, but I only tightened my hold on him, not caring. All that mattered in this treasured moment was the man in my arms.

Long minutes later, we pulled away from his wall of windows. "Cade, what are you doing?" I laughed as he carried me across the room back to his desk, my legs wrapped around him, my coat dangling from my bent arms.

"Cleaning up." He gently deposited me on his desk, then pulled up his pants and went to his wet bar. He returned with a white bar towel and cleaned me with reverent care. My hammering pulse began to calm a fraction, thoughts drifting back into moments of clarity—that I was here with Cade, panting from spectacular sex, and that I'd traveled three thousand miles on a whim to make it happen. Yet the world settled back into something resembling normal when his lips feathered over mine.

Then I fastened his pants and belt. "That'll need cleaning." I nodded toward the smudge marks my shoulders had made on the glass, grateful I hadn't been completely naked.

"Nah." He shrugged, then moved behind his desk. He held his arms out and made a wide frame with his forefingers and thumbs. "It's art. Wait..." He tugged at my coat, pulling it off my shoulders again. "I need a do-over. It won't be complete without your sexy ass print up there."

I turned on his desk and swatted his shoulder. "No way. I'm not getting up there twice."

Mischief glittered in his eyes. "I don't knowww...I'm *very* good at persuasion..."

When I shook my head with a smile, I glanced down at his desk and my gaze locked onto the top of a page that had my biological father's name typed on it. I leaned forward to get a closer look. "Is that report from the investigator?"

Cade pulled the edges of my coat together with a satisfied smirk and tied my belt into a solid knot. "I love your sexy pillow talk. You travel across the country without any warning, wearing a trench coat, have your way with me, then ask about PI's and reports. It's like you stepped off the television screen straight from a gumshoe murder mystery."

Amused at the picture he painted, I leaned forward, nipping his earlobe. "So who dunnit?"

He barked out a laugh. "You mean, besides us?"

"Quite amazingly, by the way."

He slid a finger behind my belt knot, tugging me closer. "Show up in a trench coat and heels, and I will make it worth your while every time." He pressed a soft kiss to my lips.

"And the report?"

"Oh, right. Sorry. With your nakedness underneath there, I keep getting distracted." He pulled out the thin set of stapled pages. "He checks out. Paul Gilcrest. Played in a rock band straight out of high school. Now has a successful business building custom cabinetry. No arrest record. No unpaid liens. Only been married to the woman he's with now. Twin seven-year-old kids: a boy and a girl."

"Was your investigator able to get DNA to test?"

"Yep." Cade glanced up from the report. "And, no, I didn't ask how." He flipped past the first two pages, scanning the third. "Blood type: B positive, a familial match to yours."

"Wait. How did he get *my* DNA?"

Cade grinned and ran his fingers through my hair. "I plucked one of your hair strands from your brush on your bathroom sink."

"Hmmph." I crossed my arms.

"Hey, at least I didn't pluck it from your head. And you did want to be sure, didn't you?"

I nodded. "Yeah, thanks. Didn't mean to sound ungrateful. This whole father–daughter meeting business has me a little on edge."

His hands went to my shoulders, grasping them firmly as his eyes searched mine. "Remember, you don't have to do any of this. All we did was make sure the guy was for real. Now you know he is. Doesn't mean he's a standup guy with his own family, or will in any way be a decent father to you now, but you have all the information possible to decide on whether or not you want to move forward."

The calm safety of being with Cade strengthened me. "I do want to move forward. Already have the email drafted and waiting to be sent."

"To invite him over for Thanksgiving?"

Exhaling a breath I hadn't realized I'd been holding, I nodded. "At three in the afternoon."

"After dinner but before dessert."

I smiled. "The accepted time when one entertains guests who might be family, but need to be vetted over coffee."

Cade snorted, then gave me a pointed look. "The Michaelson Clan will be more than happy to assist you."

20. UNEXPECTED MAGIC

Cade...

W orkday? *Over.*
Did I have more reports to analyze before two back-to-back meetings tomorrow? Sure. But it could wait until morning.

Hannah was here.

I still couldn't believe she'd done something so impulsive. For me.

During the ride back to my place, with Jackson driving the Bentley and no partition between us, we stayed relatively well behaved. But Hannah still never stopped touching me—her hand on my thigh, lips on my neck. A moment ago, she'd made a passing comment about a Victorian row house we passed. Jackson replied, informing her about the street of Painted Ladies that tourists flocked to for pictures. He offered to take her there tomorrow while I worked.

"That sounds nice," her tone was relaxed, but detached.

Seconds later, her teeth tugged at my earlobe. I slipped

my hand under the opening of her coat, slid it midway up her thigh. Higher.

Yeah, the only attraction she was interested in was me. I made a mental note to work her into my schedule every damn chance I had.

We pulled up to my row house. I opened the door for her and held a hand out, helping her from the car.

Her gaze traveled up the three-story building, eyes widening. "Wow. It's beautiful."

I glanced back at the dozen dark steps leading to the red front door. Two stories of bay windows rose up on either side of it, surrounded by yellow painted siding.

On a headshake, I pulled her closer. "You're the beautiful one. This is just a crash pad."

It was true. I slept here, nothing more. The company had given me one of the executive houses they owned, and I made myself comfortable there to eat and sleep when I wasn't working.

But when we stepped inside and the front door swung shut on a creek, Hannah brought new life to the place. She walked over and immediately flicked on the switch to the gas fireplace I hadn't yet touched. A blue-orange flame appeared, lighting up the realistic fake logs inside.

I set her bag on the narrow table near the staircase as she wandered toward the bookshelves along the far wall.

"I see you've made yourself at home here." Her fingers trailed along the perfect rows of CDs, moved from my room back in Philly. "Alphabetized by genre, then artist?"

Fighting a smile, I shoved the coffee table out of the way, tossed a few couch pillows onto the floor, then tugged her down onto the thick oriental rug before our fake fire. "It's only home with you here, harassing me."

She nestled into my side on a sigh: her sexy as fuck in

that trench coat, me in my dress shirt and wool pants. Yet neither of us made a move to change, or get naked.

Because I didn't want to let her go. Not even for a second.

A heavy pressure sat on my chest, and I took a deep breath. "Sure I can't convince you to move here? This house needs your touch. My OCD CD collection does not a home make."

Her arms tightened around me. "I can't, Cade. Too much of me is back there. Sweet Dreams. My friends. A father I'm hoping to know. My house..." Her voice trailed off. She didn't need to finish for me to know what she meant. Cherished memories of a past and fragile hopes of a future, both dealing with the only family she'd ever known, had a hold of her heart.

I kissed the top of her head. "I know. It's okay. Just thought I'd throw it out there."

Part of me wished *I* had a stronger hold of her heart. That I could follow the dream she'd told me to chase and have her never wanting to leave my side as I fulfilled it. But I respected the fact that she had her own dreams too.

"You nervous about meeting your father?"

Without hesitation, she nodded, still staring at the bluish flames.

"Well, don't be. You've got an inner strength I'm in awe of. Remember, *you* showed up. He didn't. And he's just a man who's already said he's hoping to know you too, asking for a second chance."

I paused, rubbing her shoulder. "Besides, my classic Thanksgiving mood should help distract you."

"Classic mood?"

"Yeah. Grumpy. Don't have an explanation for it, other than my body wakes up that way. Must be years of my family saving all their barbs for when a bird gets stuffed and marshmallows are tossed onto vegetables."

She gave out a soft laugh. "I'm looking forward to it."

I let out a long sigh, happy she was. Maybe because I was too.

She threw her leg over mine and shifted, glancing up at me. "Do you think we could fly back together? My return ticket's for the flight you normally take."

I nodded. "Don't see why not. But I'll have Maureen check my flight to be sure."

Silence followed. A tension hung heavy in the air. We were planning on heading back even while we were together. The time with each other ticked shorter and shorter with every stretch apart that loomed ahead.

"Why don't you have a private jet?"

I barked out a laugh at the left-field comment. "What? I'm here three weeks and already I'm a corporate tycoon?"

"Aren't you making an obscene amount of money? You should have a corporate jet. Or NetJets, at least."

"Don't think I haven't considered it. But the worldwide travel will be slowing after I wrap up these initial orientation months. Then it will only be the weekends commuting."

She grunted. "You should have a plane at your beck and call. Delayed and cancelled flights are wearing my patience thin. And with you making a thousand dollars a second, wasting your time seems expensive."

"I don't make a thousand dollars a second. That would be half a billion dollars a week." But although I had made good use of my delays, either working on the next proposal or drafting notes for contracts on the last, she had a valid point. And then all rational thought spun into the gutter. "You just want me to thrust you into the mile-high club."

A wicked smirk curved her lips. "I can't think of a greater travel perk."

I nudged her coat off one of her shoulders, then tugged the lapels apart, baring her gorgeous breasts. The nipples hardened as I stared.

My gaze scanned up when she bit her lip. "We already did the skyscraper-high club." I trailed my fingers over one and pinched it.

She shuddered.

I untied her belt and spread her coat apart, baring the rest of her incredible body. Never taking my gaze from hers, wide-eyed and dark with lust, I worked my shoulders between her thighs. "How about trying our hand at a new club: row house low?"

On a growl, I dipped my head, licking a path through her folds.

I took her breathy moan as a yes.

THE MIDWEEK STAY over with Hannah had been amazing, but short-lived. As promised, we traveled back together for the weekend. The few weeks that followed flew by as both of our work demands intensified, even though the time apart from one another continued to take its toll. Finally, an extended weekend had come, four whole days of being with Hannah, but I couldn't shake my sour mood. Thanksgiving had set in.

I sighed, frustrated. "Sorry, Maestro. Warned you I'd be a barrel of fun."

She simply rolled her eyes, then gave me an amused look before adjusting her hands on the steering wheel and turning her attention back to the road.

The calendar page had finally flipped to the melancholy holiday. Macy's had paraded its spectacle down Central Park West, ushering in the official start of the holiday shopping season.

Millions of Americans now hung out in their homes, surrounded by the dangers of drunk apathetic family members, cooking pressures in the face of grumbling stomachs, and high-stakes football, where, unless everyone rooted for the same team, an all-out brawl threatened to ensue before the first slice of turkey was carved.

Or maybe that was just my house.

Hannah dropped me a deadpan look. "What do you have to be worried about? I'm going to meet my father for the very first time. My emotional shit trumps your emotional shit."

I snorted, pointing to the turn she needed to take onto my parents' street. "Okay. You win. But prepare yourself. Nothing that happens here today will make your experience any easier."

When I pointed to my parents' long driveway, she nodded, but I caught her drumming her fingers nervously on her jeans-clad thigh before she took the turn. Because she'd wanted to drive today, we took Josephine out for a spin. Dad would be thrilled to check out her pristine classic Mustang, and it'd be a great distraction from the moroseness.

"Relax." On an inhale to calm myself, I reached over and slid my hand under hers.

She drummed her fingers once more, but then laced them into mine, holding my hand. She took a deep breath and slowly blew out the air through pursed lips.

I let out a relieved breath. My issues were enough to ratchet my nerves into taut guitar strings. But her anxiety added an unstable factor into the already volatile atmosphere of my house on Thanksgiving. If both of us could calm down, we'd survive the day better.

"Sorry." Her hand gripped mine. "I don't even know what I'm getting so worked up over. He's no longer just a sperm donor, he's my biological father—but not my dad. My mom did the best she could, but she, Gran, and Granpop filled in as my dad. It was Granpop who went to every Father's Day event at my school. He taught me how to work on cars and catch balls in the yard, and he was a wonderful influence in my life."

"Atta girl. This guy's just someone you happen to share DNA with, who, for whatever reason, has decided to reach out and contact you now. Could be he regrets what happened and wants to make amends. But I'm proud of you for being strong and deciding what you want, exploring the possibility of having one more tie of family in your life."

"I'm trying to be strong." Her lips quirked up on one side, but fell a second later.

"Hannah, look at me."

She glanced at me long enough to make eye contact and receive my hard stare.

"You *are* strong. And brave. And after everything you and I have been through, you're invincible. Don't ever think otherwise."

A shy smile curved onto her face. No one felt comfortable receiving flattery like that, but in her case it was the truth, and she needed to not only hear it, but believe it.

She glanced forward again as she pulled to a stop at the gate into the estate, but I continued to stare at her profile. "Promise me. Let me hear you say it. 'I'm invincible.'"

Her grin widened as her gaze strayed back toward me. "I promise...I'm invincible."

"Fuck yeah, you are."

Easy laughter rang out in the car from both of us before I told her the sequence of numbers to punch into the keypad. Seconds later, we passed through the opening gate onto my parents' cobblestone driveway.

"Okay, now I have to warn you; here's the rundown. Mom'll be in a royally bitchy mood. But only because Dad will be an argumentative asshole no one wants to be around. That's because Aunt Trix and Uncle Lou will be there, and they harass the shit out of him."

When she pulled to a stop in the motor court, she put the car in park and cut the engine. Then she turned fully toward me, arching a brow. "Aunt Trix?"

"Dad's older sister Patricia. Lou is Dad's older brother, the middle child. It's the three of them, and with Dad being the youngest with five years spread between him and Lou, Dad was always stuck being their lackey when they were kids."

She tilted her head, absorbing. "And they're here today, but they don't get along well?"

"Oh, they're here every Thanksgiving. It's the only time we see them. They stay a week, Tuesday through Monday. By the time Thursday hits, Dad's been on the butt end of their harassment for two solid days and nights. By Thanksgiving morning, his fuse has run out on a five-ton powder keg ready to blow."

Hannah blinked, eyes wide. "Wow. How do you all deal with that?"

I leaned forward to plant a kiss on her lips. "Steer clear, be overly polite, and make sure the alcohol flows and the TV remote is under Dad's control at all times."

"It's so bizarre to me that your family keeps expanding.

Just when I think I've met them all, more relatives crawl out of the woodwork."

"Stick around, Maestro. We have a big house with lots of nooks and crannies. You never know what might jump out of a closet."

She smirked. "Or who might jump in."

I snorted as we got out of the car, feeling better already. We held hands as we walked up the sidewalk, and I decided right then and there Thanksgiving was infinitely better with Hannah in it.

I didn't bother knocking; the front door was always left unlocked when family came over. Commotion echoed through the house, and we followed it into a kitchen already busy with tradition. Mom stood at the large kitchen island making her beloved green bean casserole. Kendall and Kiki were at the counter near the stove, layering apple brandy caramelized apples over baked sweet potatoes in a long, glass pan.

Kristen leaned against the far counter, glass of iced tea in hand, when she glanced up at us. "Hey guys!" She navigated the room, steering clear of the cooks on rotation. "Glad you made it before all hell broke loose."

Kendall slid her spatula under another few apple slices left in the pan and transferred them over to the dish. "Hasn't it already? Trix has Dad in rare form; she must be bored."

Like the whirlwind she was, Trix flew into the room. "My ears are buzzing. Someone must be in need of juicy gossip." This year's new hairstyle had her black hair cropped short, falling to her chin. Her blue eyes flashed brightly. "Cade! My favorite nephew."

I snorted, opening my arms before she collided into my side. "I'm your *only* nephew."

Scrunching her face, she kissed my cheek. "Exactly. And who is this delightful girl?" She glanced at Hannah.

"This is my girl, Trix." I winked at Hannah. "Hannah, this is my favorite aunt."

"I better be your favorite. Those stuffy sisters of your mother's don't deserve it."

Mom didn't bother to look up, but arched a brow. "Trix, play nice."

"Oh, please. You know it's true, Vic. That's why you never invite them."

Hannah smiled and blinked, listening to an exchange the sisters-in-law had polished into loving harassment over the years. I gave Hannah a told-you-so look before crossing over to the fridge.

Trix took Hannah's hands, spreading them wide. "Well, come here, girl. Let me get a good look at you."

I sighed, grabbing two beers from the shelf before closing the door. "She's not a prized calf, Trix."

"She does have great curves though, and delicate features."

Scowling, I spun around, ready to do battle, but paused at the feisty expression on Hannah's face.

Hannah leaned in toward Trix, lowered her voice, and added to her description, "She also bakes the best cakes this side of the Mississippi, plays a deadly game of chess, and knocks Cade flat on his ass when he deserves it."

Trix's eyes widened, her mouth dropping open. "Oh my God, girl. I love you already." She pulled Hannah into a tight hug, and everyone burst into laughter.

Hannah eased free from my aunt's embrace and took the beer I held out to her. "Can I help with anything?"

She'd been under strict orders not to bake or cook. As a guest of ours, we'd insisted upon it.

Kristen put down her iced tea. "You can help me set the table." She gathered up the linens and handed them to Hannah before lifting a heavy flatware tray with a grunt. "It's in the formal dining room. Through the doorway over there." She nodded across the room.

Hannah glanced over her shoulder at me, smiling. "I remember."

I grinned at her before she disappeared, thinking back to the Fourth of July pool party and the private tour we'd taken of the greenhouse and the garage. Which reminded me of Josephine sitting in the motor court.

I grabbed two more beers from the fridge. "I'll be out front with Dad and Lou if anyone needs me."

"Yes," Mom called out, glancing up with a grateful look. "Please keep them occupied. That's what *everyone* needs of you."

"Got it." I raised one of the beers in acceptance of my task and headed out to the garage where I knew the men were hiding out. Stepping into the cavernous space, I passed through the double lineup of collector cars with the quiet reverence I always did. The respectable display paid tribute to a style and era of years gone by, but also meant a lot to my dad; therefore it meant a lot to me.

As I approached the leather-upholstered seating area arranged around the flat-screen TV, the volume of a debate about Super Bowl hopefuls escalated.

Lou looked up when I stepped into their line of sight. "Cade, my boy. Great to see you." He stood and gave me a quick hug.

I handed each of them a beer. "Hannah and I drove up in her grandfather's Mustang, Josephine, if you want to take a look."

Dad quickly stood from a leather club chair and clapped

me on the shoulder. "That's right. You mentioned she had a '67 Mustang Fastback."

I nodded as we went out the side door that led straight to the motor court. "She's in her original condition. Been garaged except for special occasions and car shows for decades and is now Hannah's daily driver."

Sitting in the sun, the silver chrome sparkled and black paint gleamed as we walked around her. Dad whistled. Lou leaned in to examine the black interior.

Dad glanced up. "Can we pop the hood?"

"Absolutely."

He nodded toward Lou, who stood in front of the grill. "So how's San Francisco?"

I shrugged. "It's okay. The position is a dream job, the business deals—a total rush."

Lou reached under the front, pulled the latch, then lifted the hood and propped it up. "Nice." He scanned the engine compartment. "Your girlfriend keeps it clean for a daily driver."

Dad glanced at me with a heavy look. "How are the two of you handling the separation?"

I let out a slow breath. "We're dealing. It's rougher than we thought it'd be."

Lou stood upright, scrubbing a hand over his bald head. "Not that you asked for my two cents, but follow your heart. Jobs come and go. Women? Don't always stick around through rough."

Uncle Lou had remained a bachelor all his life. I suddenly wondered if he'd let one get away.

Dad glanced at me and gave me a hard nod, as if seconding his brother. Then he fell silent and returned his attention back to the car, staring at the engine. "You said this was her grandfather's?"

"Yeah. He bought it new but rarely drove it."

Dad dropped his hands into his pockets as he continued to walk around her, respectfully examining her like he did every car he admired, taking in small details and the vehicle as a whole. "She is a beauty. Worth the extra effort."

Just like Hannah.

"Boys!" Kiki shouted from the garage side door. "First game's about to start!"

And just like that, the mood shifted lighter with her spirited interjection. After the event we'd hosted at the Super Bowl party earlier this year, Kiki had become a diehard football fan. And Kristen and Kendall preferred the kitchen over the tension in the garage lounge where Dad, Trix, and Lou usually remained glued to the broadcast the entire time, breaking only when it came time to eat.

We stepped back into the garage, and I blinked, my eyes adjusting to the dimmer light. Kiki had already claimed a side chair, and Trix took a seat on the end of the couch closest to her, both of them already distracted into a conversation about which player's ass looked better. Dad and Lou took seats on the couch.

But for the first time in all the Thanksgivings we'd had here, the game held no interest for me. I kept walking through the garage toward the door that led into the house.

"Not gonna watch the game?" Kiki sounded crestfallen.

"Maybe in a bit, sis. I'd rather find Hannah."

When I stepped back into the kitchen, even though incredible aromas flooded my senses, something else entirely made my mouth water. Kendall and Kristen had abandoned the kitchen, and Mom busied herself with mixing stuffing on the stove, but Hannah sat on a stool at the far end of the counter, looking delectable as ever. She held a spatula in her hand and spread a coating of whipped cream onto a pumpkin pie.

I narrowed my eyes. "Hey, I thought we agreed, no baking or cooking for you today."

She glanced up, arching a brow as the corners of her mouth twitched. "I'm frosting. I never agreed not to put topping on a pie."

"That you didn't." I swiped the pie out from under her spatula, deciding the current amount of topping was sufficient, then shoved it into the only spare space left on the refrigerator shelf.

"Hey!" She scowled. "I wasn't done with that."

"You are now." I dropped my head, lowering my voice. "My turn with the frosting."

Amusement glittered in her eyes as I grabbed the bowl and crowded her out of the kitchen and up the stairs.

She turned around midway up, her brow furrowing as she whispered, "Cade Joseph Michaelson, what exactly are you intending to do with that? Your family is within earshot."

"Then you better be quiet." I pulled the spatula out of the bowl. It was heavy on the end, loaded with a glob of cream. "And you might want to start undressing now. Might be hard to explain if you come down in a different outfit."

She heaved in a breath, her lips parting a fraction, before she shut her mouth and obeyed, pulling her black long-sleeved T-Shirt over her head. She left it dangling on her wrist while she reached back, unfastened her bra, and bared herself to me. Brave and reckless since I had no idea where Kendall and Kristen were, but maybe Hannah did.

I sucked in a deep breath, then growled low, taking the rest of the stairs two at a time, chasing down a now-squealing Hannah who darted into my bedroom.

Laughing, I followed her inside and kicked the door shut as she ran into the adjoining bathroom.

I grinned wide, ready to get sticky.

The playful mood I'd found myself in was noteworthy, and I intended to ride the high.

On a day of potential anxiety, with her father *possibly* showing up later and one that historically etched me into a perma-snarl, neither of us seemed effected by our circumstances.

And I realized the magic had everything to do with Hannah.

21. SOLACE OF FAMILY

Hannah...

Cade shrugged for what seemed like the hundredth time during our hilarious Thanksgiving meal. "I am. I'm talented with a spatula." He gave me a pointed look, coded for only the two of us, and an ache sparked between my legs. Then he glanced around the table. "I'm damn good with frosting too."

I kicked him under the table. He squeezed my thigh while giving me a wink.

Sliding my hand under his and lacing our fingers together, I sighed, content. My cheeks hurt from laughing at everyone's jokes, and if I put one more bite into my mouth, I would be in serious danger of exploding before I ever got out of my chair. Pursing my lips together, I took deep breaths in and out, trying to get a hold of myself.

Kiki continued to giggle.

I held my hand up to her. "Stop. I'm going to be sick if my food doesn't digest."

Cade glanced at Kristen. "Wouldn't be the first time someone hurled during a meal at this table."

Kristen pointed at Cade, glaring. "No. Enough of the embarrassing stories."

Kendall leaned forward, looking at her sister. "Oh, you mean like the time you came home from college on Christmas Eve, dragging your new boyfriend into the house totally wasted?"

Kristen rolled her eyes to the ceiling. "He was sober."

Cade crossed his arms over his chest. "And you were anything but."

He leaned closer to me. "Kristen had hit her rebellious stage, believing if she brought home a rock singer covered in tats, Mom and Dad would be furious. Instead, the guy won over Dad right away, shocking the hell out of Kristen when he talked to Dad about the latest IPO and mentioned that he day traded as a hobby. Mom tried to smooth things over by feeding them the cherry pie we'd been eating for dessert."

Kendall nodded. "Kristen was so incensed over the whole thing, she inhaled three slices without taking a breath and then threw the whole thing up while we all sat around with half-eaten desserts."

Kristen flushed red with embarrassment.

I blinked. "I'm guessing no one finished their pie."

"Uh, no," Kiki said, then burst into laughter all over again.

"Gee, thanks Kendall." Kristen poked at her pumpkin pie crust.

Kendall grinned. "Anytime, sis."

The camaraderie around the room soothed my nerves. The late hour hadn't gone unnoticed by anyone at the table. Cade had filled them in earlier about the possibility of my father showing up. All of Cade's family, including his protective father, had been silent about the matter, but they'd been incredibly welcoming with me all day.

After several minutes went by with a lull in the conversation at our end of the table and napkins having been tossed onto the plates in surrender, I stood, gathering our dishes.

His mom rose from the table with me. "Coffee for everyone?"

Nods and yeses circled the table. Even Lou and Cade's dad, Garrett, mumbled something affirmative before returning to a heated debate over a local political matter.

"Say yes," Cade whispered to me, collecting the rest of the dessert plates from the table and stacking them. "She buys the fancy stuff from France."

"I heard that, Cade," his mom chided from the kitchen.

"Is it not true?" He tilted his head, arching a brow at his mom while I followed him into the kitchen. "Do you *not* purchase said coffee from France?"

His mom gave him an imperceptible glare, making me think those classic looks he gave were hereditary. "Yes. It's from France. But only because it's one of the best coffees available, it comes from a small family-owned café I'm fond of, and this is Thanksgiving."

He raised his brows, tilting his head at me. "See? The fancy stuff."

Defeated, his mom rolled her eyes, shaking her head.

I smiled, loving the banter between his family members. There had been mild tension on occasion, but most revolved around the natural rivalry between Garrett and his siblings with a smaller separate dynamic between Cade and his sisters.

"You know, I didn't think things were all that stressful here today."

Cade glanced at me, his expression unreadable. "I think it's you, Hannah. Or maybe you and me together here. I don't even know how to explain it, but things seem lighter this year than they've ever been before."

I nudged his shoulder playfully. "Well, whatever it is, I'm glad I came. Thank you for inviting me."

He brushed a soft kiss to my cheek. "I think you're a good-luck charm around here."

His mom, standing a few feet away, smiled. "It's the both of you together. Young love around all of us 'old folks' tends to soften our harder edges."

Cade put an arm around each of us. "Or maybe it's my two favorite women and my sexy ass together in the same house. No one can resist our charm."

Kiki snuck up behind us and burst out laughing. "Full of yourself much?"

Cade grabbed a kitchen towel, spun it up, then whipped the end at Kiki.

"Ow!" It cracked against her upper arm.

He immediately rolled it up again as he chased his squealing sister out of the kitchen.

While the laughter and stories continued, I helped Cade and his mom as we rinsed the plates and loaded as many as would fit into the dishwasher. When it came to the bigger platters, Cade washed, his mom rinsed, then she handed each to me to dry with a towel.

All of a sudden, the doorbell rang. I dropped one end of the china platter I held, the thick towel the only thing between it and the granite counter when it hit with a muffled clang.

Cade shot me a quick look and gave a nod.

His mom dried off her hands. "I'll get it."

Shaking my head, I took a deep breath and placed my

hand over hers. "Please, let me. I really need to do this alone."

"You sure?" Cade stepped closer to me, very much looking like he wanted to stand guard.

I nodded, grasping his hand and pulling him from the kitchen into the hallway leading toward their front entry. "Be here with me but hang back a bit? I need a few minutes alone with him."

He gathered me into his arms and kissed me softly. "Anything you need, Maestro. I'm here."

I gave him a short nod and a small smile. "Thank you."

Taking another deep breath, I steeled my courage and walked into the entryway, wrapped my hand around the cold metal knob, and opened the door.

Kind eyes looked back at me, a golden brown in contrast to my hazel. His hair was a little long, unkempt and full with a slight wave.

He blinked and stared at me a minute, exhaling a slow breath. "Wow. You look so much like your mother." He stepped forward, his motions stiffly awkward as he held out a hand. "Hello, Hannah. I'm Paul."

I gave his hand a quick shake. He looked nothing like I'd expected. Where my mom had been quiet, but strong, he seemed wild and edgy. Tall and lanky, he wore a long-sleeved shirt, but I caught a hint of tattoo curling around the side of his neck.

I left the door open, but didn't invite him in yet. Something held me back from welcoming him into Cade's parents' home. This was my space, and this stranger claiming me as his wasn't yet "mine."

My thoughts spun back to his comment of our similar appearance. "Tell me about her." I leaned into the doorframe. "She didn't mention you at all to me."

He gave a brief nod. "Doesn't surprise me. She didn't seem thrilled about the idea of me being in your life." When I continued to stand in the doorway, blocking his entrance, he leaned against the brick façade of the house's outer entryway, still facing me. "She wasn't thrilled with me being in *her* life."

Tilting my head, starving for information, yet, at the same time, unsure of how much detail I wanted, I crossed my arms over my chest. "Why?"

"I was in a rock band and hung around with a rough crowd back then. At first, my image and all that came with it attracted her. But she wanted more from me than I could give at the time." Stuffing his hands into his front pockets, he shrugged. "Half-dressed groupies throwing underwear at me didn't help matters much."

I thought back to the absentee mother I knew: always working two jobs to help pay the bills, sometimes taking a third when the opportunity presented itself, reserved whenever she did have time to relax at home, distant from her only daughter.

As his words sank in, I wondered if the detachment she'd had toward me had to do with him. The thought had never occurred to me. How could it, when my mom had never talked about him, even when I'd asked.

"Did you ever meet my grandparents?" They'd been my true close family, the ones who'd shown me the only real love I'd known growing up.

He shook his head. "Tracy never invited me. We didn't see each other for very long."

Tracy. No one had spoken her name in years, not even me. His brief description made me want to know more. "How did you meet? What was she like back then?"

He smiled, kicking a booted foot up onto the wall. "She

came to a bar where we'd been playing. The friend she'd come with was the rowdier of the two." He stared up at the ceiling. "What was her name...Mary? No, Mindy, I think. Anyway, the band sat in the back corner after the set, and your mom got dragged over by Mindy. Chatterbox that one, kept flirting with our bass player. The entire time, Tracy kept stealing glances at me. Whenever we made eye contact, she'd blush and look away. Never met a groupie like her."

"Doesn't sound like a groupie to me."

"Me either. But when I got out of the booth, I invited her over to a quieter table. Then she slowly opened up to me. I ordered us beers, and the longer we sat there, the more she shared simple things about herself, starting with her favorites of the cover songs we'd played."

Fascinated by a story of my mother, a side to her I'd never heard about, I moved closer, leaning on the opposite wall in the outer entryway. Out of the corner of my eye, I caught sight of Cade as he crossed his arms; he watched and listened, standing a dozen feet back in the entry hall of the house.

I focused my attention back toward Paul. "Which songs were her favorites?"

"Van Halen's 'Best of Both Worlds' and Depeche Mode's 'Reach Out and Touch Faith,' if I'm remembering correctly. There might've been a U2 song."

Confused still about the connection, I pushed for information. "So you two 'hooked up' that night?"

"Oh, no. Not your mom. She returned with her friend to other sets on other nights and hung out in the audience. Your mom was the first girl I'd ever asked out on a date before having sex with her."

Somehow, the knowledge of that fact made me feel

better. He wasn't a sperm donor, after all. There was more there, or at least some kind of courting.

"We went out to dinner a few times before I brought her back to my place." He paused, dropping a heavy look at me. "I'm assuming you don't want *all* the details."

"Uh, no." I blushed, thinking no one needed to know the frequency, terrain, or positions of their parents' sexual encounters, no matter how distant you were from them.

Paul continued, "Eventually she stopped coming around. Changed her number so I couldn't call her. She'd never given me her address."

"Why did she even send the letter to you, then?"

He shrugged. "Don't know. Maybe because I knew her last name. I even teased her about her driver's license picture once. I suppose she figured I could hunt her down if I wanted to. My guess is the pregnancy shook her. She even admitted to me once that I'd been the only guy she'd ever slept with, the only guy she'd ever dated."

That sad revelation didn't surprise me. As far back as I could remember, all the way up until her death, I never once saw my mom with a man. "Were you two happy when you were together?"

He smiled, and when he did, thin crinkle lines formed around his eyes. "We laughed a lot. There were things in her life I think she escaped from with me. She never wanted to share personal things about herself. There were endless questions about me, though: what religious beliefs did I have, which political party I most related to, who I admired in life—soul-searching questions."

I mumbled, "Until she became pregnant with me."

"I think so. We saw each other for a few weeks. A month, tops."

"And then life as she knew it, someone trying to find her way in the world, stopped."

His head tilted. "How so?"

His question threw me. Here I'd been grilling him for answers, breadcrumbs of my mom's life I hadn't been privy to. She'd even kept this wilder part of her life from my grandparents; when I'd gotten older, I'd grilled them incessantly about my father, only to find out that my mom hadn't told them a thing about him.

Unsure how much I wanted to reveal to Paul about my life, but comfortable sharing information regarding my mom since he'd done the same for me, I decided the truth about her wouldn't hurt.

"She never had a social life as long as I knew her. You know she died when I was young, right?"

He nodded. "I found out through the investigation."

"Investigation?" Cade had been the one to hire a PI, I hadn't realized Paul had too.

"Yeah, I had the article from the newspaper, but you only looked a lot like her with same last name. I needed to be sure and wanted to know more about you before contacting you."

A little thrown by the knowledge of his investigation, I had to force my brain back to describing my mom for him. "Well, she only ever worked. She moved into my grandparents' house and had an office day job as a secretary and another part-time job at night as a waitress. The money she made helped pay the bills and went into a bank account that she never accessed to do anything for herself. She also helped my grandparents pay off their house. By the time she died, there was enough money left over for me to go to the college of my choice twice over."

He pegged me with a penetrating stare. "Sounds like a lonely childhood."

I swallowed hard, focusing on the man in front of me who wanted to be a part of my life, instead of memories already passed. "It was."

"Well, Hannah. I'm here. I'm terribly sorry for letting you down a few weeks back. If you're willing, I'd love the chance to be even a small part of your life."

His genuineness tugged at my heartstrings. On a day when his other family had to be aware of his absence, he'd chosen to be here with mine, with new family I had, who'd embraced me because Cade did.

A landslide of emotion shifted inside of me, and I decided that I would welcome this man who'd hunted me down after all these years with no intention other than to let me know that he'd be my family too.

Moisture glistened in my eyes, my vision blurring. I shifted away from my wall, moving to the center of the outer entryway. "I'd like that."

In slow motion, he pushed off his wall and opened his arms. "Whatever you need from me, whenever you need it, I'll be here for you."

I stepped into the hug, sagging with a lifetime of relief, thankful the solace of family drew us closer, even though the past had involuntarily pulled us apart.

"Would you like to come in? I've got a boyfriend and his family I want you to meet."

He released me, pulling back on a deep breath. "That would be great."

When I turned to go inside, Cade stood in the entry hall, his hands in the pockets of his charcoal wool pants, a fierce look of pride on his face.

I exhaled, smiling, filled with gratitude for his support, for being here when I needed him, for helping me get to this point.

22. GIVING THANKS AND PLANNING CHAOS

Cade...

I stood in the dark entry hall and witnessed Hannah question, then accept, a father she'd never expected. I had only a vague idea of who Paul was from the investigator's report and the brief information he'd just provided. But I looked forward to getting to know the man who now wanted to get to know Hannah.

Part of my need for involvement stemmed from protectiveness.

The rest lay in discovering right alongside Hannah.

When she stepped back into the house, relief and hope filled her expression. She gave me a warm smile.

It took serious guts for her to put herself out there, opening her heart to a stranger, and I couldn't have been prouder. I hoped the intensity of my gaze told her so.

"Paul, this is Cade, my boyfriend." She slipped her hand into mine. "Cade, this is Paul."

I gave her hand a quick squeeze, then released it to shake Paul's. "Good to meet the father of the woman I love."

Paul huffed out a laugh. "You don't plan on going easy on me, do you?"

I arched a brow and leaned toward him. "Don't mind the customary racking of the shotgun. Happens with all new suitors at the Michaelson compound. You hold your own through the gauntlet, and we'll welcome you as one of our own."

His smile faltered. "And if I don't?"

I turned and wrapped an arm around Hannah's shoulder, separating them, before clapping Paul on the shoulder. "The bodies are buried out back."

Hannah glanced at me, her eyes widening. I winked at her. This was her first experience of a Michaelson inquisition. They only got easier from there, when someone else was in the hot seat.

In silence, we bypassed the kitchen as I led them down the hall and straight into the dining room. Like a wave of spectators in a stadium, faces popped up to look at us, eyes wide with anticipation.

"Family, this is Paul Gilcrest, Hannah's father. Paul, from the left, this is my mom, Victoria, my sisters, Kendall, Kristen, and Kiki. My father, Garrett, and his brother and sister, Lou and Trix. The only person missing from the Michaelson fold is Kristen's husband, Jason, who's overseas on business."

I pulled out a chair and nodded toward it. "Have a seat. My family's about to give you hell. The verbal flogging is best survived when your knees can't buckle from underneath you."

Paul snorted out a laugh, then took a seat, being a good sport about the imminent hazing. Hannah sat beside him, and I took the chair next to hers.

Mom stood, the hostess within her needing to take care

of her guest. "Would you like some coffee, Paul? We also have pumpkin pie left."

"Thank you. Coffee would be great."

Kiki leaned forward, sliding her forearms across the table. "So give us the deets, Paul. Where have you been all Hannah's life?"

The table fell silent. No one wanted to laugh, because the pressure was part of the fun. Kristen's lips twitched, threatening to give her away. I glared at her until she pressed them into an obedient line.

When Kristen had brought Jason home for the first time, he'd been subjected to the gauntlet. Kendall's boyfriends in college had to run the pressure-filled obstacle course of my family too. Kiki, however, had wised up to the tradition and kept anyone she dated far away from the Michaelson Clan.

The phenomenon seemed to be limited to men, however. My ex, Madison, never had to face the microscopic scrutiny of my family, yet, in retrospect, the vetting tradition might've saved me a couple years of grief—or mind-numbing fucking, depending on perspective. But then I wouldn't have met Hannah, who mysteriously hadn't been questioned at all when brought under the protective shelter of my family.

Paul leaned back, the weight of Kiki's question sobering his expression. "Wanting to meet her." He glanced at Hannah. "Your mom cut me out of your life, but I still thought about you every day."

Kendall took her turn. "What have you done for a living since then? What do you do now?"

"When I met her mother, I was in a rock band: lead singer and guitar. We played covers and traveled from bar to bar, booking whatever gigs we could get. Did that for ten years till the band broke up."

Mom brought in Paul's cup of coffee, placing it in front of him, then poured more into everyone's cups from a carafe. Kristen waved Mom off of refilling hers, taking a sip before putting her cup onto its saucer. "What broke up the band?"

"Two of the guys got girlfriends. One had already married: me. By that time bookings began to slow, and we lost our drive to keep going. Money was decent, but not enough to support two or start a family. We were ready to move on. So I gave up music and started my own custom cabinet business."

"Cabinetry?" Trix asked. "That's an odd segue, from rock music to woodworking."

Paul laughed. "Seems that way. But I love working with my hands. Been doing it on the side since woodworking in high school. Wood never lies. I like the challenge of discovering the beauty under the rough bark. There's an art in transforming it."

Kiki threw herself back in her chair. "Okay. I love him. He gets my vote."

Laughter broke out around the table.

"Not so fast." Dad's commanding tone stilled the humor. "You said you have a wife. I understand you also have children. Cade informed us you stood Hannah up at your first scheduled meeting. How does Hannah fit into your life? How's your family handling this adjustment? Did they always know, or was this news to them?"

Paul straightened in his chair and turned to face my dad. Father faced off father. Mine had been there for his family while struggling for balance. Hannah's struggled for balance now with two families from separate worlds.

But then Paul turned toward Hannah. "My family knew nothing about you. I saw no point in going there when I'd been banned from your life, from claiming you. But as my kids grew, and I became the dad I wanted to be with them, I needed to become a part of your life too. You were out there somewhere. Hell, I didn't know if you needed a father or not, but not knowing wasn't enough to stop me from trying. I had to tell you that I'd be a part of your life if you wanted me to be."

I watched Dad's expression. Recognition flickered in his eyes. Dad gave Paul an imperceptible nod. "He's okay in my book."

Hannah glanced between my father and Paul. "What about your wife and children? Are they good with your contacting me and trying to fit me into your life?"

Paul sighed. "I don't think they know what to think or how to feel yet. Before that first meeting, they seemed okay with it—until they weren't. Finding out they weren't my only children was a shock, for both my wife and my kids. I think they'll be better with it in time. Those extra few weeks between then and now have made a difference. And today we made sure we had plenty of quality family time before I headed here."

Questions continued around the table, everyone taking a random turn. Paul even chimed in with curiosities of his own: about my family, how Hannah ended up included within it.

"So Invitation Only is a side business?" Paul glanced around the room.

Kristen explained. "It's *my* main business. Jason is away often on business trips around the country and overseas, and Invitation Only gives me something to do. The idea was first tested last New Year's in the renovated barn in my backyard. Cade was brought in for his business skills. Kendall wanted something to do with us outside of her architectural design job. And Kiki's artistic side lent itself well to the outside-of-the-box themes we've come up with."

"Don't forget Cade's off-the-wall ideas." Kiki laughed.

Kendall muttered, "You mean music choices."

I slid an arm around Hannah's shoulder. "Kiki suggested Hannah as our baker, but we had no idea the level of talent Hannah had with cakes. Her legendary creations thrust us into the media spotlight, gaining feature articles in culinary, entertainment, and design magazines."

Hannah blushed, turning toward Paul. "Looks like you're not the only one who enjoys creating beautiful works of art."

Paul smiled. "I like that we have something in common." He shifted his gaze from Hannah to me. "Tell me more about these 'off-the-wall' music choices."

I raised my brows. "Oh, you mean rock and alternative classics? Don't mind my sisters. They'd play Bolton and Bublé if given free music reign."

"Speaking of Invitation Only," Kristen interjected, "How are we coming on the three Christmases?"

The topic shifted, conversation flowing easily, as if the vetting of Hannah's father had become a nonissue.

And it had.

He'd only had to make it past the tough questions. He'd been comfortable with the scrutiny, being himself with us.

Paul Gilcrest had been welcomed into the fold. As long as Hannah wanted him around, he would be considered family.

Kendall turned to Kristen. "The Andersons want theirs to be held at their estate house. Glitter Holiday is the theme."

"Good." Kristen nodded. "Phoebe wants to hold hers at

the country club. And she's insisted on having a White Christmas."

I groaned, pinching my eyes shut. "As in an *all white* party?" Visions of a total whiteout spun hideously in my head.

"All white," Kristen confirmed.

"Not a white tux. Please." I squinted an eye open to see her smug expression. Amusement flashed in her eyes. I groaned. "Somebody kill me now."

Kendall and Kiki both pressed their lips into a line while they enjoyed my suffering.

Kristen smirked. "No dying over party colors."

"White is not a color. It is the absence of color."

Hannah giggled next to me.

Narrowing my eyes, I glared at her. "What are you finding funny about this?"

"You took great pleasure in our non-dating. Why not embrace a non-color?" Hannah burst out laughing.

Kiki joined her as Kendall grinned wide.

"Go ahead, laugh." My words were moot by the time they made it out of my mouth; everyone, even the elder Michaelsons, laughed at my irritation. "I'll deal. I'll play white penguin for the night if every other male has to."

I wondered if they were set on the wardrobe detail for my party that Hannah had been kept in the dark about—with good reason. I caught Kristen's gaze, arched a brow, and mouthed, "Saturday?"

She gave me an imperceptible nod.

Good. I let out slow exhale, relieved that even from across the country, the details of my event could fall into place.

Kendall drummed her fingers on the table. "Have any of you been grilled about party details yet? While Trina is planning her party, she's pumping me for information about both of yours."

"Sure, she is." I pointed at Kristen. "Told you this would happen. Two bar mitzvahs could pale in comparison to the craziness of triple Christmases. We might have to encrypt our files."

Kiki smirked. "We should add an anti-counterintelligence addendum to the contracts."

Kristen snorted, then glanced at Hannah. "Got the cakes under control?"

Hannah nodded. "Daniel and Chloe agreed to work extra hours if needed, and one or both of them can attend the events. By that time, our two new employees should be able to handle the shop on their own. Next week we'll render the cake designs, then order supplies and do trial runs."

"Still want my help?" Kiki asked.

"Absolutely," Hannah replied, nodding. "In fact, are you free next week? Drawing the concepts can sometimes be the most challenging part."

"Can I play it by ear on the timing? I've got the gallery showing on Saturday at 7:00 p.m. You're all coming by the way, right?"

Every member of my family either nodded or said yes, and so did Hannah.

Paul glanced around the table, unsure. "Wait. By 'all,' are you including me?"

Kiki smiled warmly at him. "Would you like to be included?"

Tilting his head, he paused for a moment. "Yeah. I've never been to a gallery exhibit."

"Then consider yourself invited. Feel free to bring a guest if you'd like."

I leaned away from Hannah and pulled my phone out of my pocket. "At the Midnight Sky Gallery right?"

"Yes. I'll be the first metalwork artist they've exhibited. They have very highbrow clients with a taste for the eclectic and nature, so they're hoping the pieces will sell well."

"I'll be there." I nodded at Kiki, then leaned toward Hannah. "Want to go on our first gallery date?"

Hannah beamed me a megawatt smile. "I wouldn't miss it for the world."

I sat back and crossed my arms over my chest, grateful for this Thanksgiving with Hannah, so damn glad to be surrounded by family. I felt for Kristen missing Jason during the holiday.

It hit me again how different this Thanksgiving was with Hannah in it. Made me appreciate being around family more than usual—instead of being alone, thousands of miles away.

23. NOT A BRIDESMAID DRESS

Hannah...

The Saturday morning after Thanksgiving, Cade had taken me to breakfast at a tucked away little bistro in the Old City Arts District, not far from where Loading Zone was located. He'd also insisted on me clearing my entire day, but had remained secretive about the reason why. Not that I cared. Four whole days in a row with Cade here instead an entire continent between us? Heaven.

The midmorning air held a slight chill, but with the forecast being clear and warm, we'd decided to take Cade's bike. There wouldn't be many more days we could ride without some serious bundling up, and he'd agreed to drive either the Jeep or Josephine whenever temps dipped below fifty degrees.

After I got off his bike, stowed my helmet, and stepped down from the sidewalk into the street, I glanced at the shops across the way. The one dead center in front of us was Jeannine's Bridal Shop. The same one we'd shopped at for Candie's faux funeral. The *very* place where I'd panicked in a dressing room wearing a hideous concoction of bright pink taffeta, igniting memories of getting jilted at the altar.

"Ohhh, no." I froze in my tracks and whirled around, only to smack into the brick wall of Cade's chest. Head shaking in small, rapid movements, I lifted my brows, voice firm. "No."

A lazy smile formed on his face. "It'll be okay, Maestro. I spoke to the owner, Jeannine. She assured me the only things you will be shown are tasteful evening gowns."

His hands gripped my shoulders, and he turned me around. A horn honked as a car switched lanes to avoid us: the couple who stood in the middle of the street, impeding traffic. At his insistent pushing, I unlocked my knees and let him usher me toward the sidewalk on the other side of the street.

Once I stepped onto the curb, I spotted his sisters inside the shop, clustered in the front sitting area. Kiki turned, caught sight of us, and waved. I gave her a tight smile, then spun back toward Cade.

"This is cruel and unusual punishment," I grumbled, scowling.

"You'll be fine." He tucked a finger under my chin, forcing my gaze to his. "I'd stay to help you find the perfect petticoats, load you up on multiple glasses of Champagne, then lift your skirt when you have to pee, but something tells me my sisters want to monopolize you for the rest of the day."

In spite of my sulking mood, I smiled at his appealing naughty images. But then I glanced back inside. I couldn't hide my loud groan.

He laughed. "Text me. I'll get you through any rough spots."

I sighed, suddenly feeling like a big baby and glanced up at him. "Only tasteful gowns?"

He nodded and held up two fingers. "Scouts honor."

A laugh huffed out before I could stop it. "You were a boy scout?"

With a contemplative glance toward the sky, he arched his brows. "Not exactly. I'm too rule breaking to stick to codes of conduct, and an itchy polyester uniform never would've worked for me. But I've done many a good deed in my life, and honesty is one virtue I believe in, without exception. So, as a self-inducted honorary scout, and as your boyfriend who would never lead you astray, especially when I know your trauma with regard to weddings, I do solemnly swear that there will be no bridesmaid dresses brought out for any of you to wear. Only elegant evening gowns, which is what Jeannine assured me she'd arranged."

Confidence flowed into my veins at his words. That he knew my issues, and worked to sidestep around them to make me comfortable, meant a great deal to me.

I finally smiled, thinking I could do this. "Thank you, Cade."

In the chilly shade of the sidewalk, he leaned down and wrapped his warmth around me. His lips brushed across mine, teasing me with a soft kiss. "Have faith in me, Hannah. I promise to take care of you every step of the way."

On a deep breath, I nodded, giving him a final squeeze as we parted. I *knew* I could do this. The concept of a bridal shop had already shifted from post-traumatic-stress trigger into comical farce with Candie's faux funeral. I would redefine it, yet again, into a shopping spree of the elegant-gown variety.

Cade opened the front door, and his other two sisters turned around, eyes lighting up.

Kiki rushed over, throwing her arms around me in a fierce hug. "Finally got her into the shop. I grew worried there for a minute. You should've seen Kendall earlier, she was a wreck."

I laughed. "Let me guess. Pink taffeta flashbacks?"

Kendall shot me a deadpan look. "Of the worst kind."

Kristen laughed. "Hey, at least Cade had the sense to prep the owner before our arrival."

Cade shrugged. "I know my audience. If I want you girls in gowns, groundwork must be laid."

An attractive midforties blonde appeared from the back, followed by a familiar younger sales girl, who carried a silver tray of Champagne flutes with the ease of a seasoned waitress.

"You must be Hannah. I'm Jeannine. I was on vacation the day you girls were in for the faux-funeral party over the summer, but it's nice to finally meet you." She took two Champagne glasses from the tray and handed them to Kristen and Kendall, before taking the other two and nodding to her assistant. "This is Annabelle. We'll be taking care of your girls, Mr. Michaelson, rest assured."

Cade bowed his head slightly. "I have no doubts, Jeannine."

When Jeannine handed Kiki and me the last two Champagne glasses, she glanced at the linen on Annabelle's empty tray and then up at Cade. "Would you like a glass of Champagne, Mr. Michaelson? I have all the gown possibilities lined up, if you'd like to stay."

Cade gave her a headshake. "I've got a day filled with appointments. You girls have fun."

Unable to stop myself, I pouted. Reality finally settling in that we wouldn't be spending the day together, just Cade and me. We only had four days, and I wanted to make the most of every minute of them.

He turned me toward him, brushing a kiss to my cheek. "Remember to text me. I want dressing-room details."

I smirked, mood lightening a little. "Scandalous ones?"

He scoffed. "Is there any other kind?" He held my gaze a beat longer before glancing at the others. "Enjoy your day, ladies. Lunch at Tatum's, then have fun shopping this afternoon. Oh, and don't forget my Christmas present." He whipped a credit card out of his wallet, unzipped the purse still dangling from my shoulder, then dropped it inside. "Nothing monogrammed. No clothes. A certain level of quirkiness? Always welcomed."

Kiki lobbed a candy-coated almond at him, but he caught it in midair before popping it into his mouth. She held another up with her arm cocked back, ready to peg him again. Her eyes narrowed. "You love my quirky gifts."

He held up his hands in surrender. "I do. I swear, I do."

After a quick wink at me, he turned and left. I watched him cross the street over to his bike. Black leather jacket, jeans clinging to his tight ass, ruffled dark hair. Even from this far away, his six-foot-two stature, broad shoulders, and confident stride made that man seem larger than life. A thrill raced through me, fierce and possessive. That man was mine.

"Earth to Hannah. You joining us sometime this century, or you need more time to gawk at Cade?" Kiki teased.

My cheeks flushed hot, and I turned to find them all smirking at me. I wasn't sure which was worse. Gawking at Cade or getting caught doing it in front of his sisters.

Jeannine and Annabelle had disappeared, to the back I presumed.

Kristen lifted her Champagne flute high in the air, and the rest of us did the same. "To a fabulous girls' day. Let's find gowns to make men drool and women envious, dine while sharing secrets and gossip, and buy a king's ransom of gifts sure to make Cade's credit card keel over and die."

I fought laughter as we raised our glasses.

Kiki gasped. "Holy shit. He left us his credit card?" Kiki must've missed the stealthy drop. "I'll drink to that."

The Champagne was dry and bittersweet. I wrinkled my nose as bubbles fizzed onto my lips. Then I took a seat on a plush royal-blue settee as Jeannine and Annabelle returned, navigating a long rack of dresses toward us. I suddenly noticed we were the only customers in the store.

When Kendall settled to my left, I leaned closer. "Did Cade rent the shop out for us?"

She nodded. "They don't open until eleven. Cade made special arrangements for her to open for us early."

Deep jewel-toned gowns filled the rack, their silk fabrics swaying gently when it stopped about fifteen feet from us. They were grouped together by color. Black began on the far left, then silver, ruby, emerald, sapphire, and amethyst.

Kristen and Kiki had remained standing and descended onto the display, holding their Champagne glasses away from the gowns while perusing the choices. "Only one in the green?" Kristen asked while scanning the lineup.

Jeannine nodded. "I could order more in that color if you'd like, but I'm not sure they'd arrive in time for your event."

Kiki shook her head. "No, actually, this is perfect. There are three of the red. And it's a perfect Christmassy red. One in the emerald green." She put her glass down on a side table and pulled the green dress from the rack.

"Hannah, come over here. This color is perfect for you. It complements the olive tone of your skin and will bring out the green in your eyes."

The gown glittered under the showroom lighting, beautiful even from far away. I put my glass down and crossed over to her, taking the hanger and draping the material over my arm to lift it away from the ground. I crossed to the trifold mirrors that arced around a raised platform against the center back wall of the room and held the dress up to my body, pulling the hanger off to the side.

Kiki was right. Intricate beadwork covered the slender straps on either side as well as the low-cut bodice. The trim detail faded away beneath the bust into a floor-length silk skirt.

In the reflection of the glass, I saw the other three deciding amongst themselves over the red choices. Turning around, I crossed the room again to join them. All of them shared Cade's dark features with their brunette hair, in a shade tending toward black, and blue eyes, paler in hue than Cade's. And those red dresses would look fabulous on them.

"What do you think, Hannah? Kristen likes the one she's holding, but Kendall and I can't decide on ours."

All three were similar in styling to mine: slim straps leading to a form-fitting bodice and a straight floor-length gown. The one Kristen had chosen had no beadwork at all. A simple twist of material across the bustline led to flowing, nearly transparent, layers of silk.

I tilted my head, assessing the other two gowns. Kiki held a dress with a combination of beadwork and sequins over a sensual but conservative bodice. The fabric on the rest of the dress hung in a slim straight cut, like mine. The one Kendall held looked like the bodice had slim ties criss-crossing over the front, resembling a bustier. And the material wasn't solid red; when the light caught it, a sheer brocade-like pattern shimmered.

"I think you need to exchange dresses. The brocade Kendall's holding matches your inner artist better."

Kiki examined the other dress as Kendall held it. "It has a brocade?"

Wordlessly, Kendall and Kiki exchanged gowns, and we made our way back to the dressing rooms. My phone vibrated the back pocket of my jeans as I closed the door.

I hung the dress on the hook and pulled out my phone while toeing off my tennis shoes. Cade had texted a message.

> Still alive in the mountain of tulle and petticoats?

I laughed, typing back.

> Made it through the war zone without a single bright pink taffeta sighting.

I pulled my black peasant shirt over my head and unbuttoned my jeans before shimmying out of them.

He'd sent another text.

> What are you wearing?

I grinned, unfastening my bra to give him the truth in texting.

> At the present moment? Your favorite black lace thong.

An immediate bubble appeared, then his reply popped up.

> . . .

Laughing at our coded naughty dots, I tossed the phone onto the upholstered chair as I imagined the agonized expression on his face, thinking he probably was wishing he'd stayed, after all. I turned around and gathered the material of the gown into my hands and pulled the dress over my head, then worked it down my body.

My phone lit up again.

> Dying here.

I smiled. In a day I thought we'd be spending together, he'd spiced it with his trademark humor and a dash of naughtiness that warmed my insides. I was thankful at how only a few texts from him eased the sting of his unexpected absence. Even though he didn't stand right beside me, he'd never really left.

I bit my lip and turned fully toward the mirror, struggling with the top clasp in the back before it caught, hooking the two sides together. I grasped the tiny zipper resting at my lower back and inhaled as I zipped the gown all the way up to the hooked clasp.

My eyes widened. The dress seemed tailor-made for me, hugging my breasts and waist before the fabric whispered over my hips and draped perfectly to the floor. Not taking my eyes off the mirror, I twisted my body to see the back. The gown looked perfect on me.

I texted Cade.

Wearing the gown now.

His bubble appeared.

And?

I smiled, replying back.

You're gonna love it.

24. SHOPPING GONE WILD

Cade...

Thinking of Hannah trying on dresses—her standing in nothing but the black lace thong she'd texted me about—made me hustle through my to-do list so I could catch up with her. Holiday shopping was about to land one girl onto the naughty list this year with where my thoughts were headed.

I texted Hannah, then waited, hovering near the mall entrance of Nordstrom. I looked like a rumpled biker posing as store security. The image of her earlier pout when she'd realized we weren't going to spend the day together burned in my mind. Yeah, I intended to fix that.

Where are you?

I knew by reconnaissance texts with Kiki that they were all inside Nordstrom. Hannah replied seconds later.

Standing in front of a burlap bag.

It's black . . . with lace trim.

Why?

I groaned, imagining her lost in a sea of burlap bags. Clearly, she needed rescuing.

Just curious.

A second later, I was on the move.

My phone vibrated. I pulled it out to find another text from her.

Where are you?

I grinned.

Escalator.

On the way up, Louis Armstrong's "Cool Yule" played. I began to see racks of clothing beyond the white flocked Christmas trees that flanked the escalator. By the time the metal steps rotated up onto the second floor, I spotted her: dark brown hair, black jacket, a huge smile on her face.

Weaving my way through racks designed to clothesline unsuspecting shoppers, I walked over to her. Several items hung over her forearm, hangers dangling. Entirely too much material. Naked would be better.

"Nice burlap. They got bags with less fabric, more skin?"

A sales lady walked by, glaring at me.

"Lingerie," I corrected, bowing my head in respect to her store. "I meant nice *lingerie*."

The woman's narrowing eyes made me think she didn't appreciate my brand of humor.

Hannah burst out laughing.

"What are you doing here, anyway?" Pulling a see-through number off the rack, she flipped it over. Its lacy back plunged low and had a tiny pink bow at the bottom.

I imagined the pink bow hanging above *her* bottom and took a deep breath. "Thought I'd swing by, see how you were doing."

She glanced over her shoulder, regarding me for a moment before a gentle smile curved her lips. "Good, I kinda missed you."

Then she turned fully around. "Here, hold these." She shifted her load into my arms, and I fumbled with a mass of silk that had no substance. I finally clamped a tight fist around the damned mess to keep from dropping them.

Without looking up from the rack as she slid hangers from right to left with rhythmic clicks, she gave a large yawn. "Your sisters will be up here in a few."

She continued to scan the clothes, as if I hadn't just shown up to save her from her shopping catatonicness. In no mood for a nap for either of us, I scanned the area for busybody customers and glaring sales ladies. Satisfied everyone in the vicinity was either preoccupied, or heading in the opposite direction, I bent down, brushing my lips against her ear.

"How about we go try these burlap bags on?"

She turned toward me, arching her brows. "We?"

"We. I'm your dressing-room assistant."

Instead of debating, she scoped out the surrounding area like an illicit undercover champ. Damn, I loved how she switched from an innocent shopper to a lewd partner in crime in half a heartbeat.

Eyes scanning all around, she grabbed my hand and yanked me toward the dressing rooms. "We have about ten minutes."

"I'll have you biting a scream into my shoulder in five."

With a stern look, she held a finger up to her lips—code for shut the fuck up or you won't get any. As we entered the seemingly abandoned women's dressing-room area, a row of closed doors stretched out on either side. Hannah led me toward the right, to a propped-open door in the middle. When the door clicked shut, I tossed the lingerie I'd been carrying onto the leather cube in the corner.

We wasted no time. Hannah ripped her jacket off. Grabbing the hem of her shirt, I yanked it over her head while she fumbled with my belt buckle. I left her bra on and went for her jeans.

When I struggled with her button, I growled. "Here. We have nine minutes." I pulled her hands from my fly and put them on hers. If I wanted to bring her to orgasm, we needed to get a move on.

I ripped my fly open and sprang free while she shimmied out of her jeans. And for a few brief seconds, I could only stare in awe-filled wonder. Black lace bra, black thong, and Hannah's endless curves. *These are a few of my favorite things.*

Careful to keep the noise down, I lunged, grabbing her thighs and hoisting her into the air, ripping that scrap of lace between her legs out of my way with my fingers. Her shoulders hit the wall, and she dropped her head back a split second later, closing her eyes as I flexed my hips. My hardened cock slid upward, stroking through folds already wet and waiting for me.

I knew I'd never make a five-minute deadline by rushing. Hannah got turned on faster—and ramped up hotter—

when denied what she wanted. And so I continued to tease her, drawing my hips back and arching forward, driving her crazy.

Her eyes were open now, half lidded. She turned her head to the side to see the profile of us in the triple mirrors on the dressing-room wall. We looked sexy as fuck. Literally. Hard muscles flexing into supple curves.

Short gasps of air came from her throat. Her body began to tremble. She drifted close to the edge. I wanted to be inside when her release snapped through her, but not yet. Not until the very last moment.

I slowed my movements, letting the anticipation draw out. My breaths deepened as I tried to maintain control, hardening further with every slickened stroke.

When her face scrunched in the way it did when her ache turned into painful pleasure, I knew it was time; she rocked right on that edge.

In one last draw backward, over sensitized nerves with a final press against her clit, I hesitated. A tiny noise came from her throat as her mouth fell open.

She shuddered.

And I drove hard and deep into her wet heat, shoving her off that edge.

She fell hard, dropping her mouth onto my shoulder into a powerful bite as she released that muffled scream.

And I held her tight in my arms, catching her.

Seated deep inside her, I exhaled slowly.

Then I smirked, easing back a few inches, then thrusting up hard, murmuring into her ear. "Sure you're good with me having dropped by?" I sure as hell was. With our limited days together, I planned on getting as much Hannah time as possible.

Head falling back against the wall, she bit her lower lip before nodding frantically.

Her tight spasms surrounded me, urging me on. I drove into her in slowed movements, and she dropped her head again, whimpering softly into my shoulder. I swallowed hard, pinching my eyes shut as an electric surge fired through me, clenching hard in my balls. On a final thrust, my own release followed, and I swallowed down a growl as I held her close, riding out the pulses.

We clung to each other in the seconds that followed, heartbeats slowing.

Before the world nearly fuzzed out from lack of oxygen to my brain, she pulled back from my shoulder and gazed into my eyes with a dreamy, no-need-for-a-nap look. "Amazing."

A door to a dressing room banged shut nearby, the vibration breaking our spell.

Her eyes widened.

I held a silencing finger between our lips. Then I smiled a cocky smile and removed it, kissing her long and slow, and her panicked expression softened back into something much more along the lines of thoroughly satisfied.

A gentle knock sounded a few doors down. "How are you doing, Jane? Can I get you anything?"

"Sure." A heavy pause. "What do you have in sexy lingerie? I'm suddenly feeling inspired."

Hannah bit her lip to keep from laughing, and I pressed in for a hard kiss to help her the rest of the way.

A few moments later we collected ourselves. I buttoned up my fly, and we dressed Hannah. And everything she'd pulled off the rack was forgotten. We exited the dressing room and found the coast clear, luckily not a customer or salesperson in sight.

But when we rounded the corner to step back into the lingerie department, a line of three familiar brunettes, loaded down with shopping bags in both hands, greeted us with exasperated expressions.

Not sorry in the least for my exemplary dressing-room conduct. I gave them a wide grin. "What's up girls?"

Kendall rolled her eyes. "Two women gossiped about how some woman got the ride of her life in the dressing room."

Kiki smirked. "Took half a second to realize Hannah had been intercepted."

Feeling smug, I glanced at Hannah whose olive skin had a beautiful pink blush. "She was intercepted spectacularly."

Shaking her head, Kristen turned, muttering under her breath, "Heathen."

I gathered Hannah into my arms, unapologetic about crashing the shopping spree. "So what's next?"

Kristen flicked her wrist up, glancing at her watch. "It's almost four. How 'bout we call it a day. Jason's flying in early in the morning, and I'm beat."

"Sounds good to me," Kendall agreed as Kiki stifled a yawn.

I nodded. "I'll take you home then, Maestro."

The girls crowded in to hug her good-bye, but I refused to let her go, so we ended up in a clumsy group hug. "Thanks guys for being good sports with the gowns this morning. I really appreciate it."

My Christmas event followed both of theirs, so I needed to pull out all the stops. Besides my co-conspirator, Kristen, the others might've been tipped off with the dress code for the evening. But the details of who, what, and where I'd leave until the very last minute.

"Anytime bro. Show up to ours in whatever we demand,

and we're square." Kristen pinched my cheeks like an overzealous aunt. I narrowed my eyes at her.

We parted ways, my sisters heading out toward their cars while Hannah and I rode down the escalator. The protector in me instinctively claimed the step in front, blocking her behind me in the event of an unexpected fall. She draped her arms around my shoulders, pressing a soft kiss into my neck.

"Thanks for coming and finding me." Her low hum against my skin turned into a purr.

I turned my head, arching a brow. "You mean finding and coming with you?"

She dropped her forehead onto my shoulder. "That too. So now we're into semi-public closets?"

As the escalator steps disappeared into the floor, I walked forward, taking her hand in mine. "You know what they say, semi-public closets is the gateway drug to full-on exhibitionism."

She shook her head. "That will never happen."

"Damn straight it won't."

Spinning around, she strode backward as we entered the loud mall. "Oh? You have a line you won't cross, Mr. Michaelson?"

Dead serious, I gave her a hard nod. "Fuck yeah, I do. I don't share."

A wide grin spread on her face. "And what about our earlier dressing-room witness, Little Miss Inspired?

I tilted my head, oddly proud we'd caused a scene. "Unintended witness."

"Uh-huh." She turned back around.

"Turned you on though, didn't it? Danger. Risk of getting caught."

Biting her lip, she cast me a sidelong glance. The

naughty little shopper didn't answer, merely shoved her hands into her pockets and looked straight ahead again, ignoring my question.

I laughed hard, wrapping an arm around her as we walked past the food court. "No need to admit it, Maestro. Your teeth marks in my shoulder say it all."

A flash of guilt crossed her face a split second before she looked enormously pleased with herself. She tugged my collar away from my neck, and her eyes widened. "Wow." She ran her fingers over the welted surface. "I didn't hurt you, did I?"

Shaking my head, I scooped her into my arms. "Only in the best way. It's like a sex tattoo. Hey, there's an idea. Maybe I'll ink it permanent. You've got quite the orgasmic bite."

She elbowed me in the ribs. "Don't you dare."

"Sure. The story forever will be: remember that one time...in the dressing room?"

In spite of her stern glare, she broke out into a smile. Then she leaned into me with more of her weight, wrapping her arms around me and squeezing hard. When she pulled back, her eyes glittered with unshed tears. Her voice dropped to a whisper. "We only have one more day. The weekend's gone by too fast."

My chest suddenly burned. Her forlorn expression mirrored feelings I'd been doing my best to ignore. I gave her a serious look. "It's not over yet. We still have twenty-three hours and fifteen minutes until I have to be at the airport."

A tear fell, then rolled down. I brushed it from her cheekbone. She took a shuddering breath and stared up at me. "It's not enough." Her voice broke, and more tears flowed.

I bent down and kissed her. The salt from her tears

etched the moment into my heart. Countless weekends stretched ahead, where hours spent catching up crashed into the minutes that loomed, threatening to separate us again.

We couldn't go on like this. Something had to be done—what, I had no clue. But as we clung to each other in the middle of a mall of frenzied shoppers, holiday music blaring overhead, I whispered against her lips the only thought in my mind, "Never enough."

25. THERAPEUTIC QUALITIES OF BURLAP

Hannah...

Nervous about Kiki's gallery exhibit, for no other reason than I'd likely see my father again, and possibly his wife, I stood in a black thong while fidgeting in my closet for what to wear. My fingers played across the two dresses I'd bought the other day, but I had no idea what was appropriate for the event.

"Have you been to a gallery exhibit before?" My voice sounded artificially high to my ears. I laid the phone onto my closet shelf, trying valiantly not to be upset that Cade wasn't here with me. He'd called last night to cancel a weekend home with me for the *second* time—something he'd promised he wouldn't do.

But he was in bed with a nasty case of the flu. Yet he'd insisted on being on the phone while I got ready. A twinge of guilt pinged through me for even having selfish thoughts when what he really needed was me there, caring for him.

His nasally voice came over the speakerphone. "Yeah. A couple."

I surveyed my wardrobe choices. "What should I wear? A dress? Or dressed-up jeans?"

"You'd look amazing in either. I've gone before in dark jeans and a button-down shirt. Whatever would look great with that."

"Burlap...?" Bad girl, I know. I couldn't help teasing him.

He groaned. "Fucking flu virus. I should be there with you."

"Yeah, you should." Couldn't help ribbing him either. "I'm prescribing you massive doses of vitamin C And D. And any other letter that will help you stay strong and come home to me."

Silence followed. I'd forbidden him earlier from saying he was sorry again. He'd already done so five times, and we both knew he was in no condition to do anything other than rest and recover.

I swiped up the phone and pulled open a drawer. A smirk tugged at my lips as I laid the phone back down. I leaned forward, making certain he could hear me, then lowered my voice, giving it a sultry tone. "Feel any different?"

His short laugh was followed by a rattling cough, and I winced as I listened to his suffering. When he quieted, he asked. "Why would I feel different, babe? You doing something naughty?"

"You're now in my lingerie drawer." I pulled out a favorite demi underwire. "I'm now scooping my breasts into the black lace one you love with the violet tassel in the middle."

He groaned again. "*Fuck.* I love being in your lingerie drawer. I'm feeling better already."

I laughed. "The therapeutic qualities of burlap."

"We could write a book."

"Marvin Gaye's song is better," I countered before breaking into the "Sexual Healing" lyrics, *"Baaaby, I got sick this morning..."*

Silence followed as I continued to dress.

I picked the phone up, taking it off speakerphone. "Cade, you okay?" My off-key rendition should've garnered some kind of response, laughter at the very least.

"Yeah." His voice quieted. "What I wouldn't give for some of your sexual healing."

My heart ached, and I inhaled deeply. "I would administer it in a heartbeat if I could."

We talked for a few more tender moments before I laid the phone back down and relegated him to speakerphone spectator while I raced around. By the time I put on a blue-and-white silk dress, finished getting ready, and rushed out the door, all while giving Cade a blow-by-blow on each detail, I was running fifteen minutes late. Which, according to Cade before I'd ended our conversation, would be right on time.

The front of the gallery itself was all glass walls from floor to roof eaves, bright lights spilling onto the sidewalk of the darkened street. Enormous paintings hung on the walls made of exposed brick, beautiful on its own in sandblasted pale yellow and pink tones.

But the lighting on the art hanging on that wall had been dimmed, soft spotlights drawing attention instead to pedestal displays in the center of the gallery and along the other wall. Small metallic works of botanical art stretched from various-sized bases, steel stems reaching up to petals. Each of the surfaces were textured to appear similar to real life, some fuzzy or prickly, others soft and velvety. And only a single color appeared on any given piece: on the six-foot-tall row of sunflowers, it was a golden hue on the metal petals; on the bonsai tree, she'd given a chocolate-brown color to the trunk.

I walked over to the largest exhibit on the far wall. A framed arbor, its surface made to resemble weathered wood, spanned a good six feet wide with wisteria vines draping down between the slats. I smiled, reaching and almost touching the violet flowers, remembering the vines from the gazebo at their country club and how they'd played there as children.

I smiled, remembering the night we'd danced there for the first time. An ache panged through my heart as I wished cade could be here to see it.

"Hannah!" Kiki twirled over, catching me into a hug. She wore a gauzy emerald floral top and slim black pants. Her hair had been pinned up, but she'd left a few loose tendrils drifting down. "So what do you think?"

Hugging her tight, I looked across the room at all the sparkling works of art. "I think your very talented, Kiki. They're gorgeous."

She beamed. "Thanks. Three pieces sold in the first ten minutes. The last buyer wavered, but when I told him half of the proceeds went to The Unity Foundation, he pulled out his checkbook. Then he called his wife to have her and her friends come down."

"That's your mom's human trafficking charity, right?" The same charity that had benefited from the event held during night we'd danced in the gazebo.

"Yes, that's the one." Their mom answered me before giving Kiki a big hug. "I'm so proud of you, Katherine."

Hearing Kiki's given name threw me for a moment; I'd forgotten Kiki was only her nickname.

"Hannah, so good to see you." Their mom hugged me tight.

"Great to see you too, Mrs. Michaelson."

She drew back and gave me a stern look. "Call me Victoria or Vic. If Garrett's sister Trix does, you sure as hell can."

I laughed. "Okay, Victoria, then."

"Where's Cade? Is he running—" she cut off, then gave me a knowing look. "He can't make it, can he?"

I shook my head. "He's in bed in San Francisco with the flu."

Kiki frowned. "Poor thing. He's so needy when he's sick, depressed almost. We used to wait on him hand and foot, forcing him to eat pudding or soup—chicken noodle was his favorite."

Had he been depressed with me? I hadn't thought so. I hoped maybe I'd lightened his mood, teasing him about lingerie and with my singing.

Hearing about all of their family love made me think about my father. I wondered whether he'd take Kiki up on her offer and attend the event. Scanning the crowd, I spotted Kendall mingling near the front of the room with a group of women. Kristen was draped on Jason's arm and stood beside Cade's dad, who was near the bar toward the back.

"Has anyone seen Paul yet?"

Kiki nudged my shoulder. "I think he just walked in the front door."

Sure enough, Paul strode in, holding hands with an attractive blonde. His wife looked nothing like I'd imagined. She wore a conservative blouse and skirt with flat sandals. The polished outfit seemed at odds with my image of Paul, a former rock singer turned cabinetmaker.

Kiki nudged me, then looped an arm into the crook of my elbow. "Want to say hello?"

I nodded and she tugged me forward.

When Paul spotted us, he grinned, and they crossed the short distance between us. "Hello! Sorry we're late; the sitter was delayed. This is Melanie, my wife. Melanie, this is Hannah and..." He paused narrowing his eyes in thought for a second. "Kiki?"

Kiki gave him a quick nod.

A genuine smile lit up Melanie's face, and all my nervousness dissipated. She didn't seem threatening in any way.

"Great to meet you, Melanie." I extended a hand out, but she pulled me into a hug instead. The overwhelming greeting threw me off-balance, reminding me of when I'd met Cade's dad. Sighing in relief, I hugged her back, deciding warm family greetings were something new that I could get used to.

"Wonderful to meet you, Hannah." Then she pulled Kiki into a hug too. "Kiki."

Her outgoing personality forced me to do a double take on my first impression of her. She seemed to be perfect for my father.

When she released Kiki, she looped her arm into Paul's. "Okay, boys and girls, where's the alcohol? Mommie and Daddie don't get nights out often."

Kiki laughed. "Near the back. I'm told by the artist exhibiting" —she pointed to herself with both index fingers as she guided us over— "that organic margaritas and lemon drop martinis are the special of the night."

When Melanie sidled her way up to the bartender, my father shifted to stand beside me. "Thanks for being so welcoming of her—and me. Getting to know you in mixed company helps. And Kiki giving Melanie a chance to meet you in a relaxed way seems to have lightened Melanie's mood about the whole situation."

I smiled, watching as the bartender slid two drinks over: a margarita and a martini. "I'm glad too. Cade's family has actually been incredible to me. With Mom and my grandparents gone, they've filled a void I hadn't realized existed until they crowded in with their laughter and love."

Talking about Cade's family made me so glad I was here with them tonight, even if Cade couldn't be. Regardless of how much I enjoyed being here though, I kept getting distracted by thoughts of Cade. I hoped he wasn't suffering too badly, alone. I wished I was with him. My phone began to burn a hole in my purse, my fingers itching to text him—to call.

Paul continued, interrupting my thought tangent. "I'm sorry there was a void at all, but happy they've welcomed you, made you family."

Warmth filled my heart at Paul's words, their meaning hitting me hard. If I'd been asked about the possibility of having any semblance of family a year ago, I would've laughed. And now the only feeling I had about being a part of Cade's family, about having a fresh start with Paul, was immense gratitude.

He and I stood in the middle of a metal botanical garden, each piece finding a new home tonight. We'd been brought together from different worlds—connecting with family, making our own version of home.

The event went on with new people milling in and out of the gallery. I'd talked for over an hour with my father and Melanie, and decided they were the kind of warm and genuine people I wanted to include in my life, just like Cade's family.

Eventually, I edged my way to a quiet corner. All the people I knew at the exhibit were preoccupied in conversations. And I wanted to have an intimate one of my own.

Cade answered on the first ring. "Hey." His voice was gruff.

"Hey, yourself. How you feeling?"

"Same." He paused. "How's the gallery event?"

"It's good. Kiki's art is incredible." I thought of the arbor, and memories of our gazebo flooded in. "There's one in particular I think you'd like." My voice broke. I clutched the phone harder and closed my eyes, trying to hold it together.

"Yeah, what's it like?"

I shook my head. No way could I remain calm and describe something so intimate to him. "I'd rather show you when you're back."

His heavy sigh sounded through the phone. "I wish I was there with you. I should've come."

Thoughts of him traveling in his condition made me smile. He was probably surrounded by crumpled tissues, cold medicine, and covered in a mountain of blankets.

"No. I wish I was there with you."

"You do?" Doubt laced his tone.

"Yeah." I smiled, forcing myself not to get emotional about my care-giving fantasy. Instead, I kept it lighthearted. "I would bring you chicken soup."

He barked out a laugh. "That would be awesome."

"WHERE ARE YOU?" Cade asked.

"Your room." After the gallery exhibit ended, I needed to be near him. But surrounded by his stuff was the closest I could get. Thank God Mase hadn't asked when I'd shown up at their doorstep, he'd only given me an understanding look.

Cade insisted he felt better only moments ago. Then he refused to talk about his condition.

The phone was pressed to my ear, its glow, his existence, the only light in the darkness. I closed my eyes and turned slightly, pressing my nose into the pillow, inhaling deeply. Cade's scent mixed with my heartache for him filled me with an incomparable longing. With effort, I could almost imagine him here wrapped around me. *Almost.*

"Where in my room?"

"Your bed."

"I'm liking this bedtime story." His voice deepened, turning gruff.

His primal tone sizzled an erotic charge through me and my breath caught. Then I grinned, my melancholy shattering. He did that to me. Turned me inside out on a word, a phrase, the sexy loaded undercurrent of his voice.

On a shaky exhale, I tightened my hand on the phone. The electronic tie to him was hot on my skin. He was right there with me, and at the same time, so far away. "Wish you were here. Miss you like crazy."

"Me too, Maestro. Like you wouldn't believe."

"Really?" *Did I voice that? My doubt about his side versus mine?* "Does it hurt? Because mine does. I used to think that the good-bye was the hardest part. It's not. Not by a long shot."

"No," he agreed. "It's every moment you're dying to share in person."

I nodded. "The drop-ins and unexpected surprises. All the times I don't think I'm going to see you, and then, there you are, my sexy-as-fuck dream standing in my doorway."

A low chuckle sounded out. "Did you just call me sexy as fuck?"

My cheeks began to cramp with my huge smile. Just having him on the line was like thousand-dollar-an-hour therapy. "Maybe."

"No, I'm definitely sure I heard it. Say it again."

I swallowed hard and said in a low rumble, "Sexy as fuck."

His heavy exhale sounded over the phone. "Damn, I miss you. Three more days. I will be there by Thursday night. Count on it."

Confused about his early midweek arrival, I furrowed my brow. Then it hit me. Thursday was December 11th, my birthday. Even though I'd completely forgotten, he'd remembered. "You better. If you don't, the rest of the CDs you abandoned here are gonna get it."

He barked out a laugh. "What are you going to do? Take my favorites hostage?"

Alone in the dark, I narrowed my eyes, even though he couldn't see. "Oh, no. I'm going to put your entire collection into a random shuffle."

"You wouldn't."

"Try me, sexy boy. If you don't get here on time, as promised, all this longing I feel for you will reach a breaking point. Girl needs an outlet. I'm thinking the CDs are a great start."

He groaned. Then laughed. "Do your worst. If I am even a minute late. I'll take my licks like a man."

The thought of punishing him sent my mind guttering. Clearly I'd been exposed to him too long. "Oh, and how do you do it like a man?" My lips spit out the uncensored question before I could stop them.

His low growl vibrated in my ear. "Those are licks I'll be giving you, Maestro. That's how I do it like a man. Has it been so long that you don't remember? I think you need intensive reeducation."

His playfulness warmed my heart. Sparked the naughty girl inside of me to life. *His* naughty girl. "Maybe I do."

He dragged his words out. "Slow, unbelievably slow. To make sure you're paying attention."

On a hard swallow, I buried my face into his pillow and took another deep breath. "Oh, you have my attention."

"Teeth, dragged across skin."

A shudder ran through me. "I like…"

"I know you do." He paused. "Kiss after kiss, soft, teasing…"

"You're teasing me *now*…" I accused, not upset in the least.

"I know I am."

"Then what?" I rolled over, pulling his pillow with me, hugging it to my chest.

His low chuckle vibrated again. "Oh, no. You'll have to wait and see. You know I've never been one for itineraries."

I smiled, happy to be with him, even in this small way. We talked on the phone for another thirty minutes until he sounded sleepy. And I needed to head home for a shower and some sleep. A long bout of early mornings lay ahead to finish the cakes for the weekend's two parties.

As I walked down the hallway to leave, I called out, "Mase, I'm heading home."

His door was closed. He didn't open it or answer. Maybe he'd fallen asleep. Cade had given me a spare key to their place long ago, so I locked Mase and Ava in on my way out.

After a short drive home, I pulled in front of my garage, noticing my two porch lights were out. They were automatic lights. I looked down both sides of my street as I got out of the car. Christmas lights and holiday displays twinkled brightly from almost every neighbor's house. *So no power outage.*

I pulled my keys from my purse and headed up my

bricked walkway. "Probably a fuse blown," I muttered. Couldn't imagine what else would make them both go out.

With one foot on the first red brick step, I paused before putting weight on it. Something didn't feel right. The quiet felt too quiet. Or maybe my imagination began to run wild with a gut instinct. Yet the unusual darkness spooked me.

As a chill ran through my body, I pulled my coat tighter around me and backed up, giving the front of my house a wide berth. After another quick look down both sides of my well-lit street, I cut across my front lawn and went around back. The lights-out event extended to my back door too. But my neighbor's floodlights cast enough of a glow for me to see most of the back side of my house.

As soon as my gaze landed on my broken back window, I fished my phone out of my purse, then dialed 911.

"Yes. I think there's been a break-in at my house," I whispered.

"No, I'm not inside. I'm standing in the backyard." When the police dispatcher asked for my name, address, and phone number, I rattled the information off in hushed tones, stepping further away from my house and into the brighter light of my neighbor's yard. "No, I don't have anyone with me. Yes, I can stay on the line."

The longer I stood there in the eerie quiet, my phone only an electronic lifeline, the more nervous I got. My neighbor was typically home, but I couldn't count on it. What if whoever had broken in was still inside and decided to come out?

I huffed out a breath, beginning to freak out. "Ma'am, I'm hanging up to call someone over." After she tried to convince me to stay on, but then assured me someone would be here within minutes, I hung up.

My chest ached the moment I thought of who I wished I could call. Cade was sick in bed and a million miles away.

Then I immediately called Mase, who I *knew* was home. Thank God he answered on the third ring. "Mase, it's Hannah. Any chance you could come over right away?"

"Something wrong?" On his end, I heard a crash, then barking.

"I've called the police. Someone broke into my house."

"You inside?"

"No. I'm in my neighbor's backyard." I'd inched up onto his back porch, ready to break down his door if anyone came out of mine.

"Go to the front. Somewhere bright and visible. I'll be right there."

The line went dead. I did as he asked, rushing between the narrow stretch of yard between my house and my neighbor's until I'd crossed into their front yard. Bright blue icicle lights dangled from their eaves but stopped three-quarters of the way down. For the last four years they hung their mostly complete lighting effort, as if refusing to buy another two boxes.

I hovered near the lighted display in the middle of their yard, a trio of sparkling snowmen holding caroling books, dark mouths wide open in song as they leaned together. My gaze fell to my empty, dark house, devoid of any Christmas decorations whatsoever. I wondered if the absence of cheer had made my small cottage home a target somehow. I made a mental note to buy some security cheer.

Two marked police cars with their headlights off pulled up minutes later and parked a few doors down. As the officers approached my driveway, I waved them over. They looked charged, focused on their task. After I gave them my story, pointing toward the back of my house when I got to the part about the broken window, I handed them my keys and they left to investigate.

By the time I turned around, Mase screeched his Jeep to a halt by my curb. I glanced at my phone. He'd made it here in a record nine minutes.

He bolted out of his Jeep, left the door wide open, and jogged over to me, yanking me into a fierce hug. "You okay?" He pushed me away, grabbed my hands, then held them wide, examining me. "You aren't hurt?"

I laughed and lunged into his side again, squeezing him tightly. "Yes, I'm fine. Nothing dangerous has happened since I showed up."

He put a protective arm around me. "Good. Where the hell are the—"

I pointed to the police cars down the street. "They're already inside, checking things out." A shudder ran through me, and I let out a shaky breath. I wasn't sure if it was the chill in the air or the adrenaline pumping through me. "Thanks for coming, Mase. I didn't know who else to call."

"Of course, Hannah. You need me anytime, I'm here."

The officers returned after a few minutes. The broader one with cropped red hair stepped forward, handing me back my keys. "The house is secure. Back door was unlocked. Your belongings were ransacked, so you might want to check for valuables. We'll stay and walk through your home with you until you confirm everything's good."

After the police checked the house with us, and I confirmed nothing was missing, they advised me on safety measures, handed me my copy of their report, and gave me a business card with instructions to call if I discovered anything missing. Then Mase helped me put back together my ransacked house, folding clothes back into drawers that had been dumped, lining shelves in the closets with items that had been thrown onto the floor. Then he'd hammered two extra shelves I'd had from an unassembled new bookshelf over the broken window.

A little over an hour later, we stood on my front porch, and I nudged into him as I saw him out. "Sorry for ruining your night. I was kinda freaking."

He gave me a half hug, then kissed the top of my head before releasing me. "Don't apologize. I'm glad you called me. Trust me, Cade will be too. Sure you don't want to come back over and stay in his room for the night?"

Cade.

"No. I promise, I'll be fine." I didn't want to be in Cade's room. I needed to talk to him. As soon as possible.

"Okay." He gave me a hard look. "But do not hesitate to call me, even if you hear the wind blow the wrong way."

I nodded and closed the door behind him as he left, locking my house up tight.

I pulled my phone out of my coat pocket, desperately needing to be with Cade immediately, in the only way possible. Still hopped up from the adrenaline of the break-in, I dialed Cade's number with shaking hands. The moment it connected, I blurted, "I'm so sorry to bother you. I—I had to call you."

"You never bother me. What's wrong?"

"My house was broken into." I leaned back against my entryway wall, then slid down it, energy draining from my muscles.

"*Fuck.* Are you okay?"

"Yeah. The burglars were gone before I got home. The police were here, and after they made sure the place was clear, they gave me security suggestions. I even mentioned to them maybe Christmas lights might've helped. They agreed." I talked a million miles a minute, needing to vent all the details out. "I called Mase; he came right over."

The heavy pause that followed worried me.

"You're not upset that I called Mase, are you?"

"No. God, no." His hard sigh sounded out. "Fuck, Hannah. I hate that I'm not there. It should've been *me* there with you."

I closed my eyes. Hard to argue with his statement. I didn't have it in me to say the supportive thing. I wished it *had* been Cade here with me.

Then I told another white lie. When it came to my stuffed-down feelings, they seemed to come easier and easier. "It's okay."

"The *fuck* it is." His anger surprised me. "The very second I get back there, I'm making your house more secure: double-sided locks, lights on timers, motion sensor flood-lights. And Christmas lights. I'm going to deck the *hell* out your house."

I couldn't help but grin at the emphasis in his words, like he literally wanted to banish anything bad with glaring lights. The blinding plug-in scene in *Christmas Vacation* came to mind.

But then my smile fell at what he hadn't said in between his vows to make it better.

All of it was just stuff. None of it him.

26. MURPHY'S LAW

Cade...

T*he* worst *kind of asshole*. Hannah had dubbed me the "best kind of asshole" once in a romantic way. But in the end, an asshole was an asshole. The shining pedestal she'd put me on had tarnished. I'd made promises I hadn't kept. Let her down not once, but now twice.

My head throbbed. I could barely breathe. Yet the sad pathetic ache in my chest hurt the worst.

Getting sick hadn't been planned, but I should've been more diligent. Taken better care of myself. For her, if not for me.

Because instead of spending an incredible weekend with her and, more importantly, being there to console her through a traumatic break-in, I'd spent three days laid up in bed, head nearly exploding with snot, body convulsing with random attacks of shivers.

Then, by the time I woke up on Monday? Bored out of my fucking mind.

The worst of the flu seemed to have passed, even though

my legs felt like rubber. Regardless, I stayed in bed. I wouldn't be needed in the office for a while, anyway, due to arrangements I'd already made.

I surveyed the assortment of electronics fanned out across the covers—phone, tablet, laptop, sound system remote—and grabbed the phone, missing the fuck out of Hannah. She had her hands full with designing three cakes in addition to the chaotic holiday rush. I knew she'd be hair-on-fire busy, but I still needed to reach out to her. Our separation was driving me insane.

I fired off a quick text.

> Thinking about you . . .

I stared at my phone for a few seconds. When no reply came through, I tossed it back down onto the bed. She probably had that industrial-sized mixer whirring and couldn't hear her phone. Or maybe she was lost in thought while frosting one of her creations, unaware of her surroundings, including the dried flecks of color she often had on her arms.

Damn. I began to imagine her in a baby T-shirt and those short shorts, her ruffled apron on top.

Suddenly a round of sneezes attacked me. Three. Four. Five. *Fuck.* What a sledgehammer to the head those were. Every. Damn. Time. Wincing as the pain subsided, I dragged the tissue box closer and cleared my head with several blows. My head spun with dizziness for several seconds. My body seemed hell-bent on revolting when my thoughts got anywhere close to the gutter.

A moment after the room finally stopped spinning, my phone lit up. A text from Hannah.

> Miss you like crazy. Can't wait to see you.

I sighed, smiling. That small connection shot a thrill of adrenaline through my veins.

> Me too. Thursday.

It *would* be Thursday. I was done letting Hannah down. She volleyed back another text.

> Feeling any better?

Sure. If I ignored the headache, sinus pressure, weak muscles, and occasional chills.

> Some. Bed rest today. How are you? Busy?

Her reply bubble popped up right away.

> Very.

I grinned, remembering how damn sexy she looked when frazzled.

> Go. Be Brilliant. Call me when you have a free moment.

Which wouldn't be till late tonight, when she was exhausted. We'd probably fall asleep together like so many nights: too few words said, not enough *real* time together.

And that was the crux of it. Both of us pulled away from each other by life's demands. Her world. My world. And too much fucking real estate in between.

Either the cold medicine began working overtime or my

brain cells finally cleared from the head congestion. I sat up, an epiphany hitting me hard. Sudden resolve fired through me. I grabbed my laptop and drafted a solution to the problem, then fired off the email. The universe had thrown us all kinds of challenges. But last week at work, when I'd least expected it, a detour had edged into view.

I hadn't seen the hidden opportunity for what it was. Until now.

WEDNESDAY NIGHT FINALLY ARRIVED. With my overnight bag open on the bed, I packed the last of my things.

My level of excitement? Kids on Christmas Eve had nothing on me.

A chime on my phone went off. The flight-tracking app sent me an alert.

No. Fuck *no.*

My first call? Fixing it. "Maureen, the flight's been cancelled." I listened as she explained that she'd gotten the same alert and had already been searching for alternates. When she asked about the weather, I told her what I'd just discovered, "I guess a bad storm's starting to hit the East Coast." I continued to reply as she talked. "Please. Yeah, I understand. See how close you can get me."

I need to get home.

My next call was to Hannah. She answered almost immediately.

"Hey. Been...ing...yo...call."

I frowned. "You're cutting in and out, babe. Can you hear me?"

"Hold...cond." A pause followed. "There. Is...any better?"

"Some. I'm getting most of your words now. Where'd you go?"

"In...courtyard...hind Sweet Dreams. Phone reception's been sketchy...morning."

"Uh, isn't it dumping snow right now?"

Her laugh rang across. "Yes. Big fat snowflakes. The wind's...our way. Supposed to...forty miles an hour. They're...pred...ost three feet...areas."

"Yeah. What I'm calling about. They cancelled my flight."

Her heavy sigh cut me like a knife. "I'm sorry, babe. I've got Maureen searching for an alternate flight, but it's not looking good."

A sniff followed. "Cade, I can't...keeps happening. One thing...another."

My world crushed in on me with every disappointed word. "Hannah, I'm so sorry."

Her breath hitched, then she let a quiet sob escape. "Cade, I tried. But...can't do this anymore. Please—"

Shock imploded my heart. The ground moved. I sat on the edge of the bed, staring at the floor. A roar rumbled in my ears. For a split second, I thought my flu vertigo had returned. But shit started sliding off shelves, crashing onto the floor.

"What the fuck?"

I stood and raced down the hall, down the stairs.

In the dining room across from me, a huge cabinet filled with barware leaned forward, then toppled over, glass shattering. The row house, and everything in it, shook. Violently.

Heart pounding, I lunged and hit the floor in the center of the living room. The walls rippled as I clung to the phone.

"Hannah?" Nothing. "Hannah!" I shouted.

She was gone.

The lights cut out.

And the world around me fell apart.

LONG TERRIFYING SECONDS LATER, I scowled at the fucking universe and its twisted sense humor. The freight-train rumble ended, every car alarm in the world suddenly blaring outside. My eyes slowly adjusted to the darkness. Dim moonlight streamed through the front windows, my only aid.

Rubble surrounded me. Every damn thing that hadn't been nailed down had come down. Cracks spider-webbed across the walls. Chunks of plaster had fallen from the ceiling. Not one painting remained hanging. The chandelier dangled by the electrical cords.

I coughed, a fine powder suspended in the air fucking with my recovering lungs.

My next shallow inhale scared the shit out of me. *Rotten eggs.* I jumped up and ran around, frantic, searching for the damned gas main. The garage. I found the valve and quickly turned it off.

Suddenly feeling very alone, cut off from Hannah and stuck in a disaster zone, I made my way back through the house, opening every window to let the gas escape, before I stepped out the front door. The row house sat on a hill that overlooked downtown and San Francisco Bay.

The entire city had been rocked.

A moonlit haze of dust clouded the air, choking the panicked signs of life below. As car alarms cycled themselves off in rotation, a few horns honked. Muted shouts could be heard, somewhere off in the distance. I looked down the street. Neighbors had flocked outside, standing in the street, looking just as shellshocked as I felt.

I glanced back toward the city again. All the buildings that I remembered in the skyline appeared to be standing. Through the debris cloud, I made out the faint image of the Golden Gate. From what I could see, it still spanned across the water.

My attention returned back to my immediate neighbors. Did anyone need help? While not trained in rescue beyond CPR, I could still do something. But no one seemed in urgent need of anything. They just milled about, the entire scene playing out in slow motion before my eyes.

Well, fuck that.

No one needed my assistance. The responsibility of Fisher Holdings had been taken care of with the email that I'd sent a couple of days ago. And although Jackson had been my driver and bodyguard, I didn't need him for transportation. There was a Lincoln Navigator parked in the garage for my use, if needed.

I had somewhere I needed to be.

In under five minutes, I ran back upstairs and grabbed my packed bag and wallet. I rushed downstairs to the end kitchen drawer, pulled it open, and grabbed the keys to the Navigator.

By the time I hit the road and wove through the neighborhood side streets toward the highway, I realized just how bad it was. The entire city had been crippled. Traffic lights were flashing yellow. Worried about the structural integrity of the overpasses so close the city, I pulled over and examined a map that had been left in the center console. Thank fuck for paper maps.

Not sure if the universe was done screwing with me yet, I stayed to the larger surface streets and was grateful for the mostly clear roads. Each time traffic congestion looked to block my way, I detoured around the mess. A couple of times, I went off road to get past it, including a few spots where the asphalt had buckled.

I kept my phone on, in case anyone tried to call—really, hoping Hannah would make it through to me. I had to have heard her wrong. But every time I checked my phone, it said "no service."

After a dozen wrong turns, and nearly two hours of weaving through tangled surface streets, I finally hit the highway and headed south. And was so damn glad the rest of the way was smooth driving. Guess I'd gotten the jump on any evacuation exodus.

My best guess was LAX had to be about another eight hours away, just in time to hit rush hour in the morning. Could I luck out with a regional airport in between? Possibly. But I didn't want to take any chances. LAX would have the most amount of flight options.

And I *needed* to get home.

27. NO MORE WHITE LIES

Hannah...

The rest of the night had crawled by in a mind-numbing fog. Stuck at Sweet Dreams, working well past midnight on cakes for the events, Kiki, my four employees, and I ended up barricaded inside the shop by the severe first punch of a nasty blizzard. Then the power had gone out. And stayed out.

I'd never felt more disconnected.

Something had gone terribly wrong with Cade and me. Choked up by emotions, I'd blurted out my feelings without thinking. Bad connections on cell phones were never ever a good idea to try and communicate. I'd told him I couldn't do this long distance relationship thing any longer, and he'd hung up.

Then I couldn't get through to him. He didn't bother trying to reach me. No call. No text. Nothing.

And so, in the middle of the cold darkness of my shop, the six of us bundled in coats and sitting in the front area on the couch and chairs, we'd drank the last of the hot coffee as I poured my broken heart out to my audience.

When daylight broke, it was to a clear, blue sky. The thick blanket of snow glittered in the bright sunlight. It looked like we'd gotten hit with less than the few feet they'd predicted, but it had still ground our sleepy suburb of Glenhaven, and probably the rest of Philly, to a snow-covered halt.

"Sure you don't want a ride?" Daniel's black Mohawk bounced when he nodded toward his old Toyota Land Cruiser that the rest of them were piling into.

I glanced at Josephine. She was rebel enough to handle a little bit of snow, but doubt pinged into my brain a second later. "You have to swing back by after you drop them off, right?"

He gave a single nod. "Kiki lives up your way."

Kiki paused, one booted foot on the metal running board. "You're not coming with?"

"Not yet. I need to check on Lila." It had to be close to 8:00 a.m., and a hunch told me the other business owner would be hard at work.

Without skipping a beat, Kiki jumped down and trudged through the snow toward me. She spun around, walking backward, shielding her eyes from the glare off the snow. "Will you pick us both up here in about forty minutes?"

He gave me a proud smile before shifting his gaze to Kiki. "Take your time. I'll be back in an hour."

Kiki looped her arm in mine, then nudged me so hard, we both stumbled sideways in the snow. She laughed, tugging to keep us upright. "You are the best kind of friend, Hannah."

I glanced at her. She had dark smudges under her eyes from our all-nighter. "What makes you say that?"

She lifted her brows. "Because you take care of those you love."

Guilt gnawed at my gut as her words hit me hard. *Not* all *those I love.* One person, the one who'd meant the most to me, I'd let down. Monumentally.

My dead cell phone felt like a rock in my coat pocket. It kind of mirrored my heart at the moment.

Snow crunched under our boots as we made our way down the street. When we rounded the corner, a snowplow scraped close to the curb. We jumped out of the way of its arcing wake.

As we neared Lila's, I grinned. The back of Willard's large form came into view. Bundled in a bright yellow parka and steering a snowblower in swaying movements with a spring to his step, he was quite the sight. I fought a smile at how much fun he seemed to be having.

Lila, armed with a broom as she swept the front porch, spotted us and waved us over.

I stuffed my freezing hands into my pockets. "Willard play in the snow much?"

She leaned on her broom. "That man's a kid at heart. If he knew you two were here, he'd be all business." She glanced down. "Holy moly, no mittens?"

Kiki hid her bright red hands into her pockets too.

"You girls are gonna catch pneumonia. Get inside. I'll get the coffee."

"You have coffee?" I asked. The last of ours had disappeared with the power.

A blast of heat hit us when we stepped inside. "You have heat." Kiki's tone was awestruck.

Lila laughed. "When we'd first dreamt up the restaurant, survivalist Willard demanded we have a generator for 'just in case.' *That* would be now."

We sat at our favorite window table and Lila poured us coffees. Kiki and I clutched those individual ceramic fireplaces, warming our hands.

Lila pulled up a chair and joined us, a coffee of her own in hand. Silence followed as we watched Willard dance to his snowblowing rhythm.

Exhausted as I was, curiosity about Lila's situation filtered into my mind. "How do you manage?" I took a sip of coffee. If anyone could shed some light on the subject, it would be Lila.

"Manage what, hun?"

Kiki pulled her coffee mug to her lips, blew on its surface, then took a sip. Her attention shifted from Willard to me.

Unconcerned by Kiki being in on this, I took a deep breath and forged ahead. "How did you leave your daughter and her family? You two sound so close."

Her eyes brightened. "We are. And there ain't no trick to it, I just do."

I stared out the window at a couple of slow-moving cars that braved the dangerous streets. "How did you make the decision to be here?"

She gave a half shrug with one of her shoulders. "Willard needed me more."

I blinked. "That's how you decided? Not what you wanted or what felt right?"

The look she gave me was priceless. Her smile held understanding and sympathy all at once. Transported back in time, I could've been talking to Gran as she shared a pearl of wisdom with me.

"Live enough years, you realize life ain't about what you want or take. Life's about love. Love is about what you give

—what you sacrifice. You do that? You got everythin' you wanted but never realized."

Love is about what you give. I mulled the words over in my mind.

"Besides," she continued. "Willard was my family first. We may be brother and sister, but we fit like two missin' puzzle pieces. After seventy years of bein' on Earth with the same person, sharin' secrets and history, we know how to make each other laugh. And when either of us is ornery, we got that down too—he don't piss me off, and I stay the hell outta his way."

I smiled, remembering many times the sounds of their spirited debates in the kitchen carried into the dining room as they harassed each other. "What about friends you made in Sedona? Don't you miss them?"

"Sure. But we have computers, email, and phones. Sometimes I think we share more of our lives since we've been apart. Plus, I make sure I go back at least once a year. This year'll be twice, if I count when I go back for the Johnson's seventy-fifth anniversary."

Kiki coughed. "Seventy-fifth?"

I blinked, shocked at the number too. Gran and Granpop had celebrated their fiftieth wedding anniversary just before he'd died, and I thought that had been a long time. But they'd been in love with each other until the day he died. And she'd continued right on being in love with him until her time came to join him.

"Yep." Lila leaned back in her chair, staring beyond my shoulder, out toward Willard. "Some folks are destined to be together forever." Without moving, her gaze dropped to meet mine. "Those lucky few figure it out early enough."

Message received.

I'd been gripping the familiar so tightly, holding onto

what I'd wanted—what I thought I'd needed—I'd almost missed it entirely.

The secret to happiness didn't exist here. It wasn't in a place I took for myself.

"Thanks, Lila." I jumped up, kissed her on the cheek, and handed her my coffee mug before grabbing Kiki's hand and rushing down the porch steps.

Lila's laughter rang out behind us as we hit the freshly snow-blown path. "Where you goin', girl?"

A wide smile curved my lips, and I shouted without looking back, "To start living life!"

Kiki stared at me until I glanced at her. She raised her eyebrows. "What was that all about?"

Mind spinning, I let out a slow breath. "You'll see." I still had to work out the details.

———

INSTEAD OF DANIEL dropping Kiki and I off at our houses, we had him take us straight to Kristen's. We were about to collapse from exhaustion, but with the assistance of Lila's coffee, we'd hit that energized punchy stage. We'd also peppered each other with questions about how in the world we would still put on back-to-back parties while dealing with the aftermath of the blizzard.

Any concern we had got obliterated when we stepped into Kristen's chaotic living room. Kendall was there, and the two of them zipped back and forth, oblivious to our arrival.

Kendall had a stack of index cards. Kristen held several stapled pages on top of a notepad, pen at the ready.

Kendall held a card up. "The Coopers."

"Blaine and Carol? Or Trudy and Phil?"

"Blaine and Carol."

They go in Hannah and Mase's stack.

"What?" If I was involved in this, I needed to be clued in.

They both spun around. "Hey guys. Glad you're here. We've got Mission Whiteout underway. Everyone with a four-wheel drive gets messenger duty."

Kiki plopped down onto the couch. "What's 'Mission Whiteout?'"

I sat at the dining table, planted my elbows, and propped my heavy head onto my hands. "Yeah. What are you involving us in?"

"Cade's not back yet, but I stopped by on the way to the country club, and Mase volunteered."

A pang of heartache speared through me at the mention of Cade's name, his absence and how oddly we'd left things drilling a hole into my heart.

Kendall pointed to the index-card stacks on the kitchen counter. "All the guests are sorted by address. We figure since most live in Glenhaven's twenty-three square miles, it'll take each team about four hours."

"Ummm..." Kiki started.

Thoroughly confused, I shrugged, continuing her point. "To do what?"

"To hand deliver new RSVPs," Kendall replied, slapping down the Coopers' card. She pulled another off the top of her stack. "The Remingtons."

"My team." Kristen nodded, continuing, "We're getting a revised headcount and verifying whether the guests want to use our new transportation or their own. We've secured six motor coaches, assured by the owner of the company that they could navigate the unplowed roads. We're not taking any chances with the power out and guests wondering if the party's still on. I touched base with George, the general manager at the country club, late yesterday before the storm rolled in. The property has a permanent diesel backup generator to use in case the power isn't back on in time."

Kiki groaned. "We've been up all night. When are we supposed to sleep? I feel like the living dead."

I scowled at her. "And miss this excitement? We can sleep when today is over."

Kendall gave Kiki a pointed look. "I'm driving. You're on my team. We'll put an IV of coffee in your arm if we have to. We pull this off? Our party will be historic."

"Don't you mean Kristen's party will be?" My lack of sleep had me confused on who was in charge of which party.

Kristen shook her head. "After last night and today, these are every bit *our* parties."

Kiki flopped lengthwise onto the couch, staring up at the ceiling. "What about Saturday's party. We going through all this twice over? I don't have the stamina for that."

I groaned and slid my arms forward, resting my cheek onto the cool wood of the dining table.

Kristen flipped to the next page, then glanced up. "Power company thinks they'll have everything up by morning. Roads should be plowed by then."

My foggy mind chased the details of the second party. Kendall's was being held at the Andersons' country estate, thirty minutes out of town.

Two-and-a-half days away. I hoped the entire time was filled with either dead-to-the-world sleep, or so many tasks I wouldn't be able to think straight.

With just enough time left over to figure out the rest of my life.

28. HOME OR BUST

Cade...

After thirteen hours of travel and countless cups of coffee, I sat in the Dallas/Fort Worth International Airport. The next leg home wouldn't be for another three hours. Stations on every monitor covered the devastation from the earthquake. News of the blizzard took a short-update backseat to the earthquake's near twenty-four hour coverage. Apparently rare geological events trumped weather—even though both destroyed, injured, and killed.

I turned down the sound on the nearest TV after various news reports indicated the power was out in San Francisco and in several cities along the East Coast. My power issue? Dead phone because of a charger I'd forgotten to pack. The fix? A matching charger bought at the gift shop. *Thank fuck.*

The phone was the first thing I'd plugged in. My laptop: the second. At the booking agent's assurance that my ticket to Philly would be exchangeable if the airport didn't reopen on time, I'd purchased an exorbitantly priced first-class ticket, which entitled me to full access of their executive lounge. And I'd taken over one corner, converting it into a temporary personal command post.

I'd already pulled my half-charged phone from the wall and tried calling Hannah several times. When I hadn't gotten through, I'd tried my sisters, Mase, and Ben. Nothing.

Even though common sense told me their blackout meant the cell phone towers had to have been affected, it didn't stop me from repeatedly trying. I had gotten through to my parents and let them know I was okay. Thankfully, they lived far enough away from the storm's impact zone to be unaffected by the power outage.

I opened a packet of powdered vitamin C and dumped it into my glass of water as I read the email from Blake. He'd checked his company headquarters and confirmed the building still stood. Like the architects had planned for the modern earthquake-proof structure, it had only sustained minor damage. None of the security who'd been on duty last night had been injured.

Over the next couple hours, I sent emails off to every top-level Fisher Holdings employee. Then I replied to more than a dozen emails regarding the upcoming Christmas party I'd been tasked with before I fired off another eight more. Between every few emails, I did another round of phone calling, attempting to reach someone in Glenhaven before plugging my phone back in.

When the departure boards showed my flight leaving on time and in just over an hour, I began to pack up my electronics, stowing them into my messenger bag.

I left my phone for last. I stared at it. Until I could get home, it was my only link to Hannah. Exhausted and riding a thin edge, I refused to believe she'd left me—couldn't even go there.

So how to reach her? Would any texts get through? If

they showed delivered on my end, would Hannah get them on her end once cell service came back online?

Didn't know. But I had to try.

> I'm okay.

When that didn't seem enough, when I pictured her worrying about me, I sent another.

> I'm not hurt.

How to say everything else that needed to be said in a text?

I fired the last one right as the first boarding calls for my flight sounded over the speakers.

> I'm on my way home to you.

29. WHITEOUT

Hannah...

F riday night had officially become my least favorite day of the week—following my solitary birthday, my new least favorite day of the year. Severe detachment left me staring through my mental haze at a colorless party. Literally and figuratively.

My first without Cade.

Blinking back tears, I forced air into my lungs, past the crushing weight on my chest. I'd messed up. I wanted to fix it, but feared it was too late.

Electricity had come online four hours in advance of the party, enabling us to reconnect to the rest of the world. The power grid probably groaned with the mass simultaneous plug-ins.

My phone now lay idle in my white satin clutch, the two texts from Cade burning a hole in my mind, scorching my heart. They had both been sent, not right when we'd disconnected, but the following day. Short and to the point, both communicated all that needed to be said for me to understand so much had gone wrong.

The first?

I'm okay.

The second delivered a heavier punch.

I'm not hurt.

How could he not be hurt? I was devastated. We'd been torn apart by my selfish needs. I hadn't seen what was most important—not in time, anyway.

I hoped it wasn't too late.

No more cell phones. No more texts. We'd relied on those electronics to be our tie to get us through the difficult distance between us, but I feared it had only widened it. Cold metal and plastic, digitized conversations, visualizing touches...none of it had been enough.

The party energy vibrated around me. Guests mingled and laughed while waiters delivered flutes of Champagne. Several couples twirled on the parquet dance floor.

Yet I was in another world.

Instead of being connected with the real party around me, I imagined Cade in the room.

He'd be leaned against the back wall, brooding. Arms crossed over his chest, a deep scowl would mar his otherwise handsome face. His dark hair would be tousled, like he'd been running his hands through it, a stark contrast to the clean lines of his white tux.

I'd bite my lip, forcing myself not to laugh. Then I'd make my way over to him in my sparkling silver Jimmy

Choos, a beloved memento from a bright pink taffeta faux-funeral outfit.

He wouldn't glance my way when he grumbled, "White frothy punch. White outfits. White linens on white table-cloths. Even the damned band has white instruments. Did the musicians order that white cello just for tonight? Everything looks ridiculous."

I would nudge his shoulder to distract him from his amusing foul mood. "Even the cake tonight? Even your girl?"

He would swing his gaze my way, then take a deep breath. "You look amazing, Maestro. You always do. And I haven't had a chance to look at the cake."

I'd slip my hand into his. "Well, let me give you a private artist-guided tour."

All of a sudden, someone nudged my shoulder, jolting me out of my daydream. Phoebe Rutherford, our hostess and the person responsible for tonight's total whiteout, stood beside me. She grinned and whispered conspiratori-ally, "Isn't everything perfect? I'm certain to have *the* party of the holiday season."

I smiled, taking in the grand whiteness of it all. "It's amazing." I glanced up at the ceiling. "Did you have Kristen replace the crystal in the chandeliers?"

She nodded, beaming with pride. "They're milky quartz. Cost a fortune."

I had no doubt. I gave her a smile that I hoped appeared genuine. My heart just wasn't in a celebratory mood. "It's a beautiful party, Phoebe. People will be talking about it for months."

Phoebe drifted away toward Cade's sisters, who were all busy mingling with guests.

Cade's imaginary voice quipped loudly in my head,

embellishing my comment for my ears only. "And making fun of it for years."

With no one demanding my time at the moment, I meandered over to the cake Kiki and my shop had worked so hard on.

I visualized Cade with me again, his gaze drifting over my shoulder. "Hannah, that cake is..."

I'd turn toward the cake, then finish his sentence. "Breathtaking, spectacular, completely unique and a phenomenon in the world of cakes?"

I grinned, channeling his stark egoism for a change. Then my smile fell away, and I took in the beauty of the cake, pretending Cade was here with me.

Kiki, Daniel, Chloe, and I had spent most of the week perfecting the sugary creation. We'd erected a giant tower of crystalline snowflakes on one end, then carved snowy slopes and drifts that led to a forest of slender pine trees covered in white. Some of the trees stood almost two feet tall, the largest few with "icicles" hanging from their branches.

Kiki stepped into view, pulling me from my thoughts. She held two shot glasses and raised one a few inches higher. "Drink?"

I furrowed my brow, staring at the white liquid.

"White Russian," she clarified. "Vodka, Kahlúa, and cream."

I shook my head. "No thanks, Kiki." My emotions had tied my stomach into knots, and I wasn't sure I could keep it down.

She tossed one back, then put the empty glass onto the table beside us. "Don't worry about him. I hear he got out safe."

Thoroughly confused, I stared blankly at her. "Who? W-what?"

"Cade. The *huge* earthquake."

My heart plummeted. I'd been worried about our relationship. And he could've died?

Pulse racing, I grabbed Kiki's arm. "He's okay. He's not hurt." I repeated the texts that suddenly made sense. And were an entire world better than I'd interpreted them to be.

She put her hand over mine, repeating me. "He's okay."

I took a step backward. Then another, my eyes widening. "I have to go. You guys have the cake covered?" I darted a glance at Daniel and Chloe, who stood by the bar.

Kiki shot me a penetrating look. "*Go*. We've got this."

AFTER CONVINCING the concierge of the club to drive me home in his lifted four-wheel drive truck, and navigating the snowy streets in record time, I finally stood at the end my driveway.

A cramp choked the base of my throat as I stared beyond Cade's Jeep parked in front of my garage. Brightly colored Christmas lights hung from my eaves in a haphazard fashion, blinking on and off. An entire family of plastic reindeer surrounded a jolly, cherub-faced Santa, who presided over a nativity scene. Tears pricked my eyes at the mishmash of themes, garish, and yet...perfect.

My toes began to go numb from the cold, and I picked my way up the shoveled pathway to my front steps. Heart pounding, I tried to tamp down my excitement.

Cade was *here*. Honest-to-God here—not somewhere halfway around the world.

The front door had been left unlocked. I stepped into my dark entryway, gaze following the faint light glowing from my bedroom. I dropped my purse and keys on the table and began taking off my coat as I walked down the hall.

Ava rushed up and greeted me.

"Hey, girl." I rubbed her head, but she immediately turned around and disappeared down the hall. Measured steps brought the doorway of my bedroom into view, right as Ava curled on floor at the foot of the bed. Light flickered around the room, every surface covered in different sized candles. Cade sat on the center of the bed in jeans and a short-sleeved black T-shirt, his knees bent, his muscular arms locked around them in a lazy hold.

His hopeful expression and gentle smile undid me. My coat fell to the floor right as I burst out crying.

A blur of motion flew up from the bed until his warm arms wrapped around me. "Hey." The softest word whispered into my ear.

I slid my arms around his waist, trying not to be a sobbing mess, but failing. Relief flooded through me that he hadn't been hurt in the earthquake. That he'd made it back to me.

Real. Solid. Here.

On a shaky inhale, I tried to formulate thoughts, words, but nothing came. Only gratitude. That my idiocy hadn't scared him off. That miles and miles between us only brought him back to me when the going got rough.

When my crying slowed, I pulled back. I gave him a weak smile. "Welcome back?"

He took a deep breath, eyes shining as he scanned my face. "Best homecoming ever."

I snorted, then sniffed. "Sure it is." I wiped under my lower eyelashes with my fingertips, certain all my mascara had run onto my face. "I'm a hot mess with raccoon eyes."

With a finger, he tipped my chin up. He caressed my

cheek with his other hand, a wide smile on his face. "You're gorgeous."

Knees wobbling, I nestled back against him, closed my eyes, and breathed him in. "You're the best kind of liar."

"Did you just smell me?" His voice held an incredulous edge as his words sparked a fond memory.

I grinned. "Yeah."

"I have stale airplane all over me," he repeated from our reunion conversation so long ago.

"You need me all over you," I replied, playing along, reliving it with him.

"Fuck yeah, I do."

And just like that, with our sexy, fun banter, my uneasiness settled. I licked my lips and peered around him, taking in the room. "Those are a lot of candles. Looking to seduce me?"

With a slow headshake, he took a step back. But he grasped my hands, holding them firmly. "No. Wanting to impress you. Make you smile. Give you the birthday you deserve." His gaze held mine, expression fierce. "I'm here to win you back, Hannah."

I squeezed his hands. "You never lost me."

Brows drawing together, his mouth fell open. "But you said you couldn't handle it anymore. I thought you meant we were finis—"

When his voice broke, I pressed a finger to his lips. The horrible words were as painful for him to say as they were for me to hear. "No. Not us. I'm not done with you yet, Cade Michaelson. I just cannot do all the back and forth anymore. Missed dates. Waiting and hoping, only to be let down. I can't handle *that* anymore."

He swallowed hard and gave me a decisive nod. "Me either."

My mind whirled and my lips parted, but I couldn't manage to string cohesive words together. The news of how it would all be different tangled by the time it reached my tongue.

In a flash of movement, his lips captured mine, warm and insistent, both tender and urgent. On a soft gasp, I leaned into him, relishing his touch. A slow heat burned inside me, fueled by all the pent-up deep longing for him for hours, days...weeks.

But in this treasured space, time stopped, crystallizing. Each slightest touch became our first, our last, with every decadent brush in between melting into one magnificent moment.

As long seconds turned to minutes, us trembling together in the most amazing tender kiss, we finally slowed. He pulled back first, both of us gasping for breath. His hands cupped my cheeks and his forehead dropped, gently touching mine.

"I'm going to make love to you. Slow. Gentle. Hard. Urgent. Any way you want me, all that I can give you is yours. But first..." He took my hand and tugged me toward the bed. I climbed onto the duvet with him.

The dancing candlelight revealed the most lopsided cake I'd ever laid eyes on. I pressed my lips together, forcing myself not to laugh...or cry. Yet tears brimmed in my eyes, in spite of my efforts. A single slender candle stood in the center of dark chocolate frosting.

He grabbed a long-necked lighter from my nightstand, clicked a flame to its tip, and lit the candle. "Make a wish, Maestro."

I let out a long sigh, then gave him a huge smile. "It's already come true." But I closed my eyes anyway—wished for something grander, hoped and prayed and threw it up to the universe at large. But I wouldn't breathe a word of it.

Then I cracked my eyes open and blew out the candle. Cade leaned back behind the pillows, and a loud crinkling noise followed. He whipped out a small package between us, drumming his fingers over red foil wrapping. An iridescent ribbon crossed over the paper, both curled ends vibrating with his movements.

"Happy Birthday, Maestro."

With shaking hands, I took the present from him, staring at it.

His expression grew serious. "It's only one of your gifts."

I took a deep breath, then ripped off the wrapping in a childlike frenzy. Beneath was a rectangular black box.

When I glanced up, Cade nodded for me to continue.

I pried the case open on its hinge to reveal a sparkling stainless steel watch. A diamond-set bezel surrounded a mother-of-pearl face with white-gold stars scattered across it. The dial said Omega *Constellation*.

The irony made me huff out a soft laugh. "Shouldn't I be giving you a watch?"

He slipped his warm hand into mine, entwining our fingers. "The watch is a symbol. Wear it and know that if we're ever apart, no matter where I am, I'm wishing I was with you."

Tears welled in my eyes again, and I smiled. Then sniffed. "Cade, it's beautiful. I love it."

"There's more." He paused, then took a deep breath. "I no longer live in San Francisco."

Shocked, I blinked. "What?" I put the watch beside me on the bed.

"I no longer work for Fisher Holdings."

"But what about Blake? You said he didn't want anyone else in the position."

Cade snorted on a headshake. "Apparently old habits die hard with him. He came to my office a few days before I came down with the flu. He'd grown bored with day after day of golf and hanging out with his yacht club friends. Plus his third wife threatened to become his third divorce if he didn't give her more space. He offered his services as a consultant. A few days later, I offered him the job back."

"Wow." Mind reeling, I tried to sort all the changes. "When did you decide this?"

"Monday."

Before we'd talked Wednesday night and had somehow accidentally unplugged our relationship. Before the earthquake. Before yesterday... "What about your dream?" My heart ached for all that he'd wanted, a lifetime of goals and achievement.

His gaze burned into mine. "*You* are my dream."

My heart stuttered. He'd given up everything for me.

His expression changed, a smile playing at the corner of his lips. He shrugged. "I figure I've got icing cupcakes down. Maybe you'll hire me."

"Ummm..." And now it was my turn. "I sold Sweet Dreams."

Shock flickered across his face. "What?"

I nodded. "Yep. Yesterday. After we got disconnected, I decided none of this mattered. Me being here wasn't what was most important. All I cared about, all I wanted...the *only* thing I want—is you."

"So you sold your business." He blinked.

I nodded. "To Chloe and Daniel, on payments. They jumped at the chance."

"And I quit my job."

I tried not to laugh. "So you said. What about your consulting business? Or Loading Zone?"

He dropped his head, shaking it as his shoulders trembled with laughter. "Sold and sold. Signed the papers last month on them both." Concern etched into his expression. "What about your dream, Maestro? You love making cakes."

On a confident arm cross, I straightened as tall as sitting on a bed in an evening dress would allow. "I stipulated in my verbal negotiations with Chloe and Daniel that I reserved all rights and income to cake designing for Invitation Only, with a reasonable percentage to Sweet Dreams from each."

Pride filled his gaze, his voice softening. "Sounds like you've got great business sense."

I beamed him a smile, then leaned over and kissed him softly, murmuring against his lips. "I learned from the best."

With care, he relocated his blob of a cake to my nightstand. He picked up the torn wrapping paper and my watch and placed them beside the cake, then slid his hands over my bare shoulders.

I kicked my shoes off, sounds of their thudding on the rug making me giggle. Maybe it was the giddiness in knowing that we'd both given up everything for each other. Nothing else tugged us away from the other. There was only us.

His finger slipped under the thin dress strap. "How does it feel to be unemployed?"

I tugged his T-shirt over his head, then slid my hands over the sculpted muscles of his chest. "Feels pretty good so far." I pressed a small kiss into the dip below his collarbone. "But we're not completely unemployed. We've got Invitation Only."

He smiled. "Appropriate. The business that threw us together is the one left standing."

I dragged my lips along his jawline, dotting soft kisses in between words. "I don't care what we do next." When I reached his mouth, I gave him a long, slow kiss. I paused, pulling back to stare at him. "As long as we do it together."

He inched my gown up my thighs, sliding his strong hands over my hips. "We could run a hot dog stand on the corner."

"Hot dogs?"

"Sure. I know a girl who burns a mean hot dog." He shifted, yanking open the fly of his jeans.

I grinned, remembering our campfire fun so long ago, when I'd shown him the finer points of burning hot dogs and marshmallows. "Don't forget the cupcakes."

Suddenly, he lunged, pushing me on my back. He wore his undone jeans. The silk of my gown covered my midsection. And yet nothing was between us. Not any longer.

I closed my eyes, leaning my cheek against his, relishing this moment.

But he had other plans. He leaned back, pulling my dress over my head. Then he hooked a finger around my lace thong and dragged it down my legs before standing at the foot of the bed.

He worked his jeans down over his lean hips but never looked away from me.

Under the hot intensity of his stare, I trembled. His gaze: ravenous.

Then he crawled up my body, lips brushing soft kisses as he went, staking his claim. Every action was raw and tender. His fingers shook as they skimmed over my hip, up my waist, and caressed the curve along my breast.

With an awestruck expression, he gazed at my body, then into my eyes as if he'd never seen me before. Gentle fingertips grazed my nipple as his lips feathered over mine, teasing, asking.

I arched up, molding my lips to his in a soul-searing kiss, aching for him. I relaxed under his tender care, opening my body for him.

He shifted, covering me, but easing back. Then he slid forward. Pressing in, inch by slow inch, he filled me until all I knew was him, buried deep inside all the way to my heart, wrapped around me tight, refusing to let go. I shuddered, overcome by it all.

The man I'd never seen coming made slow love to me like he'd never done before. With every gentle thrust, with every low groan and breath catch, I felt sweetly cherished and thoroughly possessed.

The tempo increased as love and lust tangled together. I gripped his shoulders, wrapped my legs around his hips, and held him as close as possible while we rode a wave of ecstasy.

Ache twisted and spiraled into pleasure, low moans coming with every labored breath until I gasped, my orgasm hitting hard. In that instant, his whole body tensed, holding me tight as he let himself go.

Heavy breaths followed. Fast heartbeats blended together, his, mine...ours.

In the candlelit magic of my bedroom, we clung to the only dream that mattered.

30. REDEFINING REDUNDANCY

Cade...

Hannah's legs were tangled up with mine, and I rubbed my foot along her smooth calf. When she pressed her lips against my neck, purring into my skin, I rolled onto my back. She propped herself up onto a bent elbow and stared at me. "Was last night a dream? Or are you really here for good?"

I smiled and leaned up, kissing her. "It wasn't a dream, Maestro. I'm here. Not going anywhere."

And I couldn't believe what a lucky fucker I was. I didn't care about a job. Or what I would do next week. Or next month. I had Hannah—right next to me.

A heavy thump hit my shin and a rough tongue licked up the other side of my face. "Uck. *Down*, Ava."

Hannah giggled, which only made Ava's hard tail drum onto my leg faster.

Sighing heavily, I closed my eyes. "Why again did I bring her along for our slumber party?"

Hannah pressed her lips together, fighting a smile. Then

she rolled on top of me, grinding her hips down onto my hardening length.

Okay. So I guess the dog isn't dampening her mood. I groaned. "You're killing me, Maestro. The things I want to do to you."

She smirked, nipping at my lips. "You did all of those things last night. Repeatedly."

Throwing my weight to the side, I knocked her off-balance and pinned her down to the bed. "Try and stop me from doing every single one of them again, in slow succession. Redundancy will never be so much fun."

Ava finally jumped off the bed and ran out of the room.

"Mmm..." Hannah stared up at the ceiling, pretending to think about it. "Don't you mean repetitiveness? Excessiveness? Redundancy means something different, sounds like something bad."

Leaning my head down, I pressed my lips against her neck, tasting her with a slow kiss. "We'll redefine redundancy into something amazing. Doesn't it mean unnecessary? That works. We don't need to have more amazing sex after last night, but we'll do it anyway. Take our time. Memorizing. Repetition. Excessiveness. Redundant, but in the best way." I nipped at her ear, hoping to talk her into a day filled with redundancy.

Ava barked twice.

Hannah gave my chest a gentle shove. "See. Both your girls have to pee. Plus, I have to be able to walk tonight. In very high heels. Looks like your 'redundant' sexcapades will have to wait."

I sighed, releasing her. "Fine. But, just to be clear, the sexcapades are never to be referred to as 'redundant' in mixed company. People might get the wrong impression."

As she crawled toward the edge of the bed, the view of

her swaying hips gave me plenty of sexual-position images to mix up the redundancy.

On her way to the bathroom, she glanced over her shoulder, eyes mostly hidden from her messy dark hair. "And exactly when might that topic come up in mixed company? 'Oh, Hannah, do tell us about Cade's sexual acrobatics.' So I'm to reply with something other than 'Well, if you must know, he's thoroughly redundant with his sexcapades.'"

I snorted. "Smartass."

She pointed toward the kitchen. "Go let the dog out."

After I pulled on my jeans and jacket, I grabbed her leash. She barked twice more before I rounded the corner. "I'm here, girl. No need to get bossy."

The moment I opened the door, Ava bolted to the length of her tether, quickly sniffing and exploring the snow-covered grass in a random pattern before settling on a chosen place to do her business. And of course, I forgot to grab a plastic bag again. Yeah, that shit would have to wait.

A few minutes later, Ava settled down and nudged up against my leg for attention. I stood on the edge of the deck and rubbed her ears as I watched the sun rise.

A to-do list unloaded into my head as reality hit me. Tonight was Kendall's Christmas party at the client's estate house. And we had exactly one week before my party, an event I felt certain we would knock right out of the park—as long as every small detail fell perfectly into place.

Hannah stepped beside me, and I jumped in surprise. "Sorry, I didn't hear you." I wrapped an arm around her shoulder. The thick white robe she wore fell open. I smirked, then wrapped the two sides over her body once more before tying her belt and cinching it tight. "It's freezing out here, Maestro. We need to keep you bundled up."

The corners of her lips twitched. "What happened to redundant sexcapades?"

I kissed her, taking a moment to savor her taste, nipping that sexy lower lip before releasing it. "You've convinced me; I hadn't fully woken up then. No time for redefining redundancy today. Too many things to do."

Her smile nearly undid me. "This feels right."

"What feels right?"

"You...here. I'm so happy you decided to come back."

I smiled. "Me too. Best damn decision I've ever made regarding business."

She shivered, her legs exposed.

"Inside. We're not letting you get sick." I walked us back into the house, then went straight into the bedroom, took off my jacket, and grabbed my T-shirt off the floor, pulling it over my head. When I heard the refrigerator open, I called out to her. "Your dress for next weekend is all set? My sister's dresses?"

"Yep." What sounded like cereal pinged into a bowl. "We're meeting for lunch today, then we're going in afterward for a final fitting."

I nodded, mentally checking off the to-do list as I scooped up my keys and phone from the dresser. When I walked into the kitchen, Ava dragged her leash around the table leg, and I stepped on the handle before grabbing it. "Gotta run, babe. Pick you up tonight?"

She nodded, cheeks puffed out with a mouthful of cereal. Chewing, she held up an open palm plus one finger of the other.

I kissed the top of her head. "Six. Got it. I'll text you later on, between errands."

Before I made it out of the room, Hannah made a squealing noise. I turned to find her holding her phone up.

"The definition of redundant is jobless or superfluous." She burst out laughing.

I dropped her a deadpan look. "Yeah, we are so redefining that."

Running out the door in a great mood, I went over the monumental tasks of the next seven days in my mind. One party down, one to go tonight. Then a tidal wave of last-minute details to pull off the party of the year. And I was so damn happy to be *here*, taking care of it all.

Ava jumped into the passenger seat, and I shut the door ticking off how far we'd come in a year. How much I'd grown.

Last New Year's, I'd been a player who'd had girls' numbers on a sticky note list, a damaged man who'd buried himself into business and accomplishment just to be able to wake up each morning. This New Year's approached, and I'd become a changed man, all because of one Ice Queen baker who'd melted my heart.

There'd been challenges along the way and painful lessons learned, but we were now stronger together because of what we'd endured.

An excited confidence pulsed through my veins.

And a smile curled my lips as I thought of what I wanted to be doing this New Year's.

31. ALL THAT GLITTERS

Hannah...

After rushing out the door almost thirty minutes late, due to Cade getting stuck in a traffic jam across town while out on appointments, we finally settled into his Jeep and took off.

An incredible amount of energy poured off of him, and I couldn't stop staring. The way he held his shoulders back in his black collared shirt, the glint in his eye, the twitch at the corner of his lips, made it seem like he might break into a smile at any moment.

He stole a quick glance at me. "You look amazing, Maestro."

I tilted my head, thinking he'd only seen me in a blur as we rushed out of the house, and now, only in the shadow-changing lights inside the Jeep as we drove. I smiled at the compliment anyway. "Thanks. You seem...different... tonight."

"Yeah?" He cocked his head toward me, stealing another glance. "Different how?"

"I'm not sure."

He grinned. "Maybe it's because I'm happier than I've ever been."

I smiled, relaxing back against my seat, totally relating. Utter bliss at having him here had me floating up in the clouds. "Sounds like a perfect reason." I watched the reflectors blur by as we drove down the darkened road. "Me too. Pinch me. I can't believe this is real."

When I glanced up, I caught his near smirk. I pointed at him. "That! You're different somehow, even since this morning when I last saw you. Like something exciting happened today that you're hiding. Like you have a secret."

A lazy smile curved his lips. "Maybe I do. Would that be so bad?"

Surprised, I furrowed my brow, staring at him. "Are we keeping secrets from each other?"

He shook his head. "No. There will be no secrets kept between us. Only surprises."

"Oh, like a present?"

His smile widened, and he nodded. "Yes. Exactly like a present. Christmas is only a couple of weeks away, you know."

"Is it? I hadn't noticed."

He snorted. "What's with that tone in your voice? Now who's keeping secrets?"

I pursed my lips, trying to keep an impassive expression. "Nope. Only surprises."

"You got me a present, didn't you?"

"Maybe..." And really, I hadn't yet. But I enjoyed teasing him anyway.

We turned onto a dark, unmarked road, and after a couple of minutes, our headlights flashed off of metal ahead, along the shoulder. Soon vehicles appeared, parked along both sides of the street, bumper to bumper as far as our headlights would allow us to see in the darkness. "They saving energy out here? There aren't any street lights."

He passed all the cars and turned onto a narrow, winding driveway, then under a portico, parking in front of two valets who were dressed in gray-and-black uniforms.

"Too expensive to put lights up when headlights work just as well. Besides, many people prefer their neighborhood dark." He held his finger up for me to wait, ran around to my side of the Jeep, and opened the door, holding out his hand for me. I took it but watched my step, making sure my high heels hit dry concrete around the occasional chunks of snow and ice that appeared to have dropped from previous cars.

I tugged at Cade's hand and stepped to the edge of the portico, glancing up at the twinkling stars overhead. "The darkness does make for a breathtaking night sky."

"Well, tonight's theme is 'Glitter Holiday.'"

Shimmering blue lights hung from trees in the front yard, casting a soft glow onto his face as I stared at him. His lips twitched at the corners again. "What?"

Grinning, I shook my head. "Nothing. Different. Good different."

When we stepped through the front door of the modern home, flickering tea lights in stained-glass candleholders danced red-and-green hues at the floor's edge along the walls. The lit pathway took us through a living area and out toward their backyard. Tall glass windows from one side of the room to the other displayed a holiday fantasy outside.

Sliding glass doors led us onto the back patio and pool area beyond, both spaces having tall, cylindrical heaters every twenty feet or so. Trees with sculptural branches had been wrapped with solid lights, their trunks and limbs sparkling works of art, alternating in red and green. The heated pool's built-in lighting had been turned off. Mist rose off the surface of the water, and floating tea light candles on makeshift lily pads gave off a soft glow. Modern holiday music streamed from speakers mounted at the corners of the roofline. A large, white tent stood just beyond the pool area, candlelight reflecting off the stemware on tables that were covered with forest-green linens.

I squeezed Cade's hand as I took in the grounds that truly did glitter everywhere I looked. "Wow. It's beautiful."

His tug on my hand made me turn around, and I glanced back. Icicle lights appeared to "drip" white light from the house eaves to their lighted tips.

Cade laced his fingers of both hands into mine, then pulled my arms outward. "In our rush to get out here, I didn't have a chance to really see you in your dress. You look incredible, Maestro."

My cheeks flushed under the heated look he blasted at me, and I grinned, pulling away and spinning slowly for him. "You like?" The dress had narrow off-the-shoulder cap sleeves that led to a beaded bodice. Soft fabric draped from my hips to my ankles. The underlying material flashed an iridescent sheen, and the sheer overlay had clear sequins with sparkling crystal beads woven in random curling trails.

He leaned down, a low growl coming from his throat as he brushed his lips over my ear. "Without a doubt—I love."

A shiver tripped through me as my pulse quickened. My heart and mind hazed, intoxicated by this new energy coming from him. It snapped electric in the air around us.

What an amazing difference twenty-four hours made. Last night, I was at a party, miserable, wishing Cade was with me in every way. Tonight, my wish had come true.

He placed a gentle kiss on my cheek before resting his

hands on my shoulders and turning me around. When I opened my eyes in the direction he'd pointed me, my hand flew to my mouth.

Kiki and Chloe flailed their arms wildly at us from behind the cake they'd insisted on bringing. And Daniel stood next to the fiesty brunette and redhead he'd worked side by side with all week, staring at me with a pitiful expression.

I snorted, trying not to laugh as we approached. "You're Mohawk looks quite…"

"Sparkly?" Kiki smiled.

Clearing my throat, I nodded. "Uh, yeah."

Daniel sighed. "They threatened to hold me down. When that didn't work, they held a knife to the cake."

Kiki looked unremorseful.

Chloe smirked. "Don't you think it looks awesome?"

Examining the green glitter in his black hair, I crossed my arms over my chest, then raised a hand to cover my mouth again, hiding my twitching lips. "Oh, yes. Very festive."

Daniel sighed, shooting me a deadpan look, strands of his upright hair glinting green as they quivered. "I want hazard pay for this."

Drawing my brows together, I gave him my best serious look. "It's *your* business now. Pay yourself."

Daniel's expression instantly changed, a wide grin stretching across his face. "Oh, yeaaah."

Kiki stared at me with raised brows.

I winked at her. "I'll tell you later. It's a good thing."

Cade nudged me. "Guys, this cake is amazing."

Glancing down at the sparkling creation, I nodded. "The design was one hundred percent Kiki."

Enormous ornaments in deep red, purple, green, and

blue had spilled onto the flat surface of the cake that had been designed to look like dark, wood flooring. On one side of the cake, a tall pine tree stood free of colored ornaments. Instead, the green branches had been frosted with snowy icing and tiny Swarovski crystals.

Kiki beamed. "It took an act of God to wrangle the control of designing and creating it from Hannah."

I shrugged. "It's hard to stand idly by in a kitchen."

She wrapped an arm around my shoulders. "You didn't stand 'idly by.' You supervised like a champ."

"And found a million other things to be plenty busy with," Daniel added.

Cade put his arm around me, rubbing my shoulder. "How's the cake coming along for next week?"

Kiki's eyes widened imperceptibly at Cade.

But by the time I glanced up at him, whatever I'd imagined seeing between them had vanished. Kiki seemed normal again.

I shrugged. "Good, I guess. They're insisting I step back from that cake too."

Kiki rolled her eyes. "It's your fault. You invited me in there. Two creative minds in the kitchen might make the cakes explode."

Chloe nodded. "You said yourself, handling the managerial end with all the increasing orders, and baking all these elaborate cakes, made you need two of you."

When Chloe nudged Daniel, he straightened. "Exactly. For these two cakes, pretend like we are three of you."

Narrowing my eyes, I realized Cade wasn't the only one acting odd tonight. "What are you all up—"

Kendall popped beside Kiki. "Hey guys. Fabulous party, right?"

Someone tapped on my shoulder, and I turned to find

Kristen stepping in between Cade and me. "You two showed up late. Pre-party celebrating?" She winked at me.

Surprised at the redirect, I blinked. "Uh, no. Traffic. Cade got stuck across town."

Kiki leaned forward and winked. "Is 'across town' a euphemism for 'downtown?'"

I gaped at the innuendo-filled suggestion. "No. He got stuck. In *vehicular* traffic. On the other side of *Philadelphia* downtown."

Kendall smirked. "Adding more details doesn't make it less true."

Cade moved his sister out from between us. "And enunciating every syllable makes my meddlesome sisters think you're hiding more."

"Nothing is being hidden. *Nothing.*" I glared at them all, then laughed and grabbed Cade's hand, sensing the conversation degrading toward the gutter by the second.

The rumble of Cade's deep chuckle drowned out the laughter of everyone who surrounded the cake table as we walked away. "Don't let their teasing get to you. They don't mean any harm by it."

I shook my head. "I'm not. Just a little flustered tonight for some reason."

We snuck back into the empty house and veered left before the tea light pathway led to the entryway, going down a dark hallway. A gentle tug on my arm pulled me to a stop in the darkest part of the hall. "Hey."

I turned and found myself pulled into his embrace, pressed against the solid wall of his chest. I sighed in the warm comfort of his arms.

His hands rubbed up and down my back. "Why so flustered?"

I shrugged, unable to pinpoint the exact cause.

"Everyone seems to be a little different tonight, not just you."

A gentle hand caressed my cheek, and I leaned into the touch, closing my eyes. Tender lips kissed mine, heat flowing from the contact, calming me further.

"I'm not different, Maestro. This is me in the best of moods. And I can't speak for the others, but I'd imagine it's the time of year. People tend to get giddy on a daily basis during the holidays. The air is full of unexplained cheer."

Swallowing, I nodded, feeling a little foolish for questioning his demeanor. Yet I wasn't sure "cheer" defined all of it.

Pulling back, I found his hands in the dark and laced my fingers into his. "Are you sure there isn't anything going on? I'm not questioning your awesome mood; it just seems like something deeper is there. Beneath the puzzling awesome mood, you seem more serious than usual."

He lifted my hands, kissing my fingertips. "I am more serious than usual."

Tugging me forward, he led us back down the hall toward the flickering candlelight. He held my hand tightly and guided me toward a couch and sat down, pulling me down beside him. "You sure that's all?" He gave me a warm smile, brushing my hair back from my face as he gazed into my eyes.

I shrugged. "I'm not sure. Things seem so new and up in the air."

"But you're happy, right?"

"Incredibly happy. It's just...where do we go from here? You're back, but what do we do tomorrow? We're jobless. It feels like you and I are great, but there's this big question looming about what we'll be doing."

"Why don't we not worry about it for a few weeks? We'll

figure things out. First comes us, then what we want to do. Besides, I created a bar and a consulting business. You created a bakery. Together, who knows what we'll decide to dream up."

I smiled, nodding. "I like that."

He leaned forward and kissed me softly. When he pulled away, he gazed deep into my eyes.

I narrowed my eyes. "There you go, looking all serious again."

Tilting his head, he smiled. "I am serious. Very serious about you." He took my hands in his, clasping them together. "Does that scare you?"

I shook my head, certain about one thing. Nothing about Cade Michaelson scared me. "I like you serious about me."

He gave me a curt nod, a smirk twisting his lips. "Good."

Before I had a chance to think again, his lips crushed onto mine. My mind still wrestled with what our future might hold, but the deeper he kissed me, the more I got lost in all things Cade.

32. THE THIRD CHRISTMAS

Cade...

The six days leading up to the main event had broken records for whirlwind weeks, but this morning, the day of the party, I stayed in bed with Hannah for as long as I dared. Kissing her softly, after exhausting her thoroughly, I tucked her white sheets and duvet around her.

She groaned at the sunlight streaming in and buried her face under the pillows.

"Rest as long as you can, Maestro," I murmured, pressing a soft kiss to her temple.

An unintelligible mumble was my reply.

I sighed, grinning like a certifiable idiot. A man could get used to a lifetime of mornings exactly like this.

Thinking about the list of tasks I had to complete in half the time it would take a reasonably sane person to accomplish, I grabbed my tablet and keys and rushed out of her house.

After handling a few required errands, I went back to my house and barricaded myself in my room to focus. I began firing off emails and texts. Two dozen pings were sent out in under thirty minutes, and I worked diligently to fire off several more, in addition to sending directions to all the guests in gentle reminder.

One by one, replies came through from vendors. Florists confirmed. The musicians replied, double-checking the arrival time. A company I'd hired to string the lights had already arrived and begun their work.

I texted Chloe. She would be at Sweet Dreams with Daniel all morning.

> How we looking on the cake?

Another few texts and emails were sent before Chloe's reply came through.

> Cake is perfect. See you tonight. :)

My phone rang, and I answered it after checking the cake off the list. "This is Cade. Yes, thank you. Right. Wanted to be sure the lights wouldn't be a problem." I nodded. "We'll notify you the moment we leave the dock."

Drumming my fingers on the table, I thought through the plans for the night. Kristen had discovered a problem earlier this week and promised to handle it. She said she'd give me the details by this morning.

I dialed her number. "Hey, sis. What were you able to find out?"

Loud noise hummed in the background, and I assumed she was driving. "Ferdinand can't do it. But a mayor's authority is recognized."

Rapidly processing that information, I made a note on my tablet. We were bending a few rules, and likely operating outside of the rigid confines of the law to make tonight happen, but I figured we'd go ahead with the original plan and sort out legalities later.

Staying task oriented, I remembered the mayor of Glenhaven belonged to our country club. "I'm assuming you called Stan?"

"Of course. When he found out whose party it was, he said he wouldn't miss it for the world."

Unsurprised, I nodded. "Leave it to the Constantine's to draw the best dignitary guests."

"Oh, I don't know. Don't you think you could have hedged your bets and invited a few European princes?"

I snorted. "We want diplomatic relations to remain good with our country, right? Between Mom angling for their donation dollars, and Kiki and Kendall eyeing them as dating material, I'm not sure they'd leave unscathed."

Kristen's background noise got louder, and I tried to figure out the loud motor sounds. "Where are you? A wind tunnel?"

"Practically. I'm getting my car washed and just stepped outside."

"Gotcha. We all set for later?" I'd arranged to have the girls pick Hannah up and get ready at Kristen's place, since it was on the way.

"All set. Stop worrying. We've got everything covered on our end. She's safe and secure in our hands. We'll be there on time with jingle bells on."

My mind wandered at the thought of where Hannah might wear jingle bells. I took a deep breath, clearing my head to stay focused. "Okay. And hey, thanks, sis."

A pause on the other end made me smile, and I imagined a serious expression on her face. "I'm thrilled to be helping. Thank you for including us."

When I ended the call, nervous energy vibrated through me as I stared at the wood grain on my desktop. Too many things could go wrong with tonight. But as long as I knew Hannah was all right, nothing else mattered.

Missing her already, even though only a couple of hours had gone by since we'd parted, I leaned back in my chair and sent her a text.

Thinking about you . . .

Almost immediately her reply came through.

Smiling, thinking about you too . . .

I sighed. Yeah, I had it bad. But after being lost for a couple of years before Hannah, being totally whipped in love was a pretty great place to be.

LATER THAT NIGHT, I stood on the deck of the Constantine's multimillion dollar yacht, taking a breather, surveying the scene as guests began to arrive. Already lit with something in the vicinity of a hundred thousand solid white lights running along every line available, she seemed to light up the night all on her own. Pine boughs were decorated with red and white berries, and the occasional white ribbon wound around railings and trimmed the window openings.

I looked at the two other yachts moored on either side, decked with similar white lights, only two of the many neighbors we'd enlisted to join in the festivities. To my understanding, more would arrive within the hour.

The hostess, a gracious participant in my plan, stepped next to me.

"You've done well, Cade. I think before the night's over, my party will be the buzz of the season."

I smiled, glancing at the confident brunette. She'd been a friend of ours through childhood, always championing a cause with us, no matter the reason. "Thanks, Amelia. I appreciate all you've done."

She gasped, taking a step forward. "Is that Stan Harrison?"

I turned to see the mayor boarding. "Oh, did Kristen not tell you?"

A squeal was the only warning I got before she crushed me into a tight hug. "Cade Michaelson, you are the very best party planner."

"Don't thank me. That idea was all Kristen's."

Narrowing her eyes, she gave me a sidelong glance. "Really? We're competing for best party, and she invites the mayor to mine?"

"Well," I tilted my head. "In all fairness, he needed to be here, and it was only *after* her party that he was invited."

Her expression fell into mortification. "He was a last-minute invite? Oh my God. I need to go smooth things over with him."

I rolled my eyes at the formalities of high society as Amelia vanished to hobnob with the local dignitary.

But my mind stuttered when I saw the next guests arrive. In beautiful red gowns, my sisters each came aboard, the hired waitstaff assisting them. I rushed over, excusing myself as I wound my way through the thickening crowd.

I exhaled a slow breath. "Hannah."

She glanced up, and a smile lit her beautiful face.

"Cade." She took my outstretched hand and stepped aboard, leaning into my arms.

The gown she wore was magnificent, shimmering emerald fabric caressing her curves. She'd left her hair down, but parts of it were pinned back with rhinestones flashing as she moved. A dark faux fur draped across her shoulders and wound around her arms.

She smiled brightly, her cheeks pinked. "Missed you like crazy today."

I leaned down, pressing a kiss to her cheek. "Missed you something fierce too. You look gorgeous tonight."

She took a step back, tilting her head as she gave me a once over. "You look pretty handsome yourself, Mr. Michaelson. You're cummerbund is even emerald. It matches my dress."

"Imagine that." I winked at her.

I glanced at Ben, who stood at the entrance with clipboard in hand. "How we lookin'?"

He counted silently while tapping his pen, then nodded. "Only the Stevensons, Fitzpatricks, and Mrs. Moreland are unaccounted for."

I glanced at my watch. "We've got about fifteen minutes. Text me when everyone's onboard."

Hannah wrapped her hand around my waist. "Give me the tour. I've never been on a yacht before."

"Absolutely." I guided her forward.

She gazed up at me, mischief sparking in her eyes. "Did you scope out the closet situation?"

"Why, Maestro. Haven't been aboard five minutes and already with the naughty."

Arching a brow, she smirked. "You seem supremely disappointed."

Patting my breast pocket twice, I leaned down, whispering. "I have an entire diagram of the ship mapped out, closets highlighted in yellow."

She slipped her hand into mine. "Takes a guttered mind to know one."

On our way toward the cabin's side entrance, we passed my sisters, who gave the musicians additional song requests. The caterers already had waitstaff working through the crowd with platters of hors d'oeuvres on polished silver trays.

When we stepped inside, Hannah gasped. "Wow. It's luxurious in here."

And it was. Birdseye maple cabinets were the perfect complement to the ivory leather seating. Plush Persian rugs stretched across polished teak floors.

My phone vibrated in my pocket, and I pulled it out to see the heads-up from Ben.

> All here. Notified the captain.

I typed a quick reply.

> Thanks.

Moments later, the slight motion of the yacht made Hannah grip my arm. "Whoa. We're moving."

I grinned, kissing her softly. "Boats tend to do that on water."

She smelled amazing, her tropical scent surrounding me as I deepened the kiss.

Pressing further into me, she made the tiniest moan.

Not ready to make use of the fictional closet diagram just yet, I pulled away, taking a deep breath. "Tour. I promised you a tour."

Biting her lower lip, she blushed. An instant later, the heated moment vanished as she turned and gasped, then began crossing the room. "The cake!"

"You haven't seen it?" I kept my tone innocent as I slid my hands into my pockets, strolling up behind her.

She shook her head.

I remained silent as she took in its simple beauty.

When she sighed, I nudged her gently. "Well, what do you think?"

"I love it." Her voice was low, almost breathless.

Sloping hills were covered in white frosting that glittered with sugar crystals. A forest of pine trees rimmed the outer edge, some flocked with white icing, others dark green, their intricate pine needles adding texture to the varying branches.

In the center of the snowy meadow, two slender pine trees stretched upward, untouched by snow, their branches intertwined. The taller pine's canopy spanned wider in breadth, protecting its smaller companion.

I placed my hands on her hips and leaned in, whispering into her ear. "You always create symbols of us in your cakes. I thought I'd surprise you by doing the same."

She turned in my arms and gazed up at me, eyes glittering with moisture. Her whispered voice trembled. "You made this for me?"

I brushed her hair back from her face as I stared into her eyes. "Yes. Well, sort of. I designed it. Kiki created the conceptual drawing from my instructions, then she enlisted Chloe and Daniel to help her make it...and keep you out of the kitchen."

Her lips curved into a smile. "Those two trees are us."

"They are."

Her smile widened. "Standing tall."

I nodded. "Immovable."

She turned and faced the cake again, resting the back of her head onto my chest as I tightened my arms around her. "Thank you, Cade. It's beauty in simplicity. Elegant."

I kissed the top of her head. "That's what I was going for."

"Oh my God!" Kiki's loud interruption startled us, and we turned, facing my exasperated sister. She dropped her hands onto her hips, eyes flashing with mock-irritation. "The two of you can't be left unsupervised at parties anymore. The second we turn our backs, you disappear to parts unknown."

When we said nothing, Kiki waved her hands, shooing us out of the room. "Out. There is a party to attend to. Activities to oversee. A harbor master to grease. Gorgeous sparkling lights on boats to witness."

Hannah followed Kiki out into the buzzing party, but paused midstep, glancing back at me. "A harbor master to grease?"

I shook my head. "Don't ask."

We'd only been moving a few minutes, but it should've been enough time. I led her to the back of the yacht, hoping they'd all arrived.

They had, and the sight was incredible.

In the dark of a winter night, with lights on either side of The Delaware, dozens of yachts followed our lead, some on our port and some on our starboard. Every boat had a different light theme, some in all white like ours and the two smaller yachts flanking us, another vessel was decorated in blues and greens. One of the boats had lights that faded on and off in rotating colors.

Our party had its own holiday boat-light parade.

Hannah clapped her hands together, bouncing beside me. "Cade, this is wonderful!"

While gripping the rail, she watched as members of the party gathered around us. Amelia pressed in on Hannah's side. "Brilliant, Cade. I never would've thought of this on my own."

My sisters came up behind us, worming their way in to get a good view. I pulled them forward, wrapping an arm around the lot of them. "Wasn't all me, Amelia. I'm only point man on your Invitation Only event. This level of awesomeness takes a team."

Chloe and Daniel edged in beside Hannah, Chloe nudging her gently. "Have I ever told you how much I've loved working with you? I'm glad we're still helping you do the Invitation Only cakes. "

Daniel nodded, his black Mohawk bobbing, free of green glitter. "Ditto."

Soft strains of holiday music filtered through the air, inspiring me, and I slipped my hand into Hannah's. "May I have a dance?"

Nodding with a grin, she followed my lead out of the dense crowd gathered at the stern. Suddenly spotting a viewing deck up above, I quickly figured out where the stairs would be. We searched them out and climbed up to the private area.

Down below, the song changed into the perfect slow ballad, an instrumental to "What Are You Doing New Year's Eve?"

As the song played, I smiled. I already knew the answer.

33. SO NOT A WEDDING

Hannah...

The party had been amazing. Cade remained with me the entire time: as we danced, mingled with old friends, started the beginnings of new ones. But I needed a break to catch my breath, and his sisters had just pulled him away to handle some urgent matter. With all the parties we'd thrown over the year, I'd grown used to sharing him with his responsibilities.

Earlier, I'd enjoyed the twinkling lights in our very own boat parade. But I now stood on the port side with no other vessels in view, because we'd broken away from the group. The time alone brought a moment of peace I needed.

I inhaled a deep breath of fresh air and gazed into the night sky, which gave its own show as it glittered above like diamond dust blown onto black velvet. I felt the yacht slow and held onto the banister as the waves rolled gently beneath us. On a shiver, I pulled my faux fur wrap tighter around my shoulders.

A heavy presence stirred the air a split second before

warmth pressed around me, solid and true. In the quiet moment, the scent of Cade filled my lungs, spiced and earthy.

He pulled my hair aside, soft lips floating up the column of my neck. "I have something I want to show you."

I smiled, gazing out into the vast darkness. "Better than this spectacular view?"

"Depends."

Racking my brain on what could possibly be better than this, or the lightshow of the party, I glanced up at him over my shoulder. "Is it the inside of a closet?"

Amusement glittered in his eyes. "Would you like it to be?"

Without hesitation, I shook my head. "No, that's okay. Claustrophobic takes on a whole new meaning when we're talking a tiny cabin closet—with the boat rocking."

Leaning down, he growled, tugging on my earlobe with his teeth. "You won't feel the boat rocking. Trust me."

A shiver coursed through me. "You have a talent for obliterating my anxiety."

"Good. Now, come with me. I promise not to be long, and then we can do anything you want to do for the rest of the night." He slipped his hand into mine and led me away from the rail.

"A cabin-closet quickie?" I arched a brow. "*That* is the enticement to follow you?" Skeptical about his plans while guests mingled everywhere, I glanced around.

Men in tuxes and women in gowns, who'd earlier drifted all over the boat, now congregated toward the center. Cade's parents stood by the bar talking to a group of people, including Paul and Melanie, and when Cade's parents nodded toward us, Paul turned and smiled at me.

"Oh, wow. I didn't realize they were here." I smiled and waved.

Cade's sisters stood to the left side of the cabin's main entrance, their ruby gowns illuminated by sparkling lights that had been woven into pine boughs arching around the entrance. Ben, Mase, and Jason were gathered on the opposite side, facing the girls.

No matter where I looked, people stared at us, smiling. I leaned in toward Cade, murmuring, "Might be hard to steal away into a closet with everyone watching so closely."

He gazed down, an odd expression on his face. "Might be."

The music shifted into familiar romantic strains, and between one heartbeat and the next, the world spun, a puzzle I hadn't known I'd been a part of locking into place. Tiny white lights woven into the arching pine boughs formed an arbor I only now noticed. His sisters stood to one side in matching elegant gowns, his friends on the other in coordinating tuxes.

When I whirled around, the entire gathering had pressed forward like a concert crowd, each person angling for the best view—of Cade and me.

Blinking in shock, I glanced up at Cade. "Is this a wedding?"

"Oh, it's so *not* a wedding." The playful tone of his voice, and the glaring clues all around us, told another story.

"You mean as in: it's a non-wedding? Like a non-date?"

The corners of his lips twitched. "You could make a run for it, but they have strict instructions to block you in."

Speechless because I had no idea what to say, I scanned the guests who'd indeed blocked us into this area of the ship.

"Go ahead, Maestro. Run. I will run after you. Always."

His vow set my heart aglow, a promise I'd made him make to me not long ago.

Words to the song now playing filtered through the foggy haze of my thoughts, and I repeated them in a half-whispered tone, remembering our first date together and how he'd serenaded me with them, *"What are you doing for the rest of your life..."*

Cade exhaled, taking my hand. "I thought you'd never ask, Hannah. I hope to spend every breath of it with you."

Butterflies fluttered up from deep in my stomach as he pulled out a black velvet box from his pocket. His dark gaze caressed me with love so all-encompassing, the audience we had around us faded away. "Be my wife, Hannah. Put this man out of his misery and let him love you the way you were meant to be loved."

"In a closet?" My lips twitched. In that moment I knew. I'd known it long before tonight, but the breadth of what I wanted from Cade finally hit me. I wanted the crazy skirt-lifting taunts and the closet escapades. I wanted the casual picnics in the park and the naked frosting battles.

But most of all, no matter what life brought us, the breathtaking moments and every bump along the way—I wanted Cade.

He lifted a dark brow. "Most especially the closets."

"Well, then, of course." I smirked. "But only if we christen a closet at least once a week."

He gave me a hard nod. "We'll make it an itinerary requirement everywhere we go."

Kiki shouted, "Should I be taking notes for a pre-nup?"

The guests surrounding us came back into focus as I grinned.

"I didn't hear what she said," Kristen called out, her

hands cupped around the side of her mouth to echo her voice. "Was that a 'yes?'"

"Yes!" I shouted at the top of my lungs.

"But she didn't even see the ring." Kendall pointed to the black velvet box in his hand.

Cade crushed me into an embrace, then pulled back and kissed me tenderly. "Thank you, Maestro. I will make you the happiest woman on Earth."

I smirked. "Promise?"

His gaze raked down my body before locking with mine, his eyes sparking with lust. "I believe you're well acquainted with how well I deliver on promises."

A man cleared his throat, standing just inside the arbor. "Am I correct in assuming there's a ceremony to perform?"

Cade glanced at him, then turned toward me. "Stan is our town mayor and also legally able to perform wedding ceremonies. Ready to do this now?"

Not giving it a second thought, I nodded, letting Cade take charge. But I couldn't help myself questioning one little matter. "When do I get to see the ring?"

"When I slip it onto your finger. I'm not risking anything on a technicality. The offered ring was carefully chosen by your man. But if you want another, say the word and it's yours."

I could've cared less what the ring looked like as he took my hand and led me before our glittering holiday arbor. Joy burst from my heart at the great lengths he'd gone to in order to make this special moment for us and keep it secret from me.

Another puzzle piece clicked, and I turned toward him, eyes widening. "This is why you've been acting so weird lately. And your sisters. And Chloe and Daniel."

He nodded, looking smug. "Half of my 'differentness'

was nervousness, and the other half came from the excitement of knowing, believing, *hoping* you'd say yes. Of thinking that in just a few short days, we'd be married."

Gripping his hands, I took my turn at a deep breath. "And now it's only minutes."

"I'm counting the seconds," he murmured.

The mayor cleared his throat. "Let's begin, then. Shall we?"

"Do you have a quick version, Stan?"

I glanced at Cade. "This is what I get? A quickie wedding?"

He smirked. "I promise to take our time for the rest of our lives."

Biting my lip, I glanced at the mayor. "Hurry it up, Stan."

Our bridal party, and the guests within earshot, laughed.

"We're gathered here to witness the union of two people who wish to join together in the eyes of God. The union is a sacred one for each to honor, cherish, treasure, and support the other. Cade Joseph Michaelson and Hannah Noelle Martin, do you agree to do so every moment of your lives, as long as you both shall live?"

Cade gazed deeply at me. "Hannah, I promise to be with you, loving you, forever."

Tears sprang into my eyes. "Cade, I vow the same. With you, loving you, forever and ever."

The mayor nodded. "Then, by the powers vested in me, by the State of Pennsylvania, I now pronounce you husband and wife. Cade, you may now kiss your beautiful bride."

In the span of a heartbeat, Cade pulled me close, then kissed me with tender intensity. My entire world rocked, but it had nothing to do with the boat, and everything to do with the man who embraced me tightly, promising to never let me go.

After a whirlwind year I'd begun alone, hesitant to let anyone else into my sheltered life, Cade had broken down my walls and captured my heart. We'd had our share of emotional turmoil, but we clung to each other, wanting to be there together on the other side.

And now, I had the love of the most amazing man. His family had welcomed me in as their own, even before I officially was one.

I pulled away as a sudden realization hit me. "Hey." I grinned and looked at my new huge family. His sisters and parents. My father and Melanie. "I'm *officially* a Michaelson now."

Cade scrubbed a hand over his mouth. "Ummm, about that. It may or may not be official yet."

I blinked. "What?"

He sighed, glanced at the mayor, then back at me. "There may be some paperwork, an affidavit is ready for us and the mayor to sign, something about three days and a license we've skipped over in order to surprise you..."

Arching a brow, I turned toward the mayor.

He shrugged and nodded. "I'll write an official request for exception, but you may need to do the three-day route anyway."

Taking a deep breath, I blocked out the guests and stared hard at my new husband. "I don't care what legal hoops we need to go through to make it 'official' official. As far as I'm concerned, we're married. And December 20th was, and will forever be, our wedding day."

He grinned. "Have I told you lately that I love you?"

"No."

He kissed me softly. "Well, I do."

I grinned wide, heart nearly bursting from my chest

with happiness. "Good. I love you too. Now, can we consum-mate this union, or what?"

EPILOGUE
TOES IN SAND

Cade...

White sand stretched around us like sugar crystals. Gentle waves rushed onto the shore. The midday sun warmed our skin.

Cold water dripped onto my thigh.

I cracked an eye open to see Hannah's mischief-filled gaze and wide smile blocking the sun. She'd been playing in the ocean and must've sprinted straight from the water, because her chest heaved as if she'd run a marathon.

What a glorious fucking sight.

I grabbed her hand, pulling her onto me. She gasped as her knees buckled, and she fell, straddling my hips.

In a sudden mood to play, I spun around, pinning her onto the beach.

"Hey! Now I've got sand all stuck to—"

I silenced her protest with a rough kiss until she melted beneath me. "No, you've got me all stuck to you. Get used to it."

Her megawatt smile returned. "I'm already addicted to everything about you."

I gave her a hard satisfied nod, shifting to lie beside her. "Good."

I dropped my gaze down her wet, tanned body and dragged a finger between breasts hidden by turquoise scraps of fabric that I'd been earlier informed constituted a bikini top. Trailing a finger along the inner curve of her breast, I smirked. "You look good in sand."

She lifted her hand to my chest, drawing circles there with her finger. "So, I have another question."

We'd been here ten days, and she'd already asked hundreds of both on-topic and random questions. And I looked forward to a zillion more.

Last week, we'd celebrated Christmas, island style: her, me, and the ocean. Presents had been exchanged but were truly unnecessary. I already had all I ever wanted and everything I needed—Hannah.

Smiling, because I couldn't do anything else in my state of sappy perma-bliss, I kissed her with all the passion I felt. By the time I pulled away, she was breathless. And so damn beautiful.

I watched her blink, like she'd lost her mental focus. "What's your question, Maestro?"

"You had one nonnegotiable rule with Invitation Only: no weddings."

The corners of my lips twitched. "Was there a question hidden in there somewhere?"

"You *so* did a wedding." Her expression was smug. And adorable.

"*Non*-wedding. Get your facts straight. Even the State of Pennsylvania agreed."

"Nooo, they retroactively honored the ceremony."

Loving the debate, and doing my damnedest not to laugh, I pressed my lips into a hard line. "Well, then technically, there was no wedding when said ceremony occurred."

Her scathing glare could've shattered bulletproof windows. "Take it back. That was our wedding. Everything about it was perfect, and I will not have you tarnish it with technicalities."

I smirked. "Okay. I take it back."

She started to smile. "So you admit it; you broke your own rule. There *was* a wedding."

Giving her a nod, I laughed. "Yes. I'm a rule breaker. This should not surprise you. And yes, I admit, there was a wedding. Best wedding ever."

A triumphant look flashed across her face. "Why'd you toss out your rule?"

Rolling halfway onto her, I gave her a lazy smile. "You are the exception to every rule."

She reached up and gave me a soft teasing kiss in approval at my answer.

I nipped that sexy lower lip of hers before pulling back. "But just so we're clear, that was it. The rule still stands forevermore. No weddings."

"Mr. and Mrs. Michaelson!" As usual about this time of day, Philippe, our waiter from the Four Seasons, interrupted us, bringing our late lunch.

We glanced up as he politely averted his eyes.

Hannah grinned. "We're good, Philippe. No midday beach nakedness today."

In true world-class service, the Four Seasons had arranged for us to have anything we wanted, anywhere we decided to go on the island. But for the last few days, the only place Hannah wanted to be was this lonesome stretch of sand.

And truly, I was thankful for her persistence on the matter. I'd brought her to the paradise where I'd been lost and had discovered my way—when I'd realized home was in her arms.

She stared at me with that inquisitive expression I loved. "Whatcha thinkin' about?

I sighed with a smile. "You."

She tilted her head, narrowing her eyes a fraction. "Are you sure there isn't more?"

There was.

One year.

What an incredible year I'd had—we'd had. All because I'd agreed to be a part of an event-planning company but had insisted on one simple rule. Then shattered it to pieces.

I smiled at the woman who would forever be my world.

"What are you doing New Year's Eve?"

She grinned. "You mean, in a few hours?"

"I mean tonight, and every New Year's, for the rest of your life."

Her hand cupped the side of my face, happiness lighting up her eyes. She leaned down and kissed me softly, lingering there a moment before murmuring against my lips.

"I want to spend them all locked in a closet...with you."

Happily Ever After
for now . . .

Cade & Hannah's romantic adventures continue to unfold in the **No Weddings** series...

No Weddings
One Funeral
Two Bar Mitzvahs
Three Christmases
For Valentine's

Thank You!

Thank you for experiencing Cade and Hannah's romantic adventure with us in *Three Christmases*.

If you enjoyed the story, please express your love for *Three Christmases* by recommending it to friends in person, by email, on Goodreads, and through book clubs and reader groups.

And if you value reviews to help guide you into your next book, as we do, please help other readers by sharing your review of *Three Christmases* on your favorite retailer and book community sites.

Incredible thanks to everyone for extending your love of *Three Christmases*.

Reviews are cherished love notes to authors
and tantalizing invitations to readers.
Appreciated by all. ♥

Want to Read More?

Dive into the steamy romantic comedy of the
No Weddings Series...
No Weddings
One Funeral
Two Bar Mitzvahs
Three Christmases
For Valentine's

Read more of your favorite characters from the No
Weddings series in the steamy spinoff
Unbreakable Series...

Kiki & Darren's romance ignites in...
Heartbreaker

Mase & Leilani's passion flares in...
Rule Breaker

Ben & Shay flirt with danger in...
Lawbreaker

ALSO BY KAT & STONE BASTION

No Weddings Series

No Weddings · One Funeral

Two Bar Mitzvahs · Three Christmases

For Valentine's

Unbreakable Series

Heartbreaker · Rule Breaker · Lawbreaker

Forthcoming: *Ball Breaker · Icebreaker*

Highland Legends Series

Forged in Dreams and Magick

Bound by Wish and Mistletoe

Born of Mist and Legend

Found in Flame and Moonlight

THE TRAVELER: Initiate Years

Veil of Realms · Secrets of Alexandria · Panther Rising

Stones of Power · Highland Magick

Half-Baked Holidays

Half-baked Holidays:

A Romantic Comedy Holiday Collection

Kiki...

For a blessed few hours, I forgot.

Loading Zone did that to me. The nightclub's Industrial Grunge feel, which I'd helped design with its exposed brick and rusted steel, wrapped itself around me like a comfortable blanket. Heavy bass thumped, vibrating into my bones. My thighs burned from dancing back-to-back songs. Three lemon drop martinis in the last two hours hummed warmth through my veins.

"C'mon," my sister Kendall shouted above the loud music as she grasped my hand, then tugged me forward. "My toes are numb."

Out of breath, I nodded and we headed toward the corner booth the eight of us had crammed into earlier. I dance-walked in the narrow path through the crowd behind her, each step a hip shake and head toss to the pulsing rhythm.

The moment we reached the table, our oldest sister, Kristen, pulled her husband from the booth. "Time for us to go. Jason has an early flight tomorrow."

Cade, our brother and silent partner of Loading Zone, guided his new wife, Hannah, out right after them. "Last dance, Mrs. Michaelson?"

Which left Cade's two best friends: the scruffy prodigy surfer Mase, his former roommate; and clean-cut businessman Ben, the other owner of Loading Zone. I slid over the black distressed leather before landing in the center of the wide, shallow booth to face the dance floor while Mase abandoned his spot on the opposite side to anchor the end next to me.

I grasped the stem of my martini glass, sipped the last bit of the tart lemon drop, then let out a happy-buzz sigh. Being around these three—including rising-star architect Kendall —all of them with their shit together, lent some grounding *yin* to my artistic *yang*.

"Sex on a stick, twelve o'clock," Kendall announced.

My heart suddenly slammed into my ribs. But I exhaled slowly, trying to hide my reaction.

I'd been excited about tonight for several reasons: banish my secret problems from my head, surround myself with my favorite peeps, and *Darren Cole*.

Ben snorted out laughter while Mase dropped me a deadpan look. "'Sex on a *stick*'?"

I shot Mase a sidelong glare and elbowed him in the ribs.

He grunted and nudged my arm away.

By the time I glanced up, corded forearms shot over the outer edge of the table. Large hands planted with a hard smack on the brushed metal tabletop. A familiar folded strip of paper skittered out from his fingers, sliding in a wide arc toward Ben.

My breath caught as I stared into Darren's dark green eyes. A lock of his shaggy black hair fell over his forehead as he tilted his face downward. He set his jaw, expression hardening, as a scuffle between four guys unfolded right behind him, the apparent cause of his sudden hand-plant. He gave me a piercing look. "Twenty minutes."

Then he turned and grasped the nearest offender by the scruff of his shirt. Security arrived an instant later and manhandled the others into submission.

As Darren flexed his left arm while leading his guy toward the exit of the club, the tapered point of a tribal tattoo peeked out from the back collar of Darren's black T-shirt. My imagination began to paint what lay hidden from view: thick black ink arcing across sculpted back muscles, a woven design that twisted downward toward his tight...

"What's that?" Kendall leaned over the table.

I tore my gaze away from Darren and reached for the note, but Kendall snatched up the slip of paper first. She unfolded it and read its message aloud, "*Gimme a ride? K.*"

"Oh, sure." Mase took a long pull from his beer, then swallowed. "Kendall gets to innuendo the fuck out of this, but I don't?"

Ben arched a brow. "Twenty minutes. That's one helluva ride."

"Shut up. Both of you. Guys objectify women. We can do the same. And it's a ride home, smartass." I tried to shoot Ben an annoyed glare, but the corners of my mouth twitched into a smile and ruined the whole thing.

"*Suuure*...a ride home." Mase winked at me, then glanced over to where Darren strode along the edge of the room as he headed back toward his DJ booth. "I suppose he qualifies."

"Worthy of objectifying? Darren more than qualifies." I pinched the message *meant for Darren's eyes only* and ripped it from Kendall's grasp. "He doesn't say much," I continued. "Leaves the club with different women. Built like the perfect male specimen..."

Ben choked on his beer. "And what are we? Male rejects?"

"Ewww." Kendall scowled. "That's incestuous."

"You're like our brothers. Can't even..." I scrunched my nose and blanked out my mind, willing myself not to visualize it.

"Not looking for love?" Ben asked, tone softening.

At that, all of our gazes drifted toward the dance floor. One of the last songs of the night streamed a fast tempo from the speakers, but in the center of a thinning crowd, Cade and Hannah stood oblivious. Wrapped together, they swayed to a slow rhythm only they seemed to hear. The look of adoration on their faces as they stared deep into each other's eyes spoke volumes.

"No," I said with absolute conviction. "Heartache lies down that road."

Mase laid a gentle hand on mine. "As your pseudo-brother, I'm warning you: Be careful."

I had no idea whether he meant Darren specifically or men in general. It didn't really matter. I'd learned my love lesson early. And I'd never trusted a guy enough to let one hurt me since.

Darren? The only kind of guy I was willing to play with. A beautiful man I refused to form any attachment to—easy to leave.

The quintessential heartbreaker.

In Darren's truck. Again. A vast awkward distance between us. *Again.*

The drive took only about ten minutes. But the ride home from Loading Zone in Philly's Old City Arts District to the outskirts of sleepy Glenhaven—the third since last summer—stretched eternal.

Why? A hookup shouldn't be this difficult.

My gaze shifted toward him. Powerful hands gripped the steering wheel, thumbs knocking some unheard drumbeat into the silence of the cab. Sculpted forearms stretched up toward cut biceps that vanished under the thin black fabric of the T-shirt that hugged them. His expression was serious, but relaxed. As if he didn't feel the weight of the moment like I did.

Now or never, Kiki.

I took a deep breath and ran a flattened hand over the gauzy material of my skirt, trying to calm myself. Then I inched closer to him, needing some sort of validation that whatever tenuous thing we had between us was moving toward something...fun...instead of away from it.

Tonight didn't have to be a big deal. He either wanted me or didn't. Two other platonic drop-offs didn't mean anything significant. Maybe he was shy. Or a gentleman.

As we drove, yellow pools of light from wrought iron lampposts marked the passing time in a visual cadence. *Light...dark. Light...dark.* The streetlights soon began to feel like a countdown, as if they mocked me for just sitting passively in their spotlights.

Yet how to breach the uncomfortable silence? My mind tumbled over the possibilities: *How did your sound board glide tonight? Wow, how 'bout the heavy bass on that last song?*

He cleared his throat, beating me to it. "Sooo...talk to me. How's the art going?"

"Good." *Good? Really?* I winced at my pathetic attempt at conversation.

We made the second-to-last turn, my time running out, as he gave a single nod in reply.

Buck up, Kiki. You either want him or you don't. Stop being a pussy. "Actually, it's a smaller sculpture. A single orchid sprouting from a rocky riverbed."

He glanced my way. "You work with metal, right?"

"Yeah." I leaned back, staring out the windshield, finally calming a bit as I thought about my art. "This piece is bronze. The lone color is the violet on the flower."

"Sounds cool." His voice lowered. He cleared his throat again.

Had he moved closer?

Impossible. He was driving. Behind the steering wheel, as always.

Yet our legs nearly touched. The rough denim, tight over his thigh, had slid over the tan leather seat to within an inch of my bared knee; he'd spread his legs wider.

The man already consumed most of the space in the truck with his commanding presence. But instead of moving away, I automatically drew closer. My thundering pulse throbbed heavier, warmer...lower.

I swallowed hard, attempting to find my way back to the conversation. "How did your night go?" Maybe his sound board was a medium for his art, like metal was for me.

"Good." The corner of his mouth twitched into a barely perceptible grin, then relaxed.

He dropped his right hand from the steering wheel and floated it in the infinitesimal space between us. Gentle pressure rubbed through the flimsy fabric that covered my upper thigh.

My gaze lowered from the dashboard at the exact moment the knuckle of his index finger trailed in slow motion up the skin under my hem.

I held my breath.

I haven't *been imagining things.*

But then his hand suddenly lifted and fisted. His expression hardened as he stared straight ahead. We made the final turn onto my street, and he eased off the gas, letting us coast. The ride I'd been waiting all night for—six long months and two failed attempts for—appeared to be over.

We rolled to a stop in front of the white picket fence that surrounded the darling butter-yellow Victorian. Then he shifted the truck into park, letting it idle.

Refusing to give up, especially when I sensed him struggling with an attraction we both knew was real, I made a final direct attempt. "You don't have to drive right off. You could come in for a drink."

"No, I can't."

"Why not?" The two words tripped out flippant in my pitiful effort to sound nonchalant.

"You're Cade's little sister."

"No, I'm n—" I blinked.

The pad of his finger pressed to my lips. Warm. Firm. Suddenly, I thought of nothing else. My whole world became our tantalizing first contact.

He didn't move. Simply stared at me.

I closed my eyes. My head eased back against the headrest, but the contact remained as my lips pursed into the gentlest kiss against his fingertip. I wanted to flick my tongue out, taste him. But then he pulled away.

I blinked my eyes open.

He'd half-twisted on the seat toward me. "You deserve better than a one-night fuck, Kiki."

"What I deserve," I muttered, then snorted.

Damn right, I deserve better than that.

But one night was all I could handle.

"Doesn't matter." What I continued to tell myself. "What

I want right now is you." There, I'd said it. Out in the open. Bold and direct.

"What you deserve *does* matter. Don't ever forget it." His voice hardened with every word. His dark brows furrowed to the point a deep crease marred the tanned skin between them.

Without thinking, I reached up and pressed my thumb along that vertical line, massaging until his face began to relax.

He stared at me with renewed intensity. "What are you doing?"

"Trying to get you to chill out." I let my thumb slide a fraction to the right until I found a pressure point, then I spread the rest of my fingertips across the line of his eyebrow. "Is it working?"

"No." The corners of his mouth twitched again.

"Liar."

"Okay. A little."

"Seriously, though," I continued as if I hadn't been distracted by his impressive scowl. "I'm an excellent one-night fuck."

He jerked his head away, then lapsed into a coughing fit.

I arched a brow. "What? Don't think so?"

He shook his head. "No." His mouth fell open. "I mean, I'm sure you are." He blew out a heavy sigh, cheeks puffing from the effort. "You just..."

"Unnerve you?"

"*Yes.*" He thrust a splayed hand into the open air between us with the curt word. "Are you trying to kill me?"

A smile began to curve my lips. "No, I'm just trying to—"

"Don't say it."

The word hung on the tip of my tongue. "You know I'm thinking it."

"Stop thinking it." He took a measured breath, his chest gradually rising, then falling.

Enjoying the loaded tension between us, I remained still, waiting.

When he turned toward me again, I leaned closer and deeply inhaled his earthy scent. "Look. This doesn't have to be complicated just because I'm Cade's sister. You're an adult. I'm an adult. Aren't you attracted to me?"

Every telltale sign he'd shown suggested that he wanted me. But I'd never encountered so much resistance in a guy before. Then again, I'd never had one in my sights so long before either. I ignored the implications in that.

"Of course I am." He draped an arm along the top of the seatback.

His warmth lured me in, and I edged even closer until my entire side crushed against his. He made no move to stop me and didn't flinch away, but his lengthy pause indicated that he resisted committing to anything.

"All it has to be is one night," I whispered, my lips nearly touching the warm skin of his neck.

Another heavy sigh ruffled the hair above my ear, shooting chill bumps down my side. "You gotta know, if I could...I would. It *is* complicated. I can't explain. But no matter how badly either of us want to, this can't happen."

I blinked, confused and lost in uncharted territory. Never had a guy not taken the bait I'd offered. And he was being so nice about it. My mind couldn't process what was happening. "You want me."

"Fuck, yes. I mean, no." He growled in frustration. "God-dammit, Kiki. Just get out of the truck. Please."

I pulled away from him and straightened in my seat, almost laughing at the desperation in his tone. Then I dared a glance at him. His expression grew tortured. A tiny part of me felt bad for putting him in a position I didn't understand. The rest of me beamed that I wasn't the only sexually frustrated one in the vehicle.

Not yet willing to admit defeat, I gave him a smile and grasped the cold metal door handle. "Thanks for the ride, Darren."

I wouldn't ask for one again. But I didn't need to. The seeds had been planted. My work was done. Either he wanted me enough to get past whatever obstacle was cockblocking his way, or he didn't.

Meanwhile, I'd go back to the life I'd been trying to forget, once my mind-numbing buzz wore off.

I wanted to glance over my shoulder as I unfastened the painted wooden gate, double-check to see if he was still watching, but I fought the urge.

The low hum of his idling truck engine remained unchanged. But had his mind?

This lonely girl can only hope.

———

Enjoy the rest of the romance...
Heartbreaker

Sneak Peek of the final installment in our Highland Legends series

Found in Flame and Moonlight

Eight minutes was all Chelsea Smith had. All she needed. *Hopefully.*

The heavy wooden door to Professor MacLaren's private office snicked closed behind her. With a subtle suggestion from her mind, the tumblers reengaged within its lock, a deadbolt she'd "picked" with similar mental ease mere seconds ago.

On her next inhale of cooler undisturbed air, the distinctive scents of age washed over her: that certain spice of centuries-old leather, a mustiness of layered dust, the sweetness of yellowing paper in a prized collection of ancient books.

The room's furnishings echoed its owner's passion for antiquities. Within a sizable entry, a vintage coffee-colored Chesterfield sofa with matching wingchairs hovered at the edge of a burgundy-and-gold Aubusson carpet. Along the side and far wall, relics from exotic locales perched from various niches between precisely stacked scholarly tomes in massive bookcases. And beyond a sizable polished wood desk and its stately leather chair, within tall display cases that flanked a large window, treasured discoveries from historic digs rested on glass shelves.

Yet one particular artifact stood apart from the rest. The

sole reason for her break-in. And the item occupied the nearest corner of his polished wood desk, exposed. No bookcase niche. No protective case.

"Such unfathomable *power*," Chelsea murmured toward the rectangular object, at once fascinated and intrigued. More than she'd been about anything in her first twenty-two years of an immortal life hiding-in-plain sight among "normal" humans.

Her excitement even eclipsed what she'd witnessed from the other side of that window while walking to MacLaren's lecture less than an hour ago.

Though her mind still reeled about that discovery as well.

Because something very *not human* had stood near that power-drenched box, partially transparent, as if not fully materialized into the human world. And that shirtless muscular something had resembled artistic depictions of male angelic warriors, only skewed darker and more sinister with its dusky olive skin, inky black wings, and blue-green prismatic eyes.

And the enigmatic creature had stared directly at her, eyes narrowing, puzzlement twisting his sharp features as Chelsea blatantly stared back. He'd seemed surprised. That she could detect him? Or perhaps that their paths had intersected in the first place.

Yet inside the professor's locked office, no sign of the dark angel remained.

Seven minutes.

The forceful vibration of the artifact's unique power was what had caught her attention from the other side of the window. It had radiated an exhilarating and complex energy, beckoning her like a siren's call.

"Invitation accepted," she whispered.

With slow breaths, Chelsea banked her excitement. Not hard to achieve. Her kind, further evolved humans, born-and-bred assassins, had been trained through millennia to suppress emotion.

"Yeah." She let out a soft snort. "Look how well *that* turned out."

Members of her race had recently evolved again. And an underground faction had organically formed. One that no longer sought to squelch their emotions. That strong minority yearned for something greater, a deeper meaning to their eternal life.

Months ago, Chelsea had been secretly contacted by them. The founders had detected her tendency to operate on the fringe of acceptability. Of course, she'd joined their cause without hesitation.

In the hours and days following that pivotal decision, she'd eased the cognitive restraints that had hobbled her. They had warned her that she would suffer unimaginable internal struggle. Yet nothing had prepared her for the cascade of emotions. One in particular had caused an enormous dissonance with her inherited vocation.

Empathy had bled into her black-and-white world.

An *assassin's* world.

And that problematic emotion had caused a thunderstorm of chaotic gray.

Six minutes.

Focus, Chelsea. She took measured steps toward the charged artifact, noting its unusual features. A foot long, half that wide and tall, a rectangular box sat encased in layers of elaborate metallic latticework. The gleaming designs that adorned its corners and edges were comprised of various metals from differing artistry. But beneath those ornate motifs, simpler flat sides were fashioned from a beautiful bluish-silver metal with a slight sparkle to its sheen.

Indirect bright light glowed in from the large window, but as Chelsea approached, an aura of energy haloed around the box. Infinitesimal particles glittered beyond its surfaces, flashes of silver and gold visible to her preternatural eyes.

Five minutes.

Which meant MacLaren's lecture in his beloved Advanced Theories in Archaeology had concluded. Earlier, Chelsea had obediently endured the graduate-level course with fifteen other classmates until she'd politely excused herself at the last and most opportune moment. A correct amount of respectful time from a valued student. The perfect window of plausible deniability should her burglary plans go awry.

Students typically waylaid him after his lectures, but to be certain, she extended her superhuman hearing. Down a wide sidewalk between buildings, across a grassy quad, and into the cozy window-lined room that the tenured professor claimed as his own, she detected the voices of eager students who had indeed detained him. Which enabled him to wax eloquent about the week's series and his latest obsession: prehistoric artifacts handed down by gods, breadcrumbs to the secrets of mysterious civilizations.

"But you've been keeping the biggest secret of all right here in your office, haven't you?" Chelsea murmured as she paused within reach of the object.

Four minutes.

Plenty of time to abort, to walk away without detection.

"I don't *need* to be here." Sound reason.

And yet, need had become relative.

For in the months following her recent evolution, an

undefinable hunger had begun to grow that nothing satisfied. A craving for a deeper purpose. Not the deadly one mandated by her ancestry. Not even the glimmer of hope that her emerging faction offered.

"Something personal," she murmured, staring at the box. She'd been hunting a cause that matched her sudden passion for life. Unique and special. Sparked by her newfound awakening. "Worthy. And all my own."

Because every action she'd taken in life, from actual missions to basic periphery cover, had been by her race's directive. Even attending university. Particularly MacLaren's courses.

But for the first time, she operated on her own volition. Because before that morning, she hadn't been privy to any details of *why* MacLaren had become a person of interest. Until one shining detail had made itself known, flashing its undeniable energy straight toward her.

Therefore, the risk of exposure? While investigating an object as exceptional as what she hoped to discover about herself?

More than acceptable.

While she continued to listen, the distinct voices of six fellow grad students dwindled to two hardcore disciples. They peppered the professor with questions, theories, and offers of assistance on his next expedition. Groveling, as usual. But MacLaren had their number. And only a couple of minutes remained of his scheduled patience.

Chelsea drew a deep breath to calm her riotous—clearly *not* suppressed—emotions.

Instinct screamed the intricate box held her destiny. Even if she had no idea why.

But as she took a final step and reached out a hand to touch, its unique power reacted to her proximity with accelerating vibrations of energy—plenty of evidence to back up that gut feeling.

Three minutes.

MacLaren shooed out his fan club with his parting excuses and locked up the classroom.

Right as Chelsea hovered a hand over the artifact.

Energy emanated upward from that bluish-silver top, charging the air with electrons that sizzled and sparked. Warmth bathed her palm. Friendly. Inviting. *Intoxicating.*

Until a sense of grave danger spiked in those scant inches between the mysterious metal and her skin. And an unfamiliar feeling of trepidation tripped down her spine. Like some cosmic warning.

Chelsea paused, then blinked heavily, thrown by the sudden unfriendliness of the box and her own emotion about it. She wiggled her fingers within the box's charged aura and considered her impulsive actions. And their unknown ramifications. With the artifact. And MacLaren.

An extensive list of potentialities scrolled through her advanced mind. But the calculations magnified when she removed the laws of the known universe and input alternate realities. Involving energized boxes. And dark angels. And supposedly regular professors that capture the attention of a race of assassins.

Ninety seconds.

"So many possibilities," she murmured about the upside. *Too many variables to calculate.*

Chelsea snorted and shook her head with a slight smile. "I've never been afraid of anything in my life." Headlong into the adventure. The only way she saw the world.

The leather heels of MacLaren's loafers clicked down the nearest sidewalk.

Less than a minute. Before her trespass was discovered.

Urgency fired through her veins. She tensed her arm and lowered her hand, ready to touch no matter the outcome. To finally complete some circuit she'd begun to sense, as if the dark matter hovering between the spaces in the universe needed her help.

The charged air rippled with a stronger dose of caution.

Chelsea narrowed her eyes at the box.

Are you trying to communicate with me?

That the inanimate object had sentience, as opposed to some other force out in the ether, gave her pause. Deadly animals and insects often displayed vivid warnings of their lethal venom.

But why lead me here with such clear invitation? Do you not want me to touch?

The warning vibration wavered back and forth in response as the additional questions crossed her mind. Not quite a yes, not quite a no. That it wanted her there, perhaps. But not to touch? *Orrr…*

"Not yet?" Barely an inch existed.

A hot glow sparkled into existence between her and the artifact, golden and shimmering. The box's energy extended an exquisite representation of agreement in its special language.

"Fascinating." Mesmerizing.

The artifact's seductive power continued to astound.

Have you taunted MacLaren with such scandalous invitation?

No sooner had she posed the mental question, than an answer rippled forth. Only that message vibrated not from the artifact, but from somewhere out in the ether. *No.* Crystal clear. Not as any legible word, but a negative in resonance.

The energized box did not wait on that desk for the professor.

At that moment, the artifact existed for a singular purpose: to join its immense power with hers.

MacLaren's footfalls began to click down the tiles of the building's corridor.

Energy spiked from the box again. Even while its power rippled another caution: *Not yet.* The message clearly vibrated from the object, not the ether.

But unraveling the mysteries of a higher conscious-nesses in matter and space had to wait.

Adrenaline surged through her. "Out of time."

Golden sparks fountained up from its metallic top, singeing her palm. *Not yet!*

"When?" Chelsea choked out a laugh at the box. "*After* he has campus security cuff me?"

MacLaren's key slid into the lock.

Her pulse raced, the thump of her heart a drumbeat in her ears.

Now or never! she argued to the unseen gatekeepers.

Tiny clicks echoed as tumblers released in the lock's mechanism.

The door edge scraped over its frame, the only means of a clean escape swinging open and her window of opportu-nity closing right along with it.

Half-assed alibies spun through her mind, all utterly ridiculous: *I followed a burglar in, I needed to lie down and only your pin-tucked sofa would do, I saw a black-winged angel with sparkling blue-green eyes staring out your window.* Voicing that last factoid? Bordered on certifiable insanity.

But at the last split second between clean infiltration and utter discovery—right as her anxiety skyrocketed—a powerful vacuum slammed her hand down that remaining inch.

A scorching current charged up through her palm from the metal. Blinding power and incredible pleasure flashed through her being.

MacLaren's office vanished.

And a realm of absolute nothingness descended.

Gawain Brodie sucked in a stunned breath as the inside of his chest...*boomed.*

Thunder? Confused, he frowned but refused to break stride. He raced down an earthen footpath in the shadowy forest to rejoin his warriors; he'd been ambushed while scouting. And since no cloud marred the late-afternoon sky, he shook off the jarring sensation.

Faster! Scant seconds remained. Clan Brodie had been exposed. Their castle's centuries-old secret somehow breached.

Blood from three attackers speckled his arms and chest. Yet the last one's dying words bore evidence of the exposure: *Your magick castle is ours!*

A tang from the skirmish coated his tongue, pungent earth and the coppery taste of blood. Anger churned in his gut. Ferocity pumped through his veins. Single-minded determination overcame burning muscles as he sought to vanquish whatever enemy they faced.

Intent on cutting time, he broke into a sunny glade, ran across rippling purple blooms of heather, then rejoined the well-worn trail. Yet as he rounded the gnarled trunk of an ancient yew, a sudden awareness made him veer wide in the turn.

Alongside the path, lacy fronds of bracken trembled. Then a blur of motion burst forth.

Dark garb registered in his peripheral vision. As did the gleam of a swinging sword.

He unsheathed his own sword, then blocked a strike meant to cleave his neck.

Never pausing his momentum, Gawain twisted his body and shifted forward, swinging his weapon over. Then he tightened his blade down at the last moment for the killing blow.

To his surprise, the swords clashed. Punishing vibration jarred his bones from hand to arm, shoulder to neck, till they rattled a final quiver down through his teeth.

The attacker—a male with flaxen hair, of similar height and breadth to the threesome he'd more easily dispatched —merely sounded a low grunt.

With greater determination, Gawain thrust.

In equal measure, his opponent parried.

Fury darkened his attacker's eyes.

Exhilaration fired through Gawain's veins.

Their deadly battle-dance continued with strikes and blocks, thrusts and parries. Each next metallic crash rang out with echoing menace.

"At long last, a worthy opponent," Gawain murmured.

Gawain arced his sword back around, but once the tip swung skyward, he twisted, tucked, then thrust from a lower angle.

The soldier deflected then stepped aside, just as well trained, equally gifted.

"Aye. An 'opponent' who'll impale yer bloody arse like a stuck pig," the soldier replied in an English accent. A sick hunger gleamed in his eye.

Amused, Gawain relaxed his stance and drew back his weapon. He tilted his head and narrowed his eyes. "Why eat pig when you can dine like a king?"

The man's expression fell. As did the tip of his sword while he gave a heavy blink and furrowed his brow. "What're you on about?"

In the next heartbeat, Gawain lunged with incredible speed. The tip of his sword led the way, piercing the man's heart before he was able to draw a full gasp of surprise—or reengage his sword.

"The differences between us," Gawain whispered into the ear of the dying man.

Severe lack of emotion and abundance of wit.

What Gawain possessed and most did not.

With a quick jerk, Gawain freed his sword. As the body crumpled to the ground, he swiped both sides of his weapon on the cleanest patch of the soldier's woolen tunic. He believed in letting fallen men keep their blood. *Off my sword.*

English! The revelation of how far and wide their exposure had traveled still stunned him.

No time! He charged back toward the footpath and raced on.

After another few hundred yards, the clear sounds of combat filtered into the dense forest: the clatter of weapons, shouts and grunts from men.

Seconds later, he burst upon a greater battle. Or what little remained of it.

His brethren carved and sliced through their own tenacious dark-garbed attackers. One Brodie to five English. But the last of their foe fell in rapid succession, one after the other, none prepared for the skill of the unique clan of Highlanders.

With no immediate threat left to eliminate, Gawain sheathed his weapon.

A second strange thunder boomed through his chest.

And its fading vibration carried the aftertaste of something imminent...*weighty*. As if an event of great import was about to transpire. *Involving me?* Or the clan.

Dismayed by the inexplicable and unnerving sensation, Gawain stared toward the western horizon as a fiery sun dipped below jagged mountain peaks.

Two warhorses suddenly appeared below his line of vision, one snow white, the other coal black. Both materialized seemingly from nowhere. And knowing their riders as Gawain did, they likely had.

Another powerful vibration reverberated through Gawain's chest so hard, he stifled the urge to cough as his family approached.

Astride the white mare was Isobel Brodie with her long blond hair flying back in the wind. Clad in her custom deerskin hunting outfit, she braced her toddler son between her arms.

On the black stallion rode Iain, Isobel's husband, Gawain's older brother, and Laird of Clan Brodie. He cradled their lad's twin sister with a father's protective hand.

Clutched in Iain's other hand was a magickal box whose surface sparkled even in gloaming's waning light.

Yet that box had *never* left Brodie Castle.

Not in all the years of Gawain's life.

Nor in any of the legendary tales of generations past.

An unmistakable sense of foreboding washed over him as his fellow warriors gathered to watch their leader and kin draw near.

"*All* approach the battlefront?" their commander, Robert, inquired to his right.

"With the wee ones?" Duncan asked at his left.

The warriors were part of Iain's elite guardsmen. Twelve in total. Closer than brothers.

"Nay." Naught was as it seemed. A great change had begun. Those facts rang true with every heavy beat of his heart. And he'd somehow landed in the center of its shifting tides. "They'll be but a moment," he murmured.

Even if Gawain failed to comprehend *how* he knew what was about to transpire, he sensed why they'd come.

Fate had descended upon him. Though the circumstance made little sense.

"I'll not take your place!" Gawain objected to the notion. The magickal box may as well have been scepter, orb, and crown. For of the many powers it wielded, foremost among them had long been to ordain the next Brodie male as chieftain of their clan.

"*Aye*, you will." Iain lifted the hallowed box high, reaching back.

"You remain hale and whole." Fit to rule. No reason to shift the obligation.

"We've no time to explain." Isobel tightened her legs to bring her mount alongside Iain's as she glanced at her husband. "Danger abounds. And we've been summoned"— at the last word, she directed Gawain a pointed look, heavy with meaning—"*away*."

Gawain sighed. *Away through* time itself. *No explanation needed.*

A strange feeling quivered in his gut. Akin to uncertainty. And a more familiar one: dread. Of the unknown. Of the burden of a reign he had never expected to shoulder.

The obsessive focus of battle had served him well all his life, had helped him overcome childhood demons. Even to the detriment of relations with close family. Namely his sister, Brigid, who he'd wrongly blamed for the cause of those demons so long ago. But Gawain had already come to accept how he'd done Brigid a grave disservice and labored to make amends.

Of late, he'd grown more noble. Worthy of the reign.

And his brother well knew it.

"'Tis the way of it," Iain bellowed for all the guardsmen to hear in witness of the historic moment. "You'll lead the clan through."

"*Aye.*" Gawain gave a clipped nod to his brother in dutiful acceptance of the role.

Iain dipped his chin with satisfaction, punched his arm forward, and released his grip.

The box arced through the air.

With narrowed eyes, Gawain thrust his hands up to catch it.

Yet at the exact moment his fingertips made contact with its cool metal sides, several monumental events happened at once, in plain sight of their guardsmen.

A bright bolt of lightning shot from ground to sky with a true boom of thunder.

Isobel touched a hand to Iain's shoulder and Clan Brodie's former ruling family vanished, warhorses and all.

Heat sparked from the box to his fingers and flashed through his entire body.

And a raven-haired woman appeared out of thin air. Vibrant blue eyes stared straight at him. Her slender hand rested atop the box.

"*Nay!*" Gawain growled, furious.

In his disgruntled shock of becoming laird, he'd forgotten the *other* burden the ancient box bestowed.

A soul mate.

ABOUT THE AUTHOR

Kat Bastion won several awards for her bestselling debut novel *Forged in Dreams and Magick*.

Kat & Stone Bastion's bestselling first novel *No Weddings* and the No Weddings series were named Best of 2014 by multiple romance review blogs.

When not defining love and redemption through scribed words, they enjoy hiking in vivid wildflower deserts, ancient tropical forests, and historic urban jungles.

Join our Bastion Family Adventurers!

Be in the know with preorder alerts, exclusive bonus gifts, and occasional free stories:

katbastion.com/email-subscription